EMMANUEL

Titles available in this series

Yannis
Anna
Giovanni
Joseph
Christabelle
Saffron
Manolis
Cathy
Nicola
Vasi
Alecos
John
Tassos
Ronnie
Maria
Sofia
Babbis
Stelios
Kyriakos
Monika
Emmanuel

Greek Translations

Anna
published by Livanis 2011

EMMANUEL

Beryl Darby

JACH

ISBN 978-1-9997176-1-2

Printed and bound in the UK by
Berforts Ltd
Enterprise House,B52 Wrest Park, Silsoe,
Bedfordshire MK45 4HS

First published in the UK in 2017 by

JACH Publishing
92 Upper North Street, Brighton, East Sussex, England BN1 3FJ

website: www.beryldarby.co.uk

Author's Note

For the purpose of the story I have placed a bookshop in Plaka, and as visitors to the area will know there is no bookshop as such there, the nearest one is Eklektos in Elounda.

All of my characters are fictitious. Although this continues the story of Monika it is certainly not my friend Monique's life history although she agreed to be on the cover of the previous book. Monique's husband is a delightful, charming gentleman and nothing like the character I have created as Emmanuel.

I have no idea how much properties are rented for in Elounda nor the charges for building work. I have plucked the figures I have quoted out of the air and I hope they are reasonably accurate.

Rhodes 2010

Manu had not found being on remand in prison particularly unpleasant. At first he was convinced that he would be dead within months due to being infected by Natasha. He had lost a considerable amount of weight due to a prison diet and lack of alcohol. His father continually told him not to take any notice of the scare stories he heard. Many people who were HIV positive lived a normal life for many years provided they took their medication as prescribed.

'Are you taking yours regularly?' he asked.

Manu nodded. 'I'm given it each morning.'

'And you take it? You don't put it to one side and forget?'

'No. What would happen if I did forget?'

'Probably nothing if it was only an occasional slip of the memory, but if you missed your dose too often you'd find the infection was no longer under control. That's when it could begin to invade your liver and other organs. At the moment you should be pretty fit still. I hope you're taking regular exercise and not sitting in your cell feeling miserable.'

Manu glowered at his father. Of course he felt miserable and also resentful. He wanted to be out meeting his friends, drinking and playing cards during the evening, not sitting in the communal lounge with an uninteresting programme on the television.

'I'm allowed in the gym each day for as long as I want. We're sent outside during the afternoon for exercise. There's usually a game of football going on.'

Manu did not add that he no longer participated in the games of football. Twice he had been removed from the game for fighting with the other inmates and had been warned that if he offended again, although only on remand, he could receive a prison sentence. The other prisoners tended to avoid being alone with him and would only talk to him when they were in a small group.

Manu had boasted that he would certainly be released once the case had been brought to court as he was innocent of the charges. He was not a criminal and he had done nothing wrong. He was the one who had been attacked and he would lift his shirt to show the scars where Natasha had stabbed him.

'So what are you going to do about clearing your name when you are released?' asked Yiorgos. 'You say you were a detective. You should be able to find out who framed you.'

'I know who it was; it will just be a question of finding where they are hiding out. They'll certainly regret it when I catch up with them.'

It had come as a shock to Manu when he was sentenced to four years imprisonment and then a further six months for contempt of court. Even worse was the amount of compensation he was expected to pay to Monika and Natasha.

'I'm not paying them anything,' he shouted at his father. 'They should be paying me compensation. I was the one who was stabbed. I am the one who has been infected. I am the injured party.'

Elias sat and waited for his son's tirade to stop. 'Don't you realise that you'll spend the remainder of your life in jail if you don't pay. Is that what you want?'

'They don't deserve it,' replied Manu sulkily.

'The judge decided the amount and he's the one who has to be obeyed.'

'I haven't anywhere near that amount,' declared Manu.

'I know. I've discussed the situation with the bank manager. He's agreed to a loan in my name. I've had to sign over the chemist shop as security. I'll expect you to find some work when you're released and help with the repayments.'

'You're a fool,' sneered Manu.

Elias glared at his son. 'I'm not doing it for your sake. Your mother begged and pleaded with me until I finally agreed. She's distraught to know that you are locked up in here with criminals.'

Manu found that being a convicted criminal was very different from being on remand. His life was regimented from dawn until the lights in the cells were put out. Each morning he was expected to queue up with the other inmates who needed some medicine and once he had received his two tablets he had to swallow them in front of the guard and show his empty mouth afterwards. He was only allowed to spend an hour in the gymnasium once a week provided there was a guard free to escort him and any others who wished to spend some time there.

The morning was spent cleaning the basins and showers before mopping the tiled floor after each man on his level had spent his allotted ten minutes to wash and during that time they had to wash out their underwear and socks. Although he was given rubber gloves to wear his hands were checked for any cuts or abrasions when he had finished. He was then sent outside, whatever the weather, to sweep the yard free of debris, all the time being watched to ensure that nothing illegal had been thrown over the wall during the night.

'Why don't you ask if you can come and work in the kitchen?' asked Spiro. 'It's boring, peeling carrots or potatoes, but better than cleaning showers and sweeping the yard and it gives you the chance to have a bit of conversation with the others. I could put in a good word for you.'

Manu thought the idea over, but when he asked if he could join Spiro his request was refused.

'Can't have you dealing with the food. The men wouldn't be happy about that. There's other work available.'

Now Manu was not sure he had made the right decision. He was still expected to work in the shower area and sweep the yard during the morning. Once he had finished his mid-day meal, instead of being returned to his cell, he joined the other prisoners who had been detailed for kitchen duty and spent the following two hours cleaning the cooking pots that had been used that morning, followed by the work surfaces, ovens and hobs and finally the floor. Manu realised very quickly to time his efforts; if he worked slowly he was kept behind to finish his quota and if he worked speedily he was given extra work to do. Whatever work he did he was given ten Euros a day the same as the other men that he was able to spend in the prison shop on toiletries or tobacco.

Whilst taking his exercise in the yard Manu began to approach the other inmates and attempt to strike up something of a friendship. He needed to find someone he could trust. He knew it was unlikely he would be allowed to go into the Old Town to question the prostitutes again, but he needed to find out where Monika was hiding from him.

The men were a strange mixture from all walks of life and professions, but most of them seemed to have only one topic of conversation; women. Those who did not have a wife waiting outside would go immediately to the red light district. All he needed was one of them to gain the confidence of one of the girls and pry the information from her.

He did not understand the obsession the other inmates had with women. He had always managed to satisfy himself since he was a teenager. Marriage had almost been a necessity for him. There was beginning to be speculation in the police department and one or two snide remarks about his sexuality made. Monika was available and he had found her reasonably attractive and amenable. It had been a mistake. Who needed a woman? He was not interested in the foreplay that they seemed to expect. If you became dependent upon them you were no longer in control. Being in control was important.

'I know who you are, Emmanuel, known as Manu to your friends. I'm Vangelis.' A small, wiry man was standing next to him. 'I understand you had to pay out a lot of money.'

'What gives you that idea?'

'Word gets around. Your father bailed you out. Used his life savings and took out a loan from the bank using his shop as security.'

Manu nodded. 'So?'

'So I thought we ought to have a little chat. Fancy a smoke? '

Manu shook his head. 'I don't.'

Vangelis held the cigarette out to Manu temptingly. 'Helps to take the edge of things. Give it a go.'

Manu accepted the cigarette which Vangelis lit for him from the one he was smoking. Manu drew in the acrid smoke. It made him feel a little light headed but it was not unpleasant.

'I think we might be able to do a bit of business.'

'Business? What kind of business?'

'I understand your father is a chemist. He should be able to get his hands on one or two little treats for us.'

Manu laughed 'Don't be silly. Visitors are searched before they're allowed access to us. He can't just walk in here and hand me a box of tablets.'

Vangelis nodded. 'Of course not, but we have various ways of receiving items. He would probably appreciate having a bit extra to help clear that bank loan.'

'What are you suggesting?'

'No one enjoys being shut up in here. It's depressing. A few Prozac tablets or some OxyContin could help to lift our spirits. A number of the men in here are in pain and some codeine could relieve them so they get a good night's sleep. All they're given at the pharmacy is Dupon. That does no good.' Vangelis smiled slyly. 'It could also ensure that you had a good night's sleep

11

without worrying about turning your back on some of the inmates the following day.'

Manu took another drag from the cigarette. He had heard about the activities that took place in the shower and various other secluded places where the guards were not particularly vigilant. 'Those are prescription drugs. He'd lose his chemist's licence if it was found out.'

'He'd be well paid.'

Manu shook his head 'He wouldn't be willing to take the risk.'

Vangelis smiled lazily. 'I'm sure he'd think the risk worthwhile if he thought his son's life was in danger.' He drew his finger across his throat,

Manu understood the threat. He would have to persuade his father to supply forbidden medication as requested.

'When is your father due to visit again?'

Manu eyed Vangelis suspiciously. 'Next week.'

'We'll have another little chat before then.' Vangelis ground out his cigarette and walked away.

Manu thought about the conversation. Would his father be willing to supply drugs? If he was discovered he would not only lose his licence to be a chemist, he would also lose his shop and very likely be given a prison sentence as well.

During the next few days Manu watched Vangelis whilst they had their recreation time in the yard. Vangelis would make his way from one group of prisoners to another. They all seemed to know him and treat him with respect, shaking hands and often presenting him with a cigarette. As soon as a guard was seen approaching they would disperse, melting away quietly to mingle with the other inmates. Very often Vangelis was patted down or searched by one of the guards; he never resisted and nothing illegal was ever found in his possession. It was obvious to Manu that Vangelis had an arrangement with some of the guards.

A week later Vangelis approached him again when they were outside in the recreation area.

'Have you thought any more about my proposal?'

'It isn't possible. My father has to account for his stock.'

'He'd receive prescriptions so there would never appear to be any discrepancy. When he comes to visit you tell him he can expect Antonius to call on him with a business proposition.'

Manu eyed Vangelis doubtfully and accepted the cigarette he offered. 'What kind of proposition?'

'Supplying a few treats. They would be purchased for a considerable amount of money. It's an offer too good for him to refuse.' Vangelis stroked the side of his nose and smiled. 'Antonius would deal with everything. Nothing would be traced back to your father provided he kept to his side of the bargain.'

'What guarantee do you have that this Antonius would pay my father once he had the supplies he wanted?'

Vangelis shook his head. 'It would not be sensible to break the agreement. The agreed amount would be paid in cash when the goods were handed over. If Antonius tried a double cross he would soon be found floating in the harbour.'

'And if my father refuses?'

Vangelis smiled confidently and drew his finger across his throat. 'Impress upon him during his visit that he would be wise to agree. His shop could be broken into and someone could get hurt.' Vangelis walked away leaving Manu feeling sick with apprehension.

When Elias visited Manu he was surprised to see his son looking pale and nervous. Vangelis was sitting a short distance away talking earnestly to his visitor and Manu was certain they were discussing him and his father by the way they had cast furtive glances in their direction.

'You don't look as well as you did on my previous visit,' remarked Elias. 'Are you remembering to take your medicine each day?'

Manu nodded. 'I need to speak to you and make sure you

keep your voice down. I've been approached by one of the men in here. He knows you're a chemist and he's sending a man called Antonius to visit you. You'll be asked to supply him with certain products.'

'What kind of products?'

Manu dropped his voice even lower. 'Codeine, Prozac, Benzodiazepines, Amphetamines, things like that.'

Elias looked at Manu in horror. 'I can't do that. They're drugs. Prescription only. I can't just sell them over the counter.'

'You'll be well paid just to supply Antonius with whatever he wants whilst I'm in here.'

Elias shook his head. 'It isn't possible.'

'Pappa, it has to be possible. If you don't agree they will break into your shop and take whatever they can. If you or Mamma tried to stop them you could get badly hurt.'

'I'd 'phone the police,' replied Elias firmly.

'By the time they arrived it would be too late.' Manu drew his forefinger across his throat. 'That's what they've threatened to do to me if you don't comply.'

Elias looked at Manu, his eyes bulging with fear. 'What kind of people are you mixing with?'

'Criminals,' answered Manu shortly. 'I'm in prison, remember, no thanks to you and that fool of a lawyer you hired.'

Crete – August 2013

Driving from Elounda back to Heraklion Monika forced herself to put her idea of a book shop out of her mind and concentrate on driving. She wanted to be back at the apartment, shut herself in the bedroom and try to think of the practicalities such an undertaking would mean.

As soon as she returned to the apartment after depositing the car back at the garage her mother began to chatter to her about their day.

'I'm sorry, Mamma. I just need a little bit of peace and quiet for a while. I'll take a drink and go into the bedroom.'

'Have you got a headache from the sun? Maybe we should not have driven so far, even though the car had air con. Next week we won't go out for so long. Driving is probably tiring for you after a week at work.'

Monika shook her head and drew a glass of water from the tap. 'We'll talk about next week later.'

'You go and lie down. Do you want some Dupon? I have some in my bag?'

'Thank you, no, I don't have a headache.'

Litsa frowned. 'What is wrong then? Did one of your friends upset you when we were in Elounda or Plaka?'

'No, Mamma, please, just let me go and sit in the bedroom quietly for a while. I need to do some thinking.'

'What about?'

'Nothing for you to worry over.'

'You didn't damage the car when you were taking it back?'

'No, Mamma.' Monika went into the bedroom and closed the door firmly behind her. This was when she wished she still had her own apartment where she could escape from her mother's incessant talking.

Monika took a notebook and her bank book from the drawer beside her bed. She propped the pillows up behind her and picked up her pen, headed a page as "Important Questions" and sat back. The first thing she needed to know was if Yannis would rent his shop to her the following season. If so, how much was the rent? How much could she expect to pay for utilities?

She turned the page and wrote down the amounts she had calculated as being the maximum. She turned another page and headed it "Questions". She would need shelving and have to pay someone to fix it. "Measure for shelving", "cost of shelving", "cost of fixing". A computer would be a necessity to allow her to look at the brochures from book wholesalers and publishers, see which books they were offering, which ones appeared to be the most popular and the cost of transporting them from their warehouse.

Another page was turned and she wrote down price stickers, receipt book and bags. She would not consider purchasing a computerised till in the initial stages; customers could be given a hand written receipt. Ideally the bags should have the name of her shop printed on them as an advertisement and she smiled wryly. She had not thought of a name.

On a fresh page she wrote down a brief summary of her expected expenditure, added the figures up and increased the total by a thousand Euros.

Monika chewed the end of her pen thoughtfully. She would have no regular income. She was sure her mother would want to join her in Elounda which would mean leaving her shop work in Heraklion. More income lost. They still had to pay to rent an apartment and they were unlikely to find one in Elounda or Plaka with such a low rent during the season. Monika gave a deep sigh. There was so much more to her idea than she had realised when it first came to her.

She looked at the balance in her bank book. It looked a magnificent sum, but would it be sufficient? She felt a moment of panic. Did she dare take the chance? If she used all her money and then the shop was not a success she would have nothing.

Monika picked up her mobile 'phone. She would ask Vasilis Iliopolakis for advice. Half way through pressing in the numbers for the telephone at his house she stopped. She had no right to disturb him on a Sunday evening. She would speak to him at the hotel the following day and ask if she could call and talk to him about her idea and discuss the financial implications with him.

Vasilis was surprised when Monika asked if she could visit him and Cathy that evening.

'Only if it is convenient,' she assured him. 'It is to ask your financial advice as a business man.'

'Of course you may come over, unless you would rather discuss it with me now?'

Monika shook her head. 'I think Cathy could also be helpful to me.'

'Cathy does not have any business knowledge,' smiled Vasilis.

'I'm sure she would be able to give me some help.'

Monika returned to the reception desk, leaving Vasilis to ponder her request. If she wanted information about investing her money in stocks and shares he could only tell her the possible risks and refer her to a reputable broker.

'I need to go out this evening to visit Mr Iliopolakis and Cathy,' Monika informed her mother. 'I don't know what time I will be back so can you leave me some supper, please?'

'You usually visit them on a Wednesday. Why are you going

this evening?' asked Litsa.

'I need to talk to Mr Iliopolakis about something.'

'Have you got a problem at the hotel? Surely he could sort that out for you when he goes in next.'

'No, Mamma. I don't have any problem. Everything at the hotel is fine.'

'So why do you need to see him this evening? There's a film on the television that I thought we could watch together.'

'You enjoy the film and you can tell me about it tomorrow. I'm just having a quick shower and changing into something casual then I will be off.'

Monika closed the bathroom door before her mother could ask her any more questions. She had no intention of divulging her idea to Litsa. Her mother loved to gossip and Monika knew she would immediately tell her co-workers at the shop, who would tell their relatives and friends; before she knew it word would have got back to the staff at the hotel.

Now wearing cotton trousers and a T-shirt Monika checked that she had her notebook in her bag. She felt incredibly nervous. If Mr Iliopolakis advised against the venture she would be bound to respect his opinion, but she would also be desperately disappointed.

Vasilis opened the door to her and led her through to the small patio at the rear where Cathy was sitting at the garden table, an almost empty glass in her hand.

'I'm pleased you've arrived,' she smiled and held out her glass towards Vasilis. 'I'm just ready for a refill. White for you, Monika? I have a chicken salad ready for later, so I thought white wine was more appropriate.'

'I'd love a glass of wine, but I don't expect you to feed me. I asked my mother to save something for me for when I returned home.'

'Nonsense. There's far too much for just the two of us and the salad will be limp and uneatable by tomorrow.'

Vasilis handed a glass of wine to Monika and refilled Cathy's glass. 'I have already had half the amount of wine I am allowed in one evening so I will wish you good health with a glass of water.' He raised his glass and took a seat at the table. 'Now, what is it that you wish to discuss with me?'

'Well,' Monika hesitated, 'I drove my mother down to Elounda and Plaka on Sunday. I visited Saffron and she told me that Uncle Yannis is hardly ever at his shop and he is thinking of closing it next year and renting the premises out.'

'You want to take over his business?'

'Oh, no, I want to open a book shop.'

'A book shop? Why?'

'Because there isn't one down in that area. The nearest one would be in Aghios Nikolaos. Do you think he would allow me to do so?'

Vasilis shrugged. 'If he agrees to rent his shop to you he cannot stipulate the goods you sell. There are some items that would be unacceptable, but I hardly think you would consider opening a shop that sells sexual aids and toys as some do in Heraklion.'

Monika blushed. 'I certainly wouldn't.'

'What would you do with the stock that belongs to him?' asked Cathy. 'You wouldn't want it around or stored in the back room as it is now.'

'I have no idea how much stock he has. I know Saffron usually displays an item and replaces it with another if it is sold. I would be willing to do that whilst I had the space.'

'You would have to come to an arrangement with Yannis. I cannot advise you there.'

'I realise that. I will have to make an appointment to speak with him. I need to know how much rent he is likely to charge and whether I would be able to afford it, along with the utility bills. I wanted to ask you if you thought my idea was viable.'

Vasilis shrugged. 'I don't see why a book shop should not be a success. If you stocked books in Greek I'm sure the locals would be grateful and tourists often want a book to read whilst they are lying on the beach.'

'Would tourists be willing to purchase new books? Most hotels seem to have a book shelf where they can help themselves.'

'They have, but the self catering accommodation does not.'

'I have money that I could invest in more shelving suitable for books and also book stock, but if I was not successful I will have lost everything.'

Vasilis smiled sympathetically. 'You will be no worse off than you were before you received your compensation money.'

Monika shook her head. 'I will have no work and my mother and I will be without a home.'

'Your mother will still have the rental income from her shop on Rhodes.'

'Even if the book shop was a success during the season would I have made enough for us to live on during the winter? I couldn't expect my mother to use her money to subsidise my idea. She might need it later for medical expenses.'

'Provided you only agreed to renting the premises from Yannis for one season and if you found you were running at a loss you could close and he would have to rent to someone else. You would have lost your original investment but you could return to work at "The Central" as a receptionist.'

'Thank you, Mr Iliopolakis. I would certainly be very grateful to know I was able to come back and work for you.'

'I would not be able to help you with accommodation again. I do not want the responsibility of becoming a landlord to people I do not know. If you left I would sell the apartment. There is always someone who is looking for good tenants and I would give you and your mother a reference.'

Cathy frowned. 'You are both jumping ahead. Would Yannis's shop be large enough for a book shop? It is only half the size of Saffie's and books take up a lot of space. Would you have enough shelves?'

'I doubt it. I would have to ask permission to add some more, and they would have to be firmly fixed to the walls so they could not fall over. At least once they were installed I would not have to buy them again. I wanted to ask you about books, Cathy. Do your father's books still sell well?'

'Are you planning to cater for children?'

'Children and adults, but I need to know which books are popular. I cannot afford to buy a hundred books and have ninety still sitting on the shelves at the end of a season.'

'I will ask Vasilis to unearth last year's royalty statement that I received. That will tell me how many of my father's books sold. I'm afraid I take little notice of the number.'

'When I worked in the library we had catalogues stored on the machine and if we wanted to order a book we looked up the author or title. Do you know if it is possible for book shops to obtain computerised lists?'

Vasilis shrugged. 'I expect so, but I am not the person to ask. Saffie should be able to give you that information. I know she has computerised catalogues from suppliers for the gifts she sells.'

'Do they quote the cost of having the goods sent to her?'

'They would have to. No one is going to place an order and find it has cost more to have it delivered than the price of the goods. Are you going to sell only new books?'

Monika frowned. 'I hadn't really thought that far ahead. I could have a section of second hand books; ones a customer had read and no longer wanted. I could buy them back for one Euro and sell them on for two provided they were in good condition.'

'You could take some from the shelf in the hotel,' offered Vasilis. 'You know we throw away those that have loose pages or where someone has spilled their drink. I wouldn't expect you to have those. There could even be a box of books in the cupboard below and probably some of those are in French or German.'

'Is there?' Monika looked at Vasilis in surprise. 'I had no idea. I've only ever helped myself from the shelf and not looked in the cupboard. What do you think, Mr Iliopolakis? Will my idea work?'

'I cannot say with any certainty. I think the thing you need to do next is make an arrangement to speak to Yannis. You cannot really make any firm plans until you know if he will let the premises to you and allow you to add extra shelves.'

'But you don't think it's a stupid idea that's bound to fail?' Monika looked from Vasilis to Cathy anxiously.

'I think it is a good idea,' said Cathy firmly.

Vasilis nodded. 'Provided you do not become too ambitious in the first instance and find you have run out of money before you have opened. You do not want to go to the bank and ask for a loan if that can be avoided. The interest rates are extortionate.'

'I will be very conscientious about my expenses. Once I have found out the details from Mr Yannis and the cost of shelving I will put aside an amount for purchasing books. I have to remember that I will also have to rent an apartment. I thought I should divide my savings in half to start with, one half for the book shop and the other for living expenses. At least I won't have any wages to pay to anyone.' Monika gave a nervous laugh.

'What does your mother think of the idea?' asked Cathy.

'I haven't told her yet. Until I know for certain that I can go ahead I don't want her fretting that she will have no work and we won't have a home. If I'm unable to go ahead with my ideas she would have had all that worry for nothing.'

Vasilis picked up the bottle of white wine and refilled Cathy and Monika's glasses. He looked at the amount that was left and tipped it into his own glass.

'It might be a rather generous measure, but I'm sure a little extra will not hurt me.' He lifted his glass and touched Monika's. 'Here's to your success.'

Cathy took a sip and then her face fell. 'If you go down to Elounda or Plaka to live you won't be visiting me regularly.'

'I'm sure I will have plenty of reasons to return to Heraklion and I will always telephone and ask if I can see you. I hope you will come down and see my shop if and when it is open.' She giggled slightly. 'My shop! That does sound grand, but I mustn't get carried away. I will have to 'phone Mr Yannis and make an appointment to see him?' She looked at Vasilis. 'What is his surname? I cannot address him as "Yannis" or "Uncle Yannis".'

'I doubt if he would mind,' smiled Vasilis. 'He is Yannis Andronicatis, but I think it would be better if you 'phoned Giovanni Pirenzi and discussed your plans with him. Yannis is unlikely to do anything without consulting his nephew. If Giovanni does not think the idea is feasible you would be wasting your time.' Vasilis scrolled down on his mobile 'phone. 'Here is Giovanni's number. I will write it down for you.'

Monika took the slip of paper and placed it carefully in her purse. 'I'd rather speak to him face to face than over the 'phone. Do you think he would agree to meet me?'

Vasilis shrugged. 'I expect he would. He might be coming up to the airport to collect or deliver visitors and be willing to spend some time with you then.'

'I would probably be working unless it was the early hours or late at night.'

'I am sure he will be making a day time journey at some time during the week and he could meet you at "The Central".' Vasilis picked up his mobile 'phone again. 'I will see what he says.'

Monika flushed with embarrassment. 'I only came to ask your advice. I didn't expect you to make an appointment for me.'

'It's no problem. Hi, Marianne, how is everyone? Are you busy?' Vasilis waited for Marianne to reply. 'That is good. Is Giovanni around? Can I have a quick word with him?'

Again Vasilis waited. 'No, there is no problem. I want to ask him when he is planning to come up to the airport next.' He placed his hand over his 'phone. 'Marianne is looking at the diary.'

'Thursday, that sounds ideal. Can I speak to him and make a definite time?' Once again Vasilis covered his 'phone. 'She is taking the 'phone to him.'

Monika sat and waited apprehensively as Vasilis spoke to Giovanni.

'I have a lady in my employ who would like to discuss renting Uncle Yannis's shop next season with you. It would be better if you could meet and she could explain her ideas to you. If you are in agreement then she could arrange to come down to Elounda and talk to Uncle Yannis. I thought you might be able to spare some time on Thursday when you come up to the airport. You can meet at "The Central".

Monika shook her head. 'I'm working that day,' she mouthed.

Vasilis shook his head at her. 'If you're meeting a flight that is due in at ten fifteen could you manage to come to the hotel at nine? I can reserve a parking space at the rear for you and it should take no longer than half an hour so you'll still have plenty of time to get to the airport.'

Giovanni considered his reply. 'Well I suppose if I left Elounda soon after eight I should be at the hotel by nine or shortly afterwards, but it is essential that I leave at a quarter to ten to ensure I'm on time at the airport. I will have to park up and make sure I am waiting when they come through. It doesn't look efficient if I am late.'

'Suppose your car broke down?' asked Vasilis.

'Then I would call a local taxi firm and ask them to meet the visitors and bring them down to Elounda.'

'So there is no problem. I will expect you soon after nine on Thursday.' Vasilis turned to Monika with a smile. 'It is arranged. When Giovanni arrives you can be relieved of your duties and use my office for your discussion.'

'I'll be as quick as I can,' promised Monika, 'and I can make up my time by working later. I'll have all my ideas and questions written down ready for him.'

It was after nine when Giovanni arrived at "The Central" and Vasilis led him and Monika into his office.

'Do you remember Monika?' asked Vasilis. 'She visited with us when it was Annita's hundredth birthday and stayed at your apartments.'

Giovanni wrinkled his forehead. 'I have to be honest and say that I do not remember. We have so many different people staying at the apartments. I understand that you wish to rent Uncle Yannis's shop next season?'

Monika nodded. 'Saffron told me he was thinking of closing. If that is so I would like to ask him if he would rent the premises to me and allow me to open a book shop.'

Giovanni raised his eyebrows. 'A book shop?'

'There isn't a book shop in the area. I would be very unhappy if I was staying in your apartments for a week, had finished my book and needed to travel to Aghios Nikolaos to buy one.'

'You could walk into one of the hotels and pick up a book from the shelf that most of them have.'

'I don't think visitors would feel comfortable doing that. I would also want to come to an arrangement with Saffron whereby I sold guide books, maps of the area and postcards. I would not sell souvenirs as she does and if she refuses I will sell only books and magazines.'

'What kind of books would you sell?' asked Giovanni.

'A variety, but mainly easy reading novels for the tourists.'

Giovanni smiled sympathetically. 'We have many different nationalities staying here. I think it unlikely you could cater or everyone.'

'Initially I would start with English and Greek novels. If I find there is a demand for novels in other languages I could introduce them slowly. Mr Iliopolakis has said I may take some of the books at "The Central" that have been left by the visitors; they are often in other languages.'

'So you are intending to sell books in Greek?'

Monika nodded firmly. 'The Greek classics and popular novels by Greek authors. I thought I would approach the local school to find out which books would be of interest to their pupils. I would want it to be a book shop that catered for all tastes and age groups.'

'You have sufficient to fund this idea? Books are not cheap items to buy.'

'I have worked out the amount I have available. If I have not covered my expenses in the first season I would have to think seriously about continuing.'

'So what are you asking of me?'

Monika leaned forward eagerly. 'I would be grateful if you would explain my idea to your uncle. If he is willing to rent his shop to me I would probably need to add more shelving and have it fixed to the walls. I would need his permission to do that.'

'Do you know the cost for adding shelving?'

'Not yet. I need to go into the shop and take measurements. Until I know the amount of shelving I would require I cannot estimate the cost. I am sure there would be a carpenter locally who could put them up for me and I would have to ask him for an estimate for his work. If your uncle is not willing to rent the shop to me there is no point in me proceeding.'

Giovanni cast a surreptitious glance at his watch. 'If Uncle Yannis is in agreement when would you plan to start work at the shop?'

'I will need to discuss my winter working hours with Mr Iliopolakis. I certainly would not need to be at the shop every day until the shelving was completed; then I would have to place orders with the book suppliers and be at the shop to receive them. I would aim to have the shop ready to open in March at the latest.'

'Assuming you are successful would you stay open during the winter months?'

'During the summer I would tell customers that if they wished to return a book to me that they had read I would give them a small amount back on their purchase price. It is unlikely they would be in perfect condition for re-sale. I would keep them to one side and advise the local people that for a small fee they could join the library and borrow the imperfect books for one Euro a copy.'

'That would be a new idea to many people.'

Monika shrugged. 'If it was unsuccessful I would have to close down for three or four months and ask Mr Iliopolakis if I could return to work here for him whilst the conferences took place.'

'You would still have to pay the rent during that time.'

'I understand that. I hope Mr Andronicatis would be understanding and not charge me the full amount if I was closed.'

Giovanni raised his eyebrows. 'My uncle is a business man.'

'Of course, but surely it would be beneficial to him to have a proportion of the rent over the winter rather than none because I was forced to close down completely.'

Giovanni nodded. The girl did have a business head on her shoulders. 'There is much you need to discuss with him.'

'Would you be able to make me an appointment?' asked Monika anxiously.

'I am sure it can be arranged. Give me your 'phone number and I will contact you when I have spoken to him.' Giovanni rose to go.

'There is one other thing.'

Giovanni looked pointedly at his watch.

'If Mr Andronicatis is agreeable to my proposal my mother and I will need somewhere to live locally. I could not drive up and down to Heraklion each day. If you hear of an apartment to rent on a permanent basis would you be able to let me know?'

'Once the season has ended there are usually plenty of apartments available to rent. If you decide to go ahead with your ideas I will let you know if I hear of anything. Often it is better if you just visit the tavernas in the area and ask about renting. You would be able to visit them and decide if they were suitable for your needs. I must leave now or I will not be on time to meet the visitors who are arriving this morning.'

'And you will telephone me with an appointment?'

Giovanni nodded and extended his hand. 'It has been a pleasure to meet you and hear your plans.'

'Thank you for your time.' Monika watched as Giovanni hurried form the hotel. She was not sure if he was impressed by her idea and would speak favourably to his uncle.

Having deposited the tourists he had collected from the airport at the self catering apartments Giovanni decided to stop at Plaka and speak to Saffron.

'What do you know about this girl who wants to rent Uncle Yannis's shop?' he asked abruptly. 'I met her this morning at Vasilis's hotel. She said she had spoken to you.'

'She's friends with Cathy and Vasilis. She stayed with Cathy at their house whilst Vasilis was in hospital. I met her there on a number of occasions when I went up to Heraklion with Vasi.'

'So she's trustworthy?'

Saffron nodded. 'I feel sure she is. She has worked at "The Central" for a number of years. I'm sure Vasilis would give her a reference.'

Giovanni ran a hand through his thinning hair. 'What worries me is the finance involved. Opening a book shop is ambitious and costly. Could she afford it?'

Saffron shrugged. 'I don't know her financial circumstances. Why don't you ask Vasilis? He must think she has enough money or he would not have arranged for you to meet her.'

Giovanni was about to reply when a thought struck him. Was Vasilis proposing to open a book shop and let the girl run it? If that was the case it would be better for Uncle Yannis to convert his shop himself into a book shop, come to an arrangement with the girl, pay her a set wage and have the profit from the sales.

'She said she would sell the maps, guides and books that you currently stock. Would you be agreeable to that?'

Saffron frowned. 'She hasn't mentioned that to me, but then we only spoke briefly. I'd need to meet with her properly and discuss what each shop is going to sell. There would be no point in both of us stocking the same articles.'

Giovanni looked around Saffron's shop. There was a metal stand containing postcards and next to it a table with maps and guides. If she passed those to Monika it would give her more space to display her souvenirs.

'I think Uncle Yannis might be quite relieved to no longer have the responsibility of the shop but still have some income from it,' continued Saffron. 'I had thought of asking him if I could expand my business in there, but it isn't really feasible. There's a limit to how many souvenirs you can sell in one season.'

Giovanni nodded. 'I'll talk to Vasilis again; see what he says.'

Vasilis was not surprised when Giovanni telephoned him that evening. 'So, were you able to come to some arrangement with Monika?' he asked.

'She seems a very pleasant young lady, but I wanted to ask you a couple of questions before I speak to Uncle Yannis. What is your interest in this venture?'

'My interest?' Vasilis sounded puzzled. 'I have no interest at all in the shop. Monika asked if I would contact you and ask you to arrange a meeting with Uncle Yannis. It is nothing to do with me.'

'You're not planning to finance the project and just employ her for a weekly salary?'

Vasilis laughed. 'Certainly not. She is an intelligent young woman and worked in a library on Rhodes so she has a knowledge of books that I do not possess.'

'So if there is no monetary involvement from you where is she getting her money from?'

'She received a large divorce settlement about three years ago. I understand that is where the money is coming from. I have made it known to her that I would be willing to help if she runs into financial difficulties. I would give her a loan at less interest than the bank would charge, but I think she is sensible enough to budget and not overspend.'

Giovanni ran his worry beads through his fingers. 'I'll speak to Uncle Yannis and see what he decides.'

'I think it would be in his best interest to let her rent the premises from him. He's not making any money from it all the time it sits there with dormant stock.'

'You took some of his large pots for "The Central". Would any of the other hoteliers be interested?' Giovanni knew his uncle would be reluctant to pack his stock away and forget about it.

'I can ask around, maybe display a few saying they are for sale. They'd have to be at a lesser price than the museum charges for replicas. Visitors are getting canny these days about comparing prices.'

'What about Vasi? Would he take some?'

'You'd have to ask him. I understand Saffie always has two or three of the smaller ones on a shelf and passes the money on to Uncle Yannis if she makes a sale.'

Giovanni nodded. If Saffron placed the maps, guides and postcards in Monika's shop she would have space to display more of the museum replicas that belonged to Yannis.

'I'll have a word with Uncle Yannis. If he feels satisfied that his stock is still going to be available he should be happy to let the premises.'

Vasilis smiled to himself. He had an idea that Giovanni would convince his uncle that the Monika's project was in his favour and the stock would be sold gradually.

'I'll not say anything to Monika,' promised Vasilis. 'Once you have Uncle Yannis's agreement you can 'phone her and make her an appointment with him. I'm sure I can rearrange her reception duties so she can have a day off.'

Giovanni considered how best to approach his uncle. He would have to be tactful or Yannis would become stubborn and insist that he kept his shop open. He poured a glass of wine for each of them.

'Here's to a good season. It has certainly started well.'

Yannis looked at Giovanni morosely. 'It may have done for you.'

'Is someone behind with their rent?'

Yannis shook his head. 'No, there's no problem there. Trade is slow at the shop.'

'Vasilis bought four of your largest urns,' Giovanni reminded him.

'I had to give him a discount.'

'Better to do that than have them sitting there until next season.'

'I'm thinking of closing completely at the end of the month. I'm wasting money on electricity all the time I stay open.'

Giovanni nodded. 'That could be a wise decision. You're not getting any younger, Uncle. Have you thought about renting it out?'

'Why? What do you want to do with it?' asked Yannis suspiciously.

'Me? Nothing.'

Yannis shrugged. 'Business might pick up again next year.'

'You said that last year and it hasn't happened. If you rented it out you would have the income without any of the expenses.'

'Does Saffie want to expand?'

Giovanni shook his head. 'She's happy with the premises she has, but I've heard of a woman who would like to rent it from you.'

'What would she do with it?'

'She wants to open a book shop.'

'Do you know the woman?'

'I've met her. She works as a receptionist for Vasilis at his hotel and is friends with Cathy. If you are happy with the idea she would like to meet you and discuss it further with you.'

'A book shop.' Yannis mulled the suggestion over. 'What about my pots and other stock?'

'I don't think they would be particularly suitable in a book shop. If the big urns don't sell we could use some of them as flower pots.'

'Flower pots!' Yannis was horrified.

'Not with soil in them. A plant already in a container could be stood inside.'

Slightly mollified Yannis nodded. Museum replicas were works of art and not meant to be used to hold flowers. 'I can't just throw them away. They're valuable stock.'

'Of course not, but I've had an idea. You make a new label for everything. Double the price and then advertise a half price sale. That way you will get your money back and people will think they are getting a bargain.'

'Is that legal?'

Giovanni shrugged. 'I think you are supposed to have them advertised at the original price for a number of months. All the labels that are on them at present are turned so you cannot see the price. You just replace those labels with the new ones. Who is going to know?'

Yannis nodded slowly. 'It might be possible.'

'Of course it is. I'm sure Marisa will help you write the new labels. I'll write some notices saying you are closing and having a half price sale.'

'You and your notices!'

'I'll do them in different languages as I did for the hotels,' grinned Giovanni. 'Shall I 'phone Monika and arrange a day when she can visit you?'

'I'll think about it.'

'Monika really needs to know. If you keep her waiting too long for an answer she'll probably find a shop elsewhere. You might not get an offer from anyone else.'

'I'll sleep on it.' Yannis drained his glass and held it out to Giovanni to refill. He knew he was going to agree; Giovanni had always had good ideas, but it wouldn't hurt him to wait for his answer.

Giovanni telephoned Monika and told her that his uncle was in favour of letting his shop to her, but he wanted to meet her and know more details.

'That's no problem,' Monika assured him. 'Is there any day that would be most suitable? I'll ask Mr Iliopolakis if I can have some time off.'

'Whichever day suits you best. Uncle Yannis is not planning to go anywhere.'

'I'll say Friday. If I cannot be released that day I'll let you know. I can hire a car and should be in Elounda by eleven. Should I go to your house or the shop?'

'Come to the house. If you make a provisional agreement with Uncle Yannis you can always go to the shop later and ensure it is suitable.'

Monika closed her mobile 'phone with a delighted smile on her face. She would speak to Vasilis as soon as he arrived at the hotel and hope he would be agreeable to her having Friday to herself.

'I will make up my hours the following week,' she assured him.

'There is no need for you to do that unless another receptionist requests some time off. Is your mother going down with you?'

Monika smiled guiltily. 'I haven't told her yet.'

'You think she would disapprove?'

'Not at all, but she does not enjoy living in Heraklion. I would not want her to think we would be moving to Elounda until I have seen the interior of the shop and reached an agreement with Mr Andronicatis. I may find the shop is too small to be viable for a book shop or he may change his mind about renting out the premises.'

'Provided you are happy with the amount of space you will have I am sure Giovanni will persuade his uncle to allow you to use the premises. Yannis is in his eighties and his sister is a little older. He has no need to go to work to make a living.'

Week One – September 2013

Before Monika drove down to Elounda she ensured she had her notebook, a tape measure and the list of questions she needed to ask Mr Andronicatis safely stowed in her bag. She felt ridiculously nervous and chided herself. If Mr Andronicatis refused her proposal all she had lost was a day's work and the cost of hiring a car. If that was the case she could look around whilst she was in Elounda and Plaka to see if there were any other premises available that would be suitable for her to rent.

On reaching Elounda she drove into the car park and stopped in an empty space. She took a few mouthfuls of water and checked her appearance in her mirror before drawing out and continuing around the bay to Yannis's house. There was a minibus, a car and two scooters already parked and she drew in carefully beside them.

Taking her bag from the car she walked across to the front door of the house, the heat of the sun hitting her with a full force as she stood there and rang the bell. No one came and she was beginning to think she had mistaken the day and time. That would be very embarrassing. She turned to go and as she did so a woman called to her.

'Monika?'

'Yes, I believe Mr Andronicatis is expecting me.'

'I thought it must be you. Come around to the patio. We don't often use the front entrance. I'm Marianne.'

Monika nodded. 'I remember you from when I came down to help at the party.'

'That seems like a long time ago now. Would you like to sit outside or prefer to be indoors?'

Monika hesitated. 'Outside would be fine if I can be in the shade.'

'The umbrellas are up, but if you are too hot just say and you can move into the lounge.'

Monika followed Marianne to where Yannis and Giovanni sat beneath a large umbrella, both of them with a drink in front of them.

'What can I get you to drink?' asked Marianne.

'A fruit juice would be very nice, any variety, I'm not fussy.'

'Have a seat and I'll be back.'

Both men rose as Monika approached and Giovanni pulled out a chair. She shook hands with Yannis and sat down.

'It's good to see you again. May I call you Monika?' asked Yannis.

'Of course. Thank you.' Monika took the cold glass of fruit juice from Marianne and set it down carefully on the table before opening her bag and taking out her notebook and a pen. She did not know if she was expected to start the proceedings or if she should wait for Giovanni or Yannis to speak to her. She took a mouthful of the juice as a delaying tactic.

'My nephew tells me you wish to rent my shop in Plaka,' said Yannis.

Monika nodded. 'I would like to open a book shop, but before I can make a definite decision I need to know the amount of rent you expect and also see the dimensions of the shop. Books can take up a good deal of space.'

Yannis made to rise. 'We can go there now and you can see for yourself.'

Monika shook her head. 'I need to know the rent first. If it is beyond my budget there is no point in wasting your time by going to the shop.'

'It would be two thousand Euros a month. It is in a prime position.'

Monika flipped over a page in her notebook and made a swift calculation. If she rented the shop from March until October it would cost her sixteen thousand Euros. It was reasonable by rental standards, but she would try some negotiations and see if she was able to get the outlay reduced.

'Then it is not possible. At two thousand Euros a month I would need to sell books to that value each week during the season just to cover the rent. I don't think that would happen until I became known and was patronised by the local people as well as tourists. I have to take the cost of the utilities into account along with the stock I would need to buy initially. There will also be rent for an apartment in Elounda where my mother and I could live.'

Giovanni looked at his uncle. 'Suppose the rent was reduced?'

Yannis frowned at his nephew and was about to remonstrate when Giovanni shook his head.

'I would still expect to pay less during the winter when the shop would probably be closed most of the time.'

'What are you suggesting?' asked Giovanni.

'If I agreed to pay one thousand five hundred Euros a month for the weeks I was open and one thousand a month when I was closed I could probably manage that. Over the course of the year I would end up paying you sixteen thousand Euros. If I had to pay you two thousand Euros each month I would definitely have to close during the winter and cancel my agreement with you until the following season.'

'How many weeks would you plan to be open?' asked Yannis.

'From mid-March until the end of October. I could always extend the closing week into November to meet demand.'

Giovanni began to write down figures on a paper in front of him and he passed it to Yannis who scrutinized it carefully. 'I think we need a few minutes to discuss this together.'

Monika rose. 'I will go to the end of the patio and wait until you call me back.'

'Why don't you go into the kitchen and talk to Marianne rather than stand out in the heat?'

'She won't mind?' asked Monika anxiously.

'Not a bit.' Giovanni waited until Monika had entered the house then he turned to his uncle.

'You can't afford to refuse, Uncle. At the moment you are running at a loss, paying the utility bills and not making enough sales to cover them.'

'I ought to get more rent each month than two thousand Euros.'

'How much do you charge Saffie?'

'One thousand five hundred a month. She has the equivalent of two shops and that's for the whole year, whether she is open or closed. Vasi drove a hard bargain. I ought to put her rent up.'

'So you'll be making almost as much money from Monika renting one shop. It makes sense to accept. If you turn Monika's offer down you could be left with the shop sitting empty. There are already enough tavernas, gift shops and boutiques. Opening another would not be practical; at least a book shop would be something different to attract people.'

Yannis shook his head. 'I can't see it making any money.'

Giovanni shrugged. 'If she has to close at the end of the season you will have gained the rent for that time and you still have the shop to rent out to someone else the following year. If she is successful then you could renegotiate the rent with her. She won't want to lose the premises if she is making money. Trust me, Uncle. My ideas have always been profitable to you.'

'She may decide the shop is not large enough.'

'She won't know that until she has seen it. I suggest you make a provisional agreement with her using these figures, then we go up to the shop. If she decides it isn't suitable then the agreement is scrapped and it is up to you to decide whether to keep the shop open or look for someone else to rent it from you.'

Yannis sighed. 'I suppose you're right.'

Giovanni smiled. His uncle could always be talked round to agree with him.

'Don't worry,' Marianne smiled at the anxious girl. 'If Giovanni approves of your idea he'll be able to persuade Uncle Yannis to agree. He always has in the past.'

'I don't think it is the idea of opening a book shop that is the problem. I said the rent he was asking was more than I could afford.'

'I'm sure Uncle Yannis asked for the absolute maximum expecting to have to reach a compromise with you.'

Monika frowned; maybe she should have proposed less than one thousand five hundred Euros a month and she wished she had asked the annual cost of the utilities. By the time she had taken those into account, along with a telephone and internet access she would probably be looking at a further two hundred Euros each month.

'What gave you the idea of opening a book shop?' asked Marianne.

'I used to work in a library and I love books,' smiled Monika. 'If you live in this area and want to buy a new book you have to go to Aghios Nikolaos.'

'Most people would combine that with a visit to the town for something else they needed.'

'Of course, but visitors would not want to carry a book around with them all day if they were in Aghios Nikolaos sightseeing. It would be more convenient to purchase it here and leave it in their room until they wanted to read.'

'I understand that many of them purchase the electronic books rather than an actual printed book.'

'There are still readers who prefer to have a proper book in their hand rather than their iPods and the like. If you take them to the beach the sun shines on the screen and you can't see anything. If you leave them unattended whilst you go for a swim they are more likely to be stolen than a book.'

'We don't have very much crime in Elounda.'

'Ronnie told me about the two young men who were here last year systematically stealing from the tavernas and shops,' Monika reminded her.

'They just wanted money.'

'I'm sure they would have taken an iPod if they had seen one and then tried to sell it somewhere else.' Monika finished her drink and held out her glass. 'Shall I wash this up?'

'No, I have a dish washer. It will simply go in with everything else. When you have this number of people around to cater for a dish washer is the only practical answer. I would be washing up all day otherwise.'

Giovanni entered the kitchen and placed two empty glasses on the side. 'Uncle Yannis has agreed to the amount of rent you have offered,' he smiled. 'Do you wish to go up to the shop and look inside?'

'Yes, please,' answered Monika with alacrity. 'I have a tape measure with me and I would like to take some measurements. I may need some extra shelving.'

'There are shelves there now,' Giovanni assured her.

'I know, but they may not be the right size for books.'

'I will get my metal tape. It will be more accurate than a tape measure.' Giovanni disappeared into the house and returned swiftly. 'We will walk,' he announced. 'It is not possible to park in the square and I expect the car park is full at this time of the day.'

Monika waited patiently as Yannis unlocked the padlock, pushed the door open and switched on the lights.

'It was newly decorated before the start of the season,' he announced and Monika wondered if he was going to ask her for more money to compensate him for the work.

Monika gasped. 'This is amazing. I have only managed to peer through the window and I was expecting wooden shelves and all the goods stacked up like they are in other shops.'

Yannis smiled. 'My sister designed my shop in Aghios

Nikolaos. She lived in Turin for many years and was impressed by how elegantly items were displayed there. When I moved here I was happy to continue displaying my goods in the same way.'

Large urns, almost as tall as Monika were arranged against one wall, with staggered shelves of white or black marble above them holding Venetian glass work and alabaster figurines. The opposite wall had the same marble shelving, all of different heights and lengths and holding more pottery of various sizes and design, each one with the metal tag showing they were authentic museum copies.

The space between the staggered shelves was occupied by reproductions of the frescoes that had been found at Knossos. On the walls above the shelves were framed prints, similar to those sold by Saffron. A large counter stood at the back; beneath it were boxes, some bulging with tissue paper. Behind it the wooden shelves held a miscellaneous collection of photograph albums, silver photograph frames, leather purses, wooden boxes, leather book marks embossed with a scene from Knossos, along with some miniature pots with a notice that declared they were hand painted, some Phaistos discs, marble eggs and ashtrays and a box of dusty postcards.

'At the back is the stock room,' Yannis informed her and led the way past the counter into a dark room. He switched on the naked bulb and exposed the boxes that were stored in there almost to the ceiling; at the far end was a sink and on the drainer stood an electric kettle and some cups. A door on the far wall opened onto a small toilet. Taking up most of the space was a stepladder and she assumed Yannis used this if he needed to reach the goods that were on the top shelves in the shop.

'What is in all the boxes?' asked Monika.

'My stock,' announced Yannis proudly.

'Would I be able to remove this partition wall to enlarge the shop area?' asked Monika. She could see that it did not reach up to the ceiling and it was not made from stone.

Yannis looked at Giovanni. He knew the wall could easily be removed as he had had the partition erected to provide him with the storage space he wanted.

'It would be possible,' answered Giovanni cautiously.

'Could you take some measurements for me, please.' Monika took out her notebook. 'I assume the width is the same throughout, so if this wall was removed and another erected further back I could have a smaller stock room with access to the toilet and somewhere to make a drink?'

Giovanni handed the end of the metal tape to Yannis. 'Take this through to the door and we will measure the length of the room as it would be without the dividing wall.'

Monika made a quick drawing of a rectangle and wrote down the figure he called out to her at one side. 'Now could you give me the measurement of the stock room and then the shop area as it is now.'

Again she wrote down the figures, drew in the partition and showed the position of the light bulb, and an electric socket close to the floor. If she moved the dividing wall she would also need to have the electric cable extended to provide her with a light in her stock room and she might want the socket higher up. She made a quick note; that would be more expense.

'Is there a telephone line and some power points in the shop?'

Yannis looked at her in surprise. 'I have always used my mobile 'phone.'

Monika nodded patiently. 'I would need a telephone line to enable me to use a computer here, along with a socket that it could be plugged into. It would also be useful to be to be able to run a fan when it is hot.'

'I am sure a cable could be run from the electric light,' Yannis assured her, whilst Giovanni shook his head.

'That would not be safe. There would have to be a separate electric cable to provide sufficient power. It would be no big job. Dimitris could do it easily.'

Monika looked at the marble shelves. If they had not been staggered at different levels she would have been able to use them as supports for her shelves. They were ideal for displaying the items Yannis sold, but quite useless for storing books

'Would I be able to remove the marble shelves?' she asked.

'They have been set into the wall,' Yannis informed her. 'It would be more practical to have them cut back flush with the wall than try to prise them out.'

'You would allow me to do that?'

Yannis sighed and nodded. He would be sad to see his beautiful shelves removed.

'I would need full length wooden shelves; these are not suitable for books. If I removed them I could have shelves at a regular height and width along the whole length of each wall. They would not be as high as yours; that would be impractical as no one would be able to reach the books.'

'There is the ladder,' Yannis reminded her.

'I cannot expect customers to climb a ladder to read titles,' smiled Monika. 'Can you measure up two metres, please. I don't think the top shelf should be any higher than that.'

'Will you be able to reach that high?' asked Giovanni looking Monika up and down.

'I can buy a step stool so I can reach. That will be easier and safer than a stepladder. I should be able to have six shelves, but until I had sufficient stock I could display some of your smaller items on the higher shelves, Mr Andronicatis. If they sold the money would go straight to you, of course.'

Yannis nodded. At least that would mean a few less needed to be removed and stored at the house.

'What about the prints?' asked Monika. 'Are they for sale?'

'Certainly not. They are the original sketches that my mother did. I simply had them enlarged so I could display them.'

'I thought they were the same as the ones that Saffron has for sale.'

Yannis shook his head. 'The ones she has were done by little Anna when she was on the island. After Old Uncle Yannis died they were found amongst his belongings. Most of the people she drew were also dead by then so we reproduced them for people to buy as souvenirs of their visit to Spinalonga.'

'Would you allow me to keep yours up there?'

Yannis shrugged. 'I have the originals at home so I do not need these, but they are not to be sold, not to anyone, however much they might offer.'

'I would not dream of selling them. If anyone shows an interest I will send them to Saffie. I will be selling books, not prints.' Monika looked around again. 'I would need to move your large counter into the centre of the room.'

'I keep my packing materials there.'

'Very practical, but I will only need a bag for a book, so I could use it to store boxes of books and also display them on the top. I would have a smaller desk near the window so I could see the whole room. I could not afford for people to pocket a book and walk off with it.' A thought struck Monika. 'If I moved your large counter is the floor tiled underneath it?'

'Of course.' Yannis sounded quite indignant. 'It cost a good deal of money to design and pay to have the shop the way I wanted. I was not prepared to save a little on leaving part of the floor as concrete.'

'I'm so relieved.' Monika smiled at the elderly man. 'It would look horrible with a patch of concrete in the middle of the room and I don't know if I would be able to afford to have the tiles matched and laid. I would have had to leave your large counter where it is.'

'What about the window display?' asked Giovanni. 'Would you have the marble removed from there and replace it with wooden shelves?'

'Definitely not,' answered Monika firmly. 'The window would stay as it is now and I could display a book on a marble shelf.'

She looked back up at the slabs of marble that acted as shelves on the wall. 'I would like to use some more slabs when they are taken down. I could make a haphazard pile and place a book on the top or build a small bookcase in the centre of the window with them and have a different selection of books there each week.'

'Marble is expensive,' muttered Yannis.

'Of course, but if I do not use it who will? I imagine that it is off-cuts left over from a job that was being done and would probably have been thrown away.'

Giovanni gave a surreptitious smile. He had salvaged the marble from a rubbish dump on a building site in Aghios Nikolaos.

'So,' asked Yannis, 'do you wish to rent my shop?'

'I would like to work out the dimensions fully before I give you a definite answer. I need to find somewhere quiet to sit and make some calculations. Once I have done that I will walk down to your house and let you know my decision.'

Deliberately avoiding Ronnie, who was sitting in the square at her easel, Monika walked down the main road to the end of the parade of shops where she turned down a side road that led to the sea and the tavernas that specialised in fresh fish. She took a seat in the shade and asked if she could just have a frappe as she did not feel ready to eat.

Reluctantly the waiter brought it for her. He hoped she would either decide to order a meal or leave swiftly. He would want the table for his lunch time trade.

Monika placed her notebook on the table. The shop was six metres wide and the length, without the partition was seven and a half metres. The store room behind the partition was the whole width of the shop and two metres deep. Surely she would not need such a large storage space; if she reduced the stock room by one metre the area left should be sufficient. She could have a small table at the end for a kettle and cups with a fridge beneath for cold drinks.

Once the large counter had been moved into the centre of the shop there would still be sufficient space for customers to move around and she would be able to display books on the top and store copies beneath. Having electric sockets and a telephone line installed would be another expense along with buying timber of sufficient quality to hold the weight of books and having it fixed securely to the wall.

She drank half her glass of frappe. She needed to find out the price of timber that would be suitable for shelving. Quickly she calculated; she had two walls measuring roughly six metres and the partition wall was five and a half metres across. That was nearly eighteen metres for just one shelf! She was shocked and rechecked her calculations. If she then multiplied that measurement by six shelves she needed one hundred and ten metres to allow for the cutting. Could that be correct?

Monika finished her frappe and called the waiter over. 'Is there an internet cafe close by?' she asked as she paid him.

He shook his head. 'You'd need to go into Elounda. There's nothing here.'

Despondently Monika packed her notebook into her bag. She could hardly retrieve her car from Yannis's house, drive into Elounda and return when she had used the internet. It would be only polite to tell him that she wanted the shop, but needed to find out the cost of the work she planned before she made a final commitment.

Hesitantly she approached the patio and was relieved to see Yannis sitting out there with his sister. 'May I come through?' she asked.

'Of course. I will find Giovanni.'

'I'll go. You stay here.' Marisa walked into the kitchen and returned with Giovanni following her. He smiled broadly at Monika.

'Have you come to a decision?'

'That depends. I would like to rent the shop, but I have to look on the internet to find out the cost of shelving for the books.

I also have to take into account paying to have them fixed once the marble has been cut away. There is also the partition to be moved further back and some electrical work that I will need done. Until I have more idea of the costs involved I cannot give you a firm decision. I would not want to agree today and then find out tomorrow that I could not afford the necessary work. I have to keep some money in reserve for the purchase of books.'

'I have the internet here. You could look up whatever you need when you have had some lunch.'

'I could not impose upon you,' demurred Monika.

'It is no imposition. We all have to eat. More than enough food is made each day so we can all help ourselves when it is convenient. I will ask Marianne or Bryony to bring out a plate for us to share. We will then retire to my office and you can use the internet.'

Giovanni hurried back into the kitchen and Monika looked helplessly at Yannis and Marisa.

'It is better that you find the answers to all your questions today. Now I have decided to rent out the shop I will have to clear my stock. I do not want to start doing that only to find out in a week's time that you have withdrawn.'

'There would be no rush to clear your stock,' Monika assured him. 'You could continue to trade until the end of the season. We could then arrange a date when I could have access and start the work.'

Yannis nodded. He fully intended to trade until the end of October, saying he had a half price sale as Giovanni had suggested in the hope of selling as much of his stock as possible, but he also wanted a firm agreement from Monika.

'It is arranged.' Giovanni returned and took his seat beneath the umbrella. 'I have brought some beer for my uncle and myself. What would you like to drink, Monika?'

'Water would be fine with me. I had a frappe whilst I was working out measurements. They were quite frightening.'

'Yannis tells me you plan to remove the marble shelving. That is a shame,' remarked Marisa.

'I agree. The shop is beautifully laid out at the moment and I understand you designed it. Unfortunately it is not suitable for a book shop. I need rows of uninteresting shelves.'

'They will become interesting when you have books on them,' smiled Giovanni as Marianne brought out a tray loaded with plates, cutlery, glasses, water, serviettes and bread followed by Bryony carrying two large platters holding a variety of food.

'Please, help yourselves. Bryony is going to feed the girls whilst Nicola deals with little Yannis. I will be around if there is anything more you need.'

Monika helped herself to a little of everything from the platters. There was such a variety it was like being in a taverna and having a meze meal. Marisa and Yannis picked from the platter and ate sparingly. Whilst Giovanni loaded his plate and continually urged everyone to take more.

'Marianne will be offended if we send half of it back,' he announced. 'That will mean I have to eat more and she is always threatening to put me on a diet. She says I am getting too fat.' He rubbed his ample stomach with his hand and smiled ruefully. 'As you get older you eat just as much, but do not have the energy to work and get rid of it.'

Monika nodded in agreement. She had noticed that now she was no longer doing cleaning work at the hotel her waist line had expanded. She made a mental note to eat more sensibly and take more exercise.

Finally Giovanni blotted his lips with a serviette and belched discreetly. 'When you are ready, Monika, we will go to the office and use the internet.'

Monika was relieved. She could have finished her meal half an hour earlier, but eaten slowly as Giovanni seemed in no hurry to move. She followed him into the room he used as an office and waited whilst he checked the computer for any messages, then closed the programme taking it back to the main menu.

'What do you wish to look up?' he asked.

'I need to know how much timber I will need to make the shelves. The lengths it comes in and, of course, the cost.'

'What kind of wood are you looking for?'

Monika looked at him and frowned. 'I don't really know. Whatever is suitable.'

'Well, you could have mahogany, that is a very dark wood and expensive. Cherry is very attractive, but also expensive. Oak is very strong and often used for shelves that have to carry a heavy weight.'

'I don't want anything too dark. Am I able to look at colour samples on the internet?'

'That will give you an idea of the shades, but do not expect the colours to be exact. If you don't want anything too dark or expensive I would recommend pine. Do you want to do this yourself in private or are you happy for me to stay and help you?'

'I'm quite happy for you to stay. You will probably be far quicker than I am as I have never tried to look up anything like this before. I have only ever dealt with books or hotel reservations.'

Giovanni nodded and asked for the names of timber merchants in Aghios Nikolaos. 'We may as well start looking as close to home as possible. They may none of them stock the kind of timber you need, then we will have to try the merchants in Heraklion.'

He opened and closed a variety of sites before leaning forwards and studying the screen. 'This looks more likely. They have pre-cut lengths in different strengths.'

'They would need to be two millimetres thick or the weight of the books would make them bow.'

'One point nine millimetre is the strongest they are advertising. You could place a batten at the back and front to stop them from sagging.'

Monika shook her head. 'That is not practical. I would have to allow extra height between the shelves and the books would have to be lifted off, not slid out.'

'May I see your sketch?'

Monika handed him her notebook. 'I have only taken into account the side wall and doubled the quantity. I would still want the partition re-shelved, but that might have to be of lesser thickness and I would have to remember to place the lighter items there.'

Giovanni raised his eyebrows. 'May I make a suggestion?' and Monika nodded.

'Rather than try to work out the amount of timber you need it would be more practical to look for ready-made shelving. I know there is a firm in Heraklion that will make up units to the specification of the customer and then fits them.'

Monika bit her lip. 'Surely that would be more expensive than buying the timber and having them made?'

'I suggest we look at their prices and work out the total cost. You can then compare that with the price of timber. You would then need a quote for making and installing the shelving to your requirements from a carpenter so you can decide which option is more practical and cheaper.'

'I don't actually know any builders or carpenters.'

'I can recommend Mr Palamakis. He works for Vasi at the hotels during the winter and he also built the extension to Ronnie's house, along with the repairs to the main building. His grandsons know what they are doing.'

'What about the electrical work I need? Would they be able to do that?'

Giovanni shook his head. 'Dimitris would be the man for that. He's a qualified electrician and lives in Elounda. If you do not move the partition you will not need the light moved, just the extra sockets you say you require will have to be installed.'

Monika pushed her hair back from her face. 'When I first thought of this idea it all seemed so simple.'

Giovanni smiled at her sympathetically. 'All ideas seem simple at first. Do you want me to call Palamakis?'

Monika hesitated. 'Maybe I should visit the stockists in Heraklion who advertise the custom made shelving first. I feel I have taken up so much of your time today. Could I telephone you and make an arrangement to come down again, either tomorrow or next weekend?'

'It is no problem. I would be relieved if you made a firm decision as soon as possible. If you withdraw Uncle Yannis may well decide to keep the shop open for another season and it is not feasible. Sitting up there without any customers just makes him feel miserable. At one time his goods sold well, but people have to be more careful with their money now.'

'Maybe they will not buy books,' said Monika despondently.

'There is a big difference in buying a book for ten Euros and spending over a hundred Euros on an ornament.'

Marianne joined them in the office, a pleased smile on her face. 'I hope I'm not interrupting; I've just had a long distance call from my mother.'

'What is wrong?' asked Giovanni immediately.

'Nothing is wrong. Why do you always expect bad news? They are coming over to stay in the second week of October.'

'Who is "they"?' asked Giovanni suspiciously.

'Mamma and Uncle Andreas. Helena has decided she wants to visit Rome. They are going to break their journey in London and then Mamma and Uncle Andreas will fly here.'

'And Helena and Greg?'

'They will arrive a week later from Rome.'

Giovanni shook his head. 'I said things were going too well and a disaster would happen. Your mother and Uncle Andreas are very welcome. Wouldn't Helena and Greg like to spend more time in Rome or visit Florence or Venice?'

'I think Helena feels somewhat responsible for them. Mamma said they will have two nights in London and then Helena has promised she and Greg will take them to the airport and stay with them until their flight. They've booked to go to

Rome on a flight that takes off an hour later so it should be no problem.'

Giovanni sighed. 'The problems will arise when Helena arrives. I will ask Vasi if he has a room at his hotel. Your mother and Uncle Andreas can stay here in the house, but the self catering apartments would not be suitable for Helena. Nothing is ever to Helena's liking.'

Monika began to feel uncomfortable and anxious to leave. Provided the traffic was not too heavy she should be able to reach Heraklion before the carpentry workshop closed. She stood up and extended her hand to Marianne.

'Thank you for my lunch and arranging for Giovanni to spend time with me to sort out my queries regarding the shop. Is your uncle still on the patio? I would like to say goodbye to him and thank him for his help also.'

Monika drove back to the outskirts of Heraklion as rapidly as possible. She had no idea where the workshop would be situated in the industrial area and had to stop three times to ask directions before she finally drew up outside. To her relief she could see a man sitting at a desk and she hurried across and pushed open the door.

'Good afternoon, would it be possible for me to speak to someone about your custom made units?'

The man looked pointedly at his watch. 'We will be closing soon.'

'I'll not keep you long.' Monika took her notebook from her bag. 'I am contemplating renting an empty shop and turning it into a book shop. I understand you make units to the customer's requirements. If I gave you the measurements would you be able to quote me a price?'

The man sighed. 'What kind of wood do you want?'

'Pine.'

'And the measurements?'

Monika read them off. 'That is for one wall. I would want the same on the opposite wall although it is two metres shorter. I may have it altered so that it is only one metre shorter.'

'How high?'

'About two metres, maybe a little higher; depending upon the height between the shelves.'

'How many shelves?'

'Probably four.'

The man sat back in his chair. 'I cannot possibly give you a quote on such vague instructions. If you are seriously interested in our goods then it would be only sensible to make an appointment for us to visit the premises. We could measure the area ourselves and then discuss your requirements on site.'

'Oh!'

'Is that a problem?'

'Do you charge for visiting and providing an estimate?'

'Our services are free provided you then place the order with us. If you decide to go elsewhere we charge fifty Euros for the consultation.'

Monika bit at her lip. 'Would it be possible to visit tomorrow? I can telephone the owner and ask for access to the premises.'

Mr Constanakis looked at his calendar. There was very little work arranged for the winter months at present. This could be a profitable job for his firm before business picked up later when the hotels and tavernas decided on improvements and alterations ready for the next season.

'Shall we say nine thirty tomorrow morning?'

'Oh, no.' Monika shook her head. 'It cannot be that early. The shop is in Plaka. I would not be able to get there before eleven.'

'Plaka!'

'Does that make a difference?'

Mr Constanakis shook his head. 'I will have to charge you for the petrol and an extra twenty Euros for my travelling time.'

Monika took out her mobile 'phone and pressed in the numbers for Giovanni. She was answered almost immediately.

'You have made a decision?'

'No,' smiled Monika. 'I'm at the workshop where they make the customised units. The man here wants to come down and take measurements so he can give me an accurate quote. Would it be possible to visit the shop tomorrow morning at eleven?'

'Do you wish me to ask Palamakis to be there also?'

'Not at the same time, maybe an hour later.'

'Very well. I will open the shop for you at eleven tomorrow morning.'

Monika drove back to the apartment she shared with her mother full of misgivings. The amount of rent she would have to pay and the quantity and probable cost of the shelving along with the work involved had definitely made her think twice. Did she really have sufficient savings to open and equip a book shop? She would delay making a decision until she had received estimates from the workshop in Heraklion and also Mr Palamakis.

'I will be sensible,' she told herself. 'If I decide the project is too expensive I will forget the whole idea.'

Monika was awake early. She had spent a restless night turning figures over in her mind, finally falling into a deep sleep only to be awoken by a crash. A bookshelf must have fallen over! As she became fully awake she realised that was impossible. She was in the apartment that she shared with her mother, not in a book shop or the library.

Pulling her light wrap around her and pushing her feet into her mules she opened the bedroom door. Her mother looked up guiltily.

'I'm sorry. Did I wake you? I went to get out a saucepan from the back of the cupboard and tipped them all out onto the floor.'

'It was time I was up. There's quite a lot to be done today.'

'Do you have to go into work?'

Monika shook her head. 'I'm going to have a shower and get dressed and then I'll tell you my plans.'

Litsa waited impatiently until Monika emerged from the bedroom for a second time. She poured a cup of coffee and sat down at the table.

'Come and sit down, Mamma. Leave whatever that is you are doing.'

'I thought I would put some minced meat on to simmer ready for this evening's meal. I fancied making a lasagne. A packet was split and the owner said I could have it at half price as they wouldn't be able to put it out to sell. Lasagne looks quite easy, it's similar to moussaka. '

Monika raised her eyebrows. Her mother never deviated from traditional Greek cooking.

'Leave it for the time being. I want you to sit down and listen to me.'

Obediently Litsa wiped her hand and sat down at the table opposite her daughter. 'What's wrong?'

'Nothing. When we were in Plaka last week I talked to Saffron.'

Litsa nodded. 'I remember. I wrapped some of her goods for her when she made a sale. I really enjoyed doing that. Do you think she would like an assistant at the weekends?'

'Mamma, please, forget Saffie at the moment and listen to me. She told me that Uncle Yannis was considering closing his shop. It's the one with those large pots in the window. I thought about it and went down to speak to him yesterday about renting the premises.'

'You went down to Plaka yesterday? Why didn't you wait until today?'

'I needed to speak to Mr Andronicatis and find out if he was serious about closing his shop. I also wanted to look inside the shop and see how large it actually was.'

Litsa pursed her lips. 'If he can't sell his pots what makes you think that you will?'

Monika shook her head. 'I wouldn't want to sell pottery. I plan to open a book shop.'

'A book shop? Where? In Plaka? In the pottery shop?'

'That's right. I spent a long time talking to Mr Andronicatis and Mr Pirenzi. I found out how much rent I would be expected to pay each week and negotiated a little less for the weeks when I would not be open. We then visited the shop so I could see exactly how large it was and if it would be suitable. There are some alterations that I have to make and I would need to have shelves fitted to the walls. It will mean quite a large outlay, but I have more than enough on my account.'

'I could help you if you were short,' offered Litsa.

'Thank you, Mamma, but I shouldn't need to ask you for more than your share of the rental for an apartment. I went to visit a workshop in Heraklion. Apparently they make shelving to your own requirements and they are coming down to Plaka today to look at the dimensions of the shop and discuss my requirements. I'm also meeting Mr Palamakis there an hour later and will ask him for a price to build the shelving I need. Then I can compare their prices. I thought you'd probably like to come down with me and have a look inside. You can always sit over at the taverna whilst we are discussing the work if you become bored.'

'How much rent does he want?'

'He wanted two thousand Euros a month.'

'Two thousand! That's extortionate. Natasha only pays eight hundred and she lives there as well as having the shop.'

'You need to put her rent up, Mamma. The original amount was arranged by Grandma and it has never been increased. I negotiated the rent with Mr Andronicatis and I would pay him one thousand five hundred a month during the season and one thousand a month in the winter.'

Litsa frowned. 'So what would happen if you did open this book shop in Elounda? It's a long way to travel each day.'

'If, and remember, at the moment, Mamma, it is all speculation, we would rent an apartment in Elounda.'

'Are the rents there expensive?'

'I don't know,' admitted Monika. 'The prices probably go up in the summer for the tourists, but if people wanted to live there all year round they would have to be reasonable.'

'Well, we won't find anything reasonable down there at the moment. It's still the height of the season.'

'We don't need anywhere down there to live yet, Mamma. This is not going to happen overnight. I shall continue to work at the hotel until the New Year and we will live here. I would arrange with Mr Andronicatis that he removes his goods at a certain date in January and then work in the shop could commence. That would be the time to look for an apartment in the area.'

'Suppose we can't find anywhere?'

'I'm sure we will. We may have to go to the outskirts of Aghios Nikolaos or up into one of the villages, but either would be preferable to driving to and from Heraklion each day.'

Litsa shook her head. 'It's a big move, Monika.'

'I know, Mamma, but if I don't take this opportunity now I may never have it again. If I spend all my money and the shop is a failure I will have to accept that I made a mistake and return to working at "The Central".'

Litsa sighed. She was not sure if she wanted to be uprooted from the friends she had made in Heraklion, despite her declaring her dislike for the town during the summer months.

'What time do you want to leave?'

Monika looked at her watch. 'We ought to go within the next twenty minutes. You never know how heavy the traffic will be at the weekends and I don't want to keep Mr Pirenzi and Mr Constanakis waiting.'

'You've left it late to hire a car.'

'The one I hired yesterday is parked just along the road. If my idea had been impossible I would not have told you about it, but I would still have taken you somewhere to have a swim, so it seemed sensible to hire the car for three days. In fact, if I do go ahead with this idea, I may have to buy a small car. It would be more economical than hiring a vehicle to drive to Plaka from an apartment somewhere and I am sure I would have to come up to Heraklion to meet with book suppliers.'

Monika parked the car in the permitted area a short way from the square, relieved when she found there was a space there and she would not have to drive down to the car park at the bottom of the hill and walk back.

She looked at her watch. 'We are early. We'll go and have a drink at the taverna. We'll be able to see when the men arrive.'

'Do you want me to wait here whilst you talk to them?'

'No, I'd like you to see the shop as it is now. Mr Andronicatis's sister designed it and I have never seen anywhere else quite like it. You may have some ideas for things I hadn't thought of. Just don't start to tell them the work they quote for is too expensive. I have some figures worked out and I know how much I can afford to spend. I don't want them to think they will not get paid.'

Monika looked continually at her watch and over at the shop whilst they both sipped a fruit juice. The men were late. Had they forgotten that they had arranged to meet her or had Mr Andronicatis changed his mind about closing his shop?

She sighed with relief when she saw Giovanni arrive at the shop door.

Giovanni immediately apologised or his late arrival. 'I had to take a telephone call from some visitors who were due to arrive tomorrow. They have had to cancel due to a slight accident and wanted to book for two weeks time.'

Monika nodded. 'It is no problem. This is my mother, Litsa. She would love to see the shop as it is now. I have told her how attractive it is. Mr Constanakis, the man from the workshop, has not arrived yet. He insisted he had to come down to take his own measurements.'

'That is understandable. If he takes the measurements and the furnishings do not fit he would have to put the matter right. If you give him an inexact measurement he will simply blame you for any discrepancy and charge you a second time to rectify the error.'

'Would you be willing to stay with me, Mr Pirenzi? I've never done anything like this before and I don't want to make an agreement that I will regret.'

'Of course, but call me Giovanni. If you will take my advice you ask him to put his estimate in writing for you and do not make any decision until you have seen it and compared it with one from Mr Palamakis.'

Monika smiled at Giovanni gratefully. 'Here he is now.'

Mr Constanakis rounded the corner mopping his forehead. 'I should have asked you to meet me in the car park. I have been looking for you in the shops across the road. I assume I am at the correct location now.'

Giovanni unlocked the door and stood to one side to allow Monika and her mother to enter. Mr Constanakis stood inside the doorway and looked around shaking his head.

'It is not possible to fit shelving to these walls. They are uneven and they have those marble projections.'

'The marble is going to be removed,' Monika assured him.

'The walls are still uneven.'

'If they were levelled? Would it be possible then?'

Mr Constanakis pursed his lips. 'It could be.'

'Then let us assume they are level and I explain where I want the shelving fixed. That way you could take the measurements and give me an estimate.' Monika gave him what she hoped was a winning smile.

With seeming reluctance Mr Constanakis withdrew a metal tape from his pocket along with a notebook. He opened the door to its fullest extent and wedged the end of the tape beneath it before stretching it out the full length of the wall and writing down the measurement of the length, repeating the process for the opposite wall.

'You say you want the final height of the shelves to be two metres?'

'Approximately. I want the shelves to be twenty five millimetres deep so they can take regular size books. The unit may need to be a little higher as I would like six shelves.'

'The depth of the shelf is to be taken into account when you say twenty five millimetres?'

Monika shook her head. 'No, I want the actual space to be twenty five millimetres.'

'That will increase the height of the unit by twelve millimetres or a little more.'

'Then I think I may have to settle for only five shelves.'

Mr Constanakis grunted and wrote down the measurements. 'I suggest you decide exactly what you want and then I will tell you the overall height of the shelving. I cannot work on approximately.'

Monika frowned; she was rapidly taking a dislike to the man. 'I'll say five shelves.'

'Is there anything else you want me to quote for?' He looked at the partition. 'Are you removing this?' he asked.

'I may be moving it back by a metre and then it could have new shelves fitted. I don't think I need a quote for that at present. When can I expect my estimate to be ready?'

'You could collect it on Wednesday.'

Monika nodded. 'Thank you. I will come when I have finished work, about five.'

'We close at five thirty.'

Monika watched Mr Constanakis walk back towards the car park and let out her breath. 'I don't feel that was particularly successful.'

'You do not have to accept his estimate.'

'If I don't he is going to charge me seventy Euros for his visit and extra for his petrol.'

'That is reasonable. It takes an hour to drive here from

Heraklion and I know the quantity of petrol needed. He should not charge you more than eighty Euros.'

'It could be eighty Euros wasted.'

'Not necessarily. We will speak to Mr Palamakis and hear what he has to say. Whilst we wait for him we will sit across the road in the shade. Theo will not mind if you do not buy another drink. We are friends.'

Eventually a dilapidated truck stopped at the top of the Square and a young man helped Uncle Yannis out. Giovanni waved to him and he made his way over to the little group and eased himself into a chair.

'Palamakis will park and then come to join us. I was not interested in hearing about book shelves, but if you are planning any other alterations Miss Kokanides I would like to be consulted.'

'Of course.'

'You have a beautiful shop, Mr Andronicatis,' said Litsa and Yannis beamed. He loved his shop, but now Ourania had died he did not experience the same pleasure as he had when she and Marisa had spent the day up there with him and his goods had been in demand.

Mr Palamakis and his grandson, Giorgos, walked into the square and stopped before Yannis's shop. Giovanni hurried across to him with Monika and Litsa following him whilst Yannis walked over slowly to join them. Giovanni made the introductions and then unlocked the shop door.

'Miss Kokanides visited the shop yesterday and has taken measurements of the interior. She consulted a web site for the cost of shelving and has calculated the amount she will need. The marble that is inset in the wall at present would need to be removed and shelving erected. Before she can make a final decision to proceed she would like to have your professional opinion of the work she wishes to be done here and the approximate cost.'

Mr Palamakis nodded. Giovanni had told him all this on the

telephone earlier that day and he knew the information was being repeated for Monika's benefit.

'So,' he said, 'tell me what you wish to have done.'

Monika took out her notebook. 'The marble that is inset into the walls would have to be removed and I would like to keep it and use it for display purposes. The marble shelves in the window area would not be touched and stay as they are. The partition wall would be moved back by one metre and then both side walls need to be shelved all the way up to a height of two metres. The shelves need to be strong enough not to bow under the weight of the books.'

Mr Palamakis surveyed the walls and frowned. 'How are you planning to have the shelving fixed?'

'I thought you would know how to do that. Giovanni looked on the internet for me and I arranged for a firm that supplies custom made shelving and fixes them. I would really like to know if it would be cheaper to use them or ask you to make bookshelves up and fit them.'

Mr Palamakis shrugged. 'They would probably be cheaper. They would have the materials and tools to hand along with competent carpenters. The stone wall is uneven and needs to be levelled. That could be done by drilling into the wall, placing battens and having plaster board fitted. What kind of wood are you planning to have?'

'Pine,' answered Monika immediately.

'Have you decided how many shelves you want and the dimensions?'

'I think so. I thought I should find out the cost of the materials and work before I made a final decision,' admitted Monika, blushing.

'Of course, but that is the next step. If you wanted to have continuous shelving running the whole length of the wall the battens would have to be placed at the same height as you wanted the shelves. To do that you would need to double the number of battens. They would need a number of metal brackets to ensure the shelves did not fall forwards. It would be more economical to have separate units built and then fixed to the battens. Do these units you have seen come with a back panel fitted?'

'I believe so. The pictures on the internet show them with a back panel. I didn't think to ask, I just assumed.'

'If the walls were clad in plaster board there would be no need a back panel.'

Monika shook her head. 'I understand what you are saying, but if books were continually pulled out and pushed back in the plaster board would soon become damaged.'

Mr Palamakis nodded. 'You would not need to use good quality timber for the back panels Hardboard would be quite sufficient and you can specify that to the suppliers. Are all the shelves to be the same height? If you have some over sized books where will you accommodate them?'

'I could have some shelves that would take larger books. That would probably mean two less shelves in that area.' Monika wished she had spent more time designing the outlay of the shop before meeting with Mr Palamakis. 'If I had the partition moved that could also have deeper shelves to accommodate books and it would not need a backing, would it?'

Mr Palamakis shook his head. 'To ensure a partition wall was sufficiently strong to take the weight of heavier shelving and books it would have to be extended up to the ceiling or it would be in danger of falling forwards. May I make some suggestions?' and Monika nodded.

'The partition is already shelved. Is it worth the cost of removing it and having it placed further back to have a little extra wall space? If you left it in situ you would reduce the amount of shelving you needed.' Mr Palamakis shrugged. 'Of course, if you needed more at a later date the partition could always be removed then and more shelves erected.'

'I suppose so,' agreed Monika reluctantly. She was annoyed

with herself. She was showing her ignorance to Mr Palamakis and hoped he would not take advantage of it.

'You would also find,' continued Mr Palamakis, 'that the area behind the partition was hardly large enough if you planned to use it to store surplus books. I assume they would be delivered packed in boxes and once you had placed them in there you would have very little space to move any of them or unpack.'

Monika walked through the door at the end of the partition and looked at the area. Mr Palamakis was right. Making it smaller would also make storage in there difficult. She would have to place the boxes sideways to the wall rather than end on as she had envisaged.

She walked back out into the shop and nodded. 'I understand what you are saying Mr Palamakis and you are right.' It would also mean that she did not have to pay to have the electric light moved to a new position.

'Is there anything else you would like to discuss?'

Monika nodded. 'If battens were placed on the walls would it still be necessary to have plaster board? I don't want continuous shelving. I would prefer to have separate units and would definitely want back panels to the shelves; the area above them to remain as rough stone.'

Mr Palamakis crossed out plaster board and metal brackets from his list and Monika continued.

'The area above could remain as rough stone and the highest marble shelves, those above two metres, I would like left in situ so I can display one of Uncle Yannis's pots or a book at a later date. I want the large counter moved away from the partition and turned so that it is end on. That will give another display area and some storage space beneath. It will also mean that people can walk around to view the goods on the partition shelves.'

'That is no problem and could be done when the other work was completed. Leaving it where it is at present will give more work space.'

'Are you able to give me two separate estimates; one for the removal of the marble and fixing the battens and another for building the shelves?'

Mr Palamakis spread his hands. 'I cannot give you a firm figure for either until I have found out the amount and cost of the battens and timber that is required. There is also the removal of the marble to be taken into account along with wages for my grandsons. If you consider my estimate is too expensive you can obviously ask some other builders for a quote.'

'I need to receive your estimate, compare it with the one I receive from Mr Constanakis, and look at the amount I had allowed for the work before I can give a final decision. I may have to settle for fewer bookshelves to start with and add to them later. If I accepted your estimate I want you to commence the work in January and I would need it completed by the end of February. Would that be possible? I would want the shop stocked and ready to open at Easter.'

'That could be arranged. We will take some final measurements and I can work on the estimate over the weekend and send it to you on Monday. Do you have an e-mail address?'

Monika shook her head. 'I would have to ask you to send it to Mr Iliopolakis at "The Central". He would be willing to pass it through to me.'

'If you are happy to leave the keys with us, Mr Andronicatis, I will return them when we have finished our measurements.'

Monika smiled and shook hands with Mr Palamakis and Giorgos. 'Thank you for coming here and the advice you have given me. I will e-mail you with my decision regarding your estimate as soon as I have had time to consider it.'

Giovanni waited until Mr Palamakis had re-entered the shop and then turned to Monika. 'He is an honest man. He will not use inferior materials or charge you for more than he uses. Provided you decide you can afford his costs you could not do better than to use him. I doubt that any other estimate you obtained would be less.'

'I will have to add his estimate to level the walls and remove the marble to the price for the customised shelving. I don't want to agree to more work than I can afford to start with. I need to have sufficient funds in hand to purchase books.'

'Very wise. How do you plan to spend the remainder of your day?' asked Giovanni.

'I think my mother deserves a swim and then lunch at one of the tavernas.'

Giovanni nodded. 'If you need any more help please contact me.'

'Whichever estimate I decide to accept I am certain I will certainly be contacting you. I will need to speak to the man you recommend for the electrical work. Once that has been completed I would like to ask your advice about a computer. I've never bought one and only ever used those that have been pre-programmed. I will need some lessons.'

'John would probably be better to give you instructions than me. These young people appear to know exactly how to use them.' Giovanni walked towards his car. 'I will wait to hear from you. It has been a pleasure to meet you, Mrs Kokanides.'

Litsa looked at her daughter. 'It's a shame you cannot leave the shop as it is. I like the way those marble shelves are staggered at different heights.'

'So do I', agreed Monika. 'That is why I am leaving them in the shop window and also want the pieces they remove from the walls. Let's collect our swimming gear from the car and go to the beach. Now you've seen the shop for yourself I will tell you the ideas I have.'

'It sounds as though you will have to spend an awful lot of money and then you have the rent to find each week, along with buying books,' replied Litsa dubiously.

'What else will I do with my money? I can't leave it sitting in the bank forever. I'd rather invest it in a project that I know I will enjoy rather than just buy a wardrobe of new clothes and shoes.'

Monika unlocked the boot of the car and took out their swimming towels and a rug to sit on. 'We'll just have a quick swim so there's no point in paying for an umbrella. If you want to return after lunch we can hire one then.'

Week Two - September 2013

Monika waited anxiously for the estimate from Mr Palamakis to be sent through to the computer at "The Central". She had taken her mother out again on the Sunday to Agia Pelagia, appreciating that the drive was not so long.

'Why haven't we gone down to Elounda?' asked Litsa.

'We went down there yesterday. You'll soon see more than enough of the area if my idea works out and you'll be asking me to take you somewhere new. We'll probably go down again next weekend whichever estimate I decide to accept. I'll need to meet the electrician and see how much he is going to charge for his work. Then there is a computer and a desk to place it on. When I know the extent of my expenses I'll be able to think about books, and we'll be visiting the suppliers and publishers, but there's plenty of time for that. I certainly would not want them delivered down there until all the work was completed in case they were damaged.'

'You'd not have anywhere to store them anyway until all the other goods have been removed from the shop.'

Monika frowned. 'That's another thing; I don't really know what Mr Andronicatis has packed away in those boxes at the back. I thought I would keep one of his large urns and put it in the window. If it sells I can always get another from him to replace it or put some books there. I'm hoping Saffie and I can come to an arrangement. If she is agreeable to me having the maps, guides and books she is selling at the moment she would have some space for some of the smaller items from the shop. I will happily give her the box of dusty postcards,' smiled Monika, 'but I thought I would keep the leather bookmarks.'

'Won't they belong to Mr Andronicatis?' asked Litsa

Monika shrugged. 'I can always buy them from him or arrange to give him the money each time I sell one. If Saffie is willing to come to the same arrangement with him it could solve a problem. I said I would display some of his smaller pots on the top shelves until I need them for books. That would look better than having them empty.'

'If you are going to be selling Mr Andronicatis's goods for him you ought to be on commission or have your rent reduced.'

'I don't want to get into an argument with him over rent or he may decide I cannot have the shop. Once I have agreed to his terms I will want a proper agreement drawn up between us. Until I have that I cannot arrange for any work to be started.'

Monika read through Mr Palamakis's estimate for the removal of the marble, purchasing and erecting the wooden battens to provide safe fixings for the shelf units. The cost of the timber and work Mr Palamakis had calculated to be four hundred Euros. To purchase the pine for the books shelves, construction and fixing of them would be a further three thousand eight hundred and seventy five Euros, but had added a paragraph to say that once he had started the work there could be some other unforeseen expense that would have to be taken into account. Monika frowned. She was not prepared for him to suddenly add another thousand Euros to the price.

The estimate she collected from Mr Constanakis she was less pleased with. The quote for making the shelves to her requirements and fixing them she felt was extortionate. If she accepted the measurements as he quoted the quantity she wanted would cost over five thousand six hundred Euros to assemble, transport to

Plaka and erect. If she wanted to extend the length or height of the shelves or make any other alterations the cost would be extra.

Feeling far from confident she approached Vasilis and asked for his opinion of both the estimates. If he felt Mr Palamakis's estimate was reasonable she would telephone Giovanni and ask for a further meeting with his uncle at the coming weekend and draw up an agreement and also to meet Dimitris and discuss the electrical work she needed.

Vasilis read through the estimate from Mr Constanakis and looked at the drawings. 'Ridiculous,' he said and threw the papers to one side. 'The man thinks you are a simple woman with plenty of money. I suggest that you tell him his estimate was more than you had expected and pay for the cost of his visit. Palamakis will deal with you honestly.'

'Thank you, Mr Iliopolakis. I respect your judgement. I will e-mail Mr Palamakis and accept his quote for the whole job. If I accepted Mr Constanakis's estimate I would still have to pay for the marble to be removed and the battening and when added up that would mean I was paying six thousand Euros.'

'Let me know if you have any problems. You can use the computer in my office during your lunch break.'

Monika smiled. 'I will; thank you. I plan to visit Plaka again at the weekend, but in the meantime I would like to tell Mr Palamakis that I have accepted his estimate.'

When Monika e-mailed Mr Palamakis confirming acceptance of his quote, she added a paragraph of her own to say that she did not expect "unforeseen expenses" to amount to more than three hundred Euros in total, and once her agreement with Mr Andronicatis had been finalised she would like the work to commence in January.

Mr Palamakis replied with alacrity and said he would be delighted to meet her again and comply with any further instructions she had. He also requested that she paid him one thousand Euros towards the cost of the pine timber before he commenced constructing the bookshelves, but he made no mention of the "unforeseen expenses".

'Is it alright if my mother comes in?' Monika asked Giovanni. 'I can take her to the taverna and she can wait for me there if it isn't convenient, but it's too hot to leave her sitting in the car.'

'Of course, she is welcome. We will need her signature on the agreement also.'

'Why is that? My mother is not investing in the shop. It is entirely my idea and money.'

Giovanni smiled at her. 'We do not want any misunderstanding at a later date. I will sign to confirm that it is my uncle's wish to rent his shop to you and your mother will sign to say she agrees that you wish to make the investment. That way there can be no accusations later that one or the other of you was coerced into signing. If you are not happy we can have it officially drawn up by a solicitor.'

'No, I trust you, Giovanni.'

'I am pleased to hear it. I have always done business this way with my uncle whenever possible. We discuss, we argue, then we compromise and we agree. It avoids the legal fees a solicitor would charge, but if contested it would be a recognised legal agreement in court.'

Monika hoped she was not being foolish in agreeing to Giovanni's arrangement. Solicitors, as she knew to her cost, could be expensive and provided the conditions were clearly set out there should be no problem.

'I have a document ready for you, but I would like you to read it and be happy before you sign it. If there is anything that you would like to have changed please tell me and we will discuss the matter. I will bring you and your mother some drinks and leave you whilst you read.'

Monika and Litsa sat beneath the umbrella on the patio, a glass of mango juice before each of them. Giovanni placed a typewritten sheet before Monika.

'I have a copy on the computer so feel free to write any comments you may wish to make on this sheet. You have a pen?'

Monika felt her mouth go dry. Once she had signed the agreement she was committed.

She read it through swiftly and then a second time more slowly. She was to rent the shop from January first two thousand and fourteen. The rent was one thousand Euros a month whilst it was not open for business and should be paid in advance. Once she started trading her rent increased to one thousand five hundred Euros each month and again it was to be paid in advance. She was to be responsible for any utility bills throughout the whole of the time she was renting, regardless of whether the shop was open or closed. She placed a star against the paragraph.

If she wished to terminate the agreement she must give at least three months' notice and all rent and outstanding bills should be paid by the time she left. If she wished to continue with the agreement in two thousand and fifteen the rent was open to review and possible increase. She frowned. That sentence she did not like. It would mean Yannis could double the rent the following year if he felt so inclined.

'What's wrong?' asked Litsa as she saw Monika put two large stars on the paper.

'Just a couple of things I want to clarify with Giovanni and his uncle. I don't want to forget it when we start talking again.'

'Apart from that are you happy with it?' asked Litsa and Monika nodded.

'It is very straightforward. You can read it yourself if you like.'

'I suppose I should if I have to sign it along with you.' Litsa read it through quickly and stopped where Monika had starred "in advance" and again beside the possible rent increase. 'That can't be left like that. He could pluck any figure out of the air next year and if you couldn't afford to pay you would have to close and move elsewhere or lose everything. How far in advance are you expected to pay; a week, a month, the whole eight months?'

Monika nodded. 'I need to speak to him about that. I'm certainly not signing anything as vague and open ended. I'll find Giovanni and tell him we are ready to have a discussion.'

Giovanni saw that Monika had written on the paper. 'Is there a problem?' he asked and raised his eyebrows.

'Two things,' replied Monika. 'The rent has to be paid in advance. How much in advance are we talking about?'

'One month,' replied Giovanni firmly.

Monika nodded. 'The other thing is about the possible rent increase for two thousand and fifteen. I cannot sign that without having a reasonable figure to work on.'

'We do not know the state of the economy for that year. Already my uncle has had his pension cut almost in half. It could be reduced again and living expenses could increase.'

Monika looked steadily at Giovanni. 'As I understand it, your uncle is the owner of a number of properties and no doubt they subsidise his pension. He is not a poor man. I appreciate that it is unlikely the cost of living will come down or his pension be increased, but if the financial situation stays the same there should be no need to increase my rent.'

Giovanni spread his hands. 'As you say, it is most unlikely to happen.'

'If his living expenses increase then mine will have increased also. Where would you expect me to find the extra money from?'

'You are hoping to make a profit from your shop.'

'Of course, but I will have to sell a large quantity of books each week to cover my rent and also the rent for the months when I am closed. I cannot visualise making any profit for the first year. I hope to cover my costs, but more than that would be too ambitious.' Monika pushed the paper back towards Giovanni.

Giovanni picked it up and read through the paragraph regarding the possible rent increase. 'I will speak to my uncle.'

Monika sat and waited nervously. She desperately wanted the shop, but if Mr Andronicatis was not prepared to be reasonable she would walk away and look for premises elsewhere in the locale.

Giovanni returned with a broad smile on his face followed by his uncle. 'I am so sorry. There is an omission. It should read that the rent was open to review and possible increase, not exceeding two hundred Euros a month. I have also added that the rent is monthly in advance.'

Monika raised her eyebrows. She did not believe his glib excuse. 'Of course, I should be charging rent to Mr Andronicatis for the goods that remain in my shop and may be sold.'

Giovanni and Yannis exchanged glances. 'What are you suggesting?'

'I think the rent should be reduced to one thousand two hundred Euros each month whilst I am stocking Mr Andronicatis's goods. If they sell the money goes straight to him. I make nothing and they could be taking up valuable space for books. If none of Mr Andronicatis's goods have sold after three months then the rent can return to one thousand five hundred Euros each month and Mr Andronicatis will remove anything that belongs to him.'

Giovanni looked at his uncle who gave a deep sigh.

'You are a hard woman to do business with.'

Monika smiled. 'No, I am practical. I have to consider how much money I have available. I cannot afford to rent your shop and have no capital remaining to purchase books.'

'Very well, we will say the rent is one thousand two hundred Euros a month whilst you stock my uncle's goods. At the end of three months you will return the unsold items to him and your rent will increase to one thousand five hundred Euros.' Giovanni gave Monika a broad smile. 'It is a good arrangement, yes?'

Monika nodded. 'I am happy with that.'

Giovanni rose and waved the sheet of paper in the air. 'I will make the alterations as necessary and print off copies of the agreement.'

Yannis looked at Monika. 'You are a shrewd business woman.

Do you believe a book shop will be a success? Books are a luxury item; not an essential like food or chemists' products.'

'I wouldn't dream of opening a food shop. There are two supermarkets here and John has a small range of goods that can be bought at the taverna. To open a chemist's shop I would need the required qualifications. I am only familiar with books. I am hoping I can draw customers in by offering the popular magazines. If I find there is a demand I will also sell newspapers.'

'The young do not read newspapers. They use those machines they hold in their hands.' Yannis spoke scathingly.

'I am hoping some of the older Cretans or visitors might prefer to have a newspaper.'

'Maybe.' Yannis insisted on having a newspaper each day although he listened to the news on the television.

Giovanni returned and placed two copies of the agreement on the table. 'Please, read them, and then if you are satisfied we will all sign.' He sat back and waited.

Monika read it through slowly, checking the amendments that she had asked for had been added and nothing else had been altered from the one she had read earlier.

'Thank you,' she said finally. 'I will be happy to sign that.'

Yannis signed his name with a flourish and Giovanni added his beneath, printing their names beside the signatures. Monika signed hers and gave it to her mother who looked at her with raised eyebrows.

'It's fine, Mamma. Just sign your name beneath mine.'

Giovanni exchanged the papers and the four signed their names again. Giovanni added the day's date to each agreement and passed two to Monika and another to Yannis.

'So, everything is settled, everyone is happy.'

'There are still some arrangements to be settled.'

Yannis looked at her in surprise. 'What is wrong?' asked Giovanni with a frown.

'There is nothing wrong. The estimate I received from Mr

Constanakis was extortionate and I have accepted the estimate from Mr Palamakis, but we may need to clarify some details. I would also like to meet with the electrician and ask him how much it will cost for the work that I require. I cannot arrange for a computer until I know I have a telephone line and an electricity supply to run it. Also, before work can start up there Mr Andronicatis needs to place his goods somewhere safe where they will not get damaged. I will also need storage space for the books when they begin to arrive.'

Yannis sighed. He did not relish having to pack his pottery and glass away. 'I have some boxes and packing materials,' he said.

'Marisa and I will help,' Giovanni assured him. 'If the partition is not being moved they could be stored behind there temporarily.'

Monika nodded. 'Provided most of the items have been removed when I need the space that will be no problem.'

'But if you are going to sell some of my stock you will need access to it.' protested Yannis.

'Of course, but I saw at least twelve very large urns when I was up there last week. I would be happy to have one in the window as part of the display and probably another standing at the side, but I could not accommodate twelve. If I sold either of them I could always ask you to bring another to replace it. I have said I am willing to have small items stored and some displayed on the top shelf of the bookcases temporarily, but I cannot have those large urns in the store room. There would be no space for anything else.'

'We will arrange something nearer the time.' Giovanni waved his hand airily. 'Do you wish me to call Dimitris and ask him to come to the shop?'

'If it is no trouble to him I would appreciate being able to meet with him today.'

'It will be no trouble,' Giovanni assured her. 'What time to you plan to return to Heraklion?'

Monika exchanged glances with her mother. 'I would like to leave about five.'

'Then we will meet you at the shop at four thirty. Dimitris can collect Skele from John and take him back with him. It will save John having to do so when he closes.'

'Skele?'

'John and Nicola's dog. He is a stray they found some years ago. He could not come here to live as Aunt Ourania had a cat and she was frightened the dog would chase it. We still have her cat so Dimitris still looks after Skele over night.'

'Oh,' Monika smiled. 'That must be the dog I have seen lying outside the taverna and shop at your self-catering apartments.'

'He is a very good dog and very intelligent. When the original apartments were set on fire he tried to move John to safety and then he chased after the perpetrator and held him until the police arrived.'

Monika smiled politely. She found it hard to credit any dog with such intelligence, particularly the ugly mongrel that she had seen lying lazily in the shade outside the taverna and general store.

Monika picked up her copy of the agreement and rose to go. 'I will see you at four thirty with Dimitris. If he is not able to come at that time please let me know.'

'Of course,' agreed Giovanni. 'You are welcome to stay here and have lunch with us.'

Monika shook her head. 'Thank you, but no. I have promised my mother that I will take her to the beach so we can swim. She has been very patient waiting for me whilst we completed our agreement.'

Litsa sighed in relief. Although she had been sitting in the shade of the umbrella she was hot and wanted nothing more than to get into the cooling water. When the invitation had been offered she had hoped Monika would not accept.

'Well, are you satisfied?' asked Litsa as they swam a short distance away from the shore, Litsa continually putting her foot down to ensure she could still touch the ground.

'I think so, provided the estimate from Dimitris is not too much. Once the work starts I'll come down every weekend to check on progress and make sure all is being done the way I want. If it isn't right or they try to take short cuts I will insist they do the work again. That will then be the time for us to start looking for an apartment.'

'Suppose we don't find one?'

'We're sure to find something during the winter months. If it is impossible I will just have to drive down each day until Giovanni opens his self catering apartments and we will stay there.' Monika lifted her face to towards the sun. 'I am so looking forward to being able to come in for a swim every day next summer.'

'Surely you'll be working in the shop?'

'I can always come down to the beach before I open or when I have closed for the day. I might decide to shut at mid-day for a couple of hours. The tourists often return to their hotels for a siesta when they have had their lunch so it would probably be pretty quiet for a while and then trade would pick up again later in the afternoon.'

Litsa nodded. She was not sure where all the trade Monika was expecting was going to come from.

Dimitris looked at the electric socket behind the partition. 'Where is the fuse box?' he asked.

'Behind that stack of boxes,' Giovanni informed him.

Dimitris shook his head. 'A light bulb failing will trip the main switch and you will need access to re-set it and replace the faulty bulb. If the fuse box stays there it cannot have boxes stacked in front. The main electrical cables go in there and if a fault developed there could be a fire. The boxes would be set alight and before you knew it the whole of the back area would be alight.'

'It has been safe enough up until now,' remarked Giovanni.

Dimitris nodded. 'Your uncle has been lucky. I understand you want some additional wiring, Miss Kokanides, and that would increase the load the fuse box has to bear. I understand you wish to open a book shop and that will make the whole premises more vulnerable. Have you considered having sprinklers installed?'

Monika looked at the electrician in horror. 'How much would that cost me?'

Dimitris looked around. 'Ideally I would say you should have at least eight; two where you will be storing boxes of books and three on each side by your book shelves. You would be looking at around five thousand Euros.'

'I planned to have a fire extinguisher.'

'That could be sufficient if you had a fire whilst you were on the premises, but would be no protection if a fire started when the shop was closed or unattended. I know they will be expensive to install but the amount you pay for insurance cover would be reduced.'

Monika bit her lip. She had not taken insurance into account.

'The premises do not belong to me; I am only renting. If I paid to have sprinklers installed and my venture failed I will have spent a considerable amount of money for nothing. I would not be able to take them away with me if I had to close down.'

'Do you have permission from the owner for the other electrical work you require?'

Monika looked at Giovanni. She had mentioned having an additional electrical supply to enable her to run a computer and Yannis had not made any objection.

'My uncle is happy to have extra sockets installed,' he confirmed. 'I do not think he would be prepared to pay to have a sprinkler system. The building is insured against fire. Insurance of the contents would be the responsibility of whoever was trading from here.'

Dimitris looked at Monika and she shook her head.

'I cannot afford to have sprinklers. If the books were covered in water they would be ruined and I imagine any insurance company would take that possibility into account. I doubt if it would decrease the cost of insurance. I will have to take the risk. Of course, if there was a fire due to an electrical fault that could be traced back to yourself I would be asking you for compensation.'

'I am a fully qualified electrician,' replied Dimitris stiffly.

'So I am given to understand. I would not consider employing you otherwise.'

Dimitris shrugged. 'I recommend that the fuse box is moved to a more accessible area and nothing should be placed in front of it to obstruct access.'

'Where do you suggest?'

'On the wall beside the front door.'

'I had planned to have one of Mr Andronicatis's large urns standing there. A fuse box would look ugly.'

'It could be boxed in to look like a small cupboard and you could stand a smaller display item on the top, but nothing in front.'

Monika frowned. 'I suppose I could ask Mr Palamakis to make a cupboard there, but what about the wiring? I cannot have electrical wires on view.'

'That would not be necessary. From the electric light and the sockets in your storeroom they could run up the wall to the top of the partition. They would then run along the top of the shelves and drop down at the side into the fuse box. The extra sockets you have asked for would be next to the fuse box. The wires that run along the top of the shelves could be encased in a plastic sheath for safety and once secured to the shelving it is doubtful that they would be noticeable.'

Monika gave a sigh. The bills were mounting up. 'Very well. Can you send me through an estimate for the cost of your work including the materials?'

Dimitris nodded. 'It will take me a few days to get the prices. I will have to go to Aghios Nikolaos to visit the suppliers.'

'Then it might be better if I come down next weekend and collect it from you.'

'I can leave it with John. That would probably be easier for you than coming to my house. I might be out when you arrive.'

Giovanni cleared his throat. 'I think my uncle would like to have a copy of the specification. It is his property and he needs to know what is intended to take place here.'

'Do you think he will object?' asked Monika anxiously.

'Not for a minute, but he should know what has been done. His insurance company may ask for details and he would look foolish if he said he did not know.'

'When I have completed the work I will have to ask the electrical company to give me a certificate to say all has complied with their regulations. I will pass that to you, Miss Kokanides, and give a copy to Mr Andronicatis.'

'Are you sure you shouldn't have sprinklers installed?' asked Litsa as they drove away from Plaka.

Monika shrugged. 'Ideally, yes, but if Mr Andronicatis is not willing to pay to have them installed then he is hardly likely to reimburse me if I do not renew my agreement with him next year. I just hope Dimitris does not quote some ridiculous figure for the work he is going to do.'

'Are you going to get some other estimates?'

Monika shook her head. 'Dimitris is recommended by Giovanni and I am sure he would not have used him if he was not reliable. I could find someone who offered to do the work for less and it could be unsatisfactory. He did not need to tell me about the safety certificate. I would have just accepted an electrician's word that all was in order.'

'Apart from collecting the estimate next weekend what else are you proposing to do?'

Monika smiled. 'I'm sure you are tired of listening to discussions about the shop. I want to be able find some time to talk to Saffron next week and come to an arrangement regarding the goods we both sell. We don't want to be in competition with each other.'

'Do you think she would let me look after her shop whilst you are talking?' asked Litsa eagerly.

'You can always offer, but I think it is doubtful. She might appreciate some help with wrapping goods for her customers.'

Litsa nodded happily. She wished her daughter was opening a gift shop rather than a book shop. She did not think that Monika would want her assistance.

Yannis gave a deep sigh and looked around his shop. He had consulted the catalogues that advertised museum replicas and saw that all the wholesale prices had increased since he had purchased the items. He had done as Giovanni had suggested and made out new labels with a higher price crossed through and his original asking price beneath. People would think they were getting a bargain.

Whilst Marisa sat and wrote out labels for the Venetian glassware and alabaster ornaments he began to work his way steadily around the rows of pots replacing the labels. When he had finished that he would have to open up the boxes he had stored behind the partition and see what was inside each one.

Marcus had offered to come and climb the ladder to label the pottery and ornaments on the higher shelves and once that was completed he would have to put up the notices that Giovanni had prepared in Greek, English, Italian, French and German announcing that the shop was closing at the end of October and all the goods were half price.

'What price do you want me to put on the marble eggs?' asked Marisa.

'What are they now?'

'The larger ones say five Euros and the smaller three.'

'Make the larger ones six, then cross it out and put five. The same with the smaller ones; mark them as four and reduced to three. You can do just one large label for each. We'll place them in a kylix rather than a box and put them in the window. Seeing something cheap should attract people inside.'

'I can't see any kylix,' remarked Marisa looking around the shelves and Yannis clicked his tongue.

'I'll have a look in the back. In the meantime you can make out a large label saying the miniature hand-painted pots are ten Euros each. Do it on a piece of card so it can be bent and stood up amongst them. We'll change the window display tomorrow and put them at the front.'

'How much is Saffie selling them for?' asked Marisa.

'I don't remember. Better go and check. Look on the bottom of those she has there. They should have a sticky label with the price. Tell her they all have to be ten Euros.'

'Suppose her stickers are for more than ten?'

'Then come back and tell me.' Yannis was hot, tired and bad tempered. He entered the stock room, wishing there was a chair in there that he could sit on whilst he opened the boxes. He read the descriptive label on those that were still sealed and hoped they described the contents accurately. To keep Ourania occupied he had asked her to help him in the stock room. Together they had unpacked and repacked the boxes time and again, making Ourania feel she was being useful to her husband. No doubt he had allowed her to put items wherever she pleased and they fitted. Everything would be in a muddle. Now he would have to go through the painstaking job of examining the contents of each box to try to find a kylix, preferably two.

Marisa sidled over to the counter where Saffron was wrapping two T-shirts.

'I'm sure your grandsons will love them,' she smiled as the woman handed over her money and waited for her change.

'Can I have a look at the miniature pots?' asked Marisa. 'Yannis wants to know how much you are charging for them. He's busy putting new labels on everything.'

'Help yourself,' smiled Saffron, understanding little that Marisa had said. She watched as Marisa picked up one small pot after another and replaced them on the shelf.

'Does Uncle Yannis want to take them back?'

Marisa looked at her with a puzzled frown and Saffron tried again.

'Uncle Yannis – his pots – he wants?'

Marisa shook her head. 'Ten Euros,' she said firmly.

Saffron looked at the sticker on the base. 'Eight Euros.'

'I don't think so. He just wants to know how much you are selling them for. The stickers on the base say eight Euros. He says they must be ten Euros.'

Saffron looked at the sticker on the base. 'Eight Euros. Uncle Yannis said eight Euros.'

'No, no, ten Euros, Yannis say.'

Saffron smiled at Marisa again. If there was a problem Uncle Yannis could 'phone Vasi and he would explain it to her.

Marisa hurried back to Yannis. 'Saffron's pots say eight Euros on the base.'

'Make another notice from the card saying they are ten and take it in to her. Then remove all the stickers that are on them now. I still can't find the kylix.'

Marisa wrote out a second cardboard notice. "HAND PANTED MINATERS 10 E". She would take it in to Saffron and then remove the stickers from the base of the pots. Saffron would understand that they were all to be at a new price now.

Saffron read the notice a small smile playing at her lips. She would not be so rude or hurtful to Marisa to point out the errors in her spelling. Once Marisa had left she would put the notice out of sight and telephone Giovanni, explain the problem and suggest he made a new notice, in different languages, and ensured the words were spelled correctly.

Marisa stood there scratching off the sticky labels with her thumb nail and dropping them on the floor. When she finished she placed the notice she had made prominently between them, smiled at Saffron and returned to Yannis.

Immediately Saffron went over and collected up the scraps

of sticky paper from the floor and laid the notice face down. If by any chance Yannis came in or Marisa returned she could say it had fallen over.

Monika and her mother entered Saffron's gift shop. As usual it was busy, tourists picking up the goods on display, handling them and putting them back down haphazardly, whilst Saffron tried to serve and watch that no one placed an item into their pocket. Saffron nodded at them and indicated that Litsa should have the chair that was beside her desk.

Litsa sat down gratefully whilst Monika wandered around the shop.

'How do you manage every day here on your own?' asked Litsa.

'Bryony comes three days each week, so that gives me a break so I can catch up with ordering and the accounts. Occasionally we are both here for a morning or the afternoon when we know it will be busy.'

Litsa nodded. Saffron could certainly do with an assistant, if only to wrap the goods.

Monika stopped in front of the guides and maps and took down the details of the publishers in her notebook; provided Saffron was willing for her to sell the items these were the people she would need to contact. She glanced at the few novels that were on display, and again noted the publisher and distributor.

Finally she walked over to the counter where Saffron wiped her forehead. 'Sorry, it is always a bit manic when a coach party returns from the island. They know they have very little time to choose souvenirs or gifts.'

'I'll not complain if I am as busy as you,' smiled Monika.

'You're going ahead with the shop, then?'

Monika nodded. 'I've made an agreement with Mr Andronicatis, accepted the estimate from Mr Palamakis for his work, and collected Dimitris's estimate for the electrical work from John.'

'I'll be pleased to have you next door. I was a bit concerned that if Uncle Yannis did close his shop someone else would open it and try to sell the same sort of items as I do.'

'That's what I wanted to talk to you about. I've agreed that I will keep some of the pottery, glass and alabaster on display and if it is sold the money goes straight to Mr Andronicatis. I was going to ask if you would be willing to take a few more of the smaller items.'

Saffron shook her head. 'I really haven't got the space.'

'I thought if I bought whatever guides and maps you had remaining at the end of the season you would have that space available. They'd have to be in good condition still, of course.'

Saffron frowned. 'You're planning to stock maps and guides?'

'I am going to be a book shop so they would be more suitable in my shop than yours. You would still have the postcards to draw customers in. In fact there is a box of old ones next door that I would give you, just to get them out of the way.'

A customer approached the counter and looked pointedly at his watch. Monika moved to one side whilst Saffron took his money for a guide book.

'What else would you want me to take?' she asked as he left the shop.

'I honestly don't know. There are some very attractive photograph albums, but I don't think anyone uses albums any more. Everyone appears to take photos on their mobile 'phone. Even if they have a proper camera I understand they transfer them onto their computer later. I suppose they might still purchase frames to mount a special photo in. There are a number of silver ones that just need to be rubbed over to improve their appearance. You might find you have sales for those,' added Monika hopefully.

'I stock SD cards for cameras and the mini ones for mobile 'phones.'

'Then I'll avoid those,' smiled Monika. 'I want to stock magazines and I might also sell newspapers. I'll need to speak to the suppliers nearer the time and decide if it would be worth my while.'

'When are you planning to take over the shop?'

'Not until January. That will give Mr Andronicatis time to sort out and remove some of his stock before any work starts inside. I will then have to go through the remainder and agree with him what can be stored and subsequently sold by me. I might be a good idea if you were able to advise us. You know the items you have sold on his behalf.'

'It's usually the smaller items. The large ones are too expensive.'

'I'll arrange to meet with you at the end of the season and we can have a proper discussion. I've never run a shop before and I'm sure you will be able to warn me about some of the pitfalls.'

'I don't know anything about books,' Saffron warned her, 'but if I can help you with general problems I will.'

'I think you're about to have another group of tourists descend upon you,' remarked Monika as a chattering group arrived outside. 'I'll be around and about again at various times and Giovanni has my mobile number should you need to contact me.'

Saffron nodded. She knew Vasi also had Monika's phone number and could think of no reason why she should need to contact her until the end of the season when they would have an opportunity to discuss Monika's proposals without continual interruptions from customers. It might even be to her advantage to talk to Uncle Yannis and come to an arrangement regarding some of his stock.

Litsa rose reluctantly from the chair and followed Monika out. She would have loved to have stayed in the shop and wrapped the goods as they were purchased.

Week Three – September 2013

Monika waited impatiently for the tourist season to end. There was so much she wanted to get organised, but felt that until she actually held the keys to the shop in her hand she must wait. There was no point in buying a computer until she was able to install it in the shop and she went to the internet cafe to look up book suppliers, both on Crete and in Athens.

She was loath to look for an apartment in the Elounda area before January at the earliest. Once they moved down there it would mean driving up to Heraklion each day to take her mother to the shop and for her to go to "The Central". Instead she arranged with Vasilis that she would work seven days each week at the hotel to enable her to save more money and then have time off in January and February before she finally gave in her notice to him.

Monika browsed in the local library intending to make a note of titles and authors and planning to ask the assistants if certain books were available in other languages, then she realised she really was wasting her time. If she e-mailed Mrs Ethanides she was sure the librarian could give her all the information she required.

When she mentioned this her mother frowned. 'Why don't we make a quick visit to Rhodes? I ought to have a look at the shop and make sure there aren't any major repairs needed. You've told me I should put Natasha's rent up and I would want to talk to her before I did that. If we went over for a few days you could go to the library and talk to Mrs Ethanides.'

Monika considered her mother's proposal. 'I don't want to take too much time off. I told Mr Iliopolakis that I would work every day until the end of February.'

'I'm sure he would understand that you needed to come over with me.'

'I suppose we could leave one afternoon, have a day there and return the following morning. That would mean I only had to ask for two days off.'

'You should not have agreed to work every day. You should have some time off. Whilst you're working I'm just stuck here on my own at the weekends.'

'Mamma, you have friends you can visit and spend some time with. What you really mean is that you are missing driving out to some place every weekend.'

Litsa compressed her lips. It was true. She did miss being taken to Elounda or other villages and then being able to tell her envious co-workers or friends where she had been.

'I'll speak to Mr Iliopolakis and ask when it would be most convenient for him to release me. It will have to be before the direct flights stop running. I'm not prepared to go via Athens and have to spend hours waiting around in airports.'

'I'll need to know as soon as possible so I can ask for some time off also,' Litsa reminded her.

'Of course. I'll see Mr Iliopolakis tomorrow. Once we have agreed on some dates I'll tell you and book our flight. I'll also contact the hotel where we stayed before and book a room.'

'You won't be hiring a car again?' asked Litsa hopefully.

'If we are only there for the one day we'll not have time to go sightseeing,' replied Monika firmly. 'I'll obviously visit Natasha with you; then leave you to talk to her whilst I go to the library.'

Natasha was delighted to see Monika and her mother when they arrived unannounced at the shop in the Old Town of Rhodes.

'I was sorry to hear about your mother,' she said to Litsa. 'Mr Spanides told me when I went to pay the rent and I asked him to send my condolences on to you. I hope he did so.'

'He wrote me an e-mail to say he had told you the sad news and you sent your sympathy to us.'

'So what brings you both here now?' asked Natasha. 'Are you planning to come back and live in the Old Town?'

Litsa shook her head. 'I thought I ought to come over and have a look at the shop, make sure there weren't any repairs needed.'

'Not that I'm aware of. A tile blew off the roof when we had a high wind and cracked another. I just had them replaced. I didn't think I needed to trouble you. I just gave Mr Spanides the bill and he deducted it from my rent payment.'

'I remember; you did the right thing. No problems with the drains and no damp?'

'The drains are fine, the house always smells and feels a little damp until I have a fire regularly, but that's usual in these old buildings.'

Litsa nodded. She remembered how her mother had often lit a fire even during the summer months if there had been a heavy rain storm. 'How are you keeping, Natasha?'

Natasha shrugged. 'I'm as well as I can be. I take my medication each day and have check-ups regularly. The clinic seems happy enough with me. I appear to be stable, but that can change, of course.'

'And the shop? Are you making a reasonable living?'

'During the season I do quite well from passing trade. If tourists come in from the San Francisco Gate I am the first shop they see and they usually want to buy some water. If they have children with them they always start to clamour for an ice cream.' Natasha pointed to the large freezer that sat outside the shop.

'Have you bought that?'

Natasha shook her head. 'I hire it during the tourist season. It's a bit of a nuisance to have to move it in and out each day but it pays for itself each month. If the tourists are going back this way to self catering accommodation they often do a bit of shopping here for their evening meal or breakfast. The rest of the time the girls patronise me and keep me going.'

Litsa frowned. 'You've been very good about keeping up your rent payments on time.'

'I always make sure I have enough for my rent,' Natasha assured her.

'Of course you are still paying the same rent as when my mother agreed to let you have the shop and live here. Living expenses have increased for us. I am going to have to ask you for more rent each month.'

'How much more?' asked Natasha warily.

'I thought an extra hundred. That's only twenty five Euros a week increase. Can you afford it?'

Natasha shrugged. 'I will have to. I know I couldn't find anywhere else cheaper and have a shop as well. I'll just have to increase my prices a little.'

Litsa gave a sigh of relief. Monika had reminded her that morning that Natasha's rent should be increased, but they had neither of them had discussed a figure and Monika had nodded when her mother mentioned the sum.

'I'll let Mr Spanides know that as from the first of October you will be paying the extra. He'll probably say that we should draw up a new contract, but provided we agree I don't think that is necessary.'

Natasha was surprised that her rent had not been increased annually and she knew she could afford an extra hundred Euros a month. Litsa could have asked for double that amount. The little general store was doing better than she had ever expected. After she had hired the freezer the tourist trade had increased dramatically.

'Where are you living now?' asked Natasha. 'Still in Athens?'

Litsa was about to reply that they had never lived in the mainland when Monika nodded vehemently. 'We enjoy the city life. There is always something interesting taking place and the hotel where I work is busy throughout the year.'

'Monika won't be working there much longer,' smiled Litsa. 'She's going to open a book shop.'

'Is that so? What made you decide to do that?'

'Oh,' replied Monika airily, 'the opportunity arose and I've always loved books.'

'Are you buying it with the money you received from your ex?' asked Natasha curiously.

'Goodness, no. I have nowhere near enough money to buy a shop. I'm only renting. If it doesn't work out I'll return to my receptionist job at the hotel.'

'She's going to buy a car,' added Litsa and Monika shot her mother a warning glance. She did not want Natasha to know too much about their affairs. She would obviously gossip with the girls and the information about her could eventually reach Manu.

'I like to take my mother out when I'm not working. I thought that was quite a good way to use the settlement I received.'

'I'd love to visit you,' Natasha sighed enviously. 'I've never been to Athens. I wouldn't expect to stay with you, of course, but you would be able to show me around.'

'We'll think about making a date when I see how working at the book shop goes. Until I start I have no idea how many hours a week I will have to put in. It would be no good you visiting and finding that both my mother and I were working every day. We ought to make a move, Mamma. You said you wanted to visit Rebekah and I want to talk to Mrs Ethanides. We'll come back and see you later, Natasha.'

Litsa opened her mouth to argue and saw the warning frown on Monika's face. Litsa lowered her voice. 'I want to know the latest gossip from the girls. Are all my old friends still there?'

'There have been some changes. Effie has left and a new girl, Agapi is renting her rooms.'

'I'll definitely be back, Natasha.'

Once around the corner where Natasha would not be able to hear them Monika stopped. 'Mamma, please be careful what you say to Natasha. Don't tell her we are living on Crete. If Manu got to hear he might come looking for me there.'

'He can't, he's in prison.'

'He is now, but he will be released next year. He may well come up here looking for us and ask Natasha if she knows where we are. It's better that she believes we are still over in Piraeus. Let's walk down and see if Rebekah is in. I'm sure she will be pleased to see you, but don't tell her we live on Crete. When you have finished talking to her you can go back up to Natasha and I'll meet you there later.'

Litsa nodded. The last time she had visited Rebekah they had little to talk about. As Monika did not want her to mention Crete it was often difficult to make conversation. 'I can tell her about the book shop?'

'Of course, but let her think it's in Piraeus. Talk about trivial, inconsequential things, but don't tell anyone where we live.'

When Rebekah opened her door to Litsa she looked puzzled for a moment and then delighted. 'Of all people, you were the last person I expected to see at my door.'

'May I come in?'

'Of course. I have the children here so you'll have to excuse the toys that are all over the floor.'

'Your grand children?' asked Litsa and Rebekah nodded proudly.

'Both my boys are married now, but only Rueben has children. Joshua is nearly three and Elijah is eighteen months. I look after them one day a week so Sarah can get some sleep. She works as a nurse so she was on duty last night and will be again tonight. She only does the two nights, but it helps them financially.'

'I don't know how anyone copes with their children when they have to work at night if they haven't got their mother to rely on.'

'Your mother had Monika every day,' Rebekah reminded her.

'And I was grateful to her. If she had not agreed to help me I don't know what I would have done. There was no way I was going to allow Monika to be placed in an orphanage.'

'What is she doing now?'

'Who? Monika or my mother?'

'Monika. Natasha up at the shop told me your mother had died. I was sorry to hear that.'

Litsa shrugged. 'It was inevitable. The doctors tried operating and giving her treatment, but it was not successful.'

'You didn't bring her back to Rhodes for burial?'

Litsa shook her head. 'It was better that she stayed close to us. We would have had to come backwards and forwards to Rhodes for the services.'

'You didn't think she wanted to be near to your father?'

Litsa looked at Rebekah in surprise. It was years since she had thought about her father and his untimely death. 'I don't think it makes any difference once you are dead. You are together in spirit.'

'You're probably right.' Litsa and Rebekah had never fallen out over their different religions and beliefs. 'I'm forgetting my manners. I'll get some coffee and then you must tell me all about Monika.'

Mrs Ethanides greeted Monika with delight. 'How lovely that you have decided to pay me a visit. What has brought you over to Rhodes? Are you thinking of returning here to live?'

Monika shook her head. 'I've really come to ask you for advice and information.'

Mrs Ethanides raised her eyebrows. 'If you are still working at the hotel I can only advise you to look for a position in a library. Your brains are wasted doing cleaning. I could have a look on line and see if there are any vacancies. I would give you a reference, of course.'

Monika smiled. 'I'm not doing cleaning any longer. I work on reception at the moment, but I'm planning to leave at the end of the year. I'm going to open a book shop.'

'A book shop? You are going to open one?'

Monika nodded. 'I enjoy my work at the hotel, but my first love is books. I have the opportunity to rent a shop and I have signed an agreement with the owner. In January the builders will begin to put up shelves ready for my books.'

'Wait a moment and I will tell my assistant that I am taking an early lunch break. We can go to the taverna next door and you can tell me all about it.'

Monika felt hesitant about patronising the taverna close to the library. It was the one where Manu had taken her each week when he met her when she had finished work. She hoped the waiting staff would have changed by now and that having altered her appearance no one would recognise or remember her.

As they took a seat outside a girl came to take their order and Monika immediately recognised her. She bent her head and pretended to be studying the menu.

'I can recommend their keftedes,' said Mrs Ethanides.

'Very well,' said Monika without looking up. 'I will be happy with those and a salad. I would like a frappe whilst we are waiting.'

Mrs Ethanides nodded. 'That's the same for both of us, please. Keftedes and salad and we'd both like a frappe.'

The girl scribbled on her pad and walked away, calling out to the man behind the coffee machine as she passed him on her way to the kitchen.

'I'll move my chair round if you don't mind,' said Monika. 'The sun is in my eyes.'

Mrs Ethanides did not protest, although she did not understand how the sun could possibly be in Monika's eyes as they were sitting in the shade of the building.

'That's better,' announced Monika as she now sat with her back to the taverna.

'So, tell me about your book shop.' Mrs Ethanides leaned forward eagerly and Monika told her how on frequent visits to a beautiful bay she had seen Mr Andronicatis's shop hardly ever open and then heard that he was thinking of closing down.

'It isn't in Heraklion?'

Monika shook her head. 'I'll be looking for somewhere for my mother and me to live locally once I am down there every day. I wouldn't want to commute to and from Heraklion. I may have to buy a small car, depending how close to the shop we can find an apartment.'

'So that is one of your dreams that has come true,' smiled Mrs Ethanides. 'I hope your book shop dream will be as successful as learning to drive.'

'It is quite an undertaking. I didn't realise how much wooden book shelves cost. He has lovely marble shelves in there, but they are all different heights and lengths. They showed off his items beautifully, but were useless for books.'

'Why is he closing?' asked Mrs Ethanides.

'He is elderly and his wife died about a year ago. They had always been in the shop together and I think he just lost heart in it. He was hardly ever open and charged high prices for museum replicas. Tourists would look at his goods, admire them and walk away. Many of his items were too large to carry and would have to be shipped to their destination which, of course, added to their cost.'

'So what is he going to do with them when you have the shop?' Mrs Ethanides picked up her frappe, took a mouthful and wiped the froth from her lip.

'I have agreed to keep some of the smaller pottery, alabaster, bronze and onyx items. There are some beautiful Venetian glass vases. I thought I would place them on the higher shelves until I need the space for books. If they sell,' Monika shrugged, 'I will just give him the money.'

'You should receive commission for selling his goods.'

'I'm paying him less rent whilst they are stored with me. That isn't what I wanted to talk to you about, though. Can you tell me which novels are the most popular in the library? I'm planning to have books in both Greek and English to start with. I hope to encourage the local people to come and buy from me.'

Their keftedes and salad arrived as they talked and both ladies helped themselves to a portion, along with some tsatziki.

'Do they have the time to read in the summer?'

'Not really, but I thought I could stay open for an extra week at the end of the season and leave a telephone number on my door so I could be contacted if someone wanted a book. I may have to return to Heraklion and work as a receptionist in the winter months. I would then have to arrange to drive down and open up.'

Mrs Ethanides frowned. 'That would be hardly profitable once you took the cost of your petrol into consideration.'

Monika shrugged. 'I'll decide when I know how popular I am at the end of the summer. I want to visit the schools in the area and tell them that I will be stocking exercise books for their pupils. That could encourage the children to visit the shop.'

'You'll sell children's books?'

Monika nodded emphatically and waited until she had swallowed her mouthful of keftedes. 'Children's story books and those that have word or number games, along with the exercise books they need for school. The adult novels will just be in Greek and English at first. I can branch out into other languages later if there is the need. I'll offer to buy books back if they are in good condition for one Euro and sell them again as second hand for two or three Euros. I'm arranging with the gift shop next door that I will sell maps and guides and I'm planning to have a small stock of magazines, the kind people often read whilst they are on the beach or beside a pool.'

'You seem to have everything planned out. I can send you through a list of the books that have been most popular this year. Let me have your e-mail address.'

Monika finished her keftedes and shook her head. 'I haven't invested in a computer yet. I need to have a telephone line installed into the shop and then I will need some instruction on how to use a computer efficiently. Once I've mastered it I will make a list of books and then ask you to send me the supplier's details. I'm sure I will think of other things to ask you as well.'

'That shouldn't take you long. You were quick enough to learn the library computer system.'

'That was easy,' smiled Monika. 'The programme was already installed. I have to learn how to look things up, contact the suppliers and also have an efficient accounting system. I've never dealt with accounts and maths was never my best subject. I had terrible problems trying to work out how much timber I would need for my book shelves down each wall.'

'Why didn't you ask the builder to work it out for you?'

'I did eventually, but I wanted to have a rough idea of the amount and cost first. How would I know if he was being honest with me otherwise?'

Mrs Ethanides chuckled. 'I don't think you will have any problem managing your accounts.' She looked at her watch. 'I ought to be getting back. I never feel I should abuse the privilege of being the manager. I expect staff to return on time from their break so I should set an example.'

Monika turned and raised her hand for the bill and then wished she had not attracted the girl's attention. Sitting no more than two tables away was Stenos and he was looking straight at her. Horrified Monika turned to Mrs Ethanides.

'I have to go. I will meet you back at the library.' She placed a fifty Euro note on the table and before Mrs Ethanides could protest she hurried away.

'What's wrong?' asked Mrs Ethanides when she saw Monika waiting just inside the library door. 'Aren't you feeling well?'

Monika shook her head. 'I'm sorry. I saw someone there who knows my husband, well, my ex-husband. I didn't want him to recognise me.'

'I doubt if he would. You've changed your appearance considerably since you were working here. I like your hair now you've had it cut and lightened. It always looked a bit heavy before. Here, I have your change.'

'I hope you paid for your meal from it.'

'Of course not. I had every intention of paying for you. We'll pay half each. That's only fair. Are you still concerned that your ex will come looking for you?'

'I think I will always be worried. He's due to be released next year. I just hope he continues to look for me on Rhodes or in Piraeus. I feel safe at the moment on Crete.'

'If he comes to the library I'll not tell him where you are,' Mrs Ethanides assured her. 'I'd love to visit you at some time; when you have your shop up and running. I've never been to Crete. I'd come with my husband and we'd stay somewhere as ordinary tourists and visit you at the shop. We might just happen to be in the same taverna as you during the evening.'

'I'd like that,' smiled Monika. 'I know my mother would be pleased to see you again. I've left her up at the shop talking to Natasha. She's been very patient waiting for me whilst I've been dealing with the builders and electrician. I didn't think she'd want to spend time this morning discussing books.'

'Will your mother help you in the shop?'

Monika shook her head. 'I won't be able to afford to employ anyone and I couldn't expect my mother to work there for nothing. I hope she will be able to find something satisfactory. She's been working in a general store, but where we are going is only a small place. They probably have family or regular staff in their shops and no need of anyone else. There's a gift shop next door to me and she would love to work there.'

Mrs Ethanides wrote down her e-mail address on a piece of paper. 'That's my private e-mail. It would be better if you used that to contact me rather than the library mailing address. I can access it whilst I am at work. Once you have sorted out your computer send me your contact details and we can keep in touch.'

Monika placed the slip of paper safely into her purse. 'I'll certainly do that. I know someone who is very efficient on a computer and also an excellent photographer. I could ask him to send you through some photos so you can see how the shop looks. You might have some suggestions to make.'

'I doubt that. All I will say is do not make it look too austere. If you are planning to have shelves all the way around it could end up looking more like a library than a welcoming book shop.'

Monika frowned. 'I plan to have two walls shelved completely from the floor almost up to the ceiling. Above them there are some family prints that are not for sale.'

Mrs Ethanides shook her head. 'I suggest you have the shelves starting about fifty centimetres above the floor. It is not convenient for people to bend any lower.'

'I hadn't thought of that,' admitted Monika. 'I'll have to speak to my builder. Having one less shelf all the way around should reduce the cost.'

'Are they all going to be fixed at the same height? Some books are larger than others, remember.'

Monika nodded. 'I thought I could place them sideways on the shelf.'

Mrs Ethanides frowned. 'That could look clumsy. Have a look at your design again. You could have one bookcase with less shelves and more space between them to take the oversize books. You could have some shelving that was less high to break the area up and move the prints you mentioned down.'

'I'm not sure if I could move the prints. They will not belong to me. There are some plaques that are copies of the frescoes at Knossos. I'd hoped to pass those in to the gift shop, but they might be suitable to decorate a wall space.'

'These are only ideas,' smiled Mrs Ethanides. 'It is your shop and you must design it to your liking.'

'I'll think about it carefully. I can't afford to make mistakes and have them rectified later. I suppose I was thinking of the library lay out, just shelves for books. I wasn't considering how attractive I should make it look inside.'

'Your customers need to feel welcome.'

'I'll sit down later and draw out some plans. I'll have to speak to Mr Palamakis and ask if any new design I have is feasible. He won't have ordered any timber yet as he's not due to start any work there until January. Your help has been invaluable, Mrs Ethanides. I'm so pleased I agreed to come over for the day so I had the opportunity to talk to you.'

'I'm willing to give you any help I can and it has been a pleasure to see you. I'll send you through the list of most popular books when you have sent me your e-mail address. Make sure you order from the suppliers in good time. You don't want to be opening up with empty shelves.'

'I just hope they will be empty by the end of my first season.'

Monika walked slowly back up the hill to from the library to the shop. Mrs Ethanides had given her a number of ideas to think about. Once they were back on Crete she would check the measurements she had made and see if changing the number of shelves would save her money and make the shop look more attractive. Rather than do a rough sketch in her notebook it would be advisable to purchase some graph paper and draw the walls and proposed shelving to scale. Before she approached Mr Palamakis she would show Cathy and Mr Iliopolakis and ask their opinion. If they thought that her new ideas were an improvement she could then show Mr Palamakis exactly what she envisaged and provided he agreed she could amend her order accordingly.

So engrossed was she in her thoughts that she did not notice the man approaching her until he spoke to her.

'Excuse me, is it Monika, Monika Graphides?'

Monika stopped and took a deep breath. Her heart was beating uncontrollably. Stenos had obviously recognised her. She frowned and shook her head.

'I am sorry,' she muttered. 'I know of no one by that name. You have made a mistake.'

She hurried on and entered the first shop she came to. Standing at the back where the light was dim she hurriedly pressed in the numbers of her mother's 'phone.

'Mamma, listen to me. Ask Natasha to shut the shop immediately and you go down to the Navarhiou Gate and meet me there. Don't ask questions. I'll explain when I see you.'

Hoping her mother would do as she had requested and not delay saying goodbye to Natasha, Monika took her time pretending to look at the items for sale, whilst keeping a wary eye on the doorway should Stenos enter. Finally satisfied that he was not going to do so she left and began to retrace her steps down the hill towards the Navarhiou Gate, avoiding the taverna where she had eaten lunch with Mrs Ethanides.

Litsa was waiting for her daughter, looking both surprised and annoyed. 'What's all this about? Why the rush to get down here and for Natasha to close the shop?'

'Have you had some lunch?' asked Monika.

'I had an omelette with Natasha.'

'I went for lunch with Mrs Ethanides. Just as we were finishing I saw Stenos, Manu's friend who saw me in Piraeus. I was sure he had recognised me. I went back to the library and stayed there talking to Mrs Ethanides but as I began to walk up to the shop he suddenly appeared in front of me. He asked if I was Monika Graphides and I said I didn't know anyone of that name. I went into the nearest shop and 'phoned you to come and meet me.'

Litsa shook her head in puzzlement. 'But why ask Natasha to close?'

'I don't know how much he knows. He may go up to the shop and ask Natasha if she has seen me. I didn't want him to find you sitting up there with her. As far as I know he has only met you once when he came to our wedding, but if he recognised me, he could well remember you.'

'So what do you plan to do now?'

'We need to go to an area that is thronged with tourists. We'll mingle with them and be less likely to be noticed.'

'Best to stay in the Old Town, then. There are always more tourists here than anywhere else.'

'We'll go back along the road from here and then turn up into the main shopping street. We can go in and out of the shops. Some of them have entrances that lead into the next street so we can go through one and then back through the next one. If we hang around and look at the items on sale we should be able to see if anyone is following us.'

Litsa shrugged. She thought Monika was being paranoid. It was hardly likely that the man who had approached her would follow them around now she had told him she was not Monika Graphides. She had been enjoying her time talking to Natasha, hearing about the girls who still lived up in the street and laughing at the story of Lola who had suffered a broken rib from a client.

'It was accidental,' Natasha had assured her when she saw the horrified look on Litsa's face. 'He caught his foot in his trousers when he was getting dressed and fell on top of her. He realised he had hurt her and took her a big bunch of flowers along with an apology the next day. She wasn't able to work for some weeks and he called frequently to ask after her, always taking a little gift of chocolates. He felt really bad about hurting her and between you and me I think Lola made it sound far worse to him than it was. She was enjoying his attention.'

Grudgingly Litsa followed Monika through the busy streets, pretending to look at items for sale whilst Monika continually looked around for any sign of Stenos.

'There's no sign of anyone following us,' said Litsa half an hour later, wiping her perspiring face. 'We ought to go back up to Natasha and tell her she can reopen the shop. When we've done that I'd be happy to return to the hotel and have a shower.'

Monika looked doubtfully at her mother. 'He may be hanging around up there.'

Litsa looked at her daughter in exasperation. 'You say you told him you did not know anyone called Monika Graphides so why should he approach you a second time? You're over reacting.'

'I'll be pleased when we're back on Crete,' said Monika miserably.

'Well we cannot spend the time until then wandering around these shops. The owners are beginning to look at us suspiciously. They probably think we're going to start pilfering.'

Monika sighed. She knew Manu was still in prison and it was quite likely that Stenos was simply going to ask after her well being. It was unfortunate that he had been in the same taverna as herself and Mrs Ethanides earlier.

Week Four – September 2013

Now Monika felt safe again. Their journey home had been uneventful and she had arrived at "The Central" in plenty of time to relieve the morning receptionist of her duties and be brought up to date with arrivals and departures for that afternoon and evening. In retrospect she decided she had been foolish to be so frightened. When they had walked back up to Natasha's shop they had seen no sign of Stenos and Natasha assured her that no one had visited her after she had locked the shop door.

'I stayed in the shop in case one of the girls wanted something. Some tourists tried to open the fridge and I obviously missed some ice cream sales, but there's been no one suspicious hanging around.'

Somewhat reassured Monika had tried to put the incident out of her mind and returned to the hotel where she and her mother had showered, donned fresh clothes and walked to a taverna on Mandraki harbour for an evening meal. It was an area frequented by tourists and she felt they would be less conspicuous if they ate there, although the meal would cost twice as much as it would in a small taverna.

Now she was back on Crete Monika felt she was able to relax and consider the proposals Mrs Ethanides had put to her. She bought a pack of graph paper and began to draw out the dimensions of the shop to scale. On the first page she pencilled in the shelving on both walls, then removed the bottom shelf and calculated how much timber she would be saving. A second attempt saw her remove the shelves from one section and replace them with less, giving more space between to them to allow for over sized books.

Monika studied it critically. It made the shelves look unbalanced. She experimented by removing two shelves from one section to give additional wall space where she could display the replicas of the frescoes at Knossos and shook her head. It did not look right.

She showed it to her mother and asked her opinion. Litsa shrugged. 'It looks fine to me if that is how you want it.'

Disappointed that her mother was not more helpful Monika determined to show her new ideas to Cathy when she visited her the following evening. She also wanted to tell Cathy about her encounter with Stenos.

'When I've finally decided on the alterations I want at the shop I'll have to speak to Mr Palamakis. He'll probably not be very pleased that I have changed my requirements,' she told her mother. 'I'll need to telephone Giovanni and ask if he can arrange another meeting at the shop.'

'Why don't you 'phone Mr Palamakis? You have his number.'

'I'm not sure I can explain what I need over the telephone. He may want to take some new measurements or tell me something isn't possible. It will be better to be there with him.'

Monika took a final look at the plans she had drawn before placing them in a folder to take to show Cathy. She was still not happy. Everything looked very austere, more like a functional library; the friendly aspect that Mrs Ethanides had mentioned was definitely missing.

Cathy looked at them critically. 'I see what you mean, but I don't really know what I can suggest that would help. Have you thought about moving your desk to a new position or putting that large counter down by the window?'

Monika rubbed out the lines denoting the counter that she had placed in the centre if the shop and drew it in by the window. She shook her head.

'That's not right. It leaves far too much open space and it would cramp my desk area.'

What do you think, Vasilis?' asked Cathy.

Vasilis looked at the new plan and shook his head. 'Monika is right. You need to fill the space, not leave it empty. At the moment you have the counter end on, draw it across the room and see if that is better.'

Monika did so and shook her head again. 'I still don't like it.'

'Why don't you speak to Ronnie and ask her to sketch the shop as you want it?' suggested Cathy. 'From your drawings she could give you a general impression of how it would look when completed. You could then show it to Mr Palamakis and he could calculate any new measurements that were needed.'

Monika looked at Cathy in delight. 'Why didn't I think of that? Do you think she would be willing? I'd pay her for her time, of course.'

'I'm sure she would be only too pleased to help.'

'I'll arrange to hire a car the night before so we can make an early start. I'll need to ask her to complete a sketch then I could telephone Giovanni and ask to meet with him and Mr Palamakis in the afternoon.'

'You've not thought any more about buying a car?' asked Vasilis.

Monika shook her head. 'Not yet. I'll wait until the season ends and ask Mr Tammatakis at the car hire firm if he can recommend a reputable garage.'

'If you go to a garage and buy a new one you'll be paying the import tax.'

'Oh, I wasn't thinking of buying a new one.'

'Why don't you ask Mr Tammatakis if he has one he would be willing to sell at a reasonable price?' suggested Vasilis.

'I don't really need one all the time at the moment.'

'You'd probably get a better bargain if you bought now before the season ends. At the moment they all have certificates to say they are road worthy. Come November he won't bother to have them serviced or repaired before next spring. You could find you have invested in trouble.'

'I'm very happy with the one I have been hiring each week. Maybe he would sell that one to me? I'll ask him at the weekend.'

Monika and her mother arrived in Elounda shortly after nine and Monika hurried to the square, hoping she would see Ronnie sitting there and not have to go in search of her.

'You're early,' Ronnie remarked. 'The shops are only just opening.'

'It was you I wanted to see. Would you be willing to do some sketches for me?'

'Of course. How do you want Spinalonga to look, day or night, sunshine or shade, sunrise or sunset?'

Monika shook her head. 'I don't want sketches of the island. I have some designs here for my shop and I wondered if you could draw them up so I could see what it will look like when I have had the alterations done.'

'How quickly do you want them?'

'Well,' Monika hesitated 'would you be able to do them now?'

'Not really. I need to finish these two water colours and deliver them to Saffie when she arrives; special order; then I'll be taking my break. Come up to the apartment about twelve. Kyriakos will be going up to his taverna then and we can discuss what you have in mind properly.'

Disappointed Monika turned away. 'I'll see you at twelve,' she promised. 'So, Mamma, what would you like to do for the next few hours? I'm sure you don't want to sit in the car for the next three hours.'

'We didn't need to be up so early,' grumbled Litsa. 'Why

don't we drive back to Elounda? It's not too hot yet. We could have a look at the villages that are on the hill and see if there are any apartments up there. I know they'll probably have holiday makers staying, but they should have notices outside saying the properties are available to rent.'

Monika drove slowly along the coast road until she saw the turn off for Mavrikiano. She crossed the line of traffic and drove up the hill to the village, negotiating the narrow streets carefully.

'I don't think it would be practical to live here. I would have to leave the car down in the car park and we would be walking up and down this steep hill in all weathers.'

'It's very pretty and there are lovely views.' Provided Monika was willing to drive her to the door of their apartment she would have no qualms about the hill.

'I agree; but I'm sure there must be other more convenient locations where we could rent an apartment.'

'I suppose it would be more practical to be in Elounda or at least in Plaka,' sighed Litsa. 'Either place would be easier for shopping and I'd be more likely to find work down there during the season.'

'Apartments there will probably be more expensive. You'll be paying for the convenience of being in a town,' replied Monika as she drove very slowly down the hill out of the village. 'We'll go through Pano Elounda, but I don't think it would be a good idea to live up there either. I'd have to leave the car down in the car park again and the walk up is further than to Mavrikiano.'

'So why are we looking up here?'

Monika smiled. 'Really just to pass the time until I go back to meet Ronnie. It's always possible we will see something and we could make enquiries.'

They drove to Pano Elounda and down to Kato Elounda where Monika negotiated the narrow streets until they reached the top of the hill where she stopped. 'I've either got to turn around or drive down that pathway to get back to the road.' She looked in her mirrors. 'I don't think it's possible to turn, so we'll have to drive down.'

Litsa clutched at the car seat as they slipped and slithered their way down the pathway that was littered with loose stones.

'We are definitely not living up there,' declared Litsa. 'I wouldn't want to face driving down that road very often.'

'Well, that's three villages we can definitely cross off our list,' smiled Monika. 'We can take the road to Pines later, but I don't think there are any shops at all up there. I don't think either of us could cope. We're used to living in a town where we have a supermarket or a periptero on the corner. Why don't we go for a swim? There won't be many more opportunities this year. Afterwards we could have a drink and then return to Plaka to see Ronnie.'

Monika parked the car at Plaka and they walked up through the square. There was no sign of Ronnie and they walked on to the self catering apartments. Ronnie was sitting out on the balcony with some paintings spread out before her.

'Ronnie,' called Monika.

'Come into the entrance hall and I'll open up our door for you.'

By the time Monika and Litsa reached the door it was already open and Ronnie was standing there smiling at them.

'Perfect timing. Kyriakos left about ten minutes ago. I haven't cleared up yet, so you'll have to excuse the mess. I get up early and go and paint leaving Kyriakos still asleep. When I return I usually get him something to eat and we sit and talk. He goes to the taverna and I have a siesta whilst it's hot. I do some cleaning later in the day, or sit outside and add some finishing touches to my paintings.'

Despite Ronnie's declaration that the apartment was in a mess all Monika could see that was out of order were the dishes beside the sink.

'I don't want to stop you from having your siesta. If you'd rather we returned later it's no trouble.'

Ronnie shook her head. 'I just like to lie down quietly and read. I admit, some days I fall asleep. Come and sit out on the balcony and tell me what it is you have in mind.'

Ronnie checked that the additions she had made to her paintings were dry and took them inside the apartment whilst Monika laid her folder of drawings on the table.

'You know I am going to rent Mr Andronicatis's shop next year?'

Ronnie nodded. 'Of course. I think everyone in Plaka and Elounda knows by now. News travels fast around here.'

'I'm planning to open a book shop. I spoke to Mr Palamakis and he is going to fit battens to the walls so that book shelves can be fixed. I wanted shelving all the way along, but when I spoke to an old friend who works in a library she said she thought it would be rather austere and the shop should look welcoming and friendly. I drew out some plans, altering things a little and showed them to Cathy and Mr Iliopolakis. Cathy suggested that I spoke to you and asked if you could do me some quick sketches to show how it could look.' Monika took the sheets of paper from the folder and spread them out on the table.

Ronnie studied them and looked up, an amused glint in her eye. 'It's a very nice box.'

'Box!'

'That's what it looks like at the moment. Everything is too regular. What's this rectangle in the centre?'

'That's the old counter. I thought I would have it moved end on and use it to display some books.'

'And this small box here by the window?'

'That is where Dimitris says the fuse box should go. I'll have to ask Mr Palamakis to put a cupboard around it and then I will stand one of the urns on top.'

'What wood are you planning to use?'

'Pine. It's light in colour and reasonably priced.'

Ronnie nodded. 'Give me a few minutes and I'll do something

with that wall. If you're happy with my suggestions then we'll do the others.'

Monika watched fascinated as Ronnie's pencil flew over a sheet of blank paper. 'This is not drawn to scale as yours is,' she warned Monika. 'This is just an impression. If you like it you'll have to get Mr Palamakis to take new measurements.' She handed the page to Monika and Litsa craned over her daughter's shoulder.

Ronnie had placed the urn on top of the cupboard that would house the fuse box. Further along she had left a gap between the shelving and placed another urn there with some flowers before continuing the shelving to the end of the wall. Litsa looked across at Ronnie's sketches and nodded her approval to her daughter.

Monika examined the sketch carefully. 'It is more attractive to have the shelving broken up, but I don't know if the urn will look right if it is placed on the floor. I think it should be higher to match the other one.'

'Are you having a cupboard placed there also?'

'Well, no. I was told that to have bookshelves that were virtually at floor level was not a good idea. I'd planned to remove the bottom shelf from my order and ask Mr Palamakis to box the gap in.'

'That's a waste of space. Have the area below the bottom shelf and the floor made into cupboards. You may not need them for storage yet, but at least they are available for later.'

'I suppose some of Mr Andronicatis's smaller items might fit in there out of the way. I've told him I'll have some pieces on display and try to sell them on his behalf.'

'Where are you planning to have your desk?' asked Ronnie.

'Kind of there.' Monika pointed. 'I thought if I had it down by the window, on a slant, I would be able to see all round the shop.'

'How big will it be?'

Monika looked nonplussed. 'I don't really know. I need a computer, a proper one, not a laptop or anything like that, and a printer, as well as somewhere for a customer to place a book, oh, and my telephone.'

'You're talking about one hundred and fifty centimetres. You can't have books behind you, so why not have a couple of shelves, fairly high up, where you can display some of Uncle Yannis's glass or alabaster ornaments?'

'I had thought I would put them on the top shelf of the bookcases until I needed the area for books.'

Ronnie shook her head. 'They'll never be noticed up there. If there are some behind your desk people are bound to see them as they come over to pay you for their book. You could leave some of the marble shelves up there. They will catch peoples' eye. What are you planning for the partition wall at the back?'

'I was going to leave it. There are shelves already in situ and I was going to use them for lighter things, like maps and guides, maybe magazines.'

'You'll need an awful lot of maps and guides to fill those shelves and magazines won't fit. They are too large.' Ronnie took a fresh sheet of paper. 'Remove all the shelves except two and use those for your small items. Above them you could display the plaques with details of the Knossos frescoes. I'm sure Uncle Yannis has a box of them hidden away somewhere. Don't put them all in nice straight lines,' Ronnie smiled. 'An attractive, staggered display, different sizes and different designs. What colour will you paint it?'

'Colour?'

'At the moment it is painted white. If you remove some of the shelves there will be marks so it will need repainting. If you are going to hang some of the plaques up there white is not a good colour to show them off, they have a cream coloured background.'

'What colour would you suggest?' asked Monika.

'A very pale green.'

'Would that look better than blue?'

'It certainly would. Blue can look cold, green goes well with natural pine.'

'If you say so.'

Ronnie laughed. 'These are only my suggestions. You can throw my sketches in the bin when you leave. You don't have to be polite.'

'So far I'm delighted with everything you have suggested and shown me. I just hope that when I speak to Mr Palamakis he doesn't start finding reasons why they won't work. What about the big counter? I've said I'll keep it and I thought it should go end on. If I place it across the width of the shop it looks as though I'm blocking an area off.'

'What condition is the surface in?'

'I didn't actually look,' admitted Monika. 'It was covered in Mr Andronicatis's belongings.'

'That can be sorted later. If it's wood it may be able to be polished up; if not it can be covered or painted. What's underneath or is it solid?'

'There were boxes. I'm not sure if he has any of his stock in them. He said it was just packing materials he kept there.'

'So it would be a good idea if you asked Mr Palamakis to add cupboard doors. You can't have one side looking smart and the other side looking like a garbage tip.'

'I could put a curtain along.'

'You could, but people might push that to one side to see what was underneath. They're less likely to open cupboards.'

Monika sighed. 'I wish I'd asked you to do these designs for me before I went to all the trouble of working out shelf measurements and book shelf requirements. I'll call Giovanni and ask if Mr Palamakis is willing to come up to Plaka today and I can show him my changed plans. Thank goodness Cathy suggested I visited you. I really appreciate all the help you have given me and you must give me a bill for your time.'

'There's no charge. I'm pleased to help.'

'I must give you something. I've taken up almost an hour of your siesta time.'

'Have you had lunch yet?' Monika shook her head. 'Then go

up to Kyriakos at the taverna and buy your meal from him. It's always good for trade if tourists see Greeks eating there.'

Mr Palamakis closed his mobile 'phone after speaking to Giovanni. 'Women,' he remarked. 'Always changing their mind. The girl who's renting Mr Andronicatis's shop says she has a new design for the shelving. She wants us to go to Plaka in about an hour. Giovanni will meet us there with the keys.'

'Why don't you tell her we have the weekend off and we'll go on Monday?' complained Giorgos.

'She is only down here at the weekends at the moment. She works at Mr Iliopolakis's hotel in Heraklion. I don't want to lose this job by being difficult about meeting on site. You can stay here if you like and I'll tell you what she wants when I return.'

'I'll come with you, Grandpa. I don't want you agreeing to all sorts of impractical ideas that she may come up with. Remember all the changes Miss Ronnie wanted to her house at Kastelli.'

Mr Palamakis nodded. 'They all worked out well. She gave us a picture of how she wanted it to look when it was finished and we did everything else. Such a shame that all that work was ruined.'

'Could have been worse,' Giorgos shrugged. 'She could have lost the new extension as well as the original house, or even had everything finished and her relatives staying there when it happened.'

'If her relatives had been staying Babbis would not have had access,' replied Mr Palamakis.

'He would have found a way,' remarked Giorgos truculently. He hated the fact that his grandfather was always right.

Mr Palamakis looked at the sketches Ronnie had completed earlier and shrugged. 'It can be done. You will need to tell me how high off the floor you want the first shelf. We will start there and then you can decide on your new measurements for the book shelves.'

'About here.' Monika held her hand up against the wall.

Mr Palamakis held his rule up against the wall. 'You are sure that fifty centimetres is going to be of sufficient height? You will not want to change it next week?'

'No, I can't afford to lose any more shelf space. When Dimitris has placed the new fuse board in position I would like you to make a box around it that is the same height as the bottom shelf, so it is not too noticeable.'

'And the space beneath the shelves?'

'At first I thought it could just have some timber placed across the gap from the floor to the shelves to hide it; then Ronnie suggested I had cupboard doors made so I could use the area for storage. Would that be possible?' asked Monika.

'I would have to buy more timber.'

'Here,' Monika indicated approximately half way along the wall, 'I don't want any shelves, just the cupboard. I want to place one of Mr Andronicatis's urns there and I think it will look better against the white wall. If I need the space for books later I will have to ask you for more shelves.'

Mr Palamakis nodded. He would have to work out the amount of timber he would need to make the cupboard doors. If he was able to purchase sheets of pine panelling he might be able to cut two or more doors from one sheet.

'How do you want them opening?'

'I thought they could be hinged at the top and have finger holes lower down. I don't want handles that people could bang their legs on. This section here,' Monika moved to the end of the wall, 'I am going to change the measurements for the space between the shelves so I can use it for over sized books, but it will be the same height from the ground as the others.'

'May I write on this?' asked Mr Palamakis pointing to the sketch Ronnie had done.

Monika shook her head. 'I need this to show to someone. You can have the rough sketch I made from her drawing if it's any help.'

Mr Palamakis took the sketch from Monika and leaned on the counter. He scribbled the measurement of the cupboards below the lowest line of shelves, then wrote some notes to himself and turned back to Monika.

'And the other wall? Do you want the same arrangement there?'

'More or less. I'd like to have cupboards at the base and a space between the shelves about here where I can put another urn. I've decided to have one less bookcase. I'm planning to have my desk across there so I thought I would leave the marble shelves in place and put some of Mr Andronicatis's vases or ornaments up there. There's no point in having books behind me that no one can get at.'

Mr Palamakis ringed the marble shelves on the second sketch Monika had given him.

'Is that it?' he asked.

Monika shook her head. 'I'd like the higher shelves from the partition removed, just these two left. I realise they will leave marks that have to be made good and then I would like it all painted a very pale green.'

Mr Palamakis raised his eyebrows but made no comment.

'I'm not sure about the counter yet. I haven't seen the condition of the top. I may have to ask you to cover that with a laminate. The front looks fine. A polish will bring the grain up. The back will need cupboard doors again so that it looks decent when I turn it around.' Monika smiled. 'I think that's everything.'

Mr Palamakis nodded. 'You may be saving timber on the shelving and a couple of backing sheets, but you will need larger wooden panels for the cupboard doors. The cost of the timber will probably end up being about the same as my original over all estimate. Are you still planning to have pine? White block board would be just as strong and cheaper.'

Monika considered his suggestion. 'Not a lot of wood will be on show so it would be practical to opt for something cheaper.'

'You will also need hinges and they will be extra, of course.'

'I have agreed to place a thousand Euros into your account in January. I can obviously pay you more as your work progresses. I realise that I've asked you for items that you had not quoted for, but I am hoping the cost of those will be off set against using cheaper timber.'

'You are not going to change your design again when I have worked out the measurements and cost of making the doors?' asked Mr Palamakis.

Monika shook her head. 'No, I am more than happy with the design Ronnie has made. I will ask for the shelves to be fitted starting at the back. When they reach the space I have allowed for the urn the shelves can then start from the front. I don't want an ugly gap where measurements have been miscalculated.'

Mr Palamakis looked at Monika reproachfully; he did not measure incorrectly. He folded the plan he had written on and placed it in his pocket. 'I'll be in touch with you sometime next week and give you the revised cost for the timber.'

'If you think there will be any other problems you will contact me, won't you?' asked Monika anxiously.

Mr Palamakis shrugged. 'There should be no problems provided you do not telephone me next week because you want drastic changes made. I will work to this design and these measurements.'

Monika took a last look around the shop before Giovanni locked the door. January still seemed so far away.

'Now I finally have the design of the shop arranged I can concentrate on contacting the book suppliers,' smiled Monika as she drove back to Heraklion. 'I can start by going to the internet cafe and looking up the names and address of publishers. Once I have my own computer at the shop it will be easier as Mrs Ethanides has promised to send me through a complete list and also to tell me which books have been most popular at the library.'

'Why don't you leave it until you have your own computer then?'

'I need to feel I am doing something constructive; besides I won't be having the computer installed until all the renovation at the shop is completed. I'm not planning to go down to Plaka again until the season ends. I just feel impatient when I look at the shop and nothing has happened.'

'Nothing will have happened then,' Litsa reminded her.

'I know, but I need to have a meeting with Mr Andronicatis and Saffie to arrange which items of his stock he will leave at the shop for me to try to sell and which will be passed to Saffie. I'll need to see how many guides and maps she has left. I don't want to order a large quantity only to find that she has more than enough for me to start with.'

'So what will we be doing at the weekends?'

Monika smiled to herself. Her mother would have to become used to her working every day during the season and not expect an outing each weekend.

'I thought we could drive to Rethymnon and have a look at the book shops there. I might be able to pick up some ideas. Another weekend we could come down to Aghios Nikolaos and look at their shops. We can also look for somewhere suitable to live. I don't want to leave everything until the last minute to organise.'

'Would Mr Iliopolakis be able to help?'

'Help with what?'

'Well that nice son of his has a hotel down there and is Saffie's partner. He might know of an apartment to rent.'

'I can ask Saffie when I meet up with her to discuss the stock. I don't really feel I can ask Mr Iliopolakis for any more help or favours. He's been so good to us.' Monika did not add that Vasilis had also offered to give her a loan if necessary and would charge her less than the bank rate until it was repaid.

Litsa shrugged. 'You're a friend to his wife.'

Monika nodded. 'I appreciate that and I don't want to take advantage of the situation. I hope she will like the sketches Ronnie has done.'

'I don't see why she shouldn't. All you'll need once you're open is a bit of publicity so people know you are there. You could put an advertisement in the local newspaper.'

Monika frowned. She had not thought that far ahead. 'I suppose I could also have some information sheets printed and ask the hotels to display them to their guests.'

'With photographs of the shop,' insisted Litsa. 'If it turns out the way you and Ronnie envisage people will be curious and come to look at it.'

Monika showed the sketches Ronnie had made of the shop as she envisaged it when the renovation was completed to Cathy.

'Come and look, Vasilis. I think it will look splendid.'

Monika waited anxiously for his opinion and he nodded agreement.

'I can't thank you enough for suggesting that I asked Ronnie to do some sketches. All I could think about was shelves holding books. Unless someone was actually looking for a book to buy they would probably not have given me a second glance and certainly not be encouraged to come in to browse. My mother said I ought to have some publicity when I finally open. She suggested some flyers in the hotels that the guests could pick up. Do you think Mr Vasi would be willing to have some at his hotel?'

'I'm sure he will and he can encourage the other hotels to have some also.'

'You could ask Ronnie to design something for you,' suggested Cathy. 'You want more than just some typewritten information.'

'My mother said it should have some photographs.'

'Then talk to John. He's the photographer. He hoped to become professional with National Geographic before his accident.'

'What accident was that?'

'When the fire at the original self catering apartments took place. He was hit on the head by a piece of falling timber. At first no one thought it more serious than a slight concussion, but he was unable to focus properly and would have black outs. He went over to England with Saffie and she arranged for him to have a plate inserted to remove the pressure that a small piece of bone was causing. Since then he's been fine.'

'So why didn't he return to being a photographer?' asked Monika curiously.

'He didn't want to be travelling around the world on consignments, leaving Nicola and the girls for weeks on end. If there is a wedding party in Plaka or Elounda he is usually asked to take the photos, although he prefers wildlife rather than people,' smiled Cathy. 'If you see a note on their fridge it probably means there is a specimen of some sort being cooled down to make it sleepy. He puts them in little containers so it doesn't hurt them. Once he sets them free they are fine.'

'What kind of specimens?' asked Monika warily.

'Could be anything; spider, beetle, wasp, butterfly, centipede, things like that. Giovanni drew the line at him ever putting a grass snake in there.'

Monika shuddered. 'I would hope so! Giovanni suggested that I asked him to set up my computer for me when I have it installed. Would he be able to insert the photographs and put them onto a flyer so I had it on the computer? That way I would be able to run off some more copies if I needed them.'

'Talk to John. He'll be able to advise you. Will you be having a grand opening? I hope we will be invited if so.'

'Of course you are invited.'

'That would be the time to ask the local newspaper to visit and see if they were willing to insert a photo of you and write a column about the new shop,' Vasilis added. 'Most people ignore the advertisements, but a photograph catches their eye.'

'I'll do your hair and make-up,' announced Cathy. 'You'll look fantastic, like a film star.'

'It's the books I want to sell, not me,' smiled Monika.

Week Two – October 2013

Elena felt unaccountably excited. The last time she had visited Marianne and her family was on the occasion of her mother's hundredth birthday three years ago. She could still recall the pleasure she had seen on the old lady's face when she and Andreas had walked through the door. It had been such an enjoyable few weeks that she had been loath to return to New Orleans. Had she been younger she would have been willing to take a chance and move to Crete, she felt as much at home there as she did in America. Now the twin babies were proper little girls and there was the new baby boy, Yannis, who she was longing to see and cuddle.

The journey from New Orleans to Washington had gone smoothly, but now a thunder storm had delayed their take off from Washington by two hours and all the passengers had been forced to sit on the plane until a new departure slot was allocated. The Captain continually apologised, explaining that the delay was beyond his control

Just as the passengers were thinking they would soon be on their way the stewards had moved along the cabin, checking everyone's passport and travel details until the Captain made another announcement.

'Would Mr Bjorn Arlberg and Mrs Sadie Arlberg make themselves known to the cabin staff by raising their hands, please.'

No one moved, heads turned to look for the named passengers but no hand was put up. Five minutes later the captain spoke again.

'Unfortunately we have a problem. It appears that some luggage has been checked on to our plane and the owners have not boarded. For security it will be necessary to unload the hold and remove their baggage. There is probably an innocent explanation, but we are not prepared to take the risk. Obviously this will be carried out as speedily as possible and we just have to ask you to be patient.'

'Pity they didn't find that out earlier,' muttered Andreas.

'They couldn't have unloaded during the storm,' Elena remonstrated with her brother.

'If they had realised before they allowed us to board we could still be sitting in the lounge. At least we could have stretched our legs and had a cup of coffee. I could also have bought another book. If I start reading this one now I shall probably have finished it before we're half way across the Atlantic.'

'If you have I'll give you mine,' promised Elena, certain that once they had finally taken off her brother would fall asleep. She was thankful that she was sitting three rows away from Helena and Greg. She could hear Helena complaining loudly about the delay and the inefficiency of airport employees, whilst Greg tried to reason with his wife.

Elena sighed. Helena could be so difficult. She and Marianne had been close friends as children, but when Helena had met Greg she was no longer interested in spending time with her sister. Marianne had accepted the situation philosophically, immersed herself in her studies and spent her time mainly with the family who had moved next door.

Even now, Helena would make a nasty remark regarding John's parentage. She had refused to visit Crete either for the twin girls' Christening or John and Nicola's marriage. 'Hardly surprising those girls were born out of wedlock,' she had commented. 'He obviously inherited his parents' loose morals.'

Elena just hoped there would be no friction between the sisters to spoil their stay.

'This has really put our schedule out,' complained Helena when they finally landed at Heathrow five hours later than the declared arrival time.

'I expect a number of other people have also had their arrangements put into disarray,' said Greg soothingly. 'At least we were not transferring straight onto our flight to Italy. That would have caused a problem.'

'No more of a problem than I have now. Do you realise that we have been travelling for nearly twenty four hours without any proper sleep? I've not had a shower or washed my hair and the food we were offered was rubbish. It's a wonder we haven't all been ill.'

'Well, we're not,' Greg reassured her. 'Once we have checked in at our hotel you can have your shower, wash your hair and go to bed for a few hours to help you recover.'

'I can't go to bed,' declared Helena vehemently. 'If I sleep now I won't sleep tonight. My body clock will be out of rhythm. Besides, I'd planned to take Mamma and Uncle Andreas to visit Selfridges and Harrods today.'

'That was when we were expecting to land at ten this morning. It will be a bit late to take them now. I'm sure your mother and uncle must be tired. Once we've all relaxed and had an early night we'll feel considerably better and there will be plenty of time for shopping tomorrow. '

'We're booked to go on the London Eye tomorrow,' Helena reminded him. 'By the time we've done that and had some lunch most of the day will be gone.'

'You could still visit the shops today. They stay open until late.'

'Don't be stupid, Greg,' replied Helena irritably. 'By the time I've made myself ready to go out they will be closing.'

'Well, at least you have the shops in Rome to look forward to.'

'That's not the same. I wanted to look at the London shops.'

Greg shrugged. When his wife was in this mood he could not say anything to please her. 'Well, whilst you're making yourself look beautiful again I'll go down to reception. I want to make sure we are booked in for the evening meal and breakfast tomorrow.'

'We'll need an evening meal again tomorrow and an early breakfast. Whilst you're there you ought to order the taxi to take us to the airport. We don't want to be late so that Mamma and Uncle miss their flight.'

Greg nodded. 'I'll check on everything,' he assured her. He knew the meals and taxi were already booked, he had the paper confirmation in his pocket, but it was a good excuse to escape for a short while and have a beer.

He sat in the lounge, reading a London paper and sipped his beer slowly. He would have liked to go out and have a quick look in the shops, not at the fashions, but Foyle's was not far away and he always enjoyed wandering around their display of the latest historical publications. Somehow he doubted that Helena would be willing to go there with him the following day and if he slipped out now she would be certain to come looking for him.

'So, we are here finally.' Andreas sat down heavily in the seat next to him.

'Would you like a drink?' asked Greg, beginning to rise.

Andreas shook his head. 'I helped myself from the mini bar in my room. Elena should be down any minute then we are going out.'

'Out? Out where?'

'Just to look around the locality, see if there are any interesting shops.'

'Aren't you tired?'

'We both slept on the plane. It will do us good to stretch our legs for half an hour. What's Helena up to?'

'Having a shower, washing her hair and repairing her make up,' smiled Greg.

'Well you won't be wanted for a while. Come out with us.

She has your mobile number, hasn't she? She can call you if she needs you and you can tell her where you are.'

'I'm not sure.'

'Don't be silly. You know she'll be hours and you'll be sitting here bored to tears. Tell her we insisted on going out and you didn't think it safe to let us out alone.' Andreas winked at Greg. 'We could get lost. Our memories are not so good now we are older.'

Greg hesitated. 'I suppose I could. There's really no reason why I have to sit here and wait for Helena.'

'I'd like to pop into Foyle's,' continued Andreas. 'I want to check that they are still stocking my plays. The royalties have not been so good over the past two years. If they haven't any copies on the shelves I'll be giving my agent a prod when we return home. Can't expect people to buy them unless they're on display. If they can't see the title they'll often go for something different.'

Greg smiled. He had all but forgotten that Helena's uncle was a famous play write and had had some of his plays turned into films.

Helena was furious when Greg returned over an hour later. 'Why didn't you ask me to go with you? You knew I wanted to go to the shops.'

'You wanted to freshen up and your mother and uncle were not prepared to wait around. I thought I really should go out and keep an eye on them to make sure they didn't get lost. We only went around the corner to Foyle's.'

'Foyle's? I suppose that was your choice. I imagine Mamma was bored to tears.'

'Actually it was your uncle who wanted to go there and whilst we were there your mother bought a book.'

'A book? What kind of book?'

'A true account of famous murders.'

'What! Why on earth would she want a book like that?'

'She said she was interested in the way the police had managed to track the criminals down. There's Crippin and that

125

Rillington Place chap along with some of the other more recent killers like Dr Shipman and Fred and Rose West.' Greg grinned mischievously. 'Maybe she's planning to murder someone.'

'Don't be so silly,' replied Helena scathingly. 'You could at least have told me you were going out. Suppose I had needed you in an emergency?'

'I can't think of any emergency where you would have needed me. The days of calling me into the shower to scrub your back have been long gone. You could have called me on my mobile.'

'That's not the point,' pouted Helena. 'I like to know where you are.'

'I'm not a child,' Greg remonstrated mildly. 'I am a reasonably responsible adult. I bought you a magazine whilst I was there.'

'I'm not so sure of that!' Helena threw herself into the easy chair in their room and took the magazine Greg handed to her. 'What am I going to do with myself now until it is time to go to the dining room?'

'You can read your magazine whilst I go and have a shower.'

'I may not be here when you come out,' threatened Helena.

Greg shrugged. 'That's fine. You do whatever pleases you and I'll see you in the dining room at seven.'

'I shall probably faint if I go up on that,' announced Helena as she looked at the London Eye.

'Don't be ridiculous,' snapped back Elena. 'It's perfectly safe. People go up on it all the time.'

'You should never have booked us to go on this, Greg. You know I don't like heights.'

'You'll be safely strapped in and it turns very slowly. There's absolutely nothing to worry about.'

'Couldn't we cancel and ask for our money back?'

Greg shook his head. 'They don't do refunds because someone has changed their mind. You'll enjoy being able to see all over

London and it only lasts about an hour. Come on, we need to stand in the queue. We're on the next rotation.'

Andreas was beckoning to them. 'Come on, otherwise we'll probably be in separate compartments.'

'I don't think you should go, Greg. I'm sure it isn't safe.'

'They wouldn't be allowed to run it unless it had passed all sorts of stringent safety checks.' Greg took his wife's hand. 'If you really don't want to go on you can go and sit in the cafe over there. We'll wave to you.'

Helena gasped. 'You'd leave me down here alone whilst you went up on it?'

'I may never have another opportunity.'

Helena glared at her husband mutinously and went to stand beside him in the queue. 'You don't leave me any choice. If I'm sick all over you don't say I didn't warn you.'

'I thought you were planning to faint,' remarked her mother. 'Make up your mind so we can be prepared. Sit in the cafe as Greg suggested or stop being so melodramatic and come and enjoy the experience. You know you'll revel in telling all your friends about it and making them envious when you return home.'

'I'm going to take some photos,' announced Greg. 'I'm sure John will be interested. I don't think he and Nicola had the opportunity to go up when they visited London.'

'Just make sure you don't take one of me being sick,' Helena warned him.

'I don't think anyone would be interested in that. Go on, we're next.'

'Did you enjoy it after all?' asked Greg as he climbed back down on to the landing stage and helped Helena out.

'It was not quite as bad as I had expected.' She shuddered. 'I kept thinking what a long way down the ground was and what would happen if it suddenly collapsed.'

'If that had happened I doubt you would have known anything

about it. The views certainly were spectacular. Did you enjoy the experience, Uncle?'

'Very much. It's rather like going up the Empire State Building and looking across Manhattan and Long Island.'

'At least you go up there in an elevator,' muttered Helena.

'True, but if the lift supports failed you would plunge back down to the bottom of the shaft. Accidents happen however hard you try to avoid them,' smiled Andreas. 'If you were worried about something happening you would never set foot outside your door. You don't worry about flying, do you Helena?'

'Flying is the safest way to travel,' announced Helena smugly.

'I agree,' said Elena, 'but even then accidents happen occasionally. I always like to have my feet safely back on the ground after a flight. I'm not looking forward to flying to Crete tomorrow, but I do want to see everyone again, particularly the children.'

Monika drove her mother to Rethymnon and they wandered through the town together looking for book shops.

'There must be one somewhere,' said Monika in exasperation. 'I'll go into that photographic shop and ask them.'

Monika returned moments later. 'There is one down that side street that leads to the sea. If we start there we can ask them where another is situated.'

They reached the end of the road and Monika looked around. 'We must have passed it.'

'It may have closed down,' remarked Litsa.

'I'm sure the assistant in the shop where I asked would have known if it was no longer here. We'll walk back up slowly and look more carefully.'

Dog eared novels along with children's colouring books stood in a pile inside the doorway. Paper fans, bottle openers, key rings, inflatable rubber rings, assorted toys, a wooden model of Knossos and worry beads vied for a place in the shop window where a notice said "More goods inside, Come and See". Wicker baskets stood outside heaped high with trinkets and offering the goods at "special prices".

'I think this must be the shop,' said Monika. 'They may have a proper display of books inside.'

She walked into the dimly lit interior with Litsa following her, trying to avoid the eye of the man who sat behind a counter with a bored expression on his face. The silver chains attached to the pendants were tarnished, the ornaments were dusty and the collection of books that were towards the back looked second hand, much read copies.

Monika shook her head and walked back out. 'That may be called a book shop, but it's more like a junk store. The only thing I saw of any interest was the children's colouring books. I could stock some of them along with puzzle books.'

'You'd need crayons to go with them.'

'I'm sure I could get some cheap packs of miniature ones. I could even give them away as complimentary if a colouring book was bought. People like that. It makes them think they have a bargain.'

'They would have if you are giving things away.'

Monika smiled. 'If I can buy a pack of crayons for fifty cents I add the price to the colouring book. That means the customer is paying for them. Let's walk down to the sea front and then back up the next street. We might actually find a proper book shop there.'

Their second excursion was more successful. The shop they found was selling books, magazines and newspapers. The books were towards the rear of the shop and Monika began to browse, finding it difficult in some areas to see the titles of the books on display as the area was so dark and crowded. Many of them looked as if they had been sitting on the shelves for years, the pages between the covers looking dusty and discoloured. To Monika's exasperation they were not arranged in the alphabetical order of the author's names and her fingers itched to start to rearrange them correctly.

A number of customers entered whilst they were there, but they all bought newspapers or magazines and did not approach the book section that was towards the rear. Monika shook her head at her mother.

'This has only told me that the owner has no interest in books. We're wasting our time here. We'll go to the centre and have some lunch and then make our way back to Heraklion. I want to talk to Mr Tammatakis when I return the car. Mr Iliopolakis suggested that I asked him if I could buy it before the end of the season. I'm familiar with driving it and it seems in good condition.'

'Are you sure you can afford it?'

'Yes,' replied Monika firmly. 'I will need a car to go down to Plaka regularly to see how the work is progressing. Once the season is over the car hire firms close down so it is only practical to have a car of my own. I certainly can't afford to buy a new one and I'm hoping Mr Tammatakis will sell at a reasonable price as I have been a regular customer.'

'Could I buy it for you?' asked Litsa tentatively.

'You? Why would you want to buy it for me?'

'It would be a way of thanking you for everything you have done over the past few years.'

Monika squeezed her mother's hand. 'It's a lovely thought, Mamma, and I appreciate it, but I don't expect any thanks.'

'I have the extra rent coming in from Natasha so I could afford it.'

Monika shook her head. 'You save your money. I may have to ask you to contribute more to our rent when we find somewhere new to live; besides, there's no guarantee that you will be able to find any work in Elounda or Plaka. Then your only income will be the shop rent.'

'You will tell me if you need any financial help, won't you?' asked Litsa anxiously.

'Provided I am sensible and budget carefully there should be no problem, but thank you. I mustn't get carried away and order too much stock to start with. Have you finished? We ought to think about making our way back. I don't want to arrive when other people are returning their cars or Mr Tammatakis will be too busy checking them back in to spend time talking to me.'

'I don't believe it!' Monika drew up sharply as she reached the car. 'Who has done that?' She pointed to the three long scratches on the wing of the car. 'Mr Tammatakis is not going to be pleased and I will have to pay for the repair.'

'But you didn't cause the damage.'

'Whilst it is hired out in my name I am responsible. I cannot prove that someone else did it and it wasn't carelessness on my part.'

'If you want to purchase the car why don't you offer to buy it now and have the damage fixed yourself?'

Monika sighed. 'He probably has a garage that he uses regularly and will get a better price from them than I would. I'll see what he says.'

Mr Tammatakis examined the deep gouges. 'That will need to be rubbed down, filled and re-sprayed. I won't be able to hire it out again this season.'

'I was going to ask if you would sell the car to me.'

'Sell it? I can't sell it to anyone in this state.'

'I'd obviously have it repaired myself.'

'Not good for my reputation. It has my car hire name on the side. No, I can't sell it to you or anyone else until the work has been done. I'll arrange for the repairs and give you the bill. If you're still interested in buying after that we'll negotiate a price.'

Monika hesitated. 'If I bought it now I could have the whole car re-sprayed, then it wouldn't have your advert on the side.'

Mr Tammatakis shook his head. 'How do I know that you'd do that? You could drive around for months with it in that state. Everyone would think I was renting out substandard vehicles.'

Monika sighed. She had not intended to have the whole car

re-sprayed to remove the "Mercury Cars" advertisement, just scratch off the plastic lettering that had been stuck to the side.

'When shall I come back?' she asked.

'Should be completed by Wednesday evening; if not Thursday.'

'I'll come on Thursday. You can give me the garage bill and let me know how much you want for the car.'

'It's in good repair – apart from those scratches. I'll ask the garage how much they would give me for it and work from that price. I think you are looking at about three thousand Euros.'

Monika wished she had some idea about the prices of used cars. 'We'll call in briefly at the internet cafe on our way home.' she said to her mother. 'I won't be very long,' she added, when she saw the look on her mother's face. 'I just want to see how much a car of that make and year is expected to sell for and the price of a new model. I don't want to find that Mr Tammatakis has over charged me drastically.'

Monika called in on Mr Tammatakis when she finished work on Thursday. He greeted her with a bright smile. 'I have had the wing re-sprayed. The car now looks as good as new.'

Monika looked at it critically. 'The wing is not the same colour as the rest of the car,' she remarked.

'It is blue. The car is blue. It will soon weather and tone in with the body work. A new spraying always looks slightly different for a few weeks. You still wish to buy the vehicle?'

'How much are you asking for it?'

'Two thousand Euros.'

Monika shook her head. 'That is too much. I could purchase the same model from a garage for less.'

'There is the cost of the re-spraying. I have to take that into account.'

'I have already paid you for that. One thousand Euros,' said Monika firmly.

Mr Tammatakis shook his head. 'Madam, you do not

understand. I have to keep the cars in good repair. The engine has to be checked regularly, along with the brakes and the tyres. Repairs are needed. This costs money. Two thousand is the least I could take.'

'You cover your maintenance expenditure with your hire fees. One thousand five hundred and that is my final offer.' Monika turned to leave the office.

'Madam, madam, maybe we could negotiate.'

'There is nothing to negotiate, Mr Tammatakis. I have told you I will pay one thousand five hundred, nothing more.'

'The car is worth more than that.'

'Then you will have to find someone else who is willing to pay a higher price. I am prepared to transfer the money to your account tomorrow and collect the car when I finish work along with the relevant paper work. The choice is yours.'

'You do not have to negotiate with the bank for a loan?'

Monika shook her head. 'It will be a transfer from my account to yours; the equivalent of cash.'

'One thousand five hundred?'

'On condition that I collect the car tomorrow once the bank transaction is completed.'

Mr Tammatakis hesitated. If the woman was prepared to transfer the cash into his account he would be a fool to refuse. She could easily find a car that had not been used by tourists and was being advertised for less.

'Very well. I will prepare the paper work. Here is my account number.' He scribbled in the margin of a map and handed it to her. 'If the money is not transferred I will not be giving you the keys to the car.'

'It will be,' Monika assured him. 'I will see you tomorrow.'

Monika called at Mr Tammatakis's office after work on the Thursday and he handed her the registration papers and current MOT certificate.

'You will have to register the car in your name at the Ministry of Transport. The MOT certificate is valid until the end of February. You will need to take it to a garage for them to check it over, pay for any repairs that are necessary and receive a new certificate. Don't forget. If you have an accident you will need to produce the valid documents.'

'I'll not forget,' Monika assured him. As soon as she had driven it home and shown her mother she would spend the remainder of the evening removing the gold lettering that advertised "Mercury Car Hire" on both sides.

Together Monika and her mother picked away at the plastic lettering.

'This is ruining my nails,' complained Litsa. 'Couldn't we get a knife and scrape the letters off?'

'We'd be bound to make scratches on the car. I can't afford to have it re-sprayed yet. Maybe next year when the MOT is due again, provided the garage don't find any expensive repairs are necessary. Leave the big "M" in place. It will make it easier for me to find when it is in a car park.'

'Everyone will know it is your car if you leave that letter on.'

Monika shrugged. 'That's no problem. If it was a different letter I would have to remove it. At least I'm not advertising Mr Tammatakis's car hire firm, although you can still see the outlines of the letters.'

'They're not that noticeable.'

'I'll buy some car polish and see if I can rub them out.'

'Is it worth the effort?'

Monika sighed. Her mother was right. The old lettering marks hardly showed.

Week Three – October 2013

Elena and Andreas had enjoyed their week with Marianne and Giovanni. Elena had revelled in the time she spent cuddling little Yannis or playing with Elisabetta and Joanna, although she still had difficulty distinguishing one girl from another. Marisa had confided in Elena her concerns about Yannis.

'Since Ourania died he seems to have no energy or enthusiasm for anything. At first he decided to re-open the shop, but the customers were few and far between. If he sold anything it was one of the smaller items. I'm pleased he has decided to close down completely. I was so bored sitting up there all day. Yannis hardly spoke and it was miserable without Ourania.'

'So what will he do with the shop now?' asked Elena.

'He's arranged to let it to a woman from Heraklion. She wants to open a book shop.' Marisa shook her head sadly. 'She's going to remove all those lovely marble shelves and replace them with wood. The shop will never look the same again.'

'What about his stock? Has he very much left?'

'Boxes and boxes. This woman, Monika, who is going to rent the shop, has agreed to store some of it for him and have some pieces on display and will sell them if anyone is interested. Who is going to go into a book shop to buy museum replicas as souvenirs?'

'What is this woman like?' asked Elena curiously.

'She appears to be very nice, well educated and plenty of money. She's also a friend of Vasilis and Cathy. You remember them, don't you?'

Elena nodded. 'I met them when they came to my mother's birthday party. She's an English woman and walks with a stick if I remember correctly.'

'That's right. She was a famous model in England until she had a car accident. It crippled her so she couldn't work any longer. She married Vasilis and they are a devoted couple. This Monika works at Vasilis's hotel in Heraklion. I don't know how she met Cathy, but when Vasilis had to go into hospital for a minor operation she went and stayed with them to be company for Cathy.'

'Is that how she found out about Yannis's shop?'

'I don't think so.' Marisa frowned. 'She also knows Vasi and Saffron. She and her mother were visiting the area and I expect Saffie told her Yannis was thinking of closing.'

'What does her husband do?'

'She doesn't appear to be married. She doesn't wear a ring and nor does her mother. Giovanni probably knows. He's done most of the negotiations between her and Yannis.'

'When is she going to open?'

'Not until next season.'

'That's a shame. Andreas would have been interested. He loves a book shop. I went to that big one in London with him and Greg. I didn't think they would ever leave. Once I'd found a book I wanted I was ready to go back to the hotel, but I had to wait until they were ready. I wasn't certain that I knew the way on my own, but I wouldn't admit that to Helena.'

Marisa closed her eyes. 'The sun is very strong today. I never seemed to notice it when I was a girl. Now I look forward to the weather cooling, although I dislike the rain that usually arrives.'

Elena wiped her face with her handkerchief. 'It certainly is hot out here for this time of the year. I think I should go inside for a while. I don't want to make myself ill.'

'That's a good idea,' Marisa agreed readily. 'We ought to have a short siesta or we'll be falling asleep over our evening meal.'

Each morning Andreas would leave the house, announcing his intention of going for a walk.

'Where are you planning to walk to?' asked Giovanni. 'We could probably take you in the car.'

'That would not be going for a walk; that would be taking a car ride. I thought I would walk to Mavrikiano today and on to Pano. I want to see what the village looks like now that all the film set has been removed.'

'You won't over tire yourself, will you?'

'If I feel tired I will sit and rest. I can always have a taxi back if I cannot face walking any further.'

'Make sure you have your mobile 'phone with you. If you want one of us to drive out and meet you it will be no problem.'

'Thank you, but I am sure I will not have to trouble you.'

Giovanni was becoming quite concerned when Andreas did not reappear until late in the afternoon. He had never stayed out so long before, always returning about mid-day.

'I tried to call you, but your mobile was switched off,' he chided Marianne's uncle gently.

Andreas smiled at his concern. 'I was not expecting anyone to contact me so I left it off. I hope you were not concerned. I walked to Elounda and then decided I would take the donkey trail up to Pano. I sat with Constantina at her taverna and she loved telling me how she had appeared in the film along with her friends. She was quite sad when the filming finished and there was nothing of any interest happening every day.'

'So you've not had any lunch?'

'Constantina provided me with some tomato, cucumber and cheese. That was quite sufficient. I'll be able to do justice to my meal this evening. Now I plan to have a nice cold beer and then I will go to my room to shower and change. Where is everyone?'

asked Andreas as he lowered himself onto the lounger beneath the umbrella.

'Marianne will either be working on the computer or reading. Bryony is up at Saffie's shop and John is at the taverna until Marcus returns from the airport run with Helena and Greg. Nicola is probably snatching a quick nap whilst the children have a rest and Uncle Yannis is at his shop. I believe Marisa and Elena are having a siesta.'

Andreas nodded. 'My sister hasn't the same stamina as I have.'

Giovanni smiled. 'You sit there and I'll fetch a beer for you.' Andreas obviously made no allowance for the fact that his sister was five years his senior.

Giovanni looked around the office door. 'Uncle Andreas is back,' he said to Marianne.

'Where has he been?'

'Up to Pano Elounda and talking to old Constantina. I'm just getting him a beer and then he's going to shower and change.'

Giovanni selected a bottle from the fridge, uncapped it deftly and picked up a glass. He walked back out onto the patio and smiled when he saw Andreas had his eyes shut and was snoring gently. So much for having more stamina than his sister!

Marcus arrived, collected a fruit juice from the fridge and joined Giovanni on the patio.

'Good run?' asked Giovanni and Marcus pulled a face.

'I drove too slowly, I drove too fast, there was too much traffic on the road, why did you have to live so far down the island, apart from that it was fine. We made good time and had no hold ups.'

Giovanni grinned. 'Now you know why I was reluctant to go and collect them. There would have been even more complaints. The car would not have been good enough, I was not careful when I placed their luggage in the boot; it was too hot without the air con running and too cold when I switched it on.'

'Oh, I had all that as well,' sighed Marcus. 'I was reminded that the luggage was real pig skin and the boot was inspected for cleanliness before I was allowed to load it. When I took it out at Vasi's I had to carry it inside. It could not be placed outside for the porter to collect. I don't know how her husband puts up with her.'

'I think he has just become used to Helena complaining about everything over the years. He probably doesn't even listen half the time.'

'I offered to go down and collect them in a couple of hours to bring them up here, but she claimed that two hours was not nearly enough time for her to unpack and get ready. Greg said he could easily call a taxi and she told him that it would be more practical to 'phone here and ask for collection. You would think you were her servant, not her relative.'

'Why do you think I refuse to let them stay here with us? Within twenty four hours she would find her luggage sitting outside, real pig skin or not. Thank goodness Marianne didn't turn out like her or our marriage would have been doomed. I haven't anywhere near the patience that Greg appears to have.'

Giovanni parked his car a short distance away from Vasi's hotel, expecting to find Helena and Greg waiting for him. Greg was sitting outside with a beer.

'Care to join me?' he asked.

Giovanni shook his head. 'I'm driving and I'll be drinking later. Where's Helena? I thought you said you were both ready.'

'I thought we were. Then Helena decided her sandals hurt and she had to change them. She decided the new ones did not match her outfit and she would have to change that also. Her dress needed to be ironed and when she had done that she would need another shower to cool down. That probably means she will have to redo her hair and makeup. I thought if I came down here I could 'phone her when you arrived and she might hurry herself.'

Giovanni shook his head. 'I don't know how you manage to be so patient with her. I'm sure no one would have noticed if the sandals she was wearing were not the right ones to go with her outfit.'

'You have to understand that Helena has an inferiority complex. Her behaviour is a way of gaining attention.'

Giovanni raised his eyebrows. 'Why on earth should she feel inferior?'

'Marianne was always considered to be the one with the brains. She always did a little better at school than her sister. I think it really came to a head when she and Marianne both went off to college. Helena began to pay far more attention to her looks than to her studies as a way of taking attention away from Marianne's academic ability. All the boys wanted to go out with Helena whereas Marianne was virtually ignored and then she appeared to have a pretty serious relationship with Bob. I was flattered when Helena turned her attention to me.' Greg sighed. 'I am partly to blame. I spoilt her and gave in to her the whole time. I was absolutely besotted by her. I couldn't believe it when she agreed to marry me.'

'I always understood that she felt the same about you.'

Greg smiled. 'I think she did. We were very much in love, but it was a mistake to get married so young. Helena was adamant that she would not sleep with me unless we were married so I gave in. It was a good excuse for her to stop studying and leave college. Our wedding put her in the limelight and she was the centre of attention. She felt superior to Marianne, she had a husband. Again when the boys arrived her superiority was boosted further. She was a mother to two beautiful boys and Marianne was still unmarried. When their father died and Marianne returned to the States she took charge. Helena was being dramatic and no practical help to her mother at all. Marianne made all the arrangements, sorted out the finance and was there to comfort her mother. Helena felt pushed aside; the useless incompetent, inferior sister. Then when Marianne had John Helena was able to feel superior again. She was married with two boys, Marianne was an unmarried mother.'

'If Marianne had told me I would have arranged to marry her immediately. She rushed back to the States before I had a chance to ask her when she heard her father was so ill.'

'I'm sure you would, but then when Marianne went over to Athens to help her friend and subsequently married you and stayed here Helena felt secure again. Marianne was no longer around to invite comparison.'

'I hope my granddaughters don't have such rivalry between them.'

'There's no reason why they should take it to extremes. A bit of healthy rivalry between siblings is natural. When we visited and she saw your beautiful house and where you live Helena felt inadequate, or more precisely that I was inadequate. Marianne has once again surpassed her.'

Giovanni spread his hands. 'I have nothing. The house belongs to Uncle Yannis.'

'When I became an employee in the State department,' continued Greg, 'Helena expected me to enter politics; she boasted to her friends that I would end up as Governor of the State, even run for President eventually. I disappointed her as I had no ambition to be a politician. We have a very ordinary house and I have an ordinary job.'

'Had Marianne not persuaded Uncle Yannis to start the self catering units I would probably be working as a waiter in a taverna. As it is, I'm more like an odd job man. If Helena had realised the struggle we had to get back on our feet after the shooting at the hotel she would have realised she had nothing to be envious about,' remarked Giovanni dryly.

'You are a well known and respected family in the area. We are just an ordinary couple.' Greg sighed. 'I'm afraid Helena always behaves badly when she is over here. I hope you can make allowances for her. She is receiving therapy.'

Giovanni raised his eyebrows. 'You mean she is seeing a psychiatrist?'

'I finally persuaded her that she needed some help. She was putting so much pressure on both the boys. When Paul was offered an exceptionally good job in Maine I convinced him that he should accept. He needed to get away and not be at his mother's beck and call. Helena was furious that he planned to "abandon" her as she called it and did her best to persuade him to stay close to us. She has accepted his move now and is no longer 'phoning him every day to ask if he is alright and giving him advice on how to run his life.'

'What about Mark?'

'More difficult. He seems to enjoy running around after his mother and doing her bidding. I'm hoping now he's living an hour away the umbilical cord will finally break.'

'Is the psychiatrist helping?'

'I think so and I certainly hope so. He charges enough for his consultations.' Greg drained the last of his beer from his glass. 'I'd better call Helena and tell her you have arrived.'

Helena walked slowly through the hotel foyer ensuring that the visitors and staff saw her, hesitated in the doorway and looked around, although she could see where her husband was sitting. She gave Giovanni a bright smile and kissed him perfunctorily on his cheeks.

'You're looking beautiful as always, Helena.'

Helena gave a satisfied smile. 'I had expected Marianne to come with you to meet us,' she remarked.

'Marianne is busy getting everything organised at home.'

Helena raised her eyebrows. 'I would have thought there were enough women there to be able to arrange a meal.'

'Marianne doesn't expect either of our grandmothers to help; Nicola has the children to deal with and Bryony has not long returned from working all day at the shop. Do you want to sit in the front or the back, Helena?'

'Where will I feel less jolting from bumps in the road?'

'Probably in the back.' Giovanni opened the car door for her.

'You come in the front with me, Greg. You'll see some changes since you were here last. There's been a good deal of new building.'

'More hotels?'

Giovanni nodded. 'At the rate visitors are coming we never seem to have sufficient accommodation for them. I'm usually full. Some of my customers book for the following year before they leave.'

'I'm not surprised. This is one of the most beautiful areas of Crete.'

'We have the added attraction of Spinalonga. Now it's a National Heritage site a good deal of money has been invested over there; many of the old buildings had become unsafe and they have been pulled down. They've also constructed a new depository for the bones.'

'We'll have to go over.'

'I'm sure John will be only too pleased to take you.'

'It will have to be a day when the sea isn't rough,' added Helena. 'I'm not a good sailor.'

'You can always stay at the hotel if you think you might be ill.' Greg exchanged glances with Giovanni who had an idea that Helena's husband would be quite pleased not to have her company for a few hours.

'There is John,' declared Giovanni, indicating the moped ahead of them. 'I expect he's just returned Skele to Dimitris.'

'He still has that mongrel?' asked Helena.

'Wouldn't part with him. The girls love him when John brings him into the house.'

'I hope he won't be doing that when I'm there. I don't like dogs. Smelly creatures.'

'I'll tell him to make sure that Skele stays well away from you,' Giovanni promised. 'Here we are. Marianne has been looking forward to your visit for days now.'

Helena eyed her sister critically. 'I see you still don't spend time on yourself.'

'Far too much to do and no point in dressing myself up each day to sit at a computer. A pair of shorts and a T is far more comfortable. Even Uncle Andreas has invested in a pair of shorts for when he goes out walking.'

'I've brought mine,' Greg added in an undertone. 'My legs are like two white sticks, but I'm hoping they will colour up.'

'Come on in, Nicola has allowed the girls to stay up to meet you. Once they've said hello she'll pop them into bed. John is just having a shower, but everyone else is ready and waiting. I thought we would eat out on the patio. It's still too hot to be inside during the evening.'

'Provided the mosquitoes don't arrive. I have brought my repellent with me. I never travel without it over here.' Helena patted her handbag.

'Very wise, but you're not likely to need it. We're not usually troubled by them.' Marianne crossed her fingers behind her back. If a mosquito did decide to come onto the patio it was bound to bite Helena. 'I'm longing to hear all about your visit to Rome. Grandma told us that whilst you were in London you went up on the Eye and visited Harrods later.'

Helena gave a dramatic shudder. 'That was an unnerving experience. We were so high up. I was convinced we would crash. I tried to persuade Greg to cancel our tickets, but he refused.'

'Mamma and Uncle Andreas said they thoroughly enjoyed it.'

'I took some photos,' smiled Greg. 'I though John would be interested. Oh, look at these two little angels.' He crouched down to say hello to Elisabetta and Joanna as John brought them out to the patio whilst Nicola carried a sleepy Yannis. 'I enjoyed our boys, but I would have loved to have had a little girl.'

'Two children are quite enough for anyone,' remarked Helena.

John winked at Nicola. 'Do you think so? We're planning on another four at least.'

Marianne looked at her son in horror. 'I hope you don't mean that, John.'

'There are plenty of bedrooms and think of the staff you'll have to take over the apartments when you and Dad are too old,' replied John solemnly.

'You young people have no sense of responsibility. Thank goodness our boys don't plan to produce prolific numbers of children. They are far more concerned about making a success of their lives in their chosen professions.'

'Are Paul and Terri still together?' asked Marianne.

'That's a very stable relationship. Terri is such a sensible young woman. We don't see an awful lot of them as they live in Maine.'

'Probably that's why they are still together,' said John in a low voice to Nicola. 'What about Mark?' he asked. 'What is he up to now?'

Helena's lips compressed. 'He's doing very well. He decided to take an apprenticeship with an aerospace firm. He earned promotion almost immediately and is well on the way to becoming a manager. He lives no more than an hour away so visits us frequently.'

Greg looked at Giovanni and gave a slight shake of his head. Mark had tried a succession of different jobs and none of them had lasted for very long. He had only accepted his current position two months earlier and was still on probation.

'And does he have a new partner now?' asked John innocently.

Helena avoided the question. 'Thank goodness he decided to part from that silly girl who thought she was an artist.'

'Actually she's quite a successful artist. We sell a lot of her paintings.' Bryony could not help adding.

'You sell her paintings?'

'Well, I suppose Saffie does really. It's her shop.'

Greg frowned. 'How does she get them over here?'

'She lives here. She decided to come back here and paint pictures of Spinalonga. The tourists love them. You'll see her painting most days in Plaka.'

'And she actually makes a living from it?'

Giovanni nodded. 'Quite a lucrative one. She and Kyriakos live in my apartments during the summer and move back to her house at the end of the season.'

'*Her* house? You mean she has made enough money to buy a house here?' Helena could not believe it.

'Long story, Helena,' smiled Giovanni. 'Her relatives visited. Her great uncle had been born on Crete and recognised the house where he had lived as a child. It was derelict and he was the only living heir. He gave it to Ronnie.'

'He *gave* it to her?'

'He said he was too old to leave the States so Ronnie set about repairing it. She had just about completed it when it was set on fire. Fortunately she had added an annex at the back and that was virtually untouched. That's where she and Kyriakos live during the winter and she is gradually repairing the house a second time.'

'You've missed out the best bit, Dad,' said John with a smile. 'Ron asked me to do a bit of research into her family and you'll never guess where her grandmother was born.' Helena and Greg looked at him expectantly. 'On Spinalonga,' he announced.

'Really? That's amazing. You'll have to tell me more later.' Greg was genuinely interested. 'We'd like to go over to the island with you whilst we're here. Your father says a good deal of work has been done over there.'

'You'd hardly recognise it now after the way it looked thirty years ago.' Elisabetta stretched her arms up towards her father and yawned.

'Come on then.' He lifted both girls up. 'We'll just take these three off to bed and then we can catch up properly with all your news. I understand you have some photos to show me, Uncle Greg. Grandma says you took them from the London Eye.'

Helena shuddered. 'That was a horrendous experience,' she declared and Greg and Giovanni exchanged glances.

'I can't believe it,' declared Marianne when Giovanni related to her the information Greg had given him about his wife. 'Why should Helena feel inferior to anyone, least of all me? She has a happy marriage, two lovely young sons and sufficient money; what is her problem?'

Giovanni shrugged. 'I don't know. Greg said she was having therapy.'

'She needs more than therapy; she needs a brain transplant. It was her choice to drop out of college before she had any qualifications and marry Greg.'

'I think she regrets that now.'

'What; marrying Greg?'

'No, but doing so whilst they were both so young and not having a career to fall back on.'

'That was no reason for her to drop out of college. She could have continued with her studies after they were married. Many girls do.' Marianne frowned. 'I suppose, if I think about it, even as children she always wanted to be first; first to be given a present on our birthday; opening her cards first and standing them around the room leaving little space for mine. Maybe it's a twin complex. A healthy rivalry that gets out of hand until one becomes so jealous of the other that they become spiteful.'

'You didn't mind her always wanting to be first?'

'I don't think I ever thought about it. I was happy enough and that was all that mattered to me.'

'I'm going to speak to John,' determined Giovanni. 'I'll impress on him that the girls must take turns in being first. He has no patience with his aunt and her posturing. He certainly wouldn't want Jo or Lisa to turn out like that.'

Andreas sat with Yannis and looked out across the bay. 'I've made a decision,' he said, 'and I'd like to ask your help.'

Yannis raised his eyebrows. 'How can I help?'

'I've been going out walking in the area as you know and I've seen a little house in Kato Elounda that's for sale.'

Yannis nodded. 'There's often property for sale around that

area. Someone dies and the heirs think they will get a small fortune for a tumbledown cottage.'

'It's not that expensive, but it would need some money spent on it, decent bathroom and kitchen, bit of weather proofing and a lick of paint.'

'So?'

'I'm thinking seriously about buying it.'

'You are!' Yannis's eyebrows shot up. 'What for?'

'To live in. I know I have a modern apartment in New Orleans but it's incredibly lonely without Laurie. The neighbours are pleasant enough, always say hello, but there isn't one I could call a friend and invite in for a drink and a chat. Sometimes I have lunch with Elena. She's always says she's happy for me to visit, but often has to change arrangements at the last minute as she has to do something for Helena. It's different in Kato and Pano. Everyone is friendly.'

'They are during the summer when they can sit outside. It's probably a different story in the winter. You wouldn't see anyone for days on end. Have you really thought this through?'

Andreas smiled. 'I'd take that chance. I've struck up quite a friendship with a number of the villagers and I've encouraged them to tell me about their war time experiences. I'm planning to write them down and hope to be able to produce a reasonable play. I shall spend a good deal of my day writing, but I would like to feel I could drop in on a neighbour for a drink and a chat or one would knock on my door in the evening. If I find it too inconvenient and lonely during the winter I can always return to New Orleans until the weather improves here.'

'You may not enjoy living there all the time in the summer. Those villages can be a bit isolated when it's too hot to walk up and down the hills.'

'If I'm not happy I can put it up for sale and return to New Orleans. Once it has been modernised a bit I should be able to get my money back.'

'So what help do you need from me?'

'If I go ahead I'd have to stay on here for a few weeks to organise the legal transfer of the property into my name and arrange with a builder to do the work I need. May I continue to stay with you? I'm willing to pay my way. I don't expect free board and lodge indefinitely.'

Yannis shrugged. 'You'll need to speak to Giovanni and Marianne and it will be up to them. I don't mind, you can stay as long as you like, but I leave them in charge of visitor arrangements. What about Elena? Will she stay on with you?'

'I've not mentioned anything to her as yet. I don't want her telling Helena. You can imagine the kind of scene that will cause.'

Yannis nodded understandingly. He had little patience with Marianne's sister.

Week One – November 2013

Monika was feeling excited. She had arranged to meet with Uncle Yannis, Giovanni and Saffron to come to an agreement about the stock she would keep at the shop and decide which items Saffron would be willing to take. She would be firm with Mr Andronicatis and insist that he removed all the large urns whilst the shop was being refurbished. She was not prepared to compensate him for any accidental damage to his goods.

The whole area looked completely different from when she had visited during the summer months. There were no tourists around and the shops and tavernas were closed. Monika had a moment of misgiving. If it was this deserted would she and her mother dislike living down there during the winter? How would she occupy herself when the shop was closed?

Giovanni was waiting for her and unlocked the door. Monika looked around in surprise. The floor area was covered with boxes, opened to show their contents. The counter and shelves behind were crammed with vases and ornaments.

'I thought your uncle was going to clear his stock?'

'He will do so, but first he needs to know the items he can leave behind with you. It would be foolish to pack everything away and then have to unpack it again at a later date. He has already removed the large urns.'

'Did he manage to sell some more goods before the end of the season?'

Giovanni nodded and smiled. 'He held a sale and that was popular with the tourists. They always like to think they have a bargain, although they bought mainly the smaller items that they could carry back home.'

Monika looked around. If Giovanni spoke truly the amount of stock that was in the shop originally must have been tremendous.

'I hardly know where to start.'

'I will help you. As you decide upon the goods you cannot keep we will seal the box and take it to my car.'

'I think we should clear the counter first. Are there some empty boxes? We could put everything from the counter in them.'

'Should we not start with the boxes closest to the door?' suggested Giovanni. 'Uncle Yannis and my grandmother have worked hard. As far as possible the items that are the same they have placed in one box. You will only need to unwrap one item to see what the box holds.'

Monika shook her head. 'Once the counter is clear I could start to place the goods I think are suitable for Saffron on there so she can decide which she will take when she arrives. I hope there will be some space in the stock room for me to place anything I am willing to keep in there temporarily.'

'There is no space in there at present and there are no empty boxes. We need to clear some of the boxes from the shop and deal with other problems later. We will start with the boxes near the door.'

Giovanni spoke firmly and Monika realised that he was determined to work his way. Monika frowned. She wished she had been left alone in the shop to sort the stock out to her satisfaction. As she finished inspecting and rejecting the contents of each box Giovanni sealed it with some tape and took it out to his car. When ten boxes had been removed Monika smiled with relief.

'Now we have some working space we could bring out the boxes from the stock room.'

Once again Giovanni shook his head. 'The boxes Uncle Yannis left in there are the goods he thinks you will be willing to keep. We need to clear the other items first.'

As Monika began to look in the next boxes she found they often contained a variety of replicas. There would be two large items and then some smaller ones packed into the remaining space. She felt frustrated. The two large pottery urns with octopus decoration she would like to have as display items and she pushed the box to one side.

'I want to look in there more carefully. I think I could use the octopus pots, but I'm not sure about the others. I don't really want any of your uncle's goods here when the builders move in. I would hate anything to be damaged.'

'Then we look in other boxes.'

'Maybe it would be better to remove everything now and I look again later when I can bring them back?'

'That is not a good idea. It is better that you decide now. Once I have taken the boxes back to the house they will be stacked safely in one of the rooms. It would be necessary to take them all out for you to look at the contents. If you decide now on the items you want returned those boxes can be moved last and placed at the front.'

Monika shrugged; she would have to comply with Giovanni. It made sense to have the boxes stacked in some sort of order at his house.

At the end of two hours Giovanni had loaded his car with thirty two boxes and announced his intention of taking them back to his house.

'You can continue whilst I am gone. The boxes you have inspected whilst I am away can then be put into the car and we will return to the house for some lunch.'

'I had planned to work through until I had finished. I have a sandwich with me.'

Giovanni shook his head. 'It is not good to work without a

break. Saffie is coming down this afternoon to start to pack up her stock so you will have plenty of time to show her what you do not want.'

'Does Saffie remove all her stock over the winter?'

'No, she leaves it packed away. The premises are secure. It is very unlikely that anyone would break in. There are no items of great value, she is not a jeweller.'

'Do you think she would be willing to store some of your uncle's stock?' asked Monika. 'Just the boxes of goods that I am going to display and try to sell. It would save having to move them back to your house and once the builders have finished their work I could bring them back in here out of her way.'

'I will ask Uncle Yannis. He was planning to make a list of the goods you were keeping.'

'Of course. I am quite happy to list them and give him a copy.'

'That would take time and you would not know the reference terms. Only Uncle Yannis is conversant with those.'

Monika sighed. 'If only I had my telephone line and the computer installed now. I could take a photograph, put it on the computer and send it through to him.'

'You know how to do that?'

Monika gave a guilty smile. 'No, but I'm sure once I had been shown the procedure I would not find it difficult.'

'That is a good idea. I will ask John to return with us bringing his lap top and camera.'

'I'm not sure if I will be ready by then. This is taking far longer than I had envisaged. Suppose I came down again tomorrow? Would you be able to let me in?'

'That is no problem.' Giovanni cast a glance around. 'I think we should finish most of the sorting today. You will have to ask Saffie if she is willing to come down again tomorrow. I do not think you will have managed to sort out items for her by this afternoon.'

Monika gritted her teeth in frustration. She wished she had

never agreed to display any of Yannis Andronicatis's stock or ask Saffron to take anything on his behalf. It would have been far easier just to ask him to remove everything.

'Then I should get back to work or I'll not have any more boxes checked by the time you return.' Monika tried to smile brightly. 'If Saffie can come tomorrow would John be able to come with his camera and lap top? That way he could make a record of anything she is willing to display.'

Giovanni picked up a box. 'Do not eat your sandwich. When you come to the house for lunch you can ask John yourself.'

Whilst Giovanni was gone Monika worked feverishly, relieved each time she found a box that she could push to one side ready for Giovanni to seal and remove, but she found four others that she wanted to inspect more closely. The wall nearest the door that had been lined by boxes now had only six remaining at the far end and twelve by the door ready for removal. Unfortunately the opposite wall still had boxes all the way along and there was still the stock room, the counter and the shelves that needed her attention.

By the time Giovanni returned Monika had inspected the final six boxes and was just about to start examining those on the opposite wall. As she straightened up her back protested where she had been bending over for so long. Giovanni was right when he said she needed to take a break.

Over lunch Giovanni discussed his idea with Yannis that John should take photographs of everything that Monika was to stock.

'How will I cross items off once they are sold?'

'How have you done that up to now?'

'I've always known the quantity I have and once a week I would go through and check my sales; then I would know what I needed to order.'

'I'm sure John can print you off some lists and if Monika tells you if anything has sold you can simply adjust the total. It's probably easier and more accurate than your past listings.'

Grudgingly Yannis agreed. He had not relished the thought of making hand written lists and having to count the contents of a box.

'We should have finished the sorting today and Monika is coming down again tomorrow. When Saffie arrives we'll ask her to come again tomorrow and sort out items for her shop. Monika is also going to ask Saffie if she can store the boxes of goods that she will want later with her rather than bring them back here.'

Yannis nodded. He no longer felt in control of his shop and his precious stock.

'Have you any spare boxes around?' asked Giovanni. 'Everything that is sitting on the counter needs to be boxed up.'

'Those were the display items that Marcus took down from the shelves. The glass came in individual boxes and I've used most of those at different times to pack goods for customers.'

Monika sighed. There was no way the glass vases could be placed into a box without first wrapping them carefully.

'John may have some up at the taverna. We can collect them on the way back.'

'I could ask at the supermarket in Heraklion. They're not closing.'

'Good idea.' To Monika's surprise Giovanni did not linger over his lunch as he had on the previous occasion when she had visited. 'I'll have a word with John about taking the photos tomorrow and then we should get back to work or we'll be there all night.'

Saffron was already at her shop when they arrived back in the square. 'I hate this job,' she announced. 'However carefully I label everything I never seem able to find it again when I re-open.'

'I wanted to ask you a favour.'

Saffron raised her eyebrows. 'I am not prepared to take those enormous urns that Uncle Yannis has. There wouldn't be room for anything else in my shop.'

'He has already taken those back to his house,' Monika assured her. 'I wanted to ask if you would be willing to store the boxes that contain the stock I plan to keep. It would only be whilst the builders were in there working. It would be moved as soon as they had finished.'

Saffron shrugged. 'I don't see why not. If you haven't moved them when I'm ready to open up again you'll find them sitting on your doorstep.'

'Mr Palamakis is starting work in January and I'm hoping that by mid February everything will be finished. I will probably be down here every day after that. I will need to get my computer installed so I can place orders. I'd like to have everything organised before books start to arrive so I would certainly be able to take everything out of your way by March. I'm hoping that by tomorrow afternoon we will have finished sorting out the various things you might be able to sell. You don't have to take them, of course. If they're not suitable they can go into a box and be returned to Mr Andronicatis.'

'Why don't you call him Uncle Yannis as everyone else does?'

Monika blushed. 'It seems rather presumptuous of me.'

'Not at all. He's known in Elounda as Uncle Yannis. If you mentioned the name Andronicatis in the town no one would know who you meant. Ask Giovanni, I'm sure he'll agree.'

Monika turned guiltily as she heard Giovanni rattling the keys to the shop door. 'I'll speak to him. I really ought to get back to work. Giovanni has been good enough to come and help me so I mustn't spend my time talking.'

'Is your mother with you today?'

'No, I thought it would be better to leave her at home.'

'Shame,' smiled Saffron. 'She would probably have enjoyed helping me to pack up.'

'I'm sure she would have loved to, but I also think you would have regretted having her help. I can envisage her taking everything out to admire and then it would never go back into the right box. It's far better that she stays in Heraklion. I'm sure she would love to help when you unpack ready for next season if she hasn't found any suitable work by then. I'll see you tomorrow, Saffie.'

Monika was relieved that by the end of the afternoon she had checked all the remaining boxes and those from the stock room had been brought into the shop. She smiled at Giovanni.

'Thank you so much for your help today. If you are willing to unlock for me tomorrow I don't mind being here on my own.'

'It is no problem. I will collect any boxes John has at the taverna and we can start to clear the counter. When that is done the items for Saffie can be placed on there. She can decide which goods she will have and I can pack the others in a box to take back to the house. Once she has done that I can call John and he will come to photograph them.'

Monika frowned. She could envisage spending a good deal of the following day doing very little.

'Whilst John takes photographs and I pack you can examine the items in the boxes you put to one side,' continued Giovanni. 'Once the counter is clear you can start on the shelves.'

'I'm hoping Saffie will be willing to take some of those bits and pieces also.'

Giovanni shrugged. 'If we do not finish tomorrow there is always another day. If you come down next weekend you can display everything you are willing to keep on the counter and John will take more photos. We can then pack them safely into boxes and ask Saffie to store them.'

'I feel guilty taking up so much of your time.'

'If I was not here with you I would be watching the television. I can do that other weekends. This is more important. Once the shop is empty Mr Palamakis can make another visit and you can give him explicit instructions. He is going to have a very busy winter.'

'I know he always works at Vasi's hotel, but he would probably have time to do any necessary redecoration there when the building work has been finished here.'

'I believe there is some other work he is going to be asked to do. Uncle Andreas has extended his stay with us as he is buying a house in Kato and will need work done on it to make it habitable.'

Monika frowned. 'I expect him to honour his arrangement with me to start work in January and be finished by mid February at the latest.'

'I am sure he will. He is adept at keeping all his customers happy. '

Monika collected a number of cardboard boxes from the supermarket in Heraklion and placed them in her car. If everything from the shop could be sorted and cleared that day she could arrange to see Mr Palamakis the following weekend. It was disconcerting to know that he had arranged for other work over the winter and she wanted a firm agreement from him that she would be given priority in January. She was willing to transfer the money for the timber to him, but did not want it sitting in his account for weeks when she could have continued to earn interest on it.

As she arrived in Elounda she called Giovanni to say that she had arrived in the area and would continue up to the shop. She hoped that when he said he would leave immediately he meant it and she would not be sitting outside waiting for him for an indefinite amount of time.

When he finally arrived, half an hour later, he spread his hands apologetically. 'I called at the taverna to collect boxes. John was emptying the freezer. I had to wait until he had finished so I could take the food back down to the house. If I had left it until mid-day it would have spoiled.'

'Of course.' Monika curbed her annoyance. If Giovanni had unlocked the shop on his way to the taverna she could have made a start rather than sitting in her car waiting for him.

'We will clear the counter first,' he announced. 'If you plan to place the items for Saffie there we will need the space.'

Monika nodded. She would have preferred to examine some of the boxes from the stock room and those left from the previous day before tackling the miscellaneous assortment of goods on the counter.

'Are you planning to keep some of these glass vases or are you offering all of them to Saffie?' asked Giovanni.

Monika shook her head. 'She won't want all of them. It would be most sensible if you leave ten out for her and pack the others. If you could do that I'll look in some of the boxes and take out anything that I think could be useful to either of us.'

The counter gradually held an assortment of glassware, silver photo frames, miniature pots, marble eggs, onyx ashtrays, bronze figurines, alabaster busts, soap stone bowls, Phaistos discs and the photograph albums. In one of the boxes she had discovered a beautiful chess board, with the squares of inlaid marble and the chess men of carved onyx each sitting on a silver base.

She looked at it lovingly. 'I don't play chess, but this makes me want to learn. I'm going to offer it to Saffie, but if it hasn't sold by this time next year I may well buy it from Uncle Yannis.'

'I am sure he would appreciate the sale. Have you looked at the price tag?'

Monika turned the label over and gasped in horror. 'I couldn't possibly afford that amount. I do hope Saffie takes it and sells it; then I won't be tempted.'

'I'm sure Uncle Yannis could purchase another for you.' Giovanni sounded serious as he spoke.

'Please, don't even mention it to him.' Monika looked up and saw that he was laughing at her.

'If you want to learn how to play chess buy a cheap set. This is more for display than for use. Are you leaving it for Saffie?'

Monika nodded. 'If Saffie doesn't want any of those items they can all be boxed up and go to your house, including the chess set. I've taken out the bits and pieces I think I can use from the other boxes and placed them in the stock room. The boxes by the door are ready for you to seal.' Monika straightened up and pointed to the boxes that now stood on the other side of the room. 'I'll make a start on the boxes from the stock room now and then they can go back in there until the counter has been cleared.'

Giovanni shook his head. 'If they are the items that you plan to keep it would be a waste of time and effort. It is better they stay out here until the counter has been cleared and you can put them out for John to photograph. Then we can pack them properly and remove them to Saffie's shop.'

'I just want to make sure they do not get muddled up.'

'I will mark each box with the letter "M". That way you will know they are for you. The boxes that are for Saffie I will mark with "S". There will be no confusion.'

By the time Saffron drew up outside in her car Monika had arranged the counter carefully, placing similar items together.

'Is all this meant for me?' asked Saffron.

'Only if you think it will sell. Anything that you don't want can be boxed and sent back to the house for storage.'

Saffron looked over the range of items. 'I'll take the photo frames, the miniature pots, ash trays and eggs along with the kylix they are sitting in. I'm not sure if the photograph albums would sell, but I'll take three for now.'

Giovanni removed the surplus number from the table and placed them in a box.

'I'm not sure about having so many vases. Why don't I take five to start with and five bronze figurines? If I have the space when I set out the shop next season I could always take a few more then or replace them as they sell.'

'I will mark the boxes "S.S", meaning Saffron Surplus and ensure they are stored towards the front. We will ask John to photograph them so you will remember what is in there and Uncle Yannis will also know.'

Carefully Monika placed the glass vases into a box and the bronze figurines in another whilst Giovanni called John and said they were ready for him to come to take photographs.

'Is this chess set meant for me?' asked Saffron.

'Yes, isn't it beautiful?'

Saffron nodded. 'I'd like Vasi to see this. He might like to give it to his father. I don't think I would be able to sell it.'

Giovanni beamed. 'I'm sure Uncle Yannis would give him a special price.'

Saffron raised her eyebrows. 'I'm sure he would and it should be less than on this label. Vasi has also decided he wants two large urns for the Imperia. Definitely a special discount is due.'

'If you called Vasi he could come down to look at the chess set and collect the urns at the same time,' suggested Giovanni.

Saffron shook her head. 'He is busy down at the hotel. Furniture is being moved from the bedrooms so Mr Palamakis can start to decorate on Monday. Vasi likes to have it done as soon as possible so there is no smell of paint when the visitors arrive.'

'Is he doing every room? How long will that take him?' asked Monika anxiously, remembering how long it had taken to decorate each floor at "The Central".

'He will only do whatever is necessary. His grandsons will be with him to do any repairs and making good under his direction. His son, Yiorgos, and Vasi will help with the painting.'

'Mr Vasi will do the painting?'

'Yes. He is not averse to turning his hand to some manual work. He says it is quite relaxing although he would not want to do it every day of the week.'

'I'm sure Marcus and John would be willing to lend a hand,' offered Giovanni on their behalf. 'I know Monika is a bit concerned that her shop will not be finished ready for her to open if Mr Palamakis has other work to complete.'

Saffron shrugged. 'There should be no problem. The work is indoors so it does not matter what the weather is like. I'm hoping he can spend a couple of days with me to give the shop a quick paint inside. It wasn't done last year and it begins to look a bit shabby.'

'Reporting for duty.' John entered the shop, his camera slung around his neck, his laptop under his arm and a spotlight on a stand in his hand. Skele was standing docilely beside him. 'Had to bring him,' explained John. 'I couldn't leave him up at the taverna on his own.'

'Just don't let him wag his tail anywhere near the counter and knock things over,' warned Giovanni.

'He wouldn't dream of it,' replied John. 'Stay, Skele.' Obediently Skele sunk to the ground and lay with his head between his paws. 'Now, what am I doing?' asked John.

'Can you photograph everything in groups?' asked Saffron. 'That will make it easier for Uncle Yannis to know what I have. If you do the albums first we can then move them out of the way. Once all of this has been done I'll ask you to do another set of photos. That will be my reserve stock. If I sell out of some items I'll know if there are any more stored.'

John placed the spotlight behind the table and looked for a socket to insert the plug.

'It's in the stock room,' Monika told him.

'Isn't there another one nearer? The lead will never reach that far.'

'I'm having a couple of new sockets fitted down by the window.'

'That's not a lot of good to me at the moment,' muttered John. 'Dad, could you nip home and collect an extension cable? I haven't got enough light without the spot.'

Giovanni sighed and nodded. They should have thought of the light when they were discussing photographing the stock the previous evening.

'There's no point in me standing here waiting for you,' announced Saffron. 'I'll go next door and continue packing up.'

John spent most of the afternoon taking photographs, transferring them to his lap top and waiting whilst his father packed boxes and took them in to Saffron and Monika placed more items on the counter.

'You'll not have room for books if you keep this lot, Mon.'

'I don't plan to have it all out on display at the same time; just a few items on the higher shelves. If something sells I'll replace it with an item I have stored. I can't wait to get everything arranged as Ronnie suggested. Once Dimitris has finished the electrics and the dust has settled I'll be able to get my computer up and running so I can begin to order books.' Monika blushed. 'Your father suggested that you might be able to help me with the computer. Would that be possible?'

'Depends what you want. I'm no expert.'

'It's really just to set me up with the basics and give me a few instructions. I've only ever used a computer with a relevant programme installed. I need to know how to use the internet to contact suppliers. I'll have to ask you to put the photographs on for me so I can keep track of Uncle Yannis's stock. I also want to use it for listing my book stock along with my finances.'

'You plan to do internet banking?'

Monika shook her head. 'Not at first. I just want to put the balance of my account on and deduct expenditure as I go. I must be careful not to spend money that I do not have.'

'Are you planning to advertise on the internet?'

Monika looked John doubtfully. 'I wouldn't know how to do that. I thought I might have some posters made up and ask the local hotels and shops to display them.'

'Who is doing that for you? Ron?'

'I haven't asked her. She's not been around since the season ended.'

'I can knock some up for you. If you approve of my designs the master copy could be on your computer so if you needed some more you could just print them off.'

'Would you?' answered Monika eagerly. 'I'd pay you, of course.'

'We'll sort that out later. Is there anything else you would like me to photograph?'

'Just the plaques, I think. I'm planning to keep some to hang on the shelving at the back.'

'Ron's idea, no doubt,' smiled John.

Monika nodded. 'I had planned to have bookshelves all the way around and Ronnie said it looked like a box. She sketched a wall for me and then gave me new ideas for the partition wall. I'm going to paint it green.'

John raised his eyebrows. 'Uncle Yannis will have a fit.'

'Why?' asked Monika, feeling concerned. 'Will he insist I paint it white?'

'He might ask you to do so if you give the shop up. He just has this thing about everything being displayed against white walls. He says it shows everything off to its best advantage.'

'I agree with him in many ways. I wouldn't want a coloured wall to distract from the items, but Ronnie said that the plaques, being a cream colour would look better displayed on a green wall.'

'I'm sure Ron's right. Being an artist she has a good eye for colour and design. Is there anything more you would like me to photograph?'

'I think that's it, thank you. I'll seal these and take them in to Saffie. I need to speak to her about maps and guide books and see if we can come to an arrangement. I don't want to be in competition with her.'

'I'll give you a hand.' John placed his camera and lap top on the counter. Now it was devoid of artefacts, it looked far larger than Monika had realised earlier and the surface was scratched.

'Skele, guard.' The dog rose; wagged his tail at John and lay down in front of the counter. 'We can leave the door open. Everything will be safe with Skele here. He'll not let anyone in.'

Saffron sighed as Monika and John appeared inside her shop. 'Not more boxes!'

'These are the last,' Monika assured her. 'As soon as the

building work is finished I'll take them all out of your way. Have you sorted out guide books and maps for me to buy from you?'

'I've left them on the shelf.' Saffron indicated with her hand. 'Have a look and see what you think. Some are brand new and others have been on display. The display ones are certainly not perfect.'

'I could use them in the same way. Put the used ones out for customers to look through and when they bring it to the counter present them with a new copy.'

'You'll have to ask Dad to write some of his famous notices,' grinned John. '"Display only. New copies at counter."'

'What notices are those?' asked Giovanni as he appeared in the doorway. 'I thought you were next door until I tried to go in. Skele stood up and looked threateningly at me.'

John looked hurt. 'I'm sure he didn't threaten you. He knows you. I left him on guard as my camera and lap top are in there.'

'Well, I certainly would not have wanted to try to take them. He had a look in his eye. Have you finished for today, Monika? If so John can collect his belongings, including his dog, and I'll lock up.'

Monika nodded. 'I can't thank you enough for your help, you and John. Would you be able to unlock again for me next weekend if I ask Mr Palamakis to visit so I can make the final arrangements with him?'

'Is it necessary for you to make the journey? I'm sure he knows everything he has to do.'

'I'm just double checking,' smiled Monika. 'I'll have to come down here anyway as my mother and I will be looking for somewhere to live. I don't want to commute from Heraklion each day. I'm hoping now the tourists have left we will be able to find somewhere at a reasonable price. We've crossed Pano and Kato Elounda off our list along with Mavrikiano, so we'll be looking in Elounda or Plaka and maybe the outskirts of Aghios Nikolaos.'

February 2014

Monika looked around the shop. 'I'm really pleased, Mr Palamakis. You're doing an excellent job. All I need now is Dimitris to connect the electrics and have his work passed and I can have my computer installed and begin to order books.'

Christos Palamakis smiled. He took a pride in his work and enjoyed being appreciated. Ronnie had been expecting him to return to Kastelli and work on her house, but he had explained that to work there would be easier when she and Kyriakos had moved out at the beginning of the season.

'It will be noisy and dusty. You would be most unhappy living there whilst we were working.'

Mr Palamakis did not add that he was deliberately delaying returning to work on the house in Kastelli as he had agreed to work on the cottage that Andreas had purchased in Kato Elounda. He had sent his grandsons to renew the roof whilst he and his son Yiorgo had made a start on the redecoration of Vasi's hotel. As soon as the new roof was completed his grandsons had moved into Monika's shop, cut back the marble shelving and commenced fitting the battening. Provided each customer could see some results when they visited he could keep them all happy.

'We still have to erect the rest of the shelves and fix the cupboards beneath them. Once Dimitris has the certificate from the electric company we will make the box to fit around the fuse box.'

'Can't you do that now?' asked Monika.

'It is better to wait. The electric company do not like to have things hidden away.'

'You mean it is illegal to have the fuse box in a cupboard?'

'Not at all, but we do not want to give them a reason to be difficult.'

'When do you think you will be finished? I'm quite anxious to get my computer installed and begin to be able to order books.'

Christos Palamakis shrugged. 'Maybe four more weeks.'

He knew the outstanding work would not take that amount of time to complete, but the bathroom fitments ordered by Andreas had arrived and he was planning to spend the following week working up there with his grandsons. Yiorgo could come and paint the partition wall as he knew nothing about plumbing.

Monika smiled in delight. 'I can't wait to see everything finished so I can move the boxes from Saffron's shop and start to arrange the display items. Before I bring them in would you be able to give the stock room a quick lick of paint? I know it is an extra, but I hadn't realised just how marked the walls were until it was empty.'

Mr Palamakis calculated rapidly. If the stock room was now to be painted it would be another job for Yiorgo and could account for any delay in putting up the book shelves.

'That will be no problem. Do you have a colour in mind?'

'White,' replied Monika firmly. 'If I put any colour on the walls it would make it even darker in there. As it is you need the light on to be able to see anything. There is also a problem with the large counter.'

'We will move it to the position where you want it when we have finished all the other work.'

Monika nodded. 'It still needs to have cupboard doors fitted on one side and something needs to be done to make the top look respectable.'

'What do you suggest?'

'I was hoping you might be able to advise me. Which would cost more, to have it re-polished or to have a covering of some sort?'

Mr Palamakis ran his hand over the top of the counter. 'To have it re-polished would be costly. I would suggest that I placed a sheet of hardboard across the top, covered it with a laminate and put a trim around the sides.'

'How much will this add to my bill?'

'I cannot say exactly until I know the cost of the materials. No more than a hundred and fifty Euros.'

'That much?'

'I have included the cost of painting the stock room.'

Mr Palamakis had plucked the figure from the air. There was a sheet of hardboard left over from where he had made the backing for the shelves and he had a pot of white emulsion at his house that would be sufficient for painting the stock room. The only expense would be the laminate and trim along with Yiorgos' wages.

Monika nodded. 'Of course; I had forgotten that.' She wrote the figure down in her notebook. 'I need to keep track of my expenses. I mustn't spend so much on the shop that I have no money left to buy books.'

'Maybe I could give you my bill to date next weekend?'

'I have paid you for all the timber,' remonstrated Monika.

'There are the wages for my workmen.'

'I expected to pay you a final bill.'

Mr Palamakis shook his head. 'The men cannot wait indefinitely for their money. I have to pay them each week so it is better if you settle my bill every two weeks. You understand?'

'Yes, I can do that, provided your final bill does not exceed your estimate.'

Mr Palamakis spread his hands. 'I hope it will not, but there are still the cupboard hinges to purchase. When I first gave you the estimate you had not mentioned the cupboards or the painting.'

Monika gave a resigned shrug. 'I will be down here again next weekend. If you give me your bill then I can transfer money to you on the Monday.'

Monika drove her mother around the deserted streets of Elounda.

'It's very quiet down here,' observed Litsa.

'Most of the tourist areas are once the season is over. You don't notice it in Heraklion as there are always so many people around.'

'What will we do with ourselves?'

'I'm sure once we have settled in we will find plenty to occupy us, Mamma. We'll make friends with our new neighbours and go to church regularly.'

'I'd like to go to the big church in Elounda. Since meeting that nice lady there I'd like to get to know her better and I might be able to help her with the flowers.'

Monika smiled to herself. She was pleased that her mother had something positive in mind. She knew how quiet she would find it after living in the town, but at least this year she would have the organisation of the book shop to keep her occupied. She would have to think of some jobs her mother could help her with.

'Now, we'll drive up some of the side streets and see if there are any notices in the windows advertising apartments to rent.'

'Suppose we don't find one?'

'Then I will ask Giovanni and Vasi if they know anywhere. We'll look around ourselves first, but we may have to go as far as the outskirts of Aghios Nikolaos.'

'I don't want to live there,' said Litsa firmly. 'I want to be in Elounda.'

Monika made no comment. She also wanted to live in Elounda.

'Why don't we ask at the supermarket or in one of the tavernas?' suggested Litsa. 'They are bound to know everyone who lives locally.'

Monika drew her car into the side of the road and parked.. 'We'll have to hurry if we're going to a supermarket. They'll be closing soon.' She saw the puzzled look on her mother's face and explained. 'They only open for part of the day once the tourists have gone home. You have to do your shopping in the morning, no rushing out at the last minute to buy something you have forgotten.'

Together they walked back to the main road and entered the small supermarket that was devoid of customers. Monika smiled at the woman behind the counter.

'We haven't actually come in to buy anything. We wanted to ask if you knew of any apartments that are available to rent. My mother and I are planning to move down to this area in March and will need somewhere to live permanently.'

'Where do you live now?'

'In Heraklion. I'm opening a shop in Plaka so I will need to live locally.'

'There's often accommodation above a shop.'

Monika shook her head. 'There isn't anything above this one. I'm renting the premises from Mr Andronicatis.'

The woman looked at her with a puzzled frown and Monika remembered that no one would know him by that name.

'Uncle Yannis, the man who sold the museum replicas in Plaka.'

'Oh,' a broad smile spread across the woman's face. 'I heard he had a closing down sale. What kind of shop are you opening?'

'A book shop.'

The woman raised her eyebrows. 'Do you think that will be successful?'

'I hope so. Would you know of any accommodation?'

The woman shrugged. 'I can ask around. Most people prefer to let to the tourists. They can make more money during the season than letting all year round.'

'We don't need anything with a swimming pool or a view. Just an ordinary two bedroom apartment, preferably furnished with the basic necessities.'

'I'll ask. When will you be down this way again?'

'Next weekend.'

'Call in then and I'll let you know if I've heard of anything. I close at two.' The woman looked pointedly at the clock.

Monika nodded. 'I will. Thank you for your time.'

Monika looked around her shop and smiled with pleasure. The shelving was complete with the cupboards beneath, the partition had been painted a pale green and the counter moved so it no longer stood at the back of the shop and the top was covered in a white laminate with wooden trim. The marble shelves had been left in place where Monika had requested and a pile of marble slabs stood just inside the newly painted stock room.

'It looks very smart,' commented Litsa.

Monika nodded. 'All it needs now are the books. I'll speak to Saffie and arrange when I can move the boxes out of her way. There's so much to be done still. I need to speak to John about installing the computer and then I must start to place some orders.'

'It's fortunate we were able to rent that apartment as you're going to be spending most of your time down here now whilst I'm still in Heraklion.'

'Not for long, Mamma. I'll move some of my belongings down tomorrow and you can give in your notice at the supermarket. I expect they'll accept two weeks. I'll have to give Mr Iliopolakis a leaving date so we need to be organised. During the week you can begin to pack your belongings and I'll come up at the weekend to collect them.'

'Will you stay?'

'Of course. I will come up on Friday and leave on Sunday. I'll be able to help you with the cleaning whilst I'm there. I can clean the windows and wash the paintwork whilst you polish the furniture.'

'Suppose I have to stay on longer at the supermarket?'

'Then we'll re-organise things accordingly. Now, I need to go to see Uncle Yannis and pay him some rent. I expect Mr Palamakis has left his final bill for me.' Monika smiled ruefully. 'I have spent more than I originally intended, but I think it's worth it.'

'Have you sufficient money with you to pay him?'

Monika shook her head. 'I'll transfer it from the bank tomorrow. Oh, that's another thing; you'll need to tell Mr Spinades when you have moved your bank account to Aghios Nikolaos so the rent from your shop is paid in to your account there.'

Rhodes

Manu sidled up to Vangelis. 'I need to talk to you.'

Vangelis raised his eyebrows. 'Someone troubling you?'

Mani shook his head. 'They only tried that once, ended up in the infirmary. Fell out of their bunk and smashed their face.'

'So what's your problem?'

'I'm getting out in two months. I need some contacts.'

'What kind of contacts?'

'I'll need some work, nothing manual.'

'Work shouldn't be a problem. They always need doormen down in Bar Street. Easy enough to get work down there. It also puts you in touch with the right people, if you know what I mean.'

Manu did know what Vangelis meant. The drug dealers, pick pockets and petty thieves all frequented the two areas in the town that were known as Bar Street. Few locals went there to drink on a regular basis, unable to cope with the cacophony of sound that streamed forth from each bar front, each one playing different music at ear splitting level.

The young tourists appeared to love the area, paying double price for their watered down drinks and the free "chasers" that followed until they were thoroughly inebriated. Even then they continued to party until they finally passed out and had to be carried home by their companions, often finding they had parted company with their wallet at some time during the revelry.

They were offered no sympathy when they reported having been robbed. The police did not patrol the area, leaving the doormen to deal with any fights that broke out and turning away anyone whom they recognised as a regular trouble maker. Despite the tourists being warned to stay sober or only take a small amount of cash with them, the advice was ignored. They preferred to take all their money on their person rather than leave it in their room where they were convinced it would be stolen by unscrupulous landlords.

'That could suit me for a start. Good experience. Eventually I'd like to open my own bar.'

Vangelis nodded. It was unlikely Manu would be able to rent any of the premises in either street. Lucas owned them. He never visited the area. He paid a manager to look after each bar and the weekly takings were delivered to him at his office. He knew the managers would deal honestly with him, well aware that any double cross they tried, once discovered, would be dealt with by a knock on the head and a swim in the harbour. After three such occurrences when bodies had been retrieved, the managers decided to take the warning to heart.

'I also need someone who can make some enquiries for me.'

'What kind of enquiries?'

'I want to find where my ex wife is hiding out. I've a score to settle with her.'

'That could be costly. What do you want them to do? Scar her face, burn her, cripple her?'

'Nothing violent or physical. The man must appear to be decent and respectable, able to convince people that his story is genuine.'

'What story is that?' asked Vangelis.

'I'm working on it. I'll need someone who can remember the details and not contradict themselves. I've some leads they can follow up.'

'Why can't you do that yourself?'

Manu shook his head. 'They know me. This is detection work, just asking questions and letting me know the answer.'

'So employ a private detective. You must have contacts from

when you were in the force. It could be cheaper than hiring.'

'Same reason, they would know me. I need someone below the radar, so to speak. A con man who has managed to keep his nose clean, unknown to the police, no record, no suspicion attached to him if anyone looked into his background. Do you know anyone suitable?'

Vangelis nodded slowly. 'A couple of men come to mind. Where will you get the money to pay them?'

'I thought Antonius could call on my father for a few more weeks after I'm out. That should cover the cost.'

'Once you're a free man again Antonius will continue to call. Lucas relies on him for supplies. I would not recommend that your father tries to end the arrangement.'

Manu swallowed. 'I thought it was just whilst I was in here that my father was helping out.'

Vangelis smiled at Manu's innocence. 'Once you agree to supply the arrangement continues forever. You've appreciated a little something on a regular basis. It wouldn't be very fair to suddenly deprive the other men of a bit of pleasure just because you're no longer around. Besides, how would your father suddenly account for the drop in prescription requests for certain commodities? If the pharmaceutical firms became suspicious they would order an enquiry. If malpractice came to light your father would end up in here, and his sentence would be far longer than yours. Add to that the hefty fine he would receive and you are looking at a broken man. Have you considered what would happen to your mother? Homeless; on the streets; a beggar.' Vangelis spread his hands. 'I'm sure your father would not want that to happen; maybe you should explain to him. There could even be opportunities for you to earn a little extra by doing some deliveries.'

Manu clenched his fists. He was not in control of the situation.

'So what work are you planning to do?' asked Mr Graphides.

'You're due for release in three months and you can't spend your time sitting around all day at home doing nothing like you do here.'

Manu looked at his father scathingly. He did not sit around all day doing nothing. He was expected to work for at least six hours each day and attend anger management classes three times each week.

Although Manu had no choice but to attend the group anger management classes he still refused to participate. He would sit with his legs stretched out before him and a bored expression on his face. Whenever the counsellor tried to involve him in their discussions he would gaze around the room or close his eyes as if asleep. The counsellor had thought Manu might be more responsive if they had one to one sessions, but he was met with the same response. Manu would ignore whatever was said to him and look at the wall over the man's shoulder.

However hard the counsellor tried to explain that the course was for Manu's benefit he was met with silence. At the end of an hour, when the counsellor was feeling drained he would press the bell and ask for Manu to be led back to his cell. As he left Manu would smile, knowing that once again he had frustrated their attempts to get him to talk. He did not need counselling; he had every right to be resentful and angry.

'There's plenty of time for me to think about that.'

'It's never too early to make plans,' insisted Elias Graphides.

'I have plans,' answered Manu.

'You could have applied to retrain for something whilst you were in here. I know you were given a list of the courses available. You could have gone out with a trade at your fingertips.'

'They didn't interest me. I have no desire to be a plumber or electrician. I'm not designed to be a manual labourer.'

'Well you'll have to find work of some sort. You owe me a considerable amount of money.'

'Really? I understood you were being well paid due to my contacts.'

Elias shook his head. 'I still have the bank loan to pay off. The one time when I paid in a large amount I was asked where I had got it from. I told them I had won on the lottery, but since then I've not dared to bank too much at any one time. By the time you are released I should have almost enough saved to pay off the loan gradually so the arrangement can stop.'

Manu smiled at his father. 'The arrangement doesn't stop, Pappa. It's permanent.'

'What do you mean? When you're out of prison I hope I won't be seeing him ever again. The increase in requests to fulfil prescriptions has not been queried so far. One day they could come to light.'

Manu snorted in derision. 'Don't be stupid. Once you are a known supplier you stay a supplier for ever. They have that to hold over you. If you refuse they will give your name to the police and there will be a full enquiry launched.'

Elias paled. 'I thought once you had been released I wouldn't be expected to continue to be a supplier. I only agreed in the first place because you told me they would raid the shop and probably hurt your mother.'

Manu nodded. 'If you tell Antonius that you are no longer supplying him that will probably happen anyway; then the police will become involved. You'll be the one ending up in prison. There'll be nothing to connect Antonius. Have you any signed receipts from him?'

Elias shook his head. 'Everything was cash.'

Manu smiled. 'I'll also expect a little comfort as I require it. I've been used to having something on occasions when I'm feeling low. Where better to get it?'

Elias looked at his son in stunned disbelief. 'You mean you've become an addict?'

Manu ignored his father's comment. 'I'll probably need some new clothes as well and I'll have to go to the gym regularly to build myself back up. Make sure you have some savings ready for me, in cash.'

'I don't owe you. If you'd been a bit more frugal and not spent so much on gambling and drinking I wouldn't have had to take out such a large loan. You'll need to find some employment so you can contribute to your keep and start to repay me.'

'All in good time. How am I expected to go out and look for work without any money in my pocket?' Manu leaned back in his chair. 'You took all my savings when I was sentenced so I'll expect you to repay those to me before I start paying you anything.'

Crete

Monika stood back and gave a satisfied smile. She was pleased she had taken Ronnie's advice regarding the arrangements of the shelves and the decor. Two large urns stood in the space between the shelves on each side of the shop. Above them were hung some plaques and more were displayed on the pale green partition wall. All along the top shelf she had arranged specimens of pottery and on the opposite shelf she had placed most of the bronze ornaments. She had moved her desk to the side where Mr Palamakis had left the marble shelves in situ and she now displayed the glass vases there.

On the top shelf of the partition she had stood some Phaistos discs, onyx eggs and miniature pots, and below those were slim guide books and maps with a box of leather bookmarks. The lower shelf she had left empty, waiting for the children's colouring books and crayons to arrive and planning to add children's reading books to that area.

The large counter stood end on and she had glued paper table cloths that had a map of Crete printed on them to the laminated surface and covered them all with clear plastic. It was something she would be able to change quickly and inexpensively whenever the need arose. She planned to arrange a selection of books, travel guides and maps haphazardly, some standing and others lying down. That way it would not matter if customers looked at them and replaced them incorrectly.

Monika turned her attention to the window, stacking up the surplus marble shelving to different heights and eyeing them critically. It might be a good idea to ask Ronnie for help with her window display. All she needed now was her computer to arrive and she could begin to order books. John had agreed to set it up for her and show her the basic programmes that she would need, along with loading details of book suppliers and publishers.

'If you have any problems call me. It will probably be something simple, like a box that has to be ticked or has been ticked in error. Easier for me to come and put it right for you than try to explain over the telephone. Are you planning to have a web site?'

'I hadn't really thought about it,' admitted Monika.

'You should. You need to advertise the kinds of books you have in stock along with your address and telephone number. It could be a good idea to have a map showing the route to you from Elounda. Most of the other businesses here have a web site and they usually link in with each other.'

Monika looked at John, thoroughly puzzled.

John smiled patiently at her. 'It's a way of advertising. You look up tavernas in Plaka and the site will say "see also" and give names of the shops. Most people will look at those links out of curiosity or thinking they are also tavernas. Have you thought about advertising?'

'Not really. I thought I would print up some notices and ask some of the shops to display them about a week before I open.'

'Leave it with me. I'll knock something up on the computer and show it to you. If you don't like it I can always change things.'

John took a photograph of Elisabetta and Joanna with a book between them looking as if they were reading, another showed Uncle Yannis sitting beneath the umbrella on the patio pretending to be immersed in a book.

'What do you think of this one, Nick?'

John turned the computer screen around and there was Skele with a pair of glasses perched on the end of his nose and a book between his paws.

'How did you do that?' asked Nicola.

'I just asked him to sit and put his paws up on the table. All I had to do was doctor it a bit, put some glasses on his nose, take out the table and put a book between his paws.'

Nicola giggled. 'That's really clever. What's his book called?'

'"Dog Tails", of course. Do you think Monika will go for it?'

'She'd be foolish if she didn't. The photo of Skele is far more eye catching than those of people sitting reading. Make sure the title of his book is readable.'

'I need some more photos. Any ideas?'

'What about Aunt Ourania's cat? You could photograph her curled up with a book in front of her.'

'Good idea. Her photo could go opposite Skele. What shall we call her book? It can't be "Cat Tails".'

Nicola grinned. 'What about "How To Catch Mice"?'

John laughed. 'That lazy cat has never even seen a mouse, let alone caught one. I think Uncle Yannis would like that.'

'You could ask one of the boys from school if he will allow you to take a photo of him doing his homework – you know, text book and paper on the desk in front of him, but he's pushed it to one side and is actually reading a book.'

'Yes, and there could be one of you on the sun bed reading a magazine. That way it shows Monika's shop has something for everyone.'

'You should have asked Aunt Helena when she was here. She would have revelled in being a model.'

John shook his head. 'I don't think any photo I took would ever have been good enough for her. She would be bound to claim there was a hair out of place.'

Nicola looked at the photographs critically. 'Actually I think you should have Uncle Yannis reading a newspaper and then Grandma Marisa could be reading a book.'

'Good idea. Hey, we could have Mum and Dad looking at a map as if they were tourists.'

'Bryony and Marcus, what are you going to get them to do? They won't want to be left out.'

'I'll think of something. Yes, they could be customers in the shop pointing to something on a shelf. I'll put the photos down both sides of the page and the address and a list of the kinds of books Monika sells in the centre. If she likes it I could blow it up really large and we could mount it in the square for everyone to see.'

'Would that be allowed?'

John grinned. 'It would only be there for a week or so when she first opens. By the time anyone begins to complain we would have taken it down. No one will mind if we put a few smaller versions up around the area.'

'You'll probably be given commissions by the other shops wanting the same sort of publicity.'

John shook his head. 'This is a one off. Skele charges a high price for his modelling.' Nicola raised her eyebrows and John added 'Sausages.'

'I'm taking the car in today to have the MOT certificate renewed,' Monika told her mother. 'I know it isn't due until next month but it will be more practical to have it done whilst we're still in Heraklion. I'm not sure if I have to go to the same garage as issued the last certificate. I don't want to have to take it to a garage in Aghios Nikolaos and be told I have to come back to Heraklion. Besides, if there is anything major that needs repairing it could disrupt our plans for moving next week.'

Monika drove her car into the garage in Heraklion and asked if they would agree to inspect the vehicle and renew the MOT.

'Where did you get it from?' asked the mechanic.

'I bought it from Tammatakis who has the car hire service. I'd used the vehicle most weekends so I knew it was pretty decent.'

The mechanic pursed his lips. 'Have you got the original paper work?'

'Yes, I was assured that all was in order.'

'It may have been at the last MOT but who knows what has happened to it since. I'll need the MOT certificate, check it over and let you know the cost of repairs. No point in paying for an MOT and having it refused because work needs to be done. What happened to the wing?'

'It was scratched and had to be repaired and re-sprayed. I paid Mr Tammatakis for the work although the damage was not my fault.'

'Come back in two days and I'll let you know if any repairs are needed.'

'Why don't you 'phone me and tell if there's anything that needs to be fixed? Provided there is nothing major or too expensive I can authorise you to put it right. I really need the car back by Friday.' Monika tore a page from her notebook, wrote her mobile number down and gave it to him.

Monika was relieved when the mechanic 'phoned and told her he had renewed the brake pads and changed the oil. She had dreaded being told that the chassis or engine needed renewing.

'I also replaced a rear light bulb. Did you know it wasn't working?'

'I had no idea. Can it now go for the MOT?

'That can be done tomorrow. You owe me two hundred and twenty one Euros. You can pay when you come to collect the car.'

'What time should I come to collect it?'

'After three.'

Monika withdrew three hundred Euros from the bank and checked that she had some change in her purse. The hundred she was left with would pay for the MOT test. She approached the garage feeling pleased that she had her car back. She had not realised how much she had become to depend upon it.

'So it has passed the MOT?'

The mechanic shook his head. 'No.'

'Why not? You said you had made the necessary repairs.'

'The certificate says the car is white and this one is blue.'

'Mr Tammatakis must have had the car re-sprayed.

The mechanic shrugged. 'Then he should have had the MOT altered.'

'Can't you change it?'

'No. You have to go to the Town Hall.'

'May I use the car? It will be quicker if I drive into town.'

'The car stays with me until I've been paid. Two hundred Euros.'

'But I've already paid you for the work you have done on the car.'

'Standard charge for checking it over and issuing the certificate.'

Monika gritted he teeth. She should have asked Vasi or Giovanni where they took their cars to have repairs and the annual MOT.

'I can give you a hundred on account and I'll draw the rest when I'm in town.'

'You're not supposed to drive without a valid MOT.'

'I'll take a chance that I'm not stopped.'

'Don't be gone too long.'

Monika drove swiftly back into the centre of Heraklion, found a parking space a short distance from the Town Hall and hurried inside.

'Where do I go for an MOT certificate?' she asked.

'To a garage,' replied the man on the information desk without looking up.

'No,' Monika shook her head impatiently. ''I've had the MOT done, there is nothing wrong with the car, but the certificate says the car is white and the previous owner had it sprayed blue.'

'You need the information plate for the colour code.'

'Where will I find that?'

'Ask the previous owner. He should have given it to you.'

Monika looked through the papers she had received from Mr Tammatakis, not really knowing what she was searching for. She would have to visit the car hire and hope the owner was in attendance and ask for his help.

Mr Tammatakis looked at her in surprise when she walked into his office. 'What's the problem?'

'I've just taken the car you sold me to have its MOT.'

'There was nothing wrong with it when I sold it to you,' he said immediately.

'That isn't why I'm here. The garage told me they could not give me the new MOT certificate as the old one said the car was white. I was told I would find the colour code on the information plate to enable to have it amended to blue. Where is it? Do you have it?'

Mr Tammatakis rose from his desk with a supercilious smile. He walked out to the car and opened the boot. 'There,' he said, pointing to some numbers on the side.

'Oh!' Monika felt foolish. 'Why didn't they tell me to look there when I was at the garage? Thank you, Mr Tammatakis. I shouldn't have any further problem now.'

Monika hurried to the nearest cash point and withdrew a further one hundred Euros before driving back to the garage. She felt annoyed. Surely the mechanic should have known to look in the car boot for the information he needed.

She drew into the forecourt and took the hundred Euros from her bag. 'Here is the rest of your money. The colour code is in the boot. Please can you change the MOT certificate now?'

'No.' The mechanic shook his head.

'Why not?'

'No pen.'

Monika rummaged in her bag. 'Here, I have one.'

The mechanic tried to write, shook the pen and handed it back to her. 'Dried up.'

Monika looked at him in despair. 'But I need my car.'

'Then get a pen that writes.'

Feeling defeated Monika hurried from the garage searching for a periptero or a shop that was likely to have biros for sale. There appeared to be nothing in the area where every business was a small workshop of some kind.

It took her nearly half an hour before she spotted a periptero and bought a pen. She tested it on a pad of blank paper to ensure it was working and hurried back to the garage.

'I have a pen.'

The mechanic nodded and took it from her. He scratched out the word "white" and wrote "blue" before handing her the certificate and pen back. 'Now you have to take that to the Town Hall to get it stamped.'

Monika nodded. There was no way she would be able to return to the Town Hall before they closed that afternoon. Rushing backwards and forwards dealing with the colour of her car had taken up most of the afternoon. If she had examined the MOT certificate before handing it to the mechanic she would have spotted the discrepancy and could have changed the word "white" to "blue" herself. She was still driving a car without a valid MOT certificate until she had the official stamp from the Town Hall. She hoped if she was stopped by the police they would not ask to see it, or if so, accept her explanation and assurance that she would deal with it the following morning.

March 2014
Crete

Monika and her mother checked they had removed all their belongings from the drawers and cupboards, leaving only their toiletries in the bathroom some clean underwear and two changes of clothing in the bedrooms.

'I shall be sorry to leave here. Our new apartment is not so spacious and the furniture is old,' said Litsa.

'Make the most of it. Once you finish work on Friday we'll load up the car. First thing on Saturday I'll mop the floors then we can return the keys to Mr Iliopolakis. That will give us the weekend at the new apartment to get properly unpacked and settled in. If there is anything we need we can shop for it on Monday.'

'What about food? We'll need something to eat before Monday.'

'We can go to the supermarket on Saturday afternoon and stock up with the essentials. Are you ready, Mamma? I can take you to work as it's on the way to the Town Hall. I don't want to drive the car illegally. The police could insist I have to leave it in the garage and that would upset our arrangements. Mr Iliopolakis and Cathy are coming down for the opening and I want everything to be perfect on the day.'

Monika stood outside and looked at the window display she had created. On the topmost marble shelves she had placed a bronze figurine and the ones below held books, standing slightly open with a book mark between the pages. On the floor she had piled up the marble haphazardly and made a small book shelf where she had placed six books and beside it she stood two of Yannis's attractive octopus pots. Although all the goods that belonged to Yannis were for sale she rather hoped the octopus urns would never be purchased. When she had unpacked them she had fallen in love with them to the extent that she had nearly left them hidden in the stock room.

'What do you think, Saffie? How does it look to you?'

'Very attractive. All you need now is for John to erect that giant poster he has made and you'll be all set for the grand opening.'

'My mother and I have delivered posters to the local hotels and shops and ask if they will display them. I'm hoping they will keep them up for a week or two so people should be curious and come and have a look.'

'I'm sure all the locals will come. They'll probably give you advice on how to run your business, even if they've never done more than their daily shop.'

Monika smiled. 'One of the boatmen went by earlier and he told me I should have sea shells in the window. I suppose if I decided to display a selection of books to do with the sea they might be appropriate. I thanked him for his idea and I hope he won't be offended when he doesn't see any shells around.'

'Better than suggesting you had dead fish! Has your mother found any suitable work yet?'

Monika shook her head. 'She's agreed to iron table cloths for one of the tavernas and look after a little girl when she comes out of school each day as both her parents are working. Neither job is that satisfactory, but better than nothing.'

'Provided the tourists arrive as expected the shops will get busier and they could need extra staff then. They wouldn't want to take on anyone extra until they know they need them.'

Monika shrugged. 'I expect something will turn up. She has

become friendly with Brenda, the English woman and in her spare time she is helping to arrange the flowers in the church and improve Brenda's Greek. At least she is occupied. She's coming to Plaka later as she has offered to help me unpack the other boxes of books that arrived yesterday. The window might look inviting but people are going to be disappointed if they come in and see empty shelves.'

'You can always place one of Uncle Yannis's pots in a space.'

'I hope he won't be disappointed that there aren't more of them on display.'

'He knows it's a book shop. You could have refused to take any of his stock.'

'I just wouldn't want to hurt his feelings.'

'You're just too sensitive. You can't afford sentiment in business.'

Monika smiled guiltily. 'This is my first venture into the business world. Do you think I ought to offer wine to customers?'

'I'm sure they would appreciate it. Why don't you speak to Theo and ask if he'll sell you some and keep a few bottles in reserve in case you need more? Your mother will be here, won't she, and I'm sure she would enjoy being in charge of replenishing glasses and collecting more wine if it was needed.'

'That's a good idea. I was wondering what I could do to keep her occupied. I bought a pack of paper cups yesterday. I didn't think it a good idea to have glasses in case they were broken.'

Saffron shook her head. 'You cannot serve wine in paper cups. Ask Theo to lend you some glasses. If any get broken you'll have to pay for them, of course.'

'I don't really want people drinking wine inside. If they spilled any on a book it would be spoilt.'

'Are you going to be using your computer? You could unplug it and place it on your chair. You can then take your desk outside and use that as a bar. It will be a hint to people not to drink inside.'

'I can't. If people buy books I will need to put their bill through the computer.'

Saffron raised her eyebrows. 'How many more excuses are you going to make? I'll go over to Theo and ask him to bring a couple of his tables and some chairs across. Cathy will need to sit down; she can't be expected to stand up for very long.'

'Do you know where John is going to fix the poster? I don't want it obscuring the window display.'

'I'm sure he has that all organised. Why don't you drive to your apartment and collect your mother? There's really nothing more you can do here.'

'I need to unpack the books.'

'Monika! Go home. Take a break. Have some lunch and come back in an hour. With your mother helping you'll have plenty of time to unpack books and place them on the shelves.'

Monika was far too nervous to eat anything when she returned to her mother. 'I'm going down to the supermarket to buy some crisps and peanuts.'

'They won't be sufficient for a lunch.'

'They're not for me. I'm going to put them out for the visitors to help themselves. What kind of quantity should I get?'

Litsa shrugged. 'I don't know. How many people are you expecting?'

'I don't know. Cathy and Mr Iliopolakis have said they will come, Saffron will be next door and John will be fixing up the poster for me.'

'I'm sure there will be more visitors. What about Uncle Yannis and Giovanni? Buy six packs of those large bags of assorted crisps and two large packs of peanuts. That should be sufficient. You ought to get a few sweets for the children.'

Monika pulled a face; she did not want children putting sticky fingers on the books. 'I'll be back in a little while, then we can go to Plaka.'

'Wait whilst I collect some bowls. You can't serve crisps or peanuts from the bag. I'll come with you to do the shopping and we can go straight on afterwards. I might see something else we need whilst we're in the supermarket.'

Monika loaded up her shopping basket with the crisps and nuts and some packets of boiled sweets. As she took her place before the checkout her mother arrived, her basket also laden with large cartons of fruit juice, some savoury biscuits and a pack of serviettes. She glared at Monika, daring her to tell her to replace the items.

'If these items are not wanted we can always take them back and use them ourselves.'

Monika nodded. She no longer felt she was in charge of the grand opening of her book shop. Saffron had taken over arrangements with Theo and her mother had organised the supermarket shopping.

'We should have brought a plate for the biscuits.'

'I put two in,' said Litsa. 'I should have made you sit down and make out a list. Goodness knows what you would have forgotten if I hadn't been with you.'

Monika and her mother drew up outside the book shop. 'As soon as we've unloaded I'll go and park the car. Oh, look, John has put the poster up. I had no idea it would be so big.'

Standing half way down the hill and in the centre of the pathway stood a six foot high poster advertising the grand opening of Monika's shop.

'How has he fixed that?' asked Litsa.

'I don't know. We'll have a look later. Help me carry these things inside and you can start to unpack them whilst I go to park the car.'

'Don't be silly, we'll do that in the last ten minutes. I'll start opening the boxes of books whilst you're gone and you can tell me where you want me to put them when you get back.'

Monika did not argue, it was imperative that she moved her car before the other shop keepers complained that she was blocking their access. As she returned she stopped to examine the poster. John had used a metal stand that usually stood outside the self catering shop advertising ice cream and firmly taped some wooden uprights to each side. The poster was fixed on each side so it was visible to people both going up or down the hill and two heavy sandbags sat across the bottom strut.

'Do you like it?' asked John, coming up behind her.

'It's amazing. No one can miss that.'

'You can put it into the shop over night and stand it outside each day. It should last quite a while.'

'You'll have to tell me how much I owe you.'

'Two packs of sausages for Skele,' grinned John. 'He's put up his modelling prices.'

'Be serious, John.'

'I am. Skele said two packs of sausages. I asked the cat and she was too lazy to reply, just opened one eye and looked at me. Everyone else gave their services free.'

Monika felt a lump in her throat. 'You are all so good to me.'

'You go and finish whatever you have to do. We'll all be here ready for your opening.'

Monika peered out of the shop window. She could see that Theo had placed tables and chairs outside, leaving enough space for people to look in the window and also have access to the door. There were already a number of people standing outside with their backs to the window.

'Time to get the crisps out, Mamma.'

'We both need a wash before we start doing that, and you need to comb your hair.'

Monika ran some cold water from the tap in the toilet and scrubbed at her face and hands with some tissue. She must remember to bring a clean towel up with her. She dragged a comb through her hair and let out a deep sigh. Her dream was coming true.

'Monika, look!' Litsa was standing with a bemused look on her face.

'What's the matter? I'm just going to open the door.' Monika swung it back and gasped.

The people who had been standing with their backs to the window turned to face her. Each one had a glass in their hand and they raised it to her. Monika felt a moment of panic. Did they have enough wine, crisps and peanuts? Giovanni was at her side, pressing a glass into her hand.

'Where's your mother? She needs a glass so we can all drink a toast to you.'

Litsa stood self consciously beside Monika.

'What can I say?' asked Monika of her mother in a panic. 'I'll have to make a speech.'

'Just thank everyone or you'll be here all night.'

Monika took a deep breath and help up her glass. 'I have to thank everyone here today. Without all of you my shop would not have happened. Uncle Yannis, thank you.' Monika raised her glass in the direction of Yannis who had taken a seat beside Cathy. 'Thank you, Giovanni for all the good advice you gave me and for introducing me to Mr Palamakis. He and his sons have worked hard to complete everything I wanted by today. Ronnie, without your vision the shop would still look like a box, and I must not forget John who made that magnificent poster. I cannot thank all of you individually or we would be here for the remainder of the afternoon.'

'To Monika and to the success of her shop.' Vasilis Iliopolakis called out, giving Monika a broad wink and reminding her of the night when she had first mentioned her idea to him and Cathy.

Glasses were raised and before she knew it Monika was crying. 'What's wrong?' asked Bryony.

Monika shook he head. 'Nothing. It's just so perfect. I didn't expect this.'

'Then dry your eyes and enjoy it.' Bryony pushed a tissue into Monika's hands. 'You wander around and talk to people. Your mother and I will stay in the shop and call you if you are needed.'

Visitors to the area eyed the gathering curiously.

'What's going on?' asked a man.

'The opening of a new book shop,' grinned John. 'Go inside and take a look. You might find something you'd be interested in.'

'I'm not much of a reader, but my wife would probably like to have a look inside. She always has her head in a book.'

'Have a glass of wine and then go and browse.'

'Seems a bit of a nerve if it's a local celebration.'

'Not at all. It's the grand opening and everyone is welcome.'

'Can we really go inside?' asked a woman.

'Of course. If you like what you see please tell your friends.'

Vasilis helped Cathy up and into the shop. 'I think we ought to have a look now before too many people try to come in. You don't want to be crushed.'

Cathy leaned against Monika's desk and looked around. 'She's done a magnificent job. Uncle Yannis must be pleased to see so many of his items are still on display.'

'I understand Monika is hoping they will gradually be sold. Saffron says Monika has plenty more in her stock cupboard.'

'Should we buy something, Vasilis?'

'I don't think we're obliged.'

'I'd like to. How about that crystal vase up there? If we told Monika we wanted it I'm sure we could collect it tomorrow.'

'You don't know how much it costs yet.'

Cathy gave her husband a reproachful glance. She knew he would not refuse her however expensive the vase.

Monika felt quite light headed, although she had drunk sparingly of her wine. She had gradually made her way around everyone and thanked them for coming, surprised to see Mr Palamakis and his grandsons. She was introduced to Vasi's friend, Yiorgo Palamakis, who announced he had painted the stock room and the partition wall.

'That's about all I'm capable of doing,' he smiled ruefully. 'My father gave up trying to make a builder out of me and only employs me during the winter for odd jobs. I usually run boat trips over to Spinalonga.'

'So Giorgos and Yiannis are your sons.'

Yiorgo shrugged self consciously. 'They're good lads. They do as my father tells them.'

'They have worked so hard and you prefer to be out on your boat,' smiled Monika.

'I used to be in the navy. Missed the sea when I left the service.'

Someone touched Monika's arm timidly. 'Excuse me, may I interrupt. I believe some of the pottery is for sale.'

Monika nodded. 'If you show me the piece you're interested in I'll get it down and tell you the price.

'No, there's no need. It's that large urn by the door. My husband and I have bought a villa locally and that would look marvellous in our garden with geraniums growing out of it.'

'The price is on the label. If you put a deposit on it I could reserve it for you.'

'I couldn't make you an offer?'

Monika shook her head. 'The pottery does not belong to me. I can introduce you to Mr Andronicatis and you can make an offer to him. He does not speak very much English.' Monika led the way to where Uncle Yannis was sitting.

'This lady would like to make an offer for one of your urns, Uncle Yannis. Giovanni, maybe you could come and help. I ought to get back inside the shop so my mother and Bryony can come and meet everyone.'

Monika retreated thankfully into the book shop and looked around. People had obviously looked at the books as the shelves were in disarray. She could tidy them later. This was a time for her to relax and enjoy the remainder of the day.

April 2014
Rhodes

Manu stood outside the premises in Bar Street. Without the flashing lights and crowds of people to hide the drab and run down appearance the area looked very different during the day. A road sweeper was working to clear the litter that had been left behind by the previous nights' revellers and until the street was washed down it would continue to smell of alcohol.

Upon his release from prison a week earlier Manu had insisted that his father gave him a sizeable sum to enable him to buy some new clothes. As he wandered around the shops he noted the changes that had taken place, there seemed to be more expensive boutiques than ordinary clothes shops and the shirts, trousers and jackets they were displaying were far more than he could afford. Finally he took the bus to an outlying area where the cheaper shops were situated and made his essential purchases there.

Vangelis had given him a contact name and told him to be at the bar to meet the manager when the man arrived to open and prepare the premises ready for his evening trade. The previous evening Manu had walked down Bar Street to see exactly where he was supposed to meet, having a drink at the bar and trying to decide which of the men who were serving could be the manager.

He was surprised when a small man with a limp arrived and unlocked the door. He straightened up and went to follow him inside.

'Not open.' The man glared at him.

'I'm Emmanuel. I was told to be here to meet with Costas. I understood there could be some work for me.'

The man grunted. 'Better come in then.'

Manu stood there uncertainly whilst the man eyed him up and down.

'When did you come out?'

Manu swallowed uncertainly. Was it so obvious that he had recently been released? Did he have the "prison pallor" that was talked about?

'A week ago.'

'What makes you think you could be a doorman?'

'I've kept myself pretty fit and I'm planning to return to the gym regularly as soon as I have some work.'

'What were you in for?'

'Acting in self defence.'

'A bar room brawl?'

'No,' Manu shook his head. 'Nothing like that. I was in the police force and was stabbed when I tried to arrest a criminal. I defended myself and they pressed charges for assault. It was their word against mine and they were believed.'

'So why haven't you applied to return to the force?'

Manu shrugged. 'They won't accept me as I've served a prison sentence, even though I was innocent and wrongly convicted.'

Costas eyed Manu sceptically. In his experience the police looked after their officers. If Emmanuel had hurt someone in the course of making an arrest it was highly unlikely any counter charges would have been brought against him.

'We don't have any violence down here. You'll get to know the trouble makers and send them on their way.'

'What happens if they refuse to leave?'

'You pick them up and dump them out on the street. Think you could manage that?'

Manu nodded. 'Sounds easy enough.'

'If you do have to throw someone out you'll no doubt have an audience. Just remember not to use your fists. You don't want anyone coming forward to say they saw you hit them.'

'I'll remember. Have I got the job?'

'You can start tonight. It's nine 'til three. Sometimes you finish a bit earlier if we're quiet and decide to close up. Beer on the house, but no more than four bottles. A tally will be kept so don't try to be clever and buy any from next door. Word will get back and that will be the end of your job here or anywhere else in the street. Understand?'

Manu nodded. He had expected to be able to drink as much as he liked, not be restricted to only four bottles.

'I'll put you with Nikos tonight. He'll show you the ropes. I'll expect you by eight forty five at the latest and smartly dressed. You need to be recognisable as a doorman, not mistaken for a tourist.'

Manu walked back towards his father's shop, stopping at the supermarket on the way and buying some cans of beer, two packets of cigarettes and two packs of Dupon. He'd swap the tablets for some of the Benzodiazepine that were in his father's drug cupboard and place the substitutes at the bottom of the pile. There might be a chance to make some money that evening.

Once home he would have a few drinks after lunch and then sleep for the afternoon. He couldn't be expected to be awake all day and half the night as well. He would have to get into a new routine. Whilst in prison he had been woken at six every day. Now he was back home it was a luxury to lie in bed until seven or even later, but he would need to break the habit of going to sleep at ten each night.

Manu found the work as a doorman extremely boring. He and Nikos would stand either side of the door as customers walked through, stopping one occasionally and trying to ascertain if they were already so drunk that they should be turned away. At regular intervals Nikos would go inside and wander around, checking that no one was taking drugs and whilst he was absent Manu took the opportunity to smoke a cigarette.

'We don't have drugs inside,' he explained to Manu. 'They can use them before or afterwards, but not on these premises. We're clean.'

'So what do you do if you suspect someone has taken something illegal?'

'Provided they are not making a nuisance of themselves we leave them alone. If they start causing trouble that is when we throw them out. One of the bar staff will usually tip us off if they notice anything suspicious. Are you a user?'

Manu shook his head. He was not prepared to admit that he now used a small amount of cocaine, Benzodiazepine or OxyContin every day and that he regularly sold some tablets to a dealer before he reported for work.

Manu sat on the grassy ramparts overlooking the Old Town walls. A message had been left with his father at the chemist shop and Elias had handed it over to his son.

'What's this about?' he asked.

'Meeting someone about a job,' replied Manu abruptly.

'Not the usual sort of place to go for a job interview,' remarked Elias. 'What kind of job is it? Nothing illegal, I hope.'

'It's personal business, not that it's any of your affair. It's not illegal; although why that should concern you I do not know.'

'I don't want anyone coming nosing around here due to your activities.'

'I'm sure you don't!' Manu pocketed the brief note and returned to his room. His father could have given him the message when he left for work that evening rather than disturbing his siesta.

Manu lay on his bed thinking hard. He would certainly not disclose his full intentions, declaring that he wished to find his ex-wife to see if there was any chance of reconciliation between them.

He also had to think of a good reason for the man to be asking for her. He did not want Monika to hear that he was looking for her.

A non-descript man approached and sat down beside Manu. 'Warm day,' he announced and mopped his brow. 'I'm Thranassis.'

Manu nodded. 'I was expecting you.'

'I understand you have some work for me.'

'I could have. What are your charges?'

Thranassis shrugged. 'Depends what I have to do and how long it takes me. Travel has to be paid for and my lodgings if I am away over night.'

'I'm looking for someone.'

'Your ex I believe. Where do you want me to start?'

'Her grandmother has a general store in the Old Town, just down from the San Francisco gate. I'm not sure if she is still there as I've not been to the area recently. When I last looked it was closed.'

'How long ago was that?'

'About five years now.'

Thranassis nodded. 'It may have changed hands. I can ask whoever is in there if they know your wife.'

'If her grandmother is there she's unlikely to tell you anything if she thinks you've been sent by me. I've thought up a cover story for you.'

Thranassis raised his eyebrows. 'Tell me more.'

'Well,' Manu considered. 'I know my ex wife's mother, Litsa, was a prostitute. I thought if you claimed to be Monika's long lost brother you'd be more likely to get information.'

'So where have I been all this time?'

Manu shrugged. 'I don't know, Athens possibly. That's a big place.'

'And how have I found out about this supposed sister of mine?'

'Your father told you before he died; asked you to look after her.'

'I can work on that, make it sound plausible. Anywhere else I can look for her?'

'She used to work at the library in the Old Town. The woman there might know where she is. They were friends. Her name is Mrs Ethanides. She may have retired, of course.'

'I can try there. Any more ideas?'

Manu hesitated. 'When Monika and I were married her mother started work in a supermarket, but I can't remember which one. I don't think I ever knew. I'm sure her mother kept in contact with the girls who worked in the red light area. They might know something.'

Thranassis took a notebook from his pocket. He wrote down "general store", "Mrs Ethanides – library" "supermarket" and "girls". 'So give me the names of your wife and her relatives.'

'The old lady was called Monique, her mother was Litsa and my ex was also called Monika. Their surname was Kokanides. There's no one else.'

'You realise I may not find a trace of them.'

Manu sighed. 'I'm sure she's hiding out somewhere on Rhodes. She filed the divorce papers here.'

'Well that's something, I suppose. Even if I have to visit every town and village on Rhodes I should be able to find her. She may have married again, of course.'

'That's a chance I have to take.'

'Do you have the name and address of the lawyer your ex used? I may be able to pry some information out of him.'

'Angelos Spanides, he has an office in the New Town.'

Thranassis closed his notebook. 'I'll try the other sources first. They're more likely to talk to me than a lawyer.' He grinned. 'They're also cheaper. A lawyer is bound to charge for his time and his fees will be added to your bill. I charge one hundred Euros an hour and I expect it paid promptly.'

Manu looked at Thranassis sceptically. 'You could tell me you've worked for ten hours and only done two.'

'I make a note of my time. I'll meet you here in two weeks, same time, and let you know if I've made any progress. You can bring some money with you.'

Manu nodded. He would have to persuade his father to give him some more money from the amount he had hidden away.

'Pappa, I need some money,' announced Manu.

'I gave you some the other week to buy some new clothes. You're working now so you shouldn't need me to provide you with pocket money. You'll just have to cut down on the consumption of your beer and cigarettes. Neither does you any good anyway.'

'I'm talking proper money. You should have plenty hidden away that you can't pay into the bank in one large amount. When do you see Antonius again?'

'He's due next week.'

Manu nodded. 'Good timing. I'll need at least five hundred by this time next week.'

'Five hundred!' Elias gasped. 'Whatever for?'

'It's an investment. I'm employing someone to find where Monika is hiding. I plan to get my money back from her.'

'She's probably spent it by now.'

'Then she'll have to work the debt off. Her mother knew how to make a living. Monika should have a few years before she begins to look too old to attract anyone.' Manu shook his finger at his father. 'After what she did to me she deserves all she gets. I'll work her to the bone and when she's no further use I'll make sure she becomes infected and then throw her out on the street.'

'Manu! You wouldn't!' Elias was aghast at the idea.

'I certainly will. Just because she had been to University she thought herself better than me. The daughter of a prostitute – the lowest of the low. Now, where's the money, or do I have to beat the hiding place out of you?'

Thranassis walked into the old Town by way of the San Francisco Gate. Manu had accompanied him and pointed out where the red light district was situated and told him the approximate position of the shop before hurrying back through the gate to the main road.

Thranassis located the shop almost immediately, walked past and then took a turning that led down to a lower road. Once back at the San Francisco Gate he walked through the road Manu said was the red light area. It was more difficult to find during the day time as the girls rarely rose before mid-day and did not have their lights on until the evening to show they were available.

He strolled back to the shop and walked inside. There was a woman sitting behind the counter reading and Thranassis could not believe his luck. Had he found the man's ex wife already? The woman looked up as he entered and Thranassis realised that she was too old to have been Manu's wife.

He smiled widely at her. 'Hello, are you Litsa?'

'No,' answered Natasha abruptly.

Thranassis let out a loud sigh. 'I'm looking for Litsa and Monika. I understood they lived here.'

Natasha shook her head. 'They haven't lived here for some years now.'

'Do you know where I could find them? It's rather important to me.'

'I've no idea.'

Thranassis leaned on the counter. 'That's a shame. My father asked me to find Litsa. I'm Monika's half brother.'

'Really?' Natasha raised her eyebrows. Litsa had never mentioned that Monika had a half brother. 'How come?'

'Well Dad was stationed over here with the army. He met Litsa and you know how it is when you're lonely and away from home.' Thranassis smiled and spread his hands. 'He said he really loved her, but couldn't marry her because of Mum and me.'

'In the army?' This was the first Natasha had heard that Monika's father was in the army. Natasha felt even more suspicious. Litsa had always claimed he was in the navy.

Thranassis nodded. 'He came over here quite a few times, just to make sure all was well with them. He said Monika was a cute little kid and had grown into an attractive young woman. It was a shame he wasn't well enough to make the journey over to attend her wedding, although I'm not sure what excuse he would have made to my mother.'

'I'm sure he would have thought of something,' answered Natasha dryly. According to Litsa Monika's father had denied all responsibility for her from the outset and never visited Rhodes to check on their welfare.

Thranassis let out another sigh. 'Before he died he made me promise that I'd come over and find them. He asked me to take care of Litsa.'

'I believe Litsa is quite capable of looking after herself.'

'Do you have any idea where I could find them? Dad told me they lived here in this shop. It belonged to the old lady, Monika's grandmother.'

Natasha nodded. 'I took over the shop when she decided she no longer wanted to run it.'

'I understood from Dad that Litsa worked in a supermarket when she changed occupations. I would have thought she would have wanted this shop for herself.'

'Apparently not.'

'So where could I find them?' persisted Thranassis.

'I've told you, I don't know. The old lady's dead now anyway.'

'So if you own the shop there must have been a legal transaction.'

Natasha did not admit that she only rented the shop. 'It was all done through a lawyer.'

'Maybe he'd know where I can find them. Can you give me his name?'

Natasha wrinkled her brow. Surely there was no harm in telling this man the name of the lawyer to whom she paid the rent each month?

'Angelos Spanides.'

'Where will I find him?'

'He has an office in the New Town, close to the OTE building.'

Thranassis smiled and took his elbows off the counter. 'I'm grateful for your help. I'll contact Mr Spanides and see if he has an address for them. I really do want to meet my half sister.'

Thranassis turned as he reached the door. 'A thought has occurred to me. I know Litsa worked with the other ladies in the street near here. I suppose one of them wouldn't be in touch with her and know where she's living?'

'That was years ago. There are no girls living there now that she knew.'

Natasha watched as Thranassis sauntered off down the road. There was something about the man's story that did not sit easily with her. She was sure Litsa would have told the girls if Monika's father had returned to visit her on occasions and subsequently been invited to his daughter's wedding.

Thranassis took a devious route through the Old Town, looking into the gift shops hoping his behaviour made him appear like the other tourists in the area. On reaching the library he spent some time wandering around the shelves before finally approaching the desk.

Mrs Ethanides looked up. 'How can I help you?'

'I'm actually looking for Monika.'

'"Monika"? I'm not familiar with the title. Who is the author?'

Thranassis shook his head. 'No, Monika, the lady. I understand she works here.'

'There is no one here called Monika,' said Mrs Ethanides firmly.

Thranassis frowned. 'My father was quite certain this was where she worked.'

'I'm sorry, he must be mistaken.'

'I suppose that is possible. He was ill when he was telling me and he couldn't remember exactly when he had last seen her, it would have been some time ago.'

'There was a young woman called Monika who worked here about ten years ago.'

'Goodness, I didn't realise my father was going that far back in time. Did she move on to another library in a different town?'

'I have no idea.'

'You weren't asked to give her a reference?'

'No one ever wrote to me for one. I can only assume that she changed her occupation and a written reference was not necessary.'

'So you don't know where she is?'

Mrs Ethanides shook her head and hoped she would be forgiven for the half truth. She did not have Monika's home address and she had no idea whether the young woman would be at home or at her shop today. She had promised Monika that she would tell no one that she was living on Crete and she intended to keep her word.

Thranassis gave a deep sigh. 'Is there anywhere else you could suggest that I look for her? You see, I'm her half brother and before my father died he made me promise to find her and look after her.'

'I'm not able to help you. I'm sorry.'

'I believe she transacted some business with Mr Spanides, a local lawyer. Do you think he might be able to help me?'

'I have no idea. You would have to ask him. Now, if you will excuse me I do have work that I need to complete.'

Mrs Ethanides waited until Thranassis had left the building and then she exited the computer programme with the library details. She typed in the e-mail address Monika had given her and composed a brief message.

"Man looking for you. Says he is your half brother. Is approaching Spanides, lawyer, for information."

Having sent the message Mrs Ethanides deleted it and returned to the original programme that contained details of the library stock.

Monika read the message and her heart sank. It could only mean that Manu had been released from prison and was looking for her. She locked the door to her shop and pressed in the numbers for the library on Rhodes.

'Mrs Ethanides, please. It's very important,' she said to the library exchange when she was finally answered and listened to the telephone on Mrs Ethanides desk ringing to denote an incoming call.

'Hello?'

'Mrs Ethanides, it's Monika.'

'Monika! Give me five minutes and I'll call you back on my mobile.'

Monika waited impatiently for Mrs Ethanides to call and answered her telephone on the first ring.

'Please tell me what has happened?' she asked nervously.

'I'm sure it's nothing that you need to be worried about. A man came in here and asked if he could speak to you. I told him you had left some years ago and he wanted to know where you were and if he was able to contact you. He seemed genuinely disappointed when I said I didn't know and told me he was your half brother.'

'I haven't got a half brother or any siblings for that matter. Are you sure it was me he was looking for?'

'I only know what he told me. He said he had promised his dying father that he would find you and look after you.'

'Mrs Ethanides, did you tell him anything at all about me?'

'No, I told him nothing. He said he understood Mr Spanides had transacted some business for you and would ask him if he knew where you were.'

'It has to be Manu. Who else would have known that Mr Spanides had dealt with my divorce? He's obviously asked a friend to look for me. What am I going to do?'

'I suggest you call Mr Spanides and apprise him of the situation. There is no reason for him to give out your location.'

'I felt so safe over here,' replied Monika miserably.

'You are safe there. All the time Manu wastes his time looking for you on Rhodes you have nothing to worry about. When he can't find you anywhere over here he'll eventually give up. He can't search every island and the mainland.'

'If he comes back and questions you again will you let me know?'

'Of course. How is your shop doing?'

'Oh, quite well considering it is the first season I have been here.'

'That's good to hear. You concentrate on your shop and forget about Manu.'

'I'll try. Thank you, Mrs Ethanides.'

Monika turned her chair round so she could look out of her shop window onto the square where people were continually passing up and down. What would she do if she suddenly saw Manu? The door was locked, but unless she was able to climb through the small toilet window there was no other means of escape. She would be trapped and at his mercy.

Her heart was beating rapidly and Monika took some deep breaths, forcing herself to think logically. If Manu was making enquiries about her on Rhodes he obviously did not know she was on Crete. She must telephone Mr Spanides as Mrs Ethanides had suggested and request that he did not reveal her location. Now she had a business she would be far easier to find if Manu was really determined.

'Angelos Spanides.'

'Mr Spanides, can I talk to you or do you have a client with you?'

'I have no one with me at present. Who is this calling?'

'Monika Kokanides.'

'Miss Kokanides, how nice to hear from you. All is well with your mother I hope.'

'Yes, thank you.'

'So how can I help you?'

Monika took a deep breath. 'I'm sure Manu is looking for me. I received a telephone call from a friend and she said a man had visited her asking to speak to me. He claimed he was my half brother and his father had asked him to find me and my mother.'

'Yes.'

'I am sure it isn't true. I doubt if my father has ever given me a second thought. He disowned me as soon as my mother told him she was expecting a child.'

'I see.'

'He said he knew you had dealt with me in a legal capacity and would come and ask if you were able to help him find me. Please don't tell him my address, or even that I am on Crete.'

'Miss Kokanides, I do not have your private address on Crete. You insisted all correspondence should be directed to the "Central Hotel". I received the directive from your mother that her rent from the shop should be paid in to the Aghios Nikolaos bank as from March as she was transferring her account there from Heraklion. I assumed that she had left Heraklion and was living in a new location.' Mr Spanides spoke patiently to the distraught woman.

Monika let out her breath. 'Of course. I no longer work at the hotel.'

'Would you care to give me your new address?'

Monika hesitated. 'I'd rather not disclose it.'

'I would keep it entirely confidential,' Mr Spanides assured her.

'I'm sure you would, but if you do not know it you can tell anyone who makes enquiries for me quite honestly that you do not have my address.'

'I always respect my client's requests,' replied Mr Spanides stiffly. 'If anyone should approach me for your details should I advise you?'

'Yes, please. I would prefer you to 'phone me on this number. Are you able to record it safely?'

'I will transfer it to my private mobile and delete the number from the office 'phone. Would you be happy to accept that?'

'Yes,' agreed Monika eagerly. 'I'm sure you think I'm making a fuss about nothing, but I really do not want my ex husband to find out where I am.'

Rhodes

Angelos Spanides rose and extended his hand to the man who entered his room. 'Please, take a seat, and tell me how I may help you.'

'Well,' Thranassis appeared to hesitate. 'It's rather complicated. It's probably best if I start at the beginning.' He smiled ingratiatingly at the lawyer.

'Then shall we start with your name and address?'

'Oh, yes. I'm Timotheus Andopolous.'

'And your address?'

'That's not really relevant. I live in Athens.'

'Without a current address where I can send your bill I will have to insist you pay me for my time in advance. Two hundred Euros for each half hour of my time.'

Thranassis reluctantly took the notes from his wallet. 'I would appreciate having a receipt.'

'Of course. All in good time.' Angelos placed the notes in the drawer of his desk. 'Now, what is the problem you wish to discuss?'

'Many years ago now my father had an affair with a young lady who lived on Rhodes. A daughter resulted from their association. It was impossible for my father to marry and give the child his name as he was already married to my mother. I think I would have been about five or six at the time. My father never mentioned the girl and my mother and I knew nothing of her. Occasionally he would declare he had to make a business trip to Thessaloniki and would be away for a few days. It was not until my father realised he was dying that he revealed the truth to me. He had been surreptitiously visiting Rhodes to ensure the well-being of his lady friend and her daughter. He made me promise that I would come over and find them, make myself known as the girl's half brother and assist them in any way that was needed.'

'When did your father die?'

Thranassis shook his head sadly. 'It is more than seven years now since his demise.'

'So why have you not come looking for them before?'

'I had to deal with my father's business affairs, and I was also due to be married within the next few months. Shortly after that my mother was ill. I thought at first she was just grieving, but unfortunately it turned out to be more serious. My wife and I took her to live with us and Alithea nursed my mother devotedly. I could not leave Athens at that time.' Thranassis rubbed his hands across his eyes and let his voice break. 'Then further tragedy struck. We had a small son. He was involved in an accident and died. Alithea was heartbroken. So was I, of course, but I was able to deal with it better as I went out to work each day whereas she was at home where everything reminded her of our beautiful boy. I finally persuaded her that it would help her if we had another child. It was a big mistake on my part.' Now Thranassis covered his face with his hands. 'My wife died in childbirth and the baby did not survive.'

Angelos shifted uncomfortably in his chair. The poor man had certainly suffered some traumatic events.

Thranassis gave a deep sigh and straightened his shoulders. 'I am now alone in the world and I remembered my father wanted me to find my half sister. From all he had told me I thought it would be relatively easy. Her name was Monika; she worked in the library and lived with her mother and grandmother in a general store in the Old Town.'

Angelos nodded and waited for the man to continue.

'I visited the library and I was told that Monika had left their employ and they had no idea where she was working now. I found the general store where she had lived and spoke to the lady there. She told me the store now belonged to her, but she was unable to tell me where the original owner and her family were living. All she could tell me was that you had drawn up the legal agreement.'

Thranassis leaned forward earnestly. 'I was hoping you might have a current address for them.'

'The family name?'

'Kokanides.'

Mr Spanides frowned. This was obviously the man Monika had telephoned and spoken to him about, pleading with him not to divulge any information about her whereabouts.

He pressed his fingers together and frowned. 'Kokanides, Kokanides, yes, I remember the name vaguely.'

'So you can help me?' asked Thranassis eagerly.

Mr Spanides shook his head. 'Certainly not immediately. I would have to search my archived papers for the documents regarding the sale of the shop. There would probably be an address on there but they may have moved elsewhere. I would then have to try to contact the lady in question and ask her permission for me to pass her address on to you. I am not allowed by law to give out any details that are recorded on legal paper work.'

Thranassis frowned. 'So how long will this take?' He looked at the numerous filing cabinets that stood around the room.

Angelos shrugged. 'I cannot say for certain.' He looked at his calendar. 'I appear to have a free morning next week and two free afternoons the following week. I could begin to search the archives then.'

'I can't wait that long. I have to return to Athens.'

Mr Spanides spread his hands. 'I'm sorry, but that is the best I can do. These enquiries cannot be rushed. I suggest you leave me your address in Athens and I will contact you when I have any relevant information.'

Thranassis glowered at the lawyer. 'Suppose I returned in a month?'

Angelos shook his head. 'I cannot guarantee I will have any information for you at that time. Depending upon the movements of the people you are looking for I may not find a current address for them. You could be wasting your time. If you leave me your address and telephone number I would be able to advise you of the outcome of my enquiries.'

'That is not convenient. I'll telephone you.'

'As you wish.' Mr Spanides pulled a receipt book from amongst his pile of papers and wrote on it swiftly. 'Here is your receipt.'

He turned the book towards Thranassis who scowled and scrawled his name.

'Thank you.' The lawyer rose and held out his hand. Thranassis stuffed the receipt into his pocket and shook hands briefly. Manu was not going to be happy.

Angelos Spanides sat and looked at the copy of the receipt. The man had hesitated before he signed and Angelos had a suspicion the name the man had given was false. He would have to telephone Monika Kokanides and see if she was familiar with anyone called Timotheus Andopolous.

Monika looked at the number displayed on her mobile 'phone screen and gave a sigh of relief when she recognised it as belonging to Mr Spanides.

'Hello,' she said cautiously.

'It is Mr Spanides calling. Am I speaking to Miss Kokanides?'

'Yes.'

'Are you free to talk to me? I am calling on my private mobile.'

'Just one moment whilst I lock the door; then we will not be interrupted.'

Mr Spanides heard her heels click on the floor as she went across the room and turned the key in the lock.

'How can I help you, Mr Spanides?'

'A short while ago I had a visitor. He said his name was Timotheus Andopolous. Do you know anyone of that name?'

'No, no, I'm sure I don't. What did he want?'

'He told me he was looking for you and claimed to be your half brother.'

'You didn't give him my address, did you?' asked Monika

anxiously.

'No, I told him I would have to look in my archives and see if I had a current address for you. I would then have to contact you for permission to reveal it.'

Monika gave a sigh of relief. 'Thank you. He must have been sent by Manu. Is he returning to see you again?'

'I think it very unlikely. He was not willing to disclose his address and said he lived in Athens. I have a feeling that the name he gave me was false. He said he would telephone me in about a month to ask if I had made any progress.'

'So at the moment I should have no need to worry. Is there anything I can do to prevent him from contacting me if he finds out where I am?'

'To do that you would have to give a reason to the police. It is not a criminal offence to ascertain an address. You would have to prove that he was stalking you or had threatened you in some way before they could take any action.'

'You will let me know if he contacts you again, won't you?'

'Of course. My advice in the meantime is to apprise your mother of the situation and be cautious about disclosing any of your personal details to anyone.'

'Oh, that is more difficult.' Monika hesitated. 'I will tell you, again in confidence, that I have a shop and I obviously have to give my business details to my suppliers.'

Mr Spanides sighed. 'Would your ex husband have knowledge of this?'

'No. The only person on Rhodes who knows is the friend who originally telephoned me to tell me someone was making enquiries about me.'

'And you can rely on them?'

'Absolutely.'

'Then again you should not need to be concerned. It would be beyond reasoning that your ex husband could contact every wholesaler and find they were dealing with you.'

'I have a web site for publicity. It has my name and the address of the book shop. Shall I remove it, just as a further safety precaution?'

'If your ex husband has no idea about your current circumstances he is unlikely to look for you on the internet, but it would be sensible to remove any personal details temporarily.'

Monika gave a deep sigh. 'I'll speak to John. I'm sure he will know how to remove it and save it so it can be replaced later.'

Crete

John looked at Monika in surprise when she requested he removed her web site from the computer.

'Aren't you happy with it?'

'Yes, I'm delighted but I've a problem at the moment.'

'I can probably sort that out easily enough for you.'

Monika shook her head. 'I don't think so. I believe someone might be looking for me and I certainly do not want him to know where I am. If I left advertising details on the computer about my shop he could find me quite easily.'

'Does he know you are on Crete and have a book shop?'

'I don't think so, but I don't want to take a chance.'

'Your ex, I gather.'

Monika looked at John in surprise. 'How did you know? I've never mentioned anything about him to anyone.'

'You told Cathy, she told Vasilis, he told Vasi so he told Saff, Saff told Bryony, Bryony told Mum and she told Nick. You can't have secrets in a family.'

Monika was forced to smile. 'Is there anyone who doesn't know?'

'Maybe Uncle Yannis and Grandma. What's the problem with your ex?'

'He has a rather unpredictable temper.'

'You mean he might hit you?'

'It's possible.'

'You shouldn't be up here at the shop alone.'

'I don't have a choice. I only have my mother and I couldn't expect her to come up here to look after me. My only other option is to close the shop and I'm loath to do that. I've only been open a month and I'm just beginning to make a little profit.'

'You could get a dog?' suggested John.

Monika shook her head. 'Our landlord stipulated no pets of any kind; besides how long would it take me to train a dog to protect me?'

John looked around the book shop. 'I'll have a word with Dimitris.'

'Does he train dogs?'

John smiled. 'No, he looks after Skele for me, but we didn't have to train him. I'm thinking that Dimitris might be able to install an alarm system for you. He could tell you if it was feasible. I don't know anything about electrical systems.'

Dimitris arrived at Monika's shop at mid-day with John and Skele.

'Skele can sit outside if you don't want him in the shop,' offered John. 'I've told Dimitris that you want an alarm system set up.'

'Skele's welcome. Is it possible for me to have an alarm, Dimitris?'

'Are you expecting anyone to break in?'

'Not really, but I've been told that my ex husband is looking for me. It won't be for a friendly chat and I would be terribly frightened if he turned up here when I was alone.'

'You will need permission from the police to have an alarm installed that alerts them at the station.'

Monika shook her head. 'They are in Aghios Nikolaos. By the time they reached me it could be too late and Manu would have disappeared. I need something more immediate.'

'Could it be connected to Uncle Yannis's house?' suggested John.

'That's not practical. If it was connected to the house it might be activated when only Marianne was there with Nicola and the children.' Monika bit her lip. 'I certainly couldn't expect them to come to my aid and they might get hurt if they tried to help me.'

'What about the taverna, then?'

'You're not always there, John, and it could still take you some time to reach here. You'd have to turn away any customers and lock up.'

John looked at Dimitris. 'Do you have any other ideas?'

'Well,' Dimitris considered, 'you could have an alarm outside, like a fire or burglar alarm. It would make a tremendous racket and the other shop keepers would probably come out to see what was wrong.'

'You could even tell them that if they hear it you need help and they should come and see what was wrong. I'm sure one of them would 'phone the police,' added John.

'Suppose it went off accidently? If that happened a few times they would end up ignoring it.'

'There's no reason why that should happen.' Dimitris looked around the shop again. 'You could have the alarm bell outside and I could connect it to a switch beneath your desk. It would have to be wired in to the main electrical system, but that would be no problem.'

Monika frowned. 'I'm not always at my desk. Suppose I was in the stock room?'

Dimitris spread his hands. 'I could place another switch in there. How often do you go to the stock room whilst your shop is open?'

'Not often,' replied Monika. 'I usually do any re-stocking of the shelves when I close. If I need the toilet I usually lock the shop door.'

'Unless I install an alarm button in the toilet, stock room and on every book case I think you just have to be cautious and lock the door when you leave the shop unattended. If there were alarm buttons on the shelves they would probably be set off accidently by your customers. That would not be very satisfactory.'

Monika smiled. 'I think I would soon lose my customers if they continually set off an alarm. If you connected one to my desk that rang outside it should be sufficient. I mustn't be paranoid.'

'So you want me to go ahead?'

Monika nodded. 'As soon as possible, please. I feel I must be prepared in case Manu does turn up.'

Dimitris arrived at Monika's shop the following day. 'This should not take me very long. I'll have to ask you to move away from your desk and I'll also need to have the electricity switched off for a few minutes when I make the final connection.'

Dimitris crawled beneath Monika's desk and she watched as he fitted a bell push to the underside and trailed the wire to where those from her computer led to the plug socket and the fuse box. Deftly he connected the wire to the main electrical supply and the fuse. From the back of the socket he ran a cable up the side of the window, made a small hole in the top of the frame and passed a length of the cable through. He took Monika's small steps outside and proceeded to screw a metal box to the wall. A bell with a metal clapper fitted snugly inside and he clipped a protective metal cover over it.

'I'll need to check that it's working and when I've done that I'll tape the wire to the underside of the desk. You don't want to get your leg caught on it and pull it out. If you do set it off accidently just flip the switch up. Whenever you need to move the desk just switch off at the socket and remove the plugs the same as you would with the computer.' He looked at his watch. 'You ought to warn your neighbours that an alarm system has been fitted and will be tested in ten minutes.'

Monika nodded and hurried across to the taverna and spoke

to Theo.

'Can you tell your staff and customers? I don't want to frighten the life out of them.'

He grinned at her. 'You should keep a gun, the same as I do.'

'Then I'll know where to come if I need help.' She was not sure if Theo was serious.

Monika went from shop to shop, telling the owners the alarm she had installed was about to be tested, finally ending up with Saffron.

'I hope I never need to use it, but I've been told someone is looking for me on Rhodes. It can only be Manu.'

'Why should he come looking for you down here?'

'It's just a safety precaution. If I set if off accidently I can switch it off and it will stop immediately. If I do have an emergency it will continue to ring so I'll need help. Once Dimitris has finished I'll speak to everyone again and explain that if it rings continuously I need them to come and investigate.'

A horrendous clamour suddenly filled the air and by the time the shop owners had come outside to investigate the noise had abated.

'Wow,' remarked Saffron. 'That is certainly some alarm. They could probably hear it in Elounda. You ought to warn the taverna owners along by the waterfront and the taxi drivers.'

'I had no idea it would be that loud,' explained Monika. 'I thought it would be more like a door bell.'

'We would probably not have noticed it then. A racket like that will alert everyone. I hope it doesn't go off accidently at night.'

'I'll check with Dimitris, but I should be able to switch it off when I leave each day.'

Theo came across to them. 'So when I hear that I come with my gun?'

Monika smiled at him. 'Do you really have a gun?'

Theo nodded seriously. 'Of course. After those two young men were here robbing tavernas I bring it with me each day.' He pulled a revolver from the waist band of his trousers and spun it around on his finger.

'Is it loaded?' asked Monika nervously.

'Of course. You want me to show you?'

Monika shook her head. 'I'll take your word for it, Theo. Just be very careful, please.'

Rhodes

Manu placed the money he had insisted his father gave him into an envelope and headed out towards the Old Town where he was to meet Thranassis. In a short while he should know where Monika was hiding from him and he would extract some more money from his father so he could pay her a visit. He smiled to himself; he could just imagine the look on her face when she opened her door to him.

If he was able to retrieve most of the money he had been forced to pay her he would give in his notice and leave the monotonous job in Bar Street. The surreptitious deliveries he was making to the dealers was beginning to give him a sizeable amount of money that he was hiding away. So far his father had not discovered the packets where Dupon tablets had been substituted for Benzodiazepine or OxyContin. Once he had sufficient saved and recovered his money from Monika he would be able to open his own bar and it could become a new meeting and supply centre for the dealers.

He sat on the seat and looked across to the Old Town. Premises in the area close to the area that was also known as Bar Street would be ideal and if Monika was living elsewhere there was no reason for him to be forbidden to enter or have a business there. Innocent tourists would be bound to patronise him which would give his bar respectability. In a few years he could have made a fortune. He smiled happily as Thranassis sat down beside him.

'What did you find out?' he asked eagerly.

'All in good time. I'd like my money first.'

'How much?'

Thranassis pulled out his notebook and consulted it quite unnecessarily. He knew exactly how much time he had spent on Manu's behalf. 'Four hundred.'

Manu pulled a bulging envelope from his pocket, removed a hundred Euros and handed it to Thranassis.

'I'll not count it up here. I assume it's all there?'

Manu nodded. 'Four hundred.'

'That will do for the time being.'

Thranassis crossed his legs and leaned back. 'I went to the shop where you said your ex had lived. The old lady has died and the shop has been sold.'

Manu cursed his luck. 'Did the owner know where Monika and her mother had gone?'

'She said she had no idea, but the transaction had been done through Spanides, the same lawyer as acted for the divorce. I went to the library after that and the woman confirmed that Monika had left their employment years ago and she had no idea where she was now.'

'Do you think she was telling the truth?'

Thranassis shrugged. 'Who knows? I then made an appointment and visited the lawyer. I had to prompt him a bit with the name Kokanides, but he finally remembered drawing up the sale of the shop. He said the information would be in his archives and it could take him a while to unearth it.'

'So when will he let you know?'

'I refused to leave my address with him and said I would telephone in a month.'

'A month! I had expected him to give you the information in a few days.'

'There's an added problem. He said he could not disclose anything that was on a legal paper without permission. If he has contact details he will have to approach Monika and ask her permission to release her address to me.'

'She'll not agree to that. She knows she has no half brother and she'll guess it's me who is looking for her. Is there no other way of getting hold of her address?'

'In Spanides office there are a number of filing cabinets. I had no chance to examine them, of course, but lawyers tend to be well organised. They usually store their files in both date and alphabetical order. They might have separate cabinets for different legal transactions, but I would still expect those to be properly filed, not thrown in haphazardly.' Thranassis took the receipt from his wallet. 'You owe me a further two hundred. That was what Spanides charged me for his time.'

Manu frowned. 'I've only that other hundred on me. I'll have to pay you the rest later. So how do we gain access to the files?'

'No idea.'

'Could you break in?'

Thranassis shook his head. 'I don't do burglary.'

'Do you know anyone who does?'

'I might, but it will cost you.'

Manu sighed. 'How much?'

'Fifty for the initial contact, whether he agrees to do the job or not, plus the one you still owe me. If you reach an agreement you'll pay him his fee directly.'

'Suppose he doesn't find out anything useful?'

'That's a chance you have to take. You still have to pay. He will have taken a risk getting in. There'll be nothing worth stealing that would make it worth his while.'

'How soon can I meet him?'

Thranassis considered. 'This time next week, but not here. We'll meet at the kafenion up by the catacombs. You know the one I mean?'

Manu nodded. 'What time?'

'Three. That should give both of you to get a bit of sleep. He may have been out the previous night.' Thranassis winked. 'Make sure you have the money with you.'

'It could be helpful if you visited the shop again and asked when it was sold. That might narrow down the number of filing cabinets that needed to be gone through.'

'Are you employing me for another week?'

'No, just for the one visit.'

'We'll make that a round two hundred for me, then. That includes my visit to Spanides, a second visit to the shop and meeting at the kafenion.'

Manu glanced sourly at Thranassis. If he had to continue paying at this rate he would have to help himself to some more of his father's stock.

Thranassis left Manu feeling pleased with himself. The man must be desperate to find his ex wife if he was willing to keep paying out so much money. He walked leisurely along the perimeter of the Old Town walls until he reached the main entrance that led to the Grand Masters' Palace. He had no interest in the tourist attraction and continued to walk along the main road, past the Clock Tower and into a side road that would lead him towards the San Francisco Gate. He meandered through the narrow, winding streets until he was on the main thoroughfare that led to the Gate and he would reach the shop where he had called the previous week.

The door was open to allow as much air as possible to enter the shop and fan standing on the counter tried valiantly to cool the temperature. As he approached Natasha turned the fan off.

'How can I help you?'

Thranassis smiled at her. 'I called in to see you last week. Do you remember?'

Natasha nodded. She had mentioned his visit to the various girls who worked in the street and they all denied ever hearing that Monika had a half brother, although admitting that as they did not know Litsa it could be true.

'You were very helpful to me, but there was something I didn't think to ask. When I visited Mr Spanides he asked me the date you had taken over the shop. You would be amazed at the number of filing cabinets he has in his office. He cannot remember when the transaction took place and said it could take him months to go through and find out Monika's address. I thought you could probably tell me and that would save him having to search his files. Once he has the date he could probably put his hand on it immediately.'

'I don't remember exactly the date the papers were signed.' Natasha wrinkled her forehead. 'It's three years ago now. They visited me in the spring, after Easter, so it was probably May when the agreement was finalised.'

Thranassis smiled at Natasha again. 'That's a great help. It certainly narrows down the amount of files Mr Spanides will have to search through. May I have an ice cream whilst I'm here?'

'Certainly.'

Natasha watched as Thranassis opened the fridge and took his time selecting a cornet. To her annoyance he did not return into the shop to pay her, but raised his hand and walked off down the road. She stood there bewildered. Had he assumed she was giving it to him?

Thranassis telephoned Philippos and arranged to meet him in a bar in the New Town at seven. He knew it was unlikely that the premises would be busy so early in the evening and they would be able to find a quiet corner to sit and discuss business. Once agreed Philippos would be able to leave and proceed with any business of his own that he had planned for the evening.

Philippos listened to Thranassis carefully and pursed his lips. 'What more can you tell me? Which floor is he on? Is there a burglar alarm fitted? What kind of lock does he have on his door? Is there a fire escape? Do the filing cabinets have locks?'

Thranassis shook his head. 'I didn't take a lot of notice at the time. His office is on the second floor. The door was open and

I went through to a small area and knocked on a door there. He called to me to come in so that wasn't locked either.'

Philippos sighed. 'Sounds as though I need to do some investigating. If there is an alarm of any sort I'll need to know the make so I can disable it. Locked doors are not usually a problem. If he has a fire escape he must have a way to get on to it from his office; that suggests a large window. Most offices, if they bother to lock their filing cabinets, leave the keys in their desk drawer. I'll pay him a visit and let you know what I find out. Meet me at five next Wednesday down at "The Grapevine". We'll have a quick drink and then go for a walk; less likely to be overheard down on the waterfront.'

Philippos walked to the address Thranassis had given him. It was unlikely the man would still be in his office at that time and it would give him the opportunity to look at the lock on the outer door and see if there was a fire escape.

To his annoyance there was a steel shutter drawn down outside and firmly padlocked. He looked around swiftly and bent down, turning the padlock over to read the maker's name. If he was able to buy a duplicate and the same key fitted both locks entering into the building would be no problem. He walked around to the rear of the building where there were parking spaces for the clients' cars, along with designated spaces for those who conducted their business from the offices.

As he had hoped there was a metal fire escape that led up to all four of the dark floors. Quietly he made his way up until he reached the second floor and tried to peer through the window. He could see nothing. He ran his fingers over the wooden frame and could not feel any tell tale wire that declared that there was an alarm, but that did not mean there was not one installed inside that he was unable to see. The frame was wooden, with hinges at one side and the glass felt as though it was fixed with putty.

Philippos looked around. Everywhere was deserted. Taking a chance he took out a small torch and shielding the light with his hand examined the window more carefully. The glass was set in putty, but he was just able to discern the shadow of a lock inside on the base. Unless the lawyer was unconcerned with safety he probably locked it each night when he left.

Provided there was no security alarm in place it would be a relatively simple matter of removing the pane of glass and gaining access that way. He wiped the woodwork and glass down carefully; even if his prints were not removed they would be too smudged to be helpful. He would have another look at the lock tomorrow when he visited the lawyer.

Philippos had donned a stiff collar that fitted below his chin to the base of his neck and walked up the stairs with an exaggerated limp and entered the lawyer's office.

'Thank you for seeing me at such short notice,' he smiled.

'I happened to have some free time this morning between clients. Do sit down and tell me how I can help you?'

'I'd rather stand and walk around a bit if you don't mind.' Philippos walked towards the window which led out onto the fire escape. 'My leg stiffens up and becomes painful when I sit.' There were no wires visible leading to the window, but there was a lock in position on the bottom rail and also on the window sill. To remove the hinges was not an option.

'It's really my leg that I've come about. I am unable to work and I wondered if you could help me.'

Mr Spanides raised his eyebrows. This sounded like a compensation claim.

Philippos turned away from the window and appeared to adjust his collar as he looked at the labels on the filing cabinets. Those he could see were all marked with the year and letters of the alphabet that he assumed were the initial letters of the clients' names

He looked at Mr Spanides and then walked to the far side of

his desk so he could see the other filing cabinets. 'You don't seem to have very much stock here.'

'Do you have the details of the accident with you?'

'Details?'

'Yes, were you knocked over by a vehicle? Do you have the registration number and the date when it occurred? Did you report it to the police? I assume you were taken to the hospital to be treated, have you a report regarding the injuries you suffered?'

'I thought you would be able to put my leg right.'

'I'm not a doctor. I can try to get compensation for you if you can give me the details.'

'I can't remember details very well.' Philippos took another turn around the room. 'I came in on the spur of the moment. I only went out for a loaf of bread.'

Mr Spanides was not anxious to work on the man's case. His mind had obviously been affected by his accident. He drew a printed form from a folder and handed it to Philippos. 'If you can complete that and bring it back to me tomorrow afternoon we can discuss your requirements further.'

Philippos looked at the form uncomprehendingly. 'Why have I got to fill out a form?'

'I need the details of your accident before I can agree to help you in any way.'

'Oh, yes.' Philippos pushed the form into his pocket.

'My fee for this morning is one hundred Euros.'

Philippos frowned. 'A hundred Euros for a form? I'm not paying for that.' He proceeded to fumble in his pockets and finally pulled out a five Euro note and held it out to Mr Spanides with a broad smile. 'I knew I had some money somewhere. I put it in my pocket to buy my bread. Do you have any?'

Mr Spanides shook his head. 'I don't sell bread. I am a lawyer. You came to ask me about compensation for an accident you had been involved in. Five Euros is not enough to cover your bill to me.'

Philippos pushed the bill back into his pocket. 'You are a crook. Five Euros is more than enough. I'll not come here again.' Exaggerating his limp Philippos left the office and slammed the door behind him.

Mr Spanides sat back and mopped his brow. He would certainly not agree to act on behalf of the man. His unfortunate accident had obviously left him deranged.

May 2014
Rhodes

Thranassis sat with Philippos at "The Grapevine". The divers sat at one end, talking and laughing, whilst tourists sat at the tables further away. Alecos sized his customers up. He was unlikely to make any sales to them unless the two men sitting by the edge of the steps were users.

He approached them. 'What can I get for you gentlemen? Would you like the taverna special?'

'Not today if you're offering what I think you are,' replied Philippos. 'We'll just have a beer each.'

Alecos looked suitably hurt. 'I was offering you a pizza with extra topping free.'

Philippos shook his head. 'The answer is still no, just the beers.' Philippos turned to Thranassis. 'He always has that answer ready just in case we're plain clothes. We'll have our beer and then go for a walk. It's far too crowded here to talk business.'

'I'll have to curtail my curiosity, then. What have you been up to today?'

'This and that, slept late, went for a swim on the main tourist beach.'

Thranassis raised his eyebrows. 'Profitable?'

'Very. They're pretty stupid. They leave their wallet in their trouser pocket and cover it with a towel thinking no one will know where it is. They all go off into the sea together and never think to keep an eye on their belongings. I help myself and then go into the sea also, making sure they see me. I wait until they come out and then go and get myself dressed. They know I was in the sea at the same time as them so it couldn't have been me who relieved them of their cash.'

'Suppose they challenge you?'

'I don't speak their language so I don't understand. If one of them is able to speak enough Greek to tell me their problem I say I saw someone walking past when I was in the sea and it must have been them. It's a useful side line. Most of the tavernas and shop keepers take their money home each night. Easy enough to get into their homes, but most of them keep a gun and will shoot an intruder.'

Thranassis nodded. It would be easier to seize the takings from the till and make a run for it. He tipped up his bottle and drank the remaining beer. 'Shall we go?'

The two men walked down to the Navarino Gate and out onto the waterfront. Tourists were either making their way back to their hotel or searching for a taverna for their evening meal before it became dark. Boisterous youngsters elbowed their way through, talking loudly in their native tongue, whilst Thranassis and Philippos ignored them and moved aside.

By the time they reached Mandraki the people on the waterfront were less as they had moved into the tavernas on the opposite side of the road. Close to the War Memorial Thranassis and Philippos took a seat.

'So tell me what you found out.'

'The front door has a steel shutter with a padlock. I might be able to gain entry that way, but it's risky. It's on the main road and there are apartments opposite. You never know when someone will see you. I went round to the back and the fire escape window is a better proposition. I'll need to cut the glass out and climb in.'

Thranassis frowned. 'They'll know someone has been inside.'

'If I have time I'll replace it,' Philippos shrugged. 'It's a chance that I have to take if your associate wants me to get inside.'

'If you were seen would Spanides be able to identify you?'

Philippos laughed. 'Not a chance. I wore a collar, had a bad limp and told him my memory was so bad due to an accident that I thought I had gone there to buy a loaf of bread. I wandered around and had a look at the filing cabinets. They're all neatly labelled so it shouldn't take me long to find what I'm looking for.'

Thranassis nodded slowly. 'I told my client that you would charge fifty Euros for an introduction. I've arranged to meet him at the kafenion up by the catacombs and if he wants you to proceed the fees must be agreed between you. You still get the fifty even if he backs out.'

'That sounds agreeable to me. Shall we have another beer on the way home?'

'Not for me. If I have too much I'm up and down all night.'

Philippos rose and stretched, rolling his neck from side to side. 'That collar was so uncomfortable. Given me a stiff neck. Three at the kafenion next Tuesday. Don't stand me up or I'll come looking for you.'

'I'll be there, along with the man who has your money.'

Manu handed over the envelopes of money to both men grudgingly. Monika would be repaying him this expenditure along with the original amount he had been ordered to pay her by the judge. The anger inside him rose up and he forced himself to take some deep breaths to calm himself. The time to give vent to his anger was when he finally caught up with her. She would realise then how stupid she had been to think she could disappear with all his money.

'So do you want to employ me?' asked Philippos.

Manu nodded slowly. 'There's a proviso. If you are caught I know nothing.'

'Tell me exactly what you want me to do.'

'Get inside the office and find out about the sale of the shop. There must be a record of which bank the money was sent to and which account received it.'

'Assuming I am able to find the file do you want me to bring it away with me?'

Thranassis shook his head. 'Not a good idea. If that lawyer swallowed my story about being the girl's half brother he is going to be looking for the file.'

'Can you photograph it?' asked Manu.

'I can,' confirmed Philippos, 'but I'll need as much detail as you can give me to ensure I have the correct file. You won't thank me if I bring you details of someone else who happens to have sold a shop. Tell me the dates when the transaction probably took place and the woman's name.' Yiorgo pulled a paper napkin from the holder and wrote down the information as Manu relayed it to him.

'The surname is Kokanides, but I'm not sure if the old lady sold the shop before she died or her daughter, Litsa, sold it afterwards. Thranassis says the new owner bought it in the spring of two thousand and eleven. Provided you can supply me with a current address for either Litsa or Monika Kokanides that is sufficient.'

Philippos raised his eyebrows. 'Don't you want to know how much it sold for?'

'Of course. I would have thought that would have been obvious.' Manu had been so focussed on finding Monika's address that he had not considered the amount of money the sale of the shop had fetched. That inheritance should have been his as the male member of the family.

'I'll meet you here this time next week. It will cost you a thousand.'

'Suppose you haven't managed to find out anything by then?'

'It would still be a good idea for you to meet me here with my money. I wouldn't want to have to come looking for you in Bar Street. That's a very public place.'

Manu swallowed. The threat from Philippos was not lost on him.

Philippos checked he had everything he needed; a chisel, glass cutter, some spare putty and putty knife, his camera, a torch and most importantly his gloves. He waited until midnight. By then most people were in their beds, just a few stray revellers still around, and if he was spotted he would pretend to be drunk. Most people avoided a drunk if he was on his feet, and many ignored them even if they were seen to fall to the ground.

He dressed in black trousers and black cotton shirt. He wrapped his tools in a piece of cloth and pushed them deep into one pocket, in the other he placed his camera, torch and gloves. He knew that if he should be apprehended he would have a difficult time explaining away the contents of his pockets, but he had taken plenty of risks in the past. Unless he was actually seen removing the glass there should be no reason for anyone to be suspicious of him.

Approaching the offices from the bottom of the road he walked up the hill slowly. The lights were out in all but one window of the apartments opposite and the only people he saw were a young couple in a doorway who should have been in their hotel room and were running the risk of being arrested for indecency in a public place. Had he not been on an important errand he would have stopped and spoken to them, just to witness their reaction at being spotted and spoil their pleasure. He was envious of the young man and licked his lips, it was time he visited one of the girls in the street. It had been over a week since he was last there. The girl had been a new youngster but she had certainly been worth her fee. Once he had a sizeable sum of money in his pocket again he would return and enjoy her a few more times before she became unwilling to comply with some of his more unusual requests without an increase in the price of her services.

Now he must put such pleasant thoughts out of his mind

and concentrate on the job in hand. After a swift glance around, Philippos entered the deserted car park and walked over to the fire escape, pulled on his gloves and ascended quietly in his rubber soled shoes. He made a point of rubbing his hands along the rails at each side as he could not remember if he had touched them on his previous visit.

In the light of his torch he examined the putty and dug at it tentatively with his chisel. It was as hard as a rock and had been painted over a number of times. Removing it and replacing it was not an option. He ran the glass cutter up and down both sides, checking that the glass became loose when he pushed at it. He then tackled the top and steadying it with his free hand he cut half way along the bottom. The glass at that side sagged a little and he braced it with his shoulder, he did not want it falling to the ground when he made the final cut. He held it firmly in place and lowered his mouth to the handle of the glass cutter, clamping it firmly between his teeth. Gently he allowed the pane of glass to tip forwards into his waiting hands and he propped it against the safety rail.

He held his breath, waiting for an alarm to sound, but all was silent. The opening was plenty large enough for him to climb through without difficulty and once inside he switched on his torch, directing the beam to the filing cabinets. Mr Spanides was obviously methodical. The cabinets at the far end were labelled "2009 – 2010 A – L" and "2009 – 2010 M – Z".

Philippos walked to the next cabinet that bore the label "2011 -2012 A – L". This was going to be too easy. The drawer was locked and Philippos went to the lawyer's desk expecting to find the keys in there. To his annoyance all the drawers in the desk were also locked. He would have to force the cabinet open and hope that the damage would not be noticed.

Using his chisel Philippos inserted the blade between the drawer and the lip of the cabinet and forced it back towards him. He felt it give and two more pulls, using all his strength, broke the lock and the drawer opened. He replaced his chisel into his pocket and pulled the drawer fully open. Each batch of files was divided by a card with a letter on it. The last card in this drawer was marked "E". The files for "K" had to be lower down. He opened the bottom drawer and there was a card marked "K". Methodically he pulled each one up to enable him to read the name until he finally saw "Kokanides".

He pulled the file out, leaving the one behind standing up, and took it over to the lawyer's desk and opened it. This had to be the one the man was interested in, but then he frowned. There was no mention of selling the shop, only renting it to a woman named Natasha Davenidis. Each month a sum of money was to be transferred from her to a bank in Heraklion, Crete to credit Monique Kokanides. Taking a risk Yiorgo switched on the desk lamp and photographed the page. He looked at the page below and Mr Spinades had recorded briefly that the Kokanides family had visited and made the agreement with him.

Philippos returned the file to the appropriate place in the filing cabinet and pushed the door closed as far as possible. At first glance it was not obvious that it had been tampered with. Should he look further? The information he had was not conclusive. The shop could have been sold at a later date to someone else. He forced open the next cabinet that was marked to include details of the clients whose surname began with "K" and once again searched through until he found the appropriate file. There was only a single sheet of paper reporting that Monique Kokanides had requested that the monthly rent for the shop should be transferred to her daughter, Litsa Kokanides, at the bank in Heraklion. There was still no mention of a sale.

Philippos photographed the information again quickly. He would have to open the other drawers as a deed of sale should be somewhere and he did not want to be asked to make a return visit. As it was he would have to pry open the other filing cabinets so the lawyer would not know whose information had been searched for.

The filing cabinet for "2013 – 2014" was more rewarding. Once Philippos had withdrawn the relevant file the information it contained was far more interesting. The rent for the shop was still being transferred to Litsa Kokanides but this time the bank was in Aghios Nikolaos on Crete. The directive authorising this was in the form of an e-mail sent from "The Central Hotel" in Heraklion, Crete.

Pleased with his final success Philippos photographed the two pages and replaced the file. He opened two more cabinets and decided it was time to leave. He climbed back through the open window and placed some putty at the top and bottom of the opening, pushing the pane of glass back into place before running putty down the sides. Once the lawyer found his cabinets had been opened he would doubtless inform the police, they would very soon realise that access had been gained through the fire escape window, but they would not find anything missing from the premises.

Philippos hurried down the fire escape and back onto the main road where he began to walk slowly down to the bottom of the hill. To his surprise there was a still a young woman with a man in a doorway and then he realised; she was obviously a prostitute who was willing to take her chance out in the town picking up tourists, although it was illegal.

'There are better places to do that than in doorways. Probably better girls as well if you go into the Old Town,' he called out as he came level with them. The man drew back with a jerk and the woman sent a stream of invective towards Philippos before drawing the man back to her. Grinning to himself, Philippos continued home. All in all it had been a satisfactory night's work.

Mr Spanides sat at his desk and opened his diary. He was due in court that afternoon. It was only a preliminary hearing, but he ought to familiarise himself with the relevant details. He walked over to the filing cabinet with the key in his hand and was just about to insert it in the lock when he saw that the drawer was slightly open. He frowned. He was sure he had locked it the previous night.

He looked at the cabinet that stood next to it. That one was also open. Faint scratch marks could be seen around the lock where it had been forced. He took a step backwards. Someone had obviously broken in and forced the cabinets open. What were they hoping to find? He kept nothing of value on the premises. He would have to notify the police so he could send their report along with his claim to his insurance company for new cabinets.

Whilst he waited for the police to arrive Mr Spinades sat at his desk. He had been told he must not touch anything until the police had checked for fingerprints. His would be there, of course, but he had no wish to obliterate any that had been left by the intruder.

'So,' a police Inspector sat in front of the lawyer whilst another began to dust the cabinets and files for prints, 'when did you find someone had gained entry to the premises?'

'I went to look for a file. I'm due in court this afternoon and wanted to refresh my memory regarding the case.'

'How did you enter your office? Was the door unlocked when you arrived?'

Mr Spanides shook his head. 'The main door to the building was already unlocked as usual when I arrived. I came up to my office and used my key to open the door.'

'Is there an alarm system?'

'It has never been thought necessary to install one. All the rooms are used as offices. There is nothing of value kept on the premises.'

'Someone obviously thought there was something here that made it worth their while to break in. I've sent one of my officers around to the other offices to ask the occupants if they have seen any sign that they have had a break in. If your door was locked when you arrived either someone had a key or they gained access another way.' The Inspector looked around, his eye alighting on the window that led to the fire escape.

'The only other way they could have entered would have been by the fire escape, but the glass has not been broken.'

'Was that locked when you left last night?'

'Definitely. Do you want the key?'

'We'll look at that later. Are any of your files missing?'

Mr Spanides shook his head. 'I don't know. When I saw the cabinets had been opened I telephoned you and I was told I must not touch anything until after you had visited.'

'You can have access to those that have been dusted for prints. I suggest you have a quick look through.'

'They would not be of any value to anyone.'

The Inspector shrugged. 'Maybe someone wanted to remove some incriminating evidence that you were holding against them or they planned to blackmail someone by finding out information that was confidential.'

Mr Spanides looked at the files in the top drawer of the cabinet and then turned his attention to the drawer below. Finally he straightened up.

'I can't see that anything has been taken.' He smiled wryly. 'Of course I probably wouldn't know unless a client came and I needed a previous file.'

The officer who had visited the other occupants of the building entered the room and shook his head. 'No one else reports any sign of an intruder.'

'I think someone made a mistake,' said Mr Spanides wearily. 'They must have been told there was something valuable stored here and when they found only my paper work they left empty handed and didn't bother with any of the other offices.'

'That's quite possible, sir. May I have the key to the fire escape window?'

Mr Spanides pointed to the key that hung beside the window. 'It is always kept there.'

'You have never noticed that it has gone missing?'

'No. It would be no use to anyone. The window cannot be unlocked from outside. In fact you will probably have to push it quite hard as I cannot remember when it was last opened.'

The Inspector inserted the key into the lock. It turned easily, but the window stayed firmly closed. 'Not very satisfactory if you needed to leave in a hurry,' he remarked.

'I'm sure I could force it or break it if I needed to get out.'

The Inspector pushed at the frame and reluctantly the window opened and he stepped through onto the fire escape.

'When was the building last painted?' he asked.

Mr Spanides shrugged. 'I'm not sure. Maybe about five years ago.'

The Inspector nodded. 'Has the glass needed to be renewed during that time?'

'No.'

The officer joined the Inspector and together they scrutinized the pane of glass. The officer pointed to something and scratched at it with a gloved finger and handed something to the Inspector. Whilst the officer dusted for fingerprints the Inspector turned back to the lawyer.

'I think we can be fairly certain your burglar entered through the fire escape window. The putty holding the glass in place is still soft and new. If it has not been painted for about five years it would be hard. My officer pulled off a small piece and beneath it was old putty that had been painted over. Hard as a rock.'

Mr Spanides shrugged. 'It seems an awful lot of trouble to go to for nothing.'

'I agree. I think you certainly had something here that someone wanted. Have any of your clients made a request for their files or asked you to destroy them?'

'No, never. I keep all the files up here until I have no more space in the cabinets; then I box them up and they are moved to the basement. They are never destroyed or passed over to the clients.'

'Have you had any visits from new clients in the previous few weeks? They may have decided they did not want to pursue their case and thought removal of their file would ensure their visit was kept confidential.'

Mr Spanides frowned. 'I had a man asking if I had his half sister's address. I told him I would have to search through my files.'

'Do you have his name and address?'

'No, he gave me his name, Timotheus Andopolous, but he was returning to Athens and he agreed to telephone me in a month to see if I had any success.'

'Anyone else?'

Mr Spanides smiled. 'I had a very strange visitor. At first he claimed to have been hurt in an accident and insisted on wandering around as it hurt him to sit. He seemed to think I was a doctor. Then told me he had only come in for a loaf of bread and was quite annoyed when he found I didn't stock groceries.'

'And what was his name?'

'I have no idea. Whatever accident he had been involved in had obviously affected his mind, poor chap. He had a severe limp and was wearing a neck brace.'

'He wandered around, you say, whilst he was here?'

Mr Spanides nodded. 'Up and down across the room.'

'Did he walk over by the window?'

'Yes, everywhere.'

The Inspector smiled thinly. 'I think you had a visit from whoever it was who broke in. He was looking for the most accessible point of entry.'

'But what would he want to break in for? If he was the burglar he would know I had nothing of any value here.'

'You obviously have or did have something that was of value to someone. I can only assume it was information. There really is nothing more we can do I'm afraid unless you realise something is missing. I'll send you a copy of our report so you can claim on your insurance for the cabinets. In the meantime I suggest you have some bars placed across the fire escape window. Even if the glass was removed a second time they would not be able to gain access.'

Angelos looked at the dirty smudges left from the fingerprint powder on the filing cabinets and window frame. He would have to wipe them down when he returned from court. He went over to a cabinet preparing to withdraw the file he needed for the afternoon when a thought struck him. He opened the cabinet marked "A – L" and looked for Monika Kokanides's file. To his surprise it was out of order with the file marked Kostanides before hers rather than afterwards. He was meticulous in his filing, ensuring that all the files were in strict alphabetical order.

He wondered if he should call the police back, but decided it would be fruitless. Only one set of prints had been found in the office and he was sure they would match his. Whoever the burglar was he had been very careful to wear gloves to ensure he left no identifiable prints behind.

Angelos looked through the Kokanides file briefly. Nothing appeared to be missing, He replaced it and collected the file he needed ready for his court appearance. He wondered if he should 'phone the girl and make her aware that someone had been snooping, but he would think about that later. Due to having the police in his office for so long he would have to forgo his lunch and hurry to the court house.

Philippos walked to the internet cafe furthest away from his home. He was less likely to be seen by anyone who knew him if he was in a different area. He took a seat at the computer at the far end of the line and placed his bag on the seat next to him, hoping to deter anyone from sitting next to him. Taking his camera from his pocket he plugged the jack in and proceeded to download the photographs he had taken of the papers in the Kokanides file.

On the screen they looked clear and sharp and he hoped they would be as good when he printed them out. He scrutinized each one carefully as it printed and checked with the image on the computer screen before moving to the next. Finally satisfied he inserted a flash drive and transferred the photographs to the memory stick before erasing them from the computer. He folded the printed sheets carefully and placed them inside a book in his bag for safe keeping until his meeting with Manu.

Manu arrived early for his meeting. At last he would know where Monika was hiding and be able to pay her a surprise visit. Once he had her alone he would hold her by her hair and after half throttling her he would pummel her body until she cried for mercy. He smiled thinly. That would be just a start of the treatment he planned to mete out to her.

He was confident that Philippos would arrive, even if he had not found any information in the lawyer's office as he would still expect to be paid for taking the risk of breaking in. Manu looked at his watch, only five minutes had passed since he had looked at it previously. If Philippos did not put in an appearance within an hour he would have to assume the man had been arrested. He wished he had helped himself to something that would calm him down from his father's shop. He had convinced his father that when he became stressed or worried about his medical condition he found a small amount of cocaine helped him to relax.

A hand on his shoulder startled him and he jumped to his feet, nearly knocking over the bottle of beer he had been drinking.

'My, my, your nerves are a bit on edge today.' Philippos smiled and took the chair opposite.

'You shouldn't creep up on people and take them by surprise like that. You're lucky I didn't hit you.' Manu glared at Philippos.

'I was just checking that you were alone. I didn't want to find there was someone else waiting here for me as well. Have you brought the money?'

'Have you any information for me?' asked Manu.

'I might have. No money, no info.' Philippos sat back in the chair and lit a cigarette.

Manu pulled an envelope out of his pocket and Philippos seized it swiftly. 'I trust it's all there.' He opened his bag and withdrew the copied papers. 'That was all I could find. There's an agreement signed by Mrs Monique Kokanides renting the shop to a woman called Natasha Davenidis. The rents were sent to a bank in Heraklion.'

'Heraklion?'

Philippos nodded. 'That's what it says.'

'But that's on Crete. I thought she was on Rhodes.'

Philippos shrugged. 'At a later date the rents are sent to the same bank but then in the name of Litsa Kokanides. I imagine that was after the old lady died.'

Manu ran a hand over his head. Crete was far larger than Rhodes and it would be more difficult to find Monika there. 'Do you have an address for her?'

Philippos shook his head. 'No, there's a later e-mail sent from "The Central Hotel" in Heraklion saying the rents were to be transferred to a bank in Aghios Nikolaos.'

'A hotel? You mean she's living in a hotel on my money?'

'How should I know what she's doing? You asked me to take any information I could from the files and this is all I found. No private address or telephone number. You could try e-mailing her at "The Central Hotel" but she may have asked a friend to send it from there.'

Manu clenched his fists. The blood was pounding in his temples. Was she was living in a hotel on his money? Monika and her mother pretending to be ladies! He had expected her to be cowering away somewhere remote thinking he would not find her. His intention of raping her and putting her on the streets to work no longer seemed feasible. He had paid Philippos for very little useful information

'Who is it that is renting the shop?'

'I told you, a woman called Natasha Davenidis.'

Manu nodded. That had to be the prostitute who had stuck the knife in him and infected him. Her name was Natasha. She must know Monika's address and he would pay her a visit and beat the information out of her.

'Anything else you want me to do?' asked Philippos. 'If not I'll be off.'

Manu finished his bottle of beer and called for another. He needed to think calmly. He would visit Costas immediately and explain that he needed some time off from his job in Bar Street as he had some urgent family business to attend to. Provided Costas was agreeable he would book a flight to Crete as soon as possible. On his way to the airport he would visit Natasha and beat Monika's address out of her. He would make sure that she would be left unable to alert Monika that he was on his way for her.

All he needed was the money for his flight and some more in his pocket to pay for some lodgings. It could take him a week or more to find Monika and he had now revised his plans for her. He would threaten her that unless she repaid him his money he would ensure she was so badly scarred that people would shudder when they saw her face and turn away in horror. Even if she did repay him he would still make sure she was scarred for life. He smiled to himself, savouring the sounds of her screams and protests in his imagination. Before he departed to Crete he would help himself to the rest of his father's money and a plentiful supply of drugs. He was certain he would find dealers willing to purchase them.

Elias looked at his son suspiciously. 'What do you need more money for now? You have a job. You pay no rent to live here so why do you keep needing money from me?'

'When's Antonius due to call on you again?'

'Next week.'

'I shall probably be back by then. I've found out where Monika is living. I'm proposing to pay her a visit and insist that she returns all the money the judge awarded her. When I have my hands on that I will be able to repay you.'

'I doubt she'll have that money sitting around. She's probably invested it and she'll have to make an arrangement with the bank to withdraw it.'

'I'm sure she can be encouraged to part with it.'

Elias eyed Manu doubtfully. 'Where is she?'

'Living in a hotel on Crete. I've arranged some time off with Costas but I need money for the air fare and a bit to live on until I've tracked her down. It shouldn't take more than a day or two and then I'll be straight back.'

Elias sighed. Since Manu had been released from prison he had demanded money nearly every week for nebulous expenses.

July 2014
Rhodes

Manu studied the flight schedule, finally booking a flight leaving at three the following afternoon. That would give him time to visit Natasha during the morning and he would arrive on Crete in plenty of time to find somewhere to stay for the night. He might even go to "The Central". That would be a shock for Monika and her mother when they came down for breakfast to find him sitting there waiting for them.

He packed a holdall with some clean underwear and socks, two T-shirts and two casual shirts. He filled a plastic bag with as many tablets from his father's drugs cupboard as he was able to lay his hands on, replacing the Benzodiazepine and Oxycontin tablets with Dupon and left the packets on the shelf; his father would not notice they were missing until Antonius called or he was asked to fulfil a legitimate prescription. He would call on the dealers he knew and the money he was given for the drugs could be added to the money he had taken from his father's savings during the early hours. He hoped his father had not planned to go to the bank that day and would not have any more money to hide away until after Antonius had visited.

For his own consumption he had three small amounts of cocaine in his pocket and eight packs of Benzodiazepine tablets. He knew if he took sufficient they would have the same euphoric effect as the cocaine and if questioned he would claim they were given to him on prescription to help him cope with his medical condition. He had his medical card with him saying he was HIV positive and as he had only such a small quantity with him it was unlikely either drug would be taken away when he passed through customs.

Manu walked to the Old Town and entered at the main gate. Once he had extracted the necessary information from Natasha he would take a taxi to the airport and Monika was in for an unwelcome surprise. The money he had received from the various dealers felt good in his pocket and there was nothing in his bag to incriminate him.

Reaching the shop Manu stood outside and looked through the open door. He was certain the woman he could see was the same as the one who had stuck a knife in him. Her nose was misshapen where he had hit her originally. He smiled grimly to himself. If she refused to tell him Monika's address it would be more misshapen when he left her.

'Good morning, Natasha. Remember me?'

Natasha looked at him with both horror and fear on her face. 'What do you want?'

'What do you think? I want to know where Monika is.'

Natasha shook her head. 'I've no idea.'

'You must know. You pay rent to her mother for this shop. I suggest you tell me. I wouldn't want to have to hurt you again.'

'I pay the rent to Mr Spanides and he sends it on to them.'

'You must know where they are living.' Manu took a step closer.

'I don't know, honestly I don't.' Natasha groped beneath the counter. Was there anything stored there that she could arm herself with?

'A bit of persuasion could change your mind.' Manu grabbed a handful of her hair and pulled her round the counter towards him. 'Now I will ask you again, where is Monika living?'

'I can't tell you where she is as I don't know.'

'And I don't believe you.' Manu's fist contacted with her nose bringing tears to her eyes. 'Where is she?'

'I don't know, honestly. Ask Mr Spanides.' Natasha spoke thickly. Where Manu was holding her head back the blood from her nose was trickling down her throat.

'Last chance,' said Manu, 'or I really will hurt you.' He hit Natasha across her throat making her choke and gasp for breath.

'Don't know.'

Manu looked at the terrified woman before him. He felt certain that she did not know where Monika was but he could not take the chance that she would call the lawyer as soon as he left so the man could alert Monika. With all his strength he flung her back against the counter and heard a sickening crack as she crumpled to the floor.

Manu leaned on the counter trembling. Had he broken her neck? He had only meant to hurt her, not kill her. He took a last look at Natasha, grabbed his bag and left the shop, closing the door behind him. She would be out of sight to any passerby and would not be found until a customer arrived.

He hurried along the road back towards the main gate, finally stopping to light a cigarette with trembling hands. He would be able to catch a taxi from there for the airport although he would be early for his flight. Once there he could mingle with the other passengers and there would be no reason to connect him with the assault on Natasha. He would also go into the toilet and treat himself to a small amount of cocaine just to steady his nerves and calm him.

Natasha regained consciousness and tried to move. The pain in her back made her gasp, lights flashed before her eyes and everything went dark again.

Dimly she could hear someone calling her name and she struggled to open her eyes.

Agapi was standing over her. 'Natasha, what's wrong? Are

you feeling faint? Can I help you up?' She placed an arm beneath Natasha's shoulders and Natasha groaned with pain.

'No,' she managed to gasp. 'Police.'

Agapi looked at her with consternation. 'If I was able to help you to sit up and brought you some water you'd probably feel better soon.'

'Hospital – police,' Natasha gasped again. 'Can't – move.'

'What happened?'

Natasha closed her eyes. 'Manu. Mon,' her voice trailed away.

Agapi looked at the still form. She was loath to call the police and look foolish if Natasha had only fainted and given herself a slight concussion. 'Are you sure you can't get up?'

'Hospital,' muttered Natasha again.

With a shrug Agapi pulled her mobile 'phone from her purse. If an ambulance was sent out on a fool's errand then Natasha would have to pay for wasting their time. She described the situation, answering the questions about Natasha's condition as best she could.

'I offered to help her up but she says she can't move. She's on the floor of her shop. The easiest way for an ambulance to get here would be by the San Francisco Gate entrance.'

'Is she conscious?'

'Not really. She managed to speak to me, but now she is just lying there with her eyes closed. I'm frightened and don't know what to do.'

'Can you stay with her until the ambulance arrives? They are on their way.'

'Yes, how long will they be?'

'That will depend upon the traffic. Can you collect some personal belongings for her? Washing kit, nightdress, hair brush; things like that and bring them to the hospital.'

'You want me to come with her?'

'If that's possible. You'll be able to explain how you found her to the doctor and that will help his diagnosis.'

The ambulance arrived and a paramedic bent over Natasha. 'Are you able to tell me where you hurt?' he asked.

'Can't – move. Manu. Police.'

'Right, we'll soon get you sorted and taken to the hospital. The doctor there will be able to help you. I'll call my colleague and then we'll arrange to move you. Your friend is coming with you.'

The paramedics placed a support around Natasha's neck and strapped her to a back board before moving her as gently as possible to the ambulance.

Manu passed through the customs check at Rhodes airport without incident, showed his identity card along with his medical card and explained that the tablets in his possession were to combat the effect of Aids on his body and waited for his flight to be called. The cocaine had taken effect immediately, calming him down and making him feel relaxed and confident. Once he arrived in Heraklion he would take a taxi to "The Central" hotel and book a room for the night.

Agapi sat beside an empty bed for almost an hour, clutching the carrier bag of Natasha's possessions. She was not sure if she should place them in the small locker or wait until Natasha returned from the X-ray department and the doctor had visited. More than anything she wished she hadn't gone down to the shop and found Natasha.

She was relieved when she finally saw Natasha being wheeled back in and being transferred to the bed, still strapped to a back board. Her face had been wiped free of blood, but streaks of it still remained on her cheeks and around her mouth. Her nose and lips were swollen and when she tried to open her eyes they were no more than slits.

'How is she?'

The attendant shrugged. 'I'm not a doctor. She'll look better if you give her a wash. The sink is over there.'

Agapi opened the carrier bag and pulled out the face flannel she had placed in there, hoping there would be a bowl that she could fill with water and carry back to the bed. The bowls that sat beside the sink did not look particularly clean and the water when she turned on the tap was tepid. It would have to do.

Gently she sponged and wiped Natasha's face, being rewarded with a small lopsided smile. Agapi smiled back.

'Are you feeling better now?'

'No.' Natasha closed her eyes again and Agapi returned to the sink, threw the dirty water away, rinsed the bowl and tried to remove the blood stains from the soiled face cloth.

'You shouldn't be doing that without gloves.'

Agapi wheeled round and saw the doctor striding towards Natasha's bed. She wiped her hands on a paper towel and hurried across to him.

'How is she? I thought she had fainted, but when I offered to help her up she said she couldn't move.'

'Not surprising. She has cracked the vertebrae in her lower back. Any idea how it happened?'

Agapi shook her head. 'I found her lying on the floor. She wanted me to call the police, but I thought she was just confused.'

'By the look of her face I would say that someone assaulted her and as she fell down she hit her back causing the injury.'

'Maybe I should have called the police.'

'Better to wait until she has regained full consciousness. It may have been a domestic argument that she would not want reported. She will be kept sedated for the next twenty four hours and on a back board. Don't want her moving around. You'll stay with her, of course.'

'I can't stay here all the time. If she is going to be sedated surely I could go home now and return tomorrow?'

'You'll need to make arrangements to be with her. Is there another friend who could come over night?'

'I'm not sure. I'll have to ask. When do you expect her to be properly conscious?'

'Probably mid–afternoon tomorrow. Just remember to put on gloves when you attend to her. She's an Aids victim.'

Agapi gasped. 'I didn't know.'

'Give your hands a good wash and provided you haven't any breaks in your skin you should be alright. Make those arrangements for her care and I'll be back to see her tomorrow.'

Agapi went over to the sink and washed her hands thoroughly. She knew that Natasha had worked in the street originally, but thought she had retired due to her age. If Natasha was infectious she really did not want to have to attend to any of her bodily functions.

As she walked towards the bus stop across from the hospital she thought about the doctor's words. He obviously considered that Natasha had been assaulted and in which case the police should be notified. That could have been why Natasha was asking her to call the police. It was impossible that she had been a victim of domestic violence as she had no partner.

The bus taking her back into town seemed to crawl through the traffic and finally stopped at the top of the hill near to the entrance to the Old Town. Agapi rose to get off and then changed her mind. She would go down to the terminal and call in at the police station. At least her conscience would be clear and she could tell Natasha that she had reported the incident to the police.

The policeman who came to take her statement looked incredibly weary and she wondered if he had been on duty all night.

'If you would give me full details of the incident you wish to report and then my superior can decide whether we should look into it.'

Agapi suddenly wondered if she was doing the right thing. 'Maybe I'm reading more into it than I should. It might not be a police matter.'

'You tell me the problem and then we can decide if it is within our remit.' He smiled kindly at her. 'Why don't you start by telling me your name and address?'

'I'm Agapi Mavronides and I live in the Old Town.'

'Where?'

'I rent a room from Alecos down at "The Grapevine". A number of us rent rooms from him.'

'Are you talking about the "Red Light" area?'

Agapi nodded.

'How long have you lived there?'

'About three years now, but that's not important. I went down to the local shop and Natasha was lying on the floor.'

The policeman held up his hand. 'Who is Natasha? Do you know her full name?'

'Natasha Davenidis.'

'Does she also rent a room?'

'No, she runs the local convenience store. I thought she had fainted and I asked her if I could help her up. She was hardly conscious and asked for the police. She said she couldn't move.'

'Surely it would have been more logical for her to ask for an ambulance?'

'That is what I thought. Her face was a mess and when I spoke to the doctor at the hospital he thought she had been assaulted and knocked to the ground. That was when the injury to her spine would have taken place.'

'Was there any sign of a struggle or fight in the shop? Anything missing?'

Agapi shook her head. 'Everything looked in place, but I wouldn't know if anything had been taken.'

'And you are certain she asked you to call the police? Did she say anything else?'

Agapi nodded vehemently. 'She said she couldn't move, police, ambulance and Manu. That was all.'

'Who is Manu? Her partner?'

'I've no idea. To the best of my knowledge she has no partner.'

'Did you accompany her to the hospital?'

'Yes, I went in the ambulance with her and waited whilst they took her down to X-ray. The doctor told me she has cracked a bone in her back and they had sedated her so she can't move around.'

The policeman looked down at his notes and tapped his fingers together. 'You say her face was a mess. Could she have hit it when she fell?'

'She was in front of the counter. There was nothing she could have hit it on. Someone must have punched her.'

'Well, Miss Mavronides, if you would wait here for a short while I'll have a word with my colleague. Can I offer you some refreshment?'

'You're not locking me up?' asked Agapi anxiously.

'Certainly not,' he smiled kindly at her. 'Unless we find subsequently that you were the person who hit the lady and caused her injuries we have no cause to hold you.'

'Then I'd like a glass of water, please.'

As he left the room he did not close the door and Agapi breathed a sigh of relief. If he had been going to arrest her he would surely have closed and locked the door. A young police woman entered with a bottle of water and plastic cup and sat down beside her.

'We don't use glasses, I'm afraid. Some of our visitors would break them and use them as a weapon.'

Agapi poured some water into the cup and drank it gratefully. Her stomach rumbled and she realised she had not eaten anything since the previous evening. 'I'm sorry,' she apologised.

'Think nothing of it. I've been subjected to far worse than a rumbling stomach. Do you want to tell me about your experience or would you rather wait until the Inspector visits you before you go over it again?'

'There isn't much to tell.' Agapi repeated the information she had given to the policeman earlier.

'It must have been a shock when you found her.'

Agapi nodded. 'Her poor face is such a mess. It looked a bit better when I had washed it.'

'When did you do that?'

'At the hospital whilst I was waiting for the doctor. The orderly said I could do so.'

'And the doctor thinks someone hit her?'

Again Agapi nodded. 'She's a nice woman. She wouldn't give anyone cause to be violent towards her.'

The policeman returned accompanied by the Inspector and the police woman rose and left discreetly.

'Well, Miss Mavronides, I think it would be advisable if we visited your friend's premises. Someone may remember seeing a stranger around or once you go inside again you may remember something helpful. We'll take you up in one of our cars. Do you have the keys?'

Agapi looked at the Inspector in horror. 'I didn't think to lock the door and I don't know where she keeps her keys.'

'We'll have a look around whilst we're there and if we can't find them we'll make the premises secure. When do you plan to visit your friend again?'

'The doctor said she would be sedated until mid-day tomorrow. I've got to talk to some of the girls and see if they'll come up and help me to look after her. The doctor said she would need someone all day and over night. I can't do both.'

'Of course not. That would be expecting too much of you. If the doctor is expecting her to be conscious tomorrow afternoon she may be able to answer a few questions for us. Shall we go, Miss Mavronides?'

When the police car drew up outside the general store Agapi was surprised to see Marina sitting inside.

'What's going on?' she asked immediately. 'I came up to the shop, the door was open and no sign of Natasha. I thought I ought to stay here, didn't want tourists pilfering her stock.'

'Natasha has had an accident. She's in hospital.'

'What happened?' asked Marina, her eyes wide with curiosity. 'Is that her blood on the floor?'

'I'll explain later. The police need to have a look around now. Once they've finished I'll come up to your house.'

Reluctantly Marina rose from her chair. 'I've left the money for my tin of soup on the counter along with the money for the ice creams and drinks I sold.'

'Thank you, Marina.' Agapi sank thankfully onto the vacant chair. She shivered. She would rather be up at the hospital than sitting inside Natasha's shop. The intruder might return.

'We might require a word with you later, Miss. Where can we find you?'

Marina smiled widely. 'In the street. My name's Marina. It's above my door.'

Whilst the police went through to the back room and looked around the shop generally Agapi sat and watched them. What were they hoping to find? It was hardly likely that Natasha's assailant was still there. One dusted the counter top for fingerprints and then came over to Agapi.

'Could I take your prints, please Miss?'

'Mine? What for? I haven't got a record,' Agapi assured him.

The policeman smiled. 'I'm sure you haven't. This is just a formality so we can eliminate you. We've found a number of prints on the counter, probably most of them are from Miss Davenidis, and we should be able to print her tomorrow. We're looking for some that we cannot account for.'

'I have the keys.' The Inspector came through from the back room with the key ring hanging from his finger. 'They were on the table beside her bed. At least we will be able to lock up when we leave and assure your friend that her premises are secure. Her purse is in a drawer and there is some money in the till so presumably robbery was not the motive for the attack. I don't think there us anything more we can do here so you may return to your home, Miss Mavronides and we will find the lady called Marina and see if she has any information for us that could be useful.'

'Will you take her prints?'

'Naturally. She may have touched various items in the shop whilst she was here or gone through to the back room looking for Miss Davenidis. We will need to eliminate her prints from our enquiries.'

Agapi gave a sigh of relief. At least the police believed her when she said Natasha had been assaulted.

'It could be helpful if you were at the hospital when we question Miss Davenidis. You could reassure her that she was not in any trouble.'

'The doctor said she should be conscious again at mid-day.'

'We'll time our visit for then. I'll arrange a car to meet you at the San Francisco Gate at eleven thirty. Would that be convenient?'

Agapi nodded. She wanted to get home now. She needed to talk to the girls and ask them to help her by taking turns to attend to Natasha in the hospital. She was also expecting a regular customer that evening and wanted to be prepared for his arrival. If she was not there he might decide to go to one of the other girls.

Crete

Having deposited his bag in the room allocated to him Manu sat in the hotel lounge where he had a good view of the door and everyone who entered or left. Visitors of all nationalities appeared to be staying there, and he heard a variety of incomprehensible languages spoken. If anyone tried to strike up a conversation with him in any language he would simply shrug and imply he did not understand.

The time passed slowly and there was no sign of Monika or her mother. Manu felt a stirring of apprehension. Maybe they were not staying there but worked on the premises in some capacity. He would take advantage of their dining room; it was possible that Monika was a waitress or her mother worked in the kitchen.

As he ate his meal he looked up each time the swing door to the kitchen opened, but only men carrying trays of assorted food and attending to the tables entered. There did not appear to be any women serving the guests. He lingered, hoping that Monika and her mother might appear as late diners, but there was no sign of either of them.

Eventually he could stay there no longer without drawing attention to himself and he returned to the lounge. There were far fewer people around now and Manu took a chance to approach the reception desk.

'Excuse me for troubling you, but I have been waiting for a young lady called Monika. She gave me to understand that she worked here.'

The receptionist shrugged. 'We probably have a number of ladies called Monika working here. None of them would be here now as they are either our chambermaids or cleaners.'

Manu curbed his annoyance. 'Then there is little point in me sitting here any longer. I will look for her tomorrow.'

'You could ask Mr Iliopolakis when he comes in tomorrow. He would have a record of all the staff employed here.'

'Thank you. I will do that.'

Inwardly seething Manu retired to his room. He should have asked at reception when he first arrived. It would have saved him from the boring hours he had spent sitting in the lounge. He swallowed two Benzodiazepine tablets hoping it would have the same effect on him as the cocaine. He had only two small quantities of the powder left. He wanted to save them until he was really in need and he would not know where he could obtain a further supply in this unfamiliar city.

Manu awoke sweating and with a dry mouth. He pushed back the sheet and made his way to the bathroom where he filled a glass with water and drank half of it down immediately. He felt slightly nauseous and decided to take another Benzodiazepine and smoke a cigarette to counter the effect. It was probably due to flying and the large meal he had consumed the previous evening. He was tempted to return to his bed, but his desire to discover Monika's whereabouts made him enter the shower.

Manu cursed himself for not asking what time the man called Iliopolakis arrived at the hotel. He decided he would have nothing to lose by going to the dining room for an early breakfast. There was a chance that Monika and her mother had been out for the day and he had missed their return. If that were the case they should appear for breakfast. Once he had eaten he would sit where he could see the guests entering the dining room and wait until he was certain that Monika and Litsa were not amongst them.

As he left his room Manu could see the chambermaids dealing with the rooms further along the hallway. Surely they would know if Monika was working there.

'Excuse me, may I ask you something?'

The young woman looked at him and smiled. 'Certainly. I hope your room is to your satisfaction but if you have a requirement for something extra in the bathroom or another blanket I am sure I can oblige.'

Manu shook his head. 'No, I wanted to ask if you had a young lady called Monika working here?'

'Monika? She was your friend, wasn't she, Eirini?'

The older woman nodded. 'We did cleaning together until I became a chambermaid.'

'Is she still here?'

Eirini shook her head. 'She left just after Christmas. She gave me some jumpers for my boys along with a bottle of wine. I miss her. She was such a nice lady.'

'Do you know her address? I'm her brother and it's very important that I find her.'

'I don't think she's in Heraklion now.'

Manu took a chance. 'The last I heard was that she was planning to move to Aghios Nikolaos, but she didn't say when and she hasn't sent me her new address.'

'I'm sure it wasn't Aghios, but it was down that way. She was planning to open a shop.'

Manu tried to control the anger that was rising inside him. 'What kind of shop? A general store?'

Eirini shook her head. 'A book shop, she said. She collected a number of the old books that are in reception. She had bought a car and spent most weekends driving down there with her mother, probably looking for somewhere they could live and I expect she took the books down at the same time.'

'Do you think Mr Iliopolakis would have her new address?'

'Very likely. I believe she was friendly with his wife. He'll be in later and you could ask him.'

'Thank you. I will.' Manu placed a two Euro coin in Eirini's hand. 'You've been very helpful.'

Eirini looked at the coins as Manu walked away. 'I didn't know Monika had a brother. She never mentioned him.'

'Maybe they had fallen out.'

'Possibly, but she was a very private person. She never talked about herself.'

Manu continued down the hallway to the lift and walked slowly into the dining room. He didn't feel much like eating anything, but he had paid for breakfast and it would be foolish to waste the money. He looked at the assortment of cereal, hot dishes, breads, cold meat, cheese, and pastries but nothing appealed to his palate.

He sat with a cup of coffee in front of him. He might feel more interested in food when he had drunk that. He returned to the buffet and selected two sausages and four slices of bread. He would make a sandwich to take with him and eat it later. He placed a sausage between two slices of bread and waited until there were no waiters hovering around before wrapping it in a serviette and placing it in his pocket. As a waiter came to check there was still sufficient coffee in the machine he worked his jaws, pretending to chew. As soon as the man returned to the kitchen he wrapped the other sandwich and slipped it into his pocket.

Now he was anxious to leave the hotel before Mr Iliopolakis appeared. The receptionists were usually efficient and would probably tell the man that someone had been enquiring about Monika. Having been told that she was a friend of his wife it was more than likely that Mr Iliopolakis would know exactly where she was and would warn her that someone was looking for her.

Manu returned to his room, checked there was nothing belonging to him in the wardrobe or drawers and collected his bag. He would pay his bill now and leave before the man arrived. Once a short distance away from the hotel he was sure he could ask directions for an internet cafe and he would be able to look up the addresses of book shops in Aghios Nikolaos. Once he had found out how to reach the town he would visit every one of them until he found Monika.

Manu found an internet cafe two streets away from the hotel and paid for access. 'You could probably save me some time,' he said to the youth who had taken his money. 'I want to look up the addresses of book shops in Aghios Nikolaos.'

'We've plenty of book shops in Heraklion without you having to go down there.'

'I have a friend who works in one. When I see the name I can make a note of the address.'

'Be quicker just to put the name in and do a search.'

Manu shook his head. 'No, I'll need the details so I can send him an e-mail to say I am coming.'

'Still be quicker to do a search.' The young man walked away. If the man wanted to spend his time and money looking up all the book shops in Aghios Nikolaos it was up to him.

Manu copied down the name of each shop and the address,

thankful that there did not appear to be too many. He might even be able to find Monika that afternoon. Buoyed up with the idea he left the shop and went into the next general store he saw and asked for directions to the bus station.

'Depends where you want to go. Those going west leave from one station and those for the east go from the other.'

'I want to go to Aghios Nikolaos.'

'Then you need station "A". Down the hill towards the port. You can't miss it.'

Rhodes

Agapi considered her wardrobe. Yesterday she had been wearing an old blouse and shorts, not really suitable for an arranged visit to the hospital with the police. She had a few items that she wore if she needed to go into the town and finally selected a pair of white cotton trousers and a green T-shirt that did not have a plunging neckline. She felt far more self conscious as she waited for the police car to arrive than she did when she stood outside her door scantily dressed and trying to attract customers.

When the car arrived the driver opened a rear door for her and she scrambled in, hoping she did not look too ungainly. The Inspector greeted her with a nod of his head and they drove in silence to the hospital.

Agapi led the way to the ward where she had left Natasha the previous day. The Inspector drew up a chair and sat beside the bed, indicating that Agapi should do the same whilst the policeman who had driven them went in search of the doctor.

Stenos looked at the girl, firmly strapped down to the bed. There was something vaguely familiar about her.

'Should I try to wake her?' asked Agapi.

'Better to wait until we've seen the doctor. She may have woken sooner than expected and been sedated again.'

As if sensing their presence Natasha opened her eyes.

'Hello, Natasha. It's me, Agapi. I've come to see if you are feeling better today?'

'Drink,' croaked Natasha.

'Do you think I should?' asked Agapi.

'I'm sure if you wetted her lips that would not be a problem.'

Agapi looked around. 'I'll have to go to the vending machine for some water. If the doctor arrives please ask him to wait for me to return.'

Stenos leaned over so that he was in Natasha's line of vision. 'Hello, Natasha. I'm a police Inspector. I don't expect you to be able to talk, but I wanted to tell you that we are looking for the person who assaulted you. The friend who found you said you were on the floor and couldn't move. You asked her to call the police and said "Manu". Is that someone you would like us to inform?'

'No,' the answer was a whisper. 'Drink. Manu did.'

'Your friend is getting you a drink.' Stenos sat back, wishing Agapi would arrive with the water quickly. The woman appeared conscious and he did not want the doctor to send him away yet if he was able to glean a little more information.

Agapi returned with a small bottle of water and some tissues. 'I wish I'd thought to bring some with me,' she complained. 'The machine only takes one Euro coins and doesn't give change.' She moistened a tissue and placed it on Natasha's dry and swollen lips. 'No, you can't eat it,' she remonstrated as Natasha tried to take it into her mouth.

'Drink,' Natasha pleaded again.

'Alright, open your mouth and I'll squeeze some water from the tissue in.'

The liquid dripped slowly into Natasha's mouth and dribbled down her throat.

'What are you doing?'

The doctor's voice made her jump; she had been concentrating hard, ensuring the water went onto Natasha's tongue and did not dribble down her neck.

'She said she needed a drink.'

'You should have asked my permission first. We do not want her to vomit. She could choke.'

Agapi rapidly replaced the cap on the bottle. 'I'm sorry.'

'You were here when she was admitted yesterday, weren't you, so you know she has a crack in her vertebrae. She cannot be sat up and if she started to choke whilst lying on her back that could be fatal. Her mouth may feel dry, but she is not dehydrated.' He waved his hand towards the drip. 'You can moisten her lips, but she cannot have anything orally.'

'I won't do it again,' promised Agapi, almost in tears. 'I was only trying to help.'

'A patient in this condition has to be treated with great care. Are you going to look after her?'

'I can stay sometimes.' Agapi did not want to commit herself.

'Then in a few days you will be shown how to give her a drink safely. Until then, remember, she is to have nothing.'

'I won't forget, Doctor,' answered Agapi humbly. 'I'll pass the information on to the other girls who are going to come in to care for her.'

Stenos cleared his throat. 'May I have a quick word, Doctor?'

'You're the police Inspector who wanted to see me. Is that right?'

Stenos nodded and showed his identity card. 'I would obviously like to know the condition of the patient and her prognosis, but even more important I would like to know when I can take a statement from her. She has managed a few words but I need more information before I can start looking for her assailant.'

The doctor stepped a short distance away from the bed and spoke quietly. 'I believe she is fully recovered from her concussion now, but we need to keep her sedated to prevent any movement. We will gradually reduce the amount given to her over the course of a week but I think it unlikely that you could find out anything useful from her before that has worn off. Recovery will be slow.

Until we are certain that the crack is healing we are unable to allow her any movement. We will take another X-ray in a week and if we are satisfied we will place her in a plaster cast. That will enable her to have a degree of mobility in her arms and hands. She is actually very fortunate. Had the damage occurred either higher or lower in her spine she would have been completely paralysed.'

Agapi strained her ears to hear the doctor's conversation. If Natasha had been permanently paralysed she would have had to stay in hospital for the remainder of her life. Who would have looked after her then? None of the girls would want to be committed to the task and it was unlikely that Natasha could afford to pay for someone to take care of her indefinitely. The man who did this needed to be apprehended and made to pay for his act.

Stenos nodded. 'We will have to be patient and wait. If she should say anything to you in the meantime please let us know. It might seem irrelevant to you, but it could be important to us.'

'Of course. All I have heard her say so far is "Manu" and something that sounded like "Mon". I may have mistaken either word for "Mamma", of course.'

'Miss Mavronides reported the same words to us. I feel they must be of some significance.'

'Quite. Now if you will excuse me I need to sedate the lady before she becomes restless.'

Agapi stroked Natasha's hand. 'I'll come back in tomorrow to see you. Once the doctor stops sedating you one of us will be with you every day and during the night. We'll look after you.'

Natasha again gave a lopsided smile as the doctor plunged the hypodermic into her arm. '"Manu." "Mon-ka,"' she said as her eyes closed.

Stenos took Agapi's elbow as they left the ward. 'Are you alright, Miss?'

Agapi nodded. 'Just a bit shaken, hearing that doctor say she could have been completely paralysed. Thank goodness I didn't try to lift her up.'

'You did the right thing,' Stenos assured her. 'Those two words she said, do they mean anything to you?'

Agapi shook her head. 'They might to one or two of the other girls; those have lived in the street longer than me.'

'Then it could be worth my while having a quick chat with them when we take you home.'

Stenos dismissed the police car when they reached the San Francisco Gate and Agapi led the way to her house. As she arrived the girls began to appear at their doors asking for news of Natasha.

'The doctor sedated her again just before we left. She spoke a few words but apart from asking for a drink they didn't really make sense.'

'Did she say who attacked her?' asked Marina.

'I'm not sure. The Inspector has come here to ask if any of you are familiar with the names "Manu" or "Mon". I don't know anyone of either name, but you've been here longer than me.'

Marina looked at Lola who nodded her head.

'Natasha was attacked some years ago and stabbed the man. As far as I know he's in prison so it couldn't have been him, unless, of course, he sent someone to hurt her.'

Stenos frowned. 'Do you remember the name of the man? We can check our records and see if he has been released recently.'

'It was Manu something. He was Monika's husband.'

'Who is Monika? Am I able to speak to her?' asked Stenos.

Lola shook her head. 'She had already left the area when it happened. Her grandmother had closed the shop and they had all gone away somewhere.'

'Would that be the shop where Miss Davenidis was working?' Stenos took out his notebook.

'That's right,' confirmed Marina. 'I happened to see them when they were throwing out rubbish from the shop. They had come back to check on it. Monika wanted to visit Natasha but where she was living wasn't suitable for visitors. I asked Natasha to come up to the shop and the next thing we knew she had moved into the shop and re-opened it.'

'So Miss Davenidis would probably know where the family could be contacted?'

'She might, she seemed to think they were in Athens. She told me the old lady had died, so she must know where they were living.'

'Thank you.' Stenos placed his notebook back in his pocket. 'You've been very helpful. When Miss Davenidis is fit enough she may be able to help us. Just one more question; did the lady called Monika work in the shop or elsewhere?'

Lola shook her head. 'Only the old lady. Monika worked in the library and when she married her mother left the street, found a job in a supermarket and moved back into the shop to live.'

Stenos had a sick feeling in the pit of his stomach. He had seen Monika on the ferry to Piraeus and although the woman had denied her identity he felt sure he had seen her in Rhodes Old Town having lunch.

'I'll leave you in peace, ladies. Thank you for your time.'

'You know your way back to the Gate?' asked Agapi.

Stenos nodded. 'I do, but I will go through the Town. The gate lower down will be closer to my headquarters.'

As he walked away Stenos tried to get his thoughts in order. Was the girl's assailant Manu Graphides? He remembered the case now; Manu had been stabbed by one of the girls in the street as she defended herself against his violent assault. When questioned he had become rude and threatening to the Chief of Police and placed in custody. When the case went to Court he was uncooperative and abusive, consequently the Judge had increased the prison sentence he had imposed.

It was embarrassing to recall that when he had first entered the police force he had considered the man to be his friend and had spent some evenings having a drink with him. He would check with the prison authorities to confirm that Manu was still in gaol as he could not recall the length of the sentence he had finally been given.

Stenos took his mobile 'phone from his pocket. 'I'm on my way back, should be about ten minutes. Can you check something for me in the meantime? Phone the prison authorities and ask when Emmanuel Graphides is he due to be released.' He listened to the reply from the desk clerk. 'No, you don't need to call me back, but I need the information to be able to progress with my enquiries.'

As Stenos entered the police headquarters the desk clerk handed him a sheet of paper and he nodded his thanks before going through to his office. As he read the information he felt encouraged. Emmanuel Graphides had been released in June and returned to live with his parents in the New Town.

He would visit the address and see if Manu was still living there. If so he would bring him in for questioning. It was likely that Manu had assaulted the girl a second time as revenge for being sent to prison. He would be bound to deny any accusation against him, but if his fingerprints could be found in the shop the circumstantial evidence could be conclusive.

Elias Graphides saw the Inspector enter his shop and he paled and his legs felt weak. He had been found out. Antonius must have been arrested and disclosed the source of his supply. If they searched the premises the large amount of money he had hidden was bound to be found. He would be hauled off to gaol and what would happen to his shop?

Stenos showed his identity card. 'Nothing to be alarmed about, sir. I am just making a few enquiries. I understand that your son, Emmanuel, was released from prison recently.'

Elias nodded; he did not trust himself to speak.

'Is he still living here with you?'

Again Elias nodded.

'Am I able to have a few words with him?'

'He's not here.'

'When are you expecting him to return?'

Elias took a deep breath; maybe the Inspector was not looking into his activities. 'He's gone away for a few days.'

'Do you know where? It is quite important that I speak with him.'

Elias shook his head. 'He said he'd asked for some time away from work and would be back in about four or five days.'

'Are you able to contact him?'

'I can try.' Elias pressed his son's numbers into his mobile 'phone. When it rang there was a message to say the 'phone was switched off. Elias held the phone out so Stenos could hear the message when it was repeated a second time.

Stenos shrugged. 'If you could give me his number I'll try calling him later.'

Elias scribbled it down on the back of a bag and handed it to Stenos who placed it in his pocket.

'I don't disbelieve you, sir, but could I just have a quick look around? I would appear rather foolish if he was hiding in his room.'

'Why should he be hiding? I've told you, he has gone away for a few days.'

'When someone has been recently released they can be very nervous if they receive a visit from the authorities and try to avoid them. It would be far better for him, and also for you, if I was able to ascertain that he is not on the premises.'

Elias walked across and locked the shop door. 'I need to speak to my wife.'

'That's fine. I'll come with you.'

Elias looked at Stenos sourly. Evidently the Inspector expected to find Manu hiding somewhere.

Stenos walked into the stock room and glanced around. There was nowhere anyone could hide in there. He followed Elias up the stairs to the apartment above.

'We have a visitor,' called Elias to his wife. 'Nothing for you to worry about.'

Mrs Graphides looked out from the kitchen. 'Would you like me to bring some coffee?'

'No. He'll only be staying a few minutes. Get on with whatever you are doing.'

'It would be no trouble.'

'I've told you, stay in the kitchen,' ordered Elias.

Stenos smiled. 'It's really your son I came to speak to. I understand he isn't here at present.'

'That's right. He's gone away for a few days.' Mrs Graphides looked at the Inspector suspiciously. 'What's he done?'

'As far as I am aware he has done nothing unlawful. I just wish to have a few words and ascertain his whereabouts last Tuesday.'

Mrs Graphides frowned. 'That was the day he went away. He left early in the morning.'

'Did he take anything with him that would indicate that he would be absent for longer than a few days?'

'No, most of his clothes are still in his room. See for yourself.'

'Thank you. I will.' Stenos walked through the lounge and opened the first door which led into a small bathroom, the second was evidently the couples' room and the third, which was considerably smaller, was neat and tidy. Stenos opened the wardrobe and could see at a glance that it contained a man's clothing. He lifted a jacket from the hook and checked the size. It would have been too large for Elias Graphides.

'I'm sorry to have taken up your time, Mr Graphides. You understand I had to complete my investigation and I apologise if you thought I did not believe you. I will leave you my card and when your son returns I would be grateful if you would contact me. Should he telephone you I would also like you to advise me.'

'I'll tell him to get in touch with you.' Elias had no desire to have anything more to do with the Inspector.

Elias locked the shop door again behind the Inspector and returned upstairs to the kitchen. He poured himself a large glass of raki and drank it quickly.

His wife looked at him with distressed eyes. 'Is Manu in trouble?'

'How would I know?' Elias poured a second glass. 'The police don't usually come looking for people who are not!'

Stenos considered the reception he had received. Where had Manu gone? Mr Graphides was obviously unhappy about his visit which could mean he knew considerably more about his son's movements than he was prepared to disclose.

Crete

Manu looked at the timetable for the buses that went to Aghios Nikolaos. He went over to the kiosk and bought his ticket.

'How long is the journey?' he asked.

'About an hour and a half; sometimes a bit longer depending upon the traffic.'

Manu looked at his watch. It was nearly mid-day. He was unlikely to be in the town before two, but it was possible that a book shop would close during the heat of the day and re-open about two or three in the afternoon and still be open in the early evening. He had plenty of time. His mouth felt incredibly dry still and he placed his money in a vending machine for a bottle of water. He still did not feel hungry, but he had his sausage sandwiches in his pocket and could eat those as he travelled down if necessary.

Manu rose from his seat on the bus feeling slightly dizzy. He had drunk all his bottle of water and used the remaining mouthfuls to take a Benzodiazepine. He now felt desperately thirsty again and the first thing he would do would be buy a beer and have a cigarette. That would quench his thirst far better than water. He might even feel like eating his sandwich then.

He rolled the bottle of cold beer across his forehead. It appeared to be far hotter here than in Rhodes. The first two bottles he had drunk had done nothing to alleviate his thirst, but now on his third he felt better. He would find a seat somewhere and eat his sandwiches, smoke a couple of cigarettes, then go to a different taverna for another beer. After that he would have to check in somewhere to stay for the night and then he could go in search of Monika. If everything went to plan he could be returning to Heraklion the following morning and catching an afternoon flight back to Rhodes.

There were a number of houses advertising bed and breakfast at cheap prices close to the bus station and Manu booked into the first one he came across. Once he had dealt with Monika he would want to leave as quickly as possible so it was practical to stay in the area. Not bothering to unpack his bag he returned to the bus station and asked if they had a map of the town.

'You can get one from the periptero.'

Manu nodded curtly; he had hoped he might be able to have a free copy, now he would have to pay for something he would only need for a few hours.

He sat at a bar and checked the addresses he had copied from the computer. It took him some time to find each street and when he did so he placed a cross on the map. They were interspersed at intervals throughout the town and some on the outskirts and he realised it was going to take him some considerable time to visit each one.

Manu found it hard to believe that Monika could have her own shop. It was more likely that she was working in one of them. The first establishments he approached seemed quite large and well stocked. He browsed along their shelves, looking for any other assistant that might be on the premises and finally approaching the counter. Each one denied any knowledge of a woman called Monika who had a book shop in the town and he realised he had made a mistake. It was more likely that Monika would be working in a small establishment in the suburbs.

The shops were beginning to put on their lights and Manu looked at his watch. It was nearly seven; tourists were sparse now, probably at their hotels getting ready to go out for an evening meal and he had four more shops on his list, all of them some distance away and they would probably be closed by the time he reached the area. He ought to have a meal before he returned to his room. He would take some bottles of beer back with him and consult the map. He would still have to check the other book shops on his list tomorrow to ensure that Monika was not in the town.

Manu awoke with a headache. He screwed up his eyes against the light that was coming through the flimsy curtains at the window. Although he had eaten a large pork chop and chips before returning to his room the meal had obviously not been sufficient to counteract the effects of the half a dozen bottles of beer he had consumed.

He would have a quick shower, thankful that he would not need to shave having grown a certain amount of facial hair whilst in prison, and then go down for breakfast. He doubted he would be offered the assortment that had been available at "The Central" but he was not feeling unduly hungry due to the headache that was behind his eyes. He debated whether to check out and take his bag with him, convinced that he would find Monika that day and be able to return to the airport. If he was lucky he would be able to purchase a ticket for a flight that evening.

Finally he decided against it. There would be no need to carry the bag around with him. He would have plenty of time to return and collect it before he caught a bus to Heraklion airport. Checking that the map and list of book shops that he had not yet visited was safely in his pocket, along with his remaining packs of cocaine, the Benzodiazepine tablets and his cigarettes, he walked down to the breakfast room.

After two cups of black coffee and a croissant his headache seemed better. To set himself up he would take a Benzodiazepine tablet with another cup of coffee. Once he had dealt with Monika he would take one of his precious amounts of cocaine as a celebration. Until then the tablets would have to suffice. He had used Benzodiazepine tablets whilst in gaol as cocaine was at a premium and Vangelis had assured him that Benzodiazepine was cheaper and equally as effective. Having experimented with cocaine he now had to take double the quantity of Benzodiazepine tablets to achieve the same euphoric effect.

He looked at the map again. If there was a bus that went to the suburb it would save him a long walk. Once at the bus station he studied the information boards, but finally gave up and went to the kiosk to ask for help.

The attendant shook his head. 'You've missed it. There'll be another in an hour. You could walk it in that time.'

'Isn't there another that goes near?'

'No. The others go through and don't stop again until they reach Ammoudara. It would take longer to walk back from there.'

Feeling aggrieved Manu folded the map and returned it to his pocket. If Monika was not there it was a wasted morning. He should have found out the time of the buses the previous evening and made sure he arrived at the bus station earlier.

He set off along the road, consulting his map each time he came to a side road until he reached a cluster of small, shabby looking shops. There was a greengrocer, the produce limp and yellowing displayed outside, a general store, baker, a kafenion and an ironmongers.

Manu walked past the ironmongers and then retraced his steps. He wandered around the small shop and finally approached the man at the counter.

'I'm looking for a knife,' he said. 'I can only see penknives on display.'

'What kind of knife are you looking for?'

'For hunting; one that's suitable for gutting and skinning a rabbit.'

The man delved beneath the counter. 'You need something like this.'

Manu picked it up and felt the blade. It was sharp and would certainly cut through a rabbit. He nodded. 'That will do. Has it got a sheath? I don't want it cutting through my pocket.'

He handed over the money for the knife and the leather sheath that the man had produced. That would certainly do to intimidate Monika. He might even use it on her if she was uncooperative.

At the end of the row of small shops was one that advertised "hobbies". Manu shrugged, he supposed reading could be called a hobby. He looked in the window, there was knitting wool, needles, cotton, felt, writing paper, envelopes, postcards, pens, pencils, some packs of faded postage stamps and another of coins displayed, but no sign of any books.

A woman came into sight inside and for a moment Manu's heart skipped a beat, then he realised the woman was far too old to be either Monika or her mother. He pushed open the door and she looked up at him wearily.

'How can I help you?'

'I understood you were a book shop?'

'We sell books, but we don't have a vast range. I usually have to place an order for a customer. You're welcome to look, they're down the end.'

'Actually I'm looking for someone who works in a book shop. I hoped she might be here.'

'I'm the only person here. I don't employ.'

'You wouldn't happen to know a woman called Monika who works in a book shop, I suppose?'

'I know two or three Monika's, but they none of them work in a book shop. The woman at the greengrocer is called Monika. Maybe that is who you're looking for.'

'Thank you. I'll try there.'

Manu turned into the greengrocer and looked at the woman sitting at the till. She gave him a smile with her over red lips and pushed back her hair from her eyes.

'Are you Monika?' he asked.

'That's right.' Her smile widened. 'What can I do for you? My break is in half an hour.' She gave him a suggestive wink and ran her hands down her sides, pushing out her breasts.

Manu shook his head. 'You're not the lady I'm looking for.'

'I could probably take my break now.' She leaned further forwards and Manu recoiled.

'I'm not looking for a prostitute.'

She tossed her head, her hair falling back across her face. 'I don't make that offer to just anyone, you know,' she said angrily.

'Then save it for someone who might appreciate it. I'm not interested.' Manu walked out; if the door had not been held back by a hook he would have slammed it behind him; another wasted visit. His headache had returned and he entered the kafenion. He would take another tablet with a coffee; that should help. He might also be able to find out the time when the bus would come through and he could catch it to return to Aghios Nikolaos.

'You've about ten minutes,' said the proprietor as he placed Manu's coffee on the table along with a glass of water.

'Where's the bus stop?' asked Manu in alarm.

'Goes from the bus station.'

'I'd better get there then. Forget the coffee.' He slipped a tablet into his mouth, washing it down with some mouthfuls of water.

'I've made it, you pay for it.' The man crossed his arms and stood in front of the shop door.

'How much?'

'Six Euros.'

Manu had a desire to push the man out of the way and run. Grudgingly he placed a five Euro note on the table. 'That's all I have. Take it or leave it.'

The man snatched up the note and glared balefully at Manu. 'I should have asked you to pay before I served you.'

'Well you'll know better in future.' Manu pushed his way past and out of the door.

He stood outside shaking with rage and lit a cigarette to try to calm himself down. There was no way he should have paid more than three Euros for a cup of coffee. He was tempted to return and vent his temper on the man but that would mean he missed the bus and he wanted to return to the town and look for the other three book shops on his list. If he did not find Monika in one of them he did not know where else to look.

Arriving back at the bus station in Aghios Nikolaos he enquired again about buses to the suburbs. There was one about to leave and there would not be another until after three. Panic stricken Manu sprinted across to the vehicle just as it was about to draw away and wedged his foot between the doors as they closed.

The conductor looked at him sourly. 'If you'd missed your footing you would have been run over and then the bus would have been delayed. You need to consider other passengers.'

Manu caught his breath. He was being spoken to like a naughty school boy. He ignored the reprimand and pulled the map from his pocket.

'I need to go there,' he said, jabbing the cross he had made on the paper. 'Can you tell me when I need to get off?'

'I will when you've paid your fare.'

'How much?'

'Three Euros.'

Manu gave a sigh of relief. It was less than he had paid to return earlier so this suburb should not be so far away.

No sooner had Manu taken his seat than the conductor called to him. 'This is your stop.'

'Are you sure?' asked Manu. 'I thought it was further from the town.'

'This is as close as we go.'

'Will I be able to get a bus back to town?'

'Depends how long you are. There's another through in twenty minutes, then you'll have to wait until after three when the service resumes. Are you getting off?'

Manu nodded. 'I'll be as quick as I can.'

'Take your time,' muttered the conductor. 'We won't be waiting for you.'

Manu followed the roads on his map until he came to a small establishment that actually looked like a book shop. With his hopes high he opened the door. The shop was crammed from floor to ceiling with books and a bespectacled man sat at the counter reading.

'Feel free to wander around,' he said without looking up.

'Actually I need your help.'

'What exactly are you looking for?'

'I'm looking for a lady called Monika.'

The man peered over his spectacles suspiciously at Manu.

'She's my sister, you see, and I have an urgent message for her.'

'So why are you looking for her in my shop?'

'I know she moved to this area a short while ago and opened a book shop, but she's not sent me her new address.'

'Maybe she doesn't want you to know it.'

'I'm sure she has sent it,' Manu tried to speak confidently. 'It's probably been lost in the post.'

'Well, I'm not able to help you. There's no young lady working here by that name.'

'Would you have any idea which shop she might be in? I've been everywhere in town.'

'People often say they are coming to Aghios. It's a useful landmark. It doesn't necessarily mean they are living here.'

'Have you any suggestions? I'm beginning to feel quite desperate.'

'Well, she's not likely to be at Ammoudara. That's a beach resort for the tourists. Not much there except tavernas and a few general stores. You could try Elounda. I believe there's a book shop there.'

'Where's Elounda?'

'Along the coast. You can get a bus there.'

'Thank you. I imagine there won't be a bus going that way until after three?'

'That's right. Nothing into Aghios from here either until after that time.'

'Well I can always walk into town. I've one more shop to call on. Could you direct me?' Manu placed the map on the counter and put his finger on the mark he had made.

'Not much point you going there. Closed down at the end of last season.'

'It's still listed on the Internet.'

The man shrugged. 'It will be until someone thinks to take it off.'

'In that case it appears that Elounda is my last hope. Thanks for your help.'

'You wouldn't like a book to read on your journey?'

'I already have one, thanks.' Manu had no intention of buying a book that he would never read.

He hurried back to the bus stop, but when he checked his watch and the timetable the bus had already left. Unless he took a taxi he now had no option but to walk back to the bus station in Aghios Nikolaos.

Trying to take advantage of the small amount of shade that was offered by the sparse trees on the pavement Manu walked along slowly, drawing on his cigarette. There was no need to rush and end up hot, sweaty and exhausted. Once he reached the bus station he would check the time of the bus to Elounda and he would probably have time to sit and have something to eat. More than food he craved for an ice cold beer and he needed to buy some more cigarettes.

By the time he reached the bus station he felt quite light headed and turned into the snack bar. 'I'd like a beer and a sandwich,' he said, digging in his pocket for the money.

'I can do the sandwich. Take your pick from the display, but I'm not allowed to sell beer.'

Manu rammed the sandwich he had selected back into the display cabinet and walked out. His mouth was too dry to eat a sandwich without first having a beer. There had to be a taverna close by where he could purchase a drink.

He drank the beer down rapidly, sighing with satisfaction, and then called for another. He wished he had purchased the sandwich earlier, now he would have to return to the snack bar. He looked at his watch, it was already two thirty. It had taken him longer than he had realised to walk back from the suburb. He needed to find out where he caught the bus to Elounda and he also needed to find out the times of the return journeys. It could take him a while to find the book shop and deal with Monika and he did not want to be stranded in the village over night or have to pay for a taxi back to Aghios Nikolaos.

He cursed himself for not thinking earlier. He should have collected his bag from his lodgings. Now he would have to do that when he arrived back from Elounda and as a consequence he could find the last bus to Heraklion had left by then.

Bus drivers began to arrive for their afternoon shift and Manu hurried over to the kiosk, bought a return ticket for Elounda and was told whereabouts the bus would be parked. He walked into the snack bar and looked again at the sandwiches on display, ignored the one with the damaged packaging and finally selected ham and tomato. When he paid for it he added a bottle of water to his order, ignoring the glare the man at the counter gave him.

Manu walked along the row of buses until he saw the one that had a sign for Elounda in the windscreen and halted beside it. He could eat his sandwich as he travelled along and once they reached the town he would look out for a book shop. He hoped it would be on the main street and he would not have to spend precious time hunting it down.

Settled in his seat, Manu was pleased he had arrived in good time as tourists began to enter the bus, some chattering loudly about their visit to Aghios or about their impending visit to Elounda. They were annoying and once again Manu wished he had his bag with him. He could have placed it on the seat beside the window to deter anyone from sitting beside him. He opened his pack of sandwiches and took a large bite. Almost immediately the conductor appeared beside him.

'No eating on the bus, sir.'

'It's only a sandwich.'

'It's food. We don't allow the consumption of food on the buses.'

'I've not had any lunch,' protested Manu.

'That is not my fault, sir. Please put your sandwich away until you leave the bus or I will have to ask you to hand it over to me to dispose of.'

Grudgingly Manu pulled the wrapper back over and placed it in his pocket. 'Am I allowed a drink of water?'

'Make sure you don't spill it on the seats. Passengers don't appreciate sitting on a wet seat.'

A corpulent, sweating, man sat down next to Manu, leaning against him as the seat was not wide enough to accommodate him. He wiped his perspiring face with a handkerchief.

'I told you we should have left earlier to catch the bus,' he said to the woman sitting in the seat in front and leaned back again, squashing Manu further towards the window.

Throughout the journey he continually leaned forward to pass remarks to his wife, an aroma of sweat rising from him as he moved and jabbing his elbow into Manu as he sat back in his seat. Had the bus not been completely full Manu would have risen and take a seat elsewhere. At each stop more people crowded onto the bus until Manu felt he would suffocate. He was unable to take his bottle of water out of his pocket and he resolved that as soon as they arrived in Elounda he would take a Benzodiazepine to help him to recover.

He was relieved when the bus stopped at the top of a hill and the conductor called out the name of the stop and the hotels and self catering apartments it served. A number of people pushed their way to the doors and climbed out, but Manu's companion stayed firmly in his seat. At the next stop "Elounda Heights" was called and Manu forced himself to his feet and insisted the man moved to make way for him.

'Is this the stop for Elounda town?' he called.

'Next one.'

Manu stood as the bus swayed around the bends of the road, jostling him against the other passengers who seemed unconcerned, being more interested in the view across the bay and craning their necks to get a better look.

To his relief the bus finally stopped and the conductor called "Elounda." Manu could see a parade of shops across the road and a selection of tavernas. Having been unable to access his bottle of water whilst on the bus he knew it would be warm and unpleasant by now. He would visit the nearest taverna and have a beer to wash his tablet down; whilst there he would also ask directions to the book shop. He placed his hand in his pocket and felt a soggy mass where his sandwich had been continually squashed by the man who had sat next to him. He looked at it in disgust and threw it into the nearest rubbish bin.

When his beer arrived he placed his hands around the cold bottle, longing to take a drink. 'Can you give me some directions, please?'

The girl nodded. 'Where do you want to go?'

'I'm looking for the book shop that I understand is here.'

'Book shop? Do you mean the newsagent at the end of the square?'

'That's probably the one.'

'Walk to the end of the square and you can't miss it,' she waved her hand in the direction. She picked up the coins he had placed on the table and walked away.

Manu drank the beer quickly, swallowing a tablet between mouthfuls. He wanted to be on his way.

It was hot as he walked the short distance to the end of the parade of shops. Goods were displayed outside, taking up much of the pavement area; he continually had to step into the road to avoid the tourists who stood outside in groups examining items. Traffic passed continually; delivery vans parked wherever they pleased, expecting the cars and buses to go around them; whilst scooters weaved between them.

He was relieved when he finally saw the newsagents, entered the cool dimness of the shop and looked around. There was a queue of customers, mostly with newspapers clutched in their hands and a man at the counter was dealing with them. Towards the rear of the shop a woman was arranging some stock. He would have to make her get rid of the man before he could deal with her. Slowly he made his way down the narrow aisle towards her, fingering the knife in his pocket and licking his lips in anticipation.

'Are you looking for anything special?' she asked looking up.

Manu recoiled. The woman was not Monika.

'I was looking for the lady called Monika who works here.'

'There's no one called Monika here; just my husband and myself. I think you must want the new book shop in Plaka.'

'Plaka? Where's that?'

'The next village. You can catch the bus or walk; it isn't that far.'

'Where can I catch the bus?'

'Down in the centre. It's just along from the taxi rank and the car park. You can't miss it and the periptero where you buy your ticket is close by.'

Manu nodded. 'I'll try to find her in Plaka then.' He turned and walked out. If he did not find Monika in Plaka he had no idea where else he could look. He felt anger building up inside him; Monika may have told the chambermaid at the hotel she was going to Aghios Nikolaos to open a shop but she could still be in Heraklion and moved to work in a different hotel.

He walked back up the road, the full force of the sun hitting him again, as began to make his way along the narrow, congested pavement. The heat never used to worry him and he could only put his discomfort down to having spent so long in prison.

Reaching the square he walked along to the bus stop and studied the time table. The next bus was due in twenty minutes; there was time for another beer and cigarette before it arrived. The same girl attended to his order.

'Did you find the newsagents?' she asked.

'It wasn't the one I wanted. I've been told the one I'm looking for is in Plaka. I'm catching the bus. Will I know when to get off?'

'It's the end of the journey.'

Manu nodded. This sounded more like a small village where Monika would think she could successfully hide from him.

Plaka

Manu joined the queue of passengers and waited until they had boarded before he entered. He had no desire to be squashed into a seat again. The journey took less time than he had anticipated and he left the bus with the other passengers, looking around to get his bearings. They all seemed to be hurrying down a hill to where the sea could be seen with a small boat bobbing at the quay. Across the water could be seen a small island and this appeared to be their intended destination. Far from being a quiet isolated village everywhere was bustling with visitors.

Manu walked in the centre of the pathway, one side was a taverna and opposite was a gift shop; next to the gift shop was a book shop and sitting with her back to the window was a woman whom he was certain was Monika. Standing a short distance away he looked at the window display. It was difficult to be certain there were no customers in the shop but he decided he must take a chance.

The door was open and he entered silently, closing it behind him. Monika looked up in surprise. She never had the door closed; it looked unwelcoming. Manu leaned back against it, pleased at the horrified expression on Monika's face.

'You thought I would never find you. Thought you had been

clever when you left Rhodes and let everyone think you were in Athens. Well, you're not as clever as you thought. I had plans for you, but I've revised them now. When I have finished dealing with you you'll never want to look in a mirror again. The sight will be too hideous to contemplate.' Manu took the knife from his pocket and pulled it from the protective sheath as he took a step towards her. 'It will be no good you screaming. There are too many people around to hear or take any notice of you.'

Monika gripped the edge of her desk in fear. She dared not let go to press the alarm bell, convinced that if she let go of the desk her legs would give way beneath her.

'Please don't hurt me, Manu.' Seeing the knife she was convinced Manu was going to cut her throat.

He grinned mockingly at her. 'Frightened now? So you should be. When I've finished with you I'm going to visit your mother.'

'No, please don't touch my mother. She's done nothing to you.'

'She's a liar. Told me she didn't know where you were. Liars need to have their tongues cut out.'

Monika swallowed; the vision before her too horrible to contemplate. 'Ring the alarm' her brain kept registering, but she was too frightened to release her grip on her desk.

Manu took another step towards her; one more and he would be able to touch her and once he had hold of her she would be helpless. In desperation she brought her knee up beneath the desk and pressed the alarm bell.

The sudden raucous noise filled the air, tourists stopped and looked around; Saffron ran out from her shop leaving customers standing there bewildered, and Theo rushed across the road.

'Stand back,' he shouted, brandishing his gun, as he opened the door to Monika's shop. Manu stood there, the open knife in his hand and Monika was white and shaking, still gripping the edge of her desk.

'Put that knife down on the floor, now.'

Manu stood there, grinning wildly. 'You'll have to take it from me, old man.'

'Throw it down or I'll shoot. My gun is loaded.'

Manu shook his head and threw the knife at Theo. As he did so Theo pressed the trigger and a bullet landed close to Manu and ricocheted off the floor. Theo clutched his arm where the knife had grazed him. Monika screamed and having begun to scream she was unable to stop.

'Sit down,' commanded Theo, pointing his gun Manu. 'Sit down there on the floor and if you move I'll really shoot you.' He walked backwards to the shop door. 'Police. We need the police. Someone call the police,' he shouted.

'I've done so. They're on their way. What's happened, Theo?'

'See to Monika and find out how to stop that racket.'

'Is she hurt?' asked Saffron as she edged past the bulk of Theo. She was not sure if Theo was referring to the alarm or Monika's screaming. She clasped Monika in her arms, feeling the girl trembling uncontrollably.

Saffron shook her gently. 'Stop screaming, Monika. I know you've been frightened but you're safe now. Show me how to switch the alarm off.' Saffron stroked Monika's hair as she buried her head in Saffron's shoulder. 'The alarm, Monika, we need to switch it off,' Saffron tried again.

Skele raced into the shop, John following him, panting hard. 'What's happened? Skele heard the alarm and started barking.'

'Turn it off, John,' shouted Saffron.

John walked over to Monika's desk and flipped the switch up. Saffron gave a sigh of relief as the quietness descended. She became conscious of the crowd of tourists who were gathered outside, craning their necks to catch a glimpse of whatever was going on inside.

Saffron still held Monika in her arms. 'Quieten down, Monika. We need you to tell us exactly what happened.'

'Manu,' gasped Monika. 'Manu.'

'Did he hurt you?'

'Theo came.'

Theo beamed. 'I saved her. I will shoot this bad man. He is a robber with a knife.'

'You mustn't shoot him, Theo.' Saffron looked at the man sitting on the floor. He did not appear to be hurt, but the casing and the bullet lay on the floor beside him, the tiles on the floor dented and cracked.

Theo shrugged. 'That time I did not aim at him. Next time I will make sure I do not miss. John, take Monika over to my taverna and look after her. I'll stay here until the police arrive.'

John looked at Theo doubtfully. 'Are you sure you'll be safe?'

'I have my gun.'

John shook his head and picked up the spent bullet and the casing. 'Give me your gun, Theo. It will be better if the police do not see you in possession of a fire arm. I'll leave Skele with you. He'll make sure the man doesn't try to get away.' John kicked Manu's knife to the side of the room. 'Don't touch that. The police will need it for prints.'

'What about the floor tiles? How do we explain the damage to those?' asked Saffron.

'Happened when the large counter was moved, of course.' John answered glibly and pushed at the loose chippings with his foot until they were underneath the counter.

Manu glared at him. At the first opportunity he would make his escape.

Saffron placed her arm around Monika. 'Come on, we'll go over to the taverna and wait for the police there.'

At the door John turned to Skele. 'Guard,' he commanded.

Once over at Theo's taverna Monika collapsed into a chair and buried her head in her hands. 'I'm sorry. I was so frightened.'

'Well, the alarm certainly works well. I was at the shop and Skele began to bark like crazy. Once I had quietened him I could hear the alarm going and ran up a fast as I could.' John placed Theo's gun in the waistband of his trousers. 'We won't mention the gun,' he said. 'It will be your ex's word against ours.'

'When he showed it to me I didn't believe it when he said it was loaded. Thank goodness he didn't hit Manu.'

'Actually, he must be quite a good shot,' observed John. 'He was close enough to have hit him in the body so he must have aimed at the floor.'

'How am I going to explain to Uncle Yannis about the damage?'

'We'll worry about that later. I'm sure he'll be relieved to know that you are unhurt.'

'Here,' Saffron placed a glass of water in front of Monika. 'I don't think you ought to have anything stronger until the police have been and taken your statement. You don't want them to think you were intoxicated.' A look of alarm came over Saffron's face. 'I'd forgotten about my shop. I've left it unlocked.'

'Go and make sure it's secure. Take this with you and put it somewhere out of sight.' John handed Saffron Theo's gun and she looked at it in horror. 'Put it up your T-shirt and fold your arms. No one will notice. I'll stay here with Monika.'

Saffron hurried across the road. No one seemed interested in her shop. Everyone was looking through the windows of the book shop to try to ascertain what exactly was happening in there. She slipped inside and locked both the doors, then looked for a hiding place for the gun, finally placing it on a shelf behind a pile of T-shirts where it could not be seen.

She unlocked one of the shop doors and locked it behind her as she went next door to where Theo was effectively blocking the doorway to prevent anyone from entering. Saffron touched his shoulder.

'Everything under control?'

Theo nodded. 'He tried to get up, but John's dog soon put a stop to that idea. I'm not sure he would actually let me leave the premises.'

Saffron smiled. 'I'll ask John to come over. As you were here when John told Skele to be on guard he probably thought he was meant to guard you as well. What's happened to your arm?'

Theo shrugged. 'Just a graze where he threw the knife at me.'

'When you come back to the taverna I'll have a look at it. I hope you have a first aid box.'

'Under the counter.'

'Fine. I'll not place a dressing on it until after the police have been, but you should have it properly cleaned.' Saffron lowered her voice. 'Deny all knowledge of a gun.'

'Suppose the police search my taverna? They'll be bound to find it.'

'It isn't there. John has dealt with it.'

Theo was about to remonstrate when the sirens of police cars could be heard. 'Remember, Theo. Say nothing.'

Saffron stood outside Monika's shop and beckoned to the police to come over as they drew up 'I'm the person who called you. A man threatened the owner of the book shop with a knife.'

'Is he still around?'

A police man looked over at Theo. 'Is that the man?'

'No, he's inside. I think you ought to wait until I ask my friend to come over and call his dog off.'

The policeman took his gun from his belt. 'We may have to shoot the dog if he's dangerous.'

'No, he's not a bit dangerous.' Saffron clutched at the policeman's arm. 'John. John,' she called, 'Come and save Skele.'

John elbowed his way through the small crowd of onlookers in front of the shop. 'What's wrong with Skele?' he asked.

'Are you the owner of the dog?' asked the policeman, barring John's way with his arm. 'We've been told he's dangerous.'

'Dangerous? He's not dangerous. I left him on guard and he'll not let anyone near the man until I call him off. Let me through and I'll show you.'

The gun still in his hand the policeman allowed John to enter Monika's shop whilst his companion stood outside with his hand on his gun.

Manu glared at him balefully. 'This dog attacked me,' he said.

'That's not true.' Theo declared loudly. 'The dog did not arrive until later.'

'Skele, come here. There's a good dog.'

Obediently Skele walked over to John's side and sat down. Manu went to get to his feet and Skele growled.

The policeman turned to Saffron. 'As you called us, Madam, maybe you can tell us exactly what happened.'

'The lady who owns the book shop is across the road recovering from shock. The man on the ground is her ex husband. He threatened her with a knife and she rang her alarm bell.' Saffron pointed to Theo's arm. 'He threw the knife at Theo when he came in to help, then John arrived with his dog and left him on guard. The knife is over there.'

'That's not true,' shouted Manu. 'He shot at me.'

'Is that true, sir? Did you attempt to shoot the man?'

Theo looked at the policeman innocently, pulled out his pockets, spread his arms and turned in a full circle. 'Where is my gun? I cannot shoot anyone if I do not have a gun.'

The policeman eyed Skele warily as he went over to where Manu was sitting. 'I am going to place you in temporary custody whilst I take statements from everyone involved. You will be released if I decide there are no charges against you.' He clicked handcuffs around Manu's wrists and took him outside to the waiting police car, pushed him into the back seat and locked the doors, leaving the second policeman to stand beside it.

The policeman returned to the shop. 'Is that the knife?' He pointed to where the knife was lying, a small amount of blood on the blade and Theo nodded.

'I'll be taking this as evidence.' Lifting it up by the tip the policeman slipped it inside a polythene bag. 'Now, maybe we could go somewhere to take the statements from those people who are involved.'

'My taverna,' smiled Theo. 'It is only across the road and Monika is already in there.'

'Do you have the keys to lock the premises? Until we have

taken statements and examined the area we do not want people coming in and contaminating evidence.'

'I'll ask Monika where they are.' Saffron hurried across to Monika and returned moments later.

'They're in her bag under the desk.'

'Then if you will be good enough to get them out I will lock up when we leave.'

Whilst Saffron rummaged in Monika's bag, finally pulling out a bunch of keys, the policeman took a last look around. Apart from the damaged tiles there did not appear to be anything out of place. He ushered Saffron, Theo and John out of the shop, keeping a wary eye on Skele, who walked docilely beside John, and locked the door behind them.

'I regret I have to ask you to close your taverna whilst I take statements from those involved.'

'I'll be losing trade,' remarked Theo.

'That is unfortunate, but I'll keep you no longer than necessary. Now, maybe if the owner of the shop would like to make herself known to me I could start to take some details of the incident.'

Saffron shook her head. 'John, please explain that I need to look at Theo's arm and dress it.'

John nodded and explained rapidly that Saffron was once a doctor and was quite capable of dressing the scratch. 'I'll take a photo first,' he said.

'Whatever for?' asked Saffron.

'Evidence that Manu threw a knife at him and caused the injury. You find some raki, Saff.'

'I'm sure you are all very shocked, but I would prefer you not to have an alcoholic drink before I have finished my enquiries.'

'It's not to drink,' smiled John. 'It's for Saff to clean Theo's arm and help it to heal.'

The policeman looked at John scathingly, but did not protest when Saffron appeared from behind the bar with a bottle of raki and proceeded to wash Theo's arm with a tissue soaked in the liquid. She replaced the bottle and returned with the first aid box from behind the counter.

'Theo, this is useless,' she exclaimed as she examined the contents. There was a pair of scissors, a pair of tweezers, a small piece of dirty bandage and two tiny strips of Elastoplasts. 'I'm throwing that bandage away. I'll place a pad of tissue over the cut and secure it with the plaster temporarily. I'll go and get my box later. I have a clean bandage in there and larger plasters.'

Theo nodded. His arm stung a little from the application of the raki, but he did not think a bandage was necessary.

The policeman settled himself next to Monika who looked pale and nervous.

'Where is he?' she asked anxiously.

'If you mean the man who was in your shop he is sitting in the police car until we have finished our enquiries.'

'You won't let him go, will you?'

'That will depend. Now, if we can start at the beginning. Why should this man be looking for you and why are you so frightened of him?'

Monika licked her lips and told the policeman that Manu was her ex husband, Emmanuel Graphides. She had divorced him due to his violent behaviour towards her, run away from Rhodes and made a new life for herself on Crete, thinking he would not find her.

'If you were not expecting him to find you why did you have the alarm installed at your shop?'

'I was told that he had been making enquiries about me, trying to find out my address.'

'And that was sufficient information for you to think you should have a panic alarm fitted?'

'I was frightened that if he found me he would hurt me. He has injured people before. I used to live in an area in the Old Town of Rhodes close to the street where the prostitutes worked. He assaulted one of them when he tried to find out my address once before. He was sent to prison.'

The policeman frowned. 'How long did he serve?'

'He was sentenced to over four years.'

The policeman raised his eyebrows. The assault must have been serious for the man to be given such a lengthy term of imprisonment.

'So what happened when he accosted you today?'

Monika closed her eyes and spoke tremulously. 'He closed the shop door and began to come towards my desk. He took out a knife and said he was going to scar my face so badly that I would never want to look in a mirror again. He then said he would attack my mother.' She wrinkled her forehead. 'I think that was when I pressed the alarm bell with my knee. Theo came rushing across and Manu threw the knife at him and grazed his arm, then John arrived with his dog so Manu couldn't escape before you arrived.'

Theo and John nodded vehemently.

'You can see where the knife cut me. It is lucky I put my hand up to defend myself or it may have gone into my chest.'

The policeman looked at the wound on Theo's arm. If the man had raised his arm to defend himself he would have expected the cut to have been on the underside and nearer to the elbow. 'You're quite sure you put up your arm to defend yourself?'

'Of course. It was a reflex action.'

'You didn't put your hand out to try to take the knife away from him?'

Theo raised his eyes heavenwards. 'I would not do anything so foolish. Had I done that my hands would be cut to ribbons.'

'Did the man make no attempt to run from the shop? I would have thought that having been unsuccessful in his attempt to injure Miss Kokanides he would have wanted to make his escape.'

John interrupted quickly before Theo could answer. 'That was when I arrived with my dog and placed him on guard. We brought Monika over to the taverna to wait until you arrived. When we heard your sirens Saff went back over to meet you.'

'You were happy to allow the lady to return to the shop so she was in the vicinity of a man who had wielded a knife a little earlier?'

'Skele knows Saff. He wouldn't hurt her, but he wouldn't let anyone else hurt her either. I can trust him.'

'I waited outside for you,' added Saffron.

The policeman looked at the large mongrel that lay at John's feet, his full attention on cleaning one of his paws.

'What happens now?' asked Monika.

'We will take the man in our car back to headquarters and hear his version of the events. There may be an innocent explanation, his actions misconstrued.'

Theo rose to his feet. 'There can be no innocent explanation. He intended to hurt Monika. If that was not his intention why did he have a knife? You have that in your possession and you will find it has his fingerprints on it.'

'We will obviously send that to be tested and his background will be investigated.'

'You'll keep him in prison won't you?' asked Monika anxiously. 'If you let him out he'll come looking for me again.'

'Just for the record, can you give me the name of the person he attacked previously?'

'Natasha Davenidis, she has the general store where we used to live.'

The policeman frowned. 'I thought you said she was a prostitute?'

'She was, but she became ill. We allowed her to rent the shop so she had somewhere to live and an income.'

'She would no doubt confirm the attack that she suffered?'

'Of course, and it should be in the police records and also the lawyer's, Mr Spanides.'

The policeman closed his notebook and rose. 'I don't think there is any more I can do here today. If I have any more questions I will return. In the meantime, Miss Kokanides, you are quite safe.'

'You will tell me what happens won't you? I wouldn't want you to release Manu without me knowing. If he was released I would have to close my shop and go elsewhere and hope he did not find me.'

Manu was driven to the police station and pushed inside. Still handcuffed, he was searched and the cocaine and Benzodiazepine tablets found and removed.

'I need those,' protested Manu. 'I'm HIV positive and they are part of my medication.'

'Really?' The policeman raised his eyebrows. By the look of the trembling, sweating man in front of him he had taken something more than conventional medication. 'I'll have a word with the police doctor and if he confirms that it will be returned to you. Now we need to take your prints.'

'What for? I've done nothing wrong.'

'I understand that you threatened the shop keeper with a knife.'

'Rubbish. She's my ex wife and I went there to find out how she was; did she need anything. She's deranged. She obviously keeps a knife under the counter and threw it at me. It hit the man who walked in. It was nothing to do with me.'

The policeman nodded. 'In that case you won't have to stay with us for very long. Now, your prints, then we can compare them with those we find on the handle of the knife.'

Rhodes

Natasha lay flat on her back. Provided she did not move she had nothing worse than a dull ache in her back. Whenever she had to be moved the pain would stab through her like a knife, making her gasp. The doctor leaned over her.

'I'm pleased with your progress, Miss Davenidis. We are only sedating you at night now and giving you some pain killers during the day when you need them to combat the pain in your spine. Now, can you move your fingers?'

The doctor waggled his fingers before her face and Natasha did her best to copy him.

'That's good. Try to lift your hands.' Again the doctor nodded as she complied. 'And your toes?' he asked as he pulled back the sheet that was covering her. Try as she might Natasha could not move her toes.

'Hmm. I'm going to give you a little prick. Close your eyes and tell me if you feel it.'

Natasha felt only the slightest sensation.

'Nothing to worry about. We'll give it a few more days.'

'Am I paralysed, doctor?' asked Natasha in a whisper.

'You can move your fingers and hands. If you were paralysed you would be unable to do that,' he replied cheerfully. If the feeling in her feet or legs did not return fully within the next few days it was possible that she was paralysed from the waist down, but there was plenty of time for her to recover full mobility.

'Do you feel able to give a statement to the police this afternoon?'

'Sleep,' she answered.

'Yes, you'll want to sleep now as we've given you some pain killers. The police really do need to speak to you this afternoon. They are unable to catch the person who assaulted you until you have given them some more details.'

'Manu,' muttered Natasha as her eyes closed.

Stenos sat patiently beside Natasha's bed. The doctor has assured him that she would be able to give him a statement when she woke up.

'Give her about ten minutes and then speak to her. She'll open her eyes when she hears you. Treat her gently and don't be any longer than necessary. Let me know when you leave and I'll ask if she needs some more medication for her pain.'

'Natasha, are you awake?'

Natasha's eyelids fluttered. She did not want to wake up.

Whenever she was awake she was conscious of the pain in her back.

'Natasha, I do need to speak to you. I believe you know the name of the man who assaulted you. Please tell me. We want to arrest him before anyone else is hurt.'

'Manu.'

'Manu? Is that the man's name?'

Natasha opened her eyes and Stenos came into focus. 'Manu Graphides.'

'You're quite sure it was him?'

Natasha tried to nod, the movement causing so much pain in her spine that she gasped and groaned.

Stenos regarded her anxiously. 'Do you want me to call the doctor?'

'Not yet. It was Manu Graphides, Monika's husband.'

'Why would he want to hurt you?'

'He's looking for her and thought I would know where she was living.'

'Do you know where she is?'

'No. I think she might be in Athens.'

'If you do know her address, please tell me. Monika could be in danger.'

'I don't know. Truly I don't.' Tears welled up in Natasha's eyes.

Stenos patted her hand. 'I believe you. Is there anyone else who might know where she is living?'

'Spanides; the lawyer. I pay my shop rent to him.'

'So if you pay your rent to him he must have an address for Monika where he sends it.'

'Must do. My back hurts.'

'You've been very helpful to me, Natasha. One more question, then I'll speak to the doctor and ask him to administer your medication. If Manu Graphides is the man who injured you are you willing to press charges against him?'

'Yes, oh, yes. Please get the doctor.'

Stenos rose. 'I'll speak to the doctor as I go out and I'm sure he will be with you very soon. I may have to return to ask some more questions of you, but I'm sure they can wait until you are a little stronger. You are already looking considerably better than when I first saw you.'

Natasha tried to give Stenos a smile.

Stenos called the police headquarters to say he had visited Miss Davenidis and been given details of the suspect. He was now going to consult with the woman's lawyer and would place a full report when he returned to the office. He drove from the hospital to the New Town where Angelos Spanides' office was located. His name was vaguely familiar and Stenos wondered if he had dealt with the man at any time in the past.

Mr Spanides was studying the papers he had received that day about an impending court case where he would be expected to represent the claimant. It was the usual problem concerning the ownership of a strip of land, usually such a small amount that it was virtually useless, but still disagreements arose.

Stenos introduced himself and showed his identity card.

'Have a seat, how can I help you?'

'I understand that you receive rent for a general store in the Old Town on behalf of the Kokanides family and send it on to them?'

'I do that on behalf of a number of my clients,' answered Angelos Spanides cautiously.

Stenos nodded. 'The young woman who runs the store is currently in hospital,'

'Not seriously ill, I hope.'

'Not ill, but badly injured. A man went to the shop and assaulted her. She has spinal damage from which she may not recover fully. She claims it was Emmanuel Graphides who attacked her whilst trying to discover the whereabouts of his ex wife.'

'What!' Mr Spanides' eyebrows shot up. 'Not again! The poor girl.'

'You mean she has been attacked before by him?'

'I acted on her behalf when she brought assault charges against him previously. I trust she will again once she has recovered sufficiently.

'I'm sure she will. The reason I am visiting you is to ask if you have an address for Miss Kokanides. Miss Davenidis insisted she did not know where they were living, but thought you might know as you forward the rent from her.'

Angelos Spanides rested his head on his hands. 'Let me think a minute.' Finally he raised his head. 'May I see your identity card again?'

Stenos took it from his pocket and handed it to Mr Spanides who laid it on the desk. 'Excuse me for one moment.' He pressed in the number of the local police headquarters on his mobile 'phone. When he was answered he asked for Stenos only to be told he was unavailable, he had visited someone in hospital and having taken their statement was on his way to visit a lawyer.

Mr Spanides handed Stenos back his identity card. 'I'm sorry to be suspicious, but someone broke into my office a while back. My filing cabinets had been forced open. Nothing was taken, but I did find that my file for the Kokanides family was out of order.'

'Would the file have had Miss Kokanides address?'

'No, she was most particular that I did not have her address. I transferred the rent to her mother's bank account each month. I imagine the bank would have her current address.'

Stenos took out his notebook. 'If you could give me the name of the branch and their address I will call on them and see if they can help me.'

Mr Spanides gave a small smile. 'The bank account is held on Crete.'

'Crete! So I have to assume Miss Kokanides is living there and not on Rhodes.'

'It would appear so.'

'I cannot see that I will be sent over to Crete to track the lady down. Is there any further information you can give me?'

'Not at this moment. If I find I can give you some more help I will obviously contact you.'

Stenos had shaken hands with the lawyer and placed a card with his name and telephone number on the desk. 'You can reach me on my mobile number at any time. If I am giving evidence in court I will be unable to answer, but if you leave me a message I will reply to you as soon as possible.'

Now he sat in his car and tried to get his thoughts into order. He felt sure the lawyer knew more than he had been prepared to disclose to him. The girl in the hospital bed had been adamant that it was Manu Graphides who had attacked her in an attempt to find out where Monika was living. The lawyer said his office had been broken into and the file containing the bank details relating to the shop rent had been moved. When he had visited Elias Graphides he had said his son had gone away for a few days. Had Emmanuel Graphides gone to Crete? Another visit to the chemist was necessary to see if his son had returned.

Angelos Spanides pressed the numbers for Monika into his mobile 'phone.

'Miss Kokanides,' he said when she answered, 'This is Angelos Spanides. I have just had a visit from the police. The lady who rents your mother's shop has been assaulted and she has named her assailant as Manu Graphides. He is obviously looking for you.'

Monika made a sound between a gasp and a sob. 'He found me, Mr Spanides.'

'Are you alright?'

'Thanks to my friends he didn't touch me. He has been taken into custody whilst the police make some enquiries. Did he hurt Natasha badly?'

'I'm not aware of her injuries, but according to the police Inspector who visited me she is in hospital. The Inspector wanted to know if there was any way he could contact you.'

Monika gave a deep sigh. 'There's no point in trying to keep my location a secret now. Yes, you can give the Inspector my telephone number and I will tell him my address.'

No sooner had Stenos pulled up outside the chemist's shop than his mobile alerted him to a call. He sighed. He had not wanted to give Mr Graphides the time to tell his son that he was visiting and give him the opportunity to leave the premises.

'Yes?' he said tersely.

'It's Angelos Spanides here. Is that you Inspector?'

'Have you remembered something?'

'No, but I have spoken with Miss Kokanides and she is happy for me to give you her telephone number. Apparently Mr Graphides is in custody in Crete whilst the police there make some enquiries about him. I believe he may have tried to attack her.'

Stenos wrote the number Mr Spanides gave him in his notebook. 'Thank you. I'm on my way back to headquarters and I will telephone her from there.' He gave a pleased smile. His visit to the chemist would have been a waste of time.

Stenos spent some time on the telephone speaking to Monika. He asked her for a statement regarding the events that had taken place in Plaka, although she assured him she had already given one to the local police.

'I need to contact them and ask that they hold Mr Graphides until they hear from me. The Cretan police could decide that he has no case to answer as you were not injured and release him. He could then disappear and we don't want that to happen. We wish to interview him with a view to prosecuting him for the injuries Miss Davenidis sustained. She has named him as her attacker.'

'How is Natasha? Is she badly hurt?'

'I believe she may be in hospital for a considerable amount of time. She has spinal damage.'

'Oh, that's awful. If I came over to Rhodes would I be allowed to visit her?'

'I'm sure that would be no problem, but I would have to ask you to advise me of your proposed dates. You are a material witness to the events that took place on Crete. I would have to guarantee your return should you be called upon to give evidence.'

'Does that mean I would be under arrest?' asked Monika, suddenly frightened at the prospect.

'Not at all. You would have to be escorted to Heraklion airport and I would undertake the responsibility for meeting your flight, escorting you to the hospital and ensuring that you boarded your return flight. You would then be met at Heraklion and allowed to go on your way.'

'Could my mother come with me?'

'Of course, as far as I understand she is not involved in any way, apart from being the owner of the shop.'

'Thank you, Inspector. I'll contact you as soon as I have made some arrangements.'

Stenos walked into the chemist shop and Elias looked at him warily. 'How can I help you?'

'I just wondered if your son had returned.'

'No.'

'I thought you said he was only expected to be away for a few days.'

'That was what he told me.'

'And you still do not know where he is?'

Elias shook his head.

'I happen to know that he is in Crete.'

'Crete! Whatever is he doing there?' Elias was truly surprised.

'I believe he went there looking for his ex wife. Unfortunately when they met it appears that he threatened her. He is currently in custody over there.'

'You can't be placed in custody for threatening someone,' replied Elias.

'You can when there is a knife involved. Apparently there are conflicting statements. Your son said Miss Kokanides had the knife and she threw it, injuring a man who was in the shop. Both the man and Miss Kokanides say the knife was thrown by your son. He is being held in custody until the prints on the handle of the knife have been checked against his. Should they not be his he will obviously be released without charge.'

Elias swallowed. Manu was in trouble again. He should never have been so foolish as to go looking for Monika.

August 2014
Rhodes

Monika twisted her fingers together nervously as the plane began its descent into Rhodes airport. She and her mother had been met at Heraklion airport by a policeman and she had felt like a criminal when he stood behind her watching her check in and receive her boarding card. If she was to be escorted around by the police in Rhodes Old Town it was going to be embarrassing.

'When we've visited Natasha I'd like to go to the shop. There could be some produce in there that needs to be thrown out. I could give it a quick clean through and tidy up so it was all ready for when Natasha returns.'

'You'll have to ask the police if you're allowed in there,' Monika warned her.

'Why shouldn't I be? It's still my shop.'

Monika shrugged. 'I don't know, but according to the Inspector it is a crime scene. You may not be allowed to touch anything even if you are able to go inside.'

'If there's food there that has gone bad how can that be relevant? Better to have it thrown out.'

'Just see what they say, Mamma.' Monika tried to placate her mother as she felt the wheels touch the runway and bump gradually to a standstill.

As Monika and Litsa walked through passport control they

were stopped by a policeman. Monika's heart missed a beat. Had the policeman in Heraklion reported an irregularity?

'There is a gentleman waiting over there for you.'

Monika looked to where he indicated and could see Stenos waiting for her. She should have asked the name of the Inspector she had spoken to; Stenos was Manu's friend, but at least he was wearing casual clothes and not in police uniform.

Stenos held out his hand to her. 'Hello, Monika.' He eyed her up and down. 'I was sure it was you I saw in the Town although you denied it.'

Monika blushed. 'I'm sorry.'

'Had you given me the opportunity I could have reassured you that I would not tell Manu I had seen you. I'm pleased to see both you and your mother looking well. Crete seems to agree with you.'

'It did until Manu arrived,' replied Monika glumly.

'I hope you're not planning to run away to another island?'

Monika sighed. 'Wherever I go Manu will find me.'

Stenos shook his head. 'I'll do my utmost to prevent that happening again. Now, would you like to stop for some refreshment or go straight to the hospital?'

'The hospital, please. When we've seen Natasha my mother would like to go to the shop. She wants to check that there is no mouldy food lying around and make sure all is in order for Natasha's return.'

Stenos nodded. 'I anticipated her request and I have brought the keys with me. I think it unlikely Miss Davenidis will be able to return for some considerable time. The vertebrae has to be given time to heal and she will have to take life very easy for a while.'

'She isn't paralysed, is she?' asked Litsa. 'Monika told me she had injured her back.'

'I understand her prognosis is good. She has feeling in her limbs.'

'Have you any idea how much longer she will need to be in hospital?' asked Monika.

'That would be a question for the doctor. I'm not qualified to answer. I'll come into the hospital with you and wait outside the ward until you have completed your visit. We can then go to the shop.'

'Would I be able to visit Mrs Ethanides whilst I'm here?' asked Monika.

'Who is Mrs Ethanides?'

'She is the chief librarian. I worked for her years ago.' Monika blushed again. 'She was the lady you saw me having lunch with.'

'Certainly you can visit her, but again I will have to come with you.'

'I'd like to see some of my old friends whilst we're here,' added Litsa.

Stenos smiled. 'That is no problem. Once we have visited your shop and I have locked it again you will be free to go wherever you wish. It is only your daughter I have to accompany everywhere.'

'She's not a criminal,' protested Litsa.

'Of course not, but she is a witness that the Cretan police do not want to disappear.'

Monika looked at Natasha lying flat in the hospital bed. 'I am so terribly sorry, Natasha. It's my fault that you've been hurt again.'

Natasha smile was returning now her face was not so swollen. 'It isn't your fault, Monika. I didn't infect Manu deliberately. I think he would have come looking for me at some time to get his revenge. Looking for you was a good excuse in his mind. Have they arrested him?'

'He's in custody in Crete at the moment.'

'Crete? Did he try to hide over there?'

'No,' Monika shook her head. 'He came looking for me.'

'I didn't tell him you were on Crete, honestly I didn't. I said you were in Athens.'

'That's alright, Natasha, I believe you. He broke into Mr Spanides's office and found out where the rent for the shop was being sent each month.'

'I'm not going to be able to send any rent this month. I don't even know if I will be able to open up again next month. They say I'll be allowed to sit up for a short while next week and they hope I can be allowed out of bed the following week.' Natasha's eyes filled with tears. 'I feel so helpless lying here.'

Litsa patted Natasha's hand. 'You lie there for as long as the doctors say you should. You don't need to worry about the rent. Have you enough money at the moment for anything you need?'

Natasha nodded. 'The girls are being very good. They are taking it in turns to come in and be with me. Agapi organised a rota. When I'm back on my feet I'll be able to make it up to them. Some of them will have lost out financially by spending time in here with me; they may even have lost a regular. I'm pressing charges against Manu and I will be asking for substantial damages. I should be quite a wealthy woman eventually.' Natasha gave a wry smile.

'If you do need any money please let me know,' insisted Monika and was rewarded with another smile from Natasha.

'All I want is to recover. I'm very fortunate. The doctor said had the injury been higher or lower in my spine I would probably have been completely paralysed. No amount of money would make up for that.'

Monika nodded sombrely. If Manu could injure Natasha so badly what would he have done to her if she had not been able to raise the alarm? She was tempted to tell Natasha about Theo and his gun, but realised that she would probably tell the girls and the knowledge would get back to Stenos. He could feel compelled to pass the information on to the Cretan police.

'How long are you here for?' asked Natasha.

'We have to return to Crete this evening. I have to be escorted everywhere by the Inspector to ensure I don't abscond.'

'Is he here now?'

'Waiting outside.'

'He's been very kind and patient with me. Nice man.' Natasha gasped and winced. 'I'm sorry, I need some more pain medication. Once I've had that I shall drift off to sleep again. They say that is the quickest way for me to recover.'

'We'll ask the doctor on the way out. If there is anything at all that you need, Natasha, ask one of the girls to contact Stenos. He has my 'phone number.'

'I will,' promised Natasha and winced again.

Monika bent over and kissed her forehead. 'I feel so guilty. If I had told you where I was you could have told Manu and he would not have hurt you.'

'It would have made no difference. Even if I had told him he would have hurt me.'

'Now, for the shop,' said Litsa. 'I'm not worried about the loss of rent, but if Natasha can't go back there for a while the customers will get used to going elsewhere and may not return.'

'Maybe one of the other girls could run it temporarily,' suggested Monika.

'That wouldn't be possible. You couldn't expect them to be up most of the night and then have the shop open all day. It wouldn't be worth it to them.'

'You could pay them.'

'The amount I could afford to pay them a week they can make in a night. It isn't practical.'

Monika shrugged. Whatever her mother decided about the future of the general store was her affair.

Monika stood just inside the doorway with Stenos beside her. The stain from Natasha's blood had dried leaving what looked like a rusty mark on the floor.

'Is it alright if I go through to the back room?' asked Litsa and Stenos nodded, returning swiftly to say that everywhere was clean and tidy, just smelling a little stale where it had been closed up.

'What's all this dust?' asked Litsa as she looked at the counter.

'We took prints from the counter,' explained Stenos. 'We're

still awaiting the results, but we're hoping Manu leaned against it. It will be no use him denying ever having been here if his fingerprints are found.'

'Can I clean it off?' asked Litsa. 'And that blood from the floor?'

'There's no reason why you shouldn't. We've taken samples and confirmed it belongs to Miss Davenidis. Make sure you wear gloves and dispose of them afterwards.'

Litsa nodded. 'I know she's positive. I'll be careful. Can I throw away the fruit and vegetables? They're no use to anyone.'

'Are you happy to stay here for a while on your own, Mamma?' asked Monika. 'I want to go down to Mrs Ethanides and Stenos has to accompany me. I won't be that long.'

'Take as long as you like. I'll be up in the street talking to the girls when I've finished here.'

Monika raised her eyebrows at Stenos and he smiled and nodded. He had no jurisdiction over Litsa's movements.

Mrs Ethanides greeted Monika in surprise. 'What are you doing over here?'

'I'm here for a number of reasons. I had to come and visit Natasha. Manu hurt her very badly. I also had to come and thank you for telling me someone was looking for me.'

'I've no idea who he was. It certainly wasn't Manu.'

'That doesn't matter. You probably saved my life. It gave me time to arrange to have an alarm system fitted at the shop.'

'You mean he found you?' Mrs Ethanides was aghast.

Monika nodded. 'He just arrived in my shop with a knife and threatened me. I pressed my alarm and the local shop keepers came to see what was happening. Manu threw his knife at one of them and then a friend arrived with his dog and he was kept there until the police arrived.'

Mrs Ethanides crossed herself. 'You were not hurt?'

'Not at all, thankfully, just very frightened.'

'So where is Manu now?'

'He's in custody in Aghios Nikolaos. I'm not sure what is going to happen. They say they are making enquiries, but apart from the scratch on Theo's arm no one was actually hurt.'

'So they may let him go?'

'The police on Rhodes want him for questioning. He attacked Natasha thinking she knew my address and would give it to him. When he is released from prison in Crete it will be into their custody.'

'And you will be safe again?'

Monika laughed shakily. 'I will be provided he is sent back to prison here. If he's set free I will have to make plans to disappear somewhere else.'

Mrs Ethanides lowered her voice. 'That man needs to be dealt with. I could ask my husband; he might know someone who could help.'

Monika shook her head. 'No, I couldn't expect anyone else to deal with my problem.'

'How long are you here for?'

'My mother and I have to fly back to Crete this evening.'

'Can't you extend your stay for a few days?'

'It's not possible. I had to get permission to leave Crete for one day and wherever I go I am accompanied by the Inspector.'

'You're not a criminal.'

'No, but I am a witness and as such my movements are restricted. Have you made any definite plans to visit me now my shop is open?'

'We thought we'd come at the beginning of October, whilst there are still direct flights and before everything closes down. If we stayed for a week in Heraklion and hired a car we should be able to see quite a bit of the island. Then we could drive down to Aghios Nikolaos and visit you and see that area.'

'Let me know your dates and I'll arrange a hotel for you in Heraklion,' promised Monika. 'It will be the one where I used to work so I know it is good.'

'Not too expensive, I hope.'

Monika shook her head. 'It's very reasonable.' She had every intention of making an arrangement with Vasilis Iliopolakis so half the bill would be paid by her. 'I think you would prefer to stay in Elounda rather than Aghios Nikolaos and I can arrange a hotel there for you also. It's only a short distance from Aghios and you would still be able to drive around and see the area.'

Stenos approached and pointed to his watch.

Monika smiled. 'I have to go. We need to go back to the shop and meet my mother and we both have to be at the airport in time for the flight back to Crete. You won't forget to e-mail me with your dates, will you?'

'Of course not, and you'll keep me updated with whatever happens with Manu. I don't want to arrange to come to Crete only to find you have run away to a different island.'

Stenos accompanied Monika back up to the shop, which was locked. 'My mother is obviously up in the street talking to the girls. Do you mind coming up there? I could 'phone her.'

'It's no problem. I was up there interviewing the ladies after Miss Davenidis was admitted to the hospital.'

Monika knocked on Marina's door and there was no answer. She shrugged. 'I'll try Lola.' Again the door remained firmly closed. Monika frowned. 'I think they are the only girls left of her original friends. If she isn't there I don't know where else to look for her.'

Stenos sighed. He had no authority over Litsa's movements, but he could see that Monika would refuse to leave Rhodes until she knew her mother's whereabouts.

Agapi opened her door and looked out. 'Thought I heard someone knocking. If you're looking for Litsa she's in here. We've been making arrangements. Come on in.' Agapi looked at Stenos and winked. 'You're welcome, Inspector.'

'It might be better if I waited outside. Please don't be long, Monika.'

Litsa was sitting on Agapi's bed with Lola and Marina standing beside her. She looked up at Monika doubtfully.

'I suppose we have to leave now? We've been very busy recalling old times and making plans for the future.'

'What plans are those, Mamma?'

'I'll tell you on the plane back.' Litsa winked at the girls. 'See you again soon. May I keep my shop keys, Inspector?'

'Certainly.' Stenos knew the police had no reason to hold the keys to the shop now the owner requested their return. Fingerprints had been taken and swabs from the blood on the floor; there was no reason why they should require access to the shop.

Antonius entered Elias Graphides's shop with a collection of prescriptions in his pocket.

'Morning, Mr Graphides. We're running a bit low. Would you have time to make these up for me today and I'll collect them later?'

Elias nodded. 'Provided I don't have too many interruptions they should be ready for you by five.' He liked to take his time when fulfilling any prescriptions for Antonius and was meticulous about checking the overall quantity of the drugs. He knew Antonius would check the number of packets before he handed them over to Lucas and he would have to answer for any unexplained shortage to the courier.

Elias went into the back room and unlocked the drugs cupboard. He took out fifty packs of Benzodiazepine and twenty packs of OxyContin. There were sufficient quantities remaining to fulfil any other prescriptions he might receive from genuine customers. He placed the packets in a bag and back in the cupboard, locking it securely.

When Antonius returned Elias handed over the bag and Antonius counted the packets that were inside. He nodded and handed it back for Elias to seal with his sticky label showing his name and address. Elias wished he could just staple it closed but

Antonius insisted his label with his name and address was always placed on the outside.

'I have other collections to make,' he explained. 'I need to ensure I have completed my calls as Lucas checks my list and the bags. I would not want to have to explain to him if I was a packet short and did not know which chemist had omitted it.'

Antonius placed the bags into his holdall between the dirty washing he was ostensibly taking to the laundry. Elias breathed a sigh of relief as the man left and hurried upstairs for a glass of raki to steady his nerves. This was all Manu's fault for involving him whilst he was in prison and now the boy was in trouble again.

Elias was surprised when Antonius entered his shop the following day. He frowned. 'I doubt if I can let you have any more supplies yet. I will need to have a delivery from my supplier.'

Antonius leaned on the counter. 'Did you check the packets you gave me yesterday?'

Elias nodded. 'I always check them carefully. Fifty packs of Benzodiazepine and twenty packs of OxyContin. I'm sure that was the quantity you asked for.'

Antonius nodded. 'The number of packets was quite correct. It was the contents that Lucas was not happy about.'

'The contents?'

'Did you look inside the packets?'

'No. I shook them and there was no movement so I knew it was a full pack. I always keep the full ones separate from any that have been opened and used for a customer's prescription.'

'So you didn't look inside?'

Elias shook his head miserably. He must have made an error somewhere.

'Shall we go into your stock room and check on the packets you have in there?'

Elias licked his dry lips. 'I'll just lock the shop door.'

Antonius followed Elias into the stock room where the chemist unlocked the drugs cupboard. Antonius pushed him to one side and picked up a packet of Benzodiazepine, pulling it open and shook the contents into his hand.

'Dupon!' exclaimed Elias.

'Exactly. Are you able to explain how the packets you sent to Lucas all contained Dupon?'

'The suppliers. It must have been a mistake on their part.'

'Lucas doesn't think so. I've been instructed to collect the prescriptions I delivered to you yesterday.'

'If I return those I'll not be able to order the quantity I need from my suppliers.'

'Lucas wants to meet with you this evening and hear any explanation you are able to give. If he is satisfied no doubt he will return the prescriptions.'

Elias spread his hands. 'It can only have been an error by my suppliers; whoever did the packaging there.'

'He expects you to meet him at eight this evening. He'll be waiting for you at "Pandora". You know where that is? At the end of Bar Street. Don't be late.' Antonius turned the key, opened the shop door and let himself out.

Elias was shaking visibly when Antonius left the shop. How could he explain the error to Lucas? He had not changed the tablets in the packets. He hurried into the stock room and began to check the other packets that were still stored there. Each one contained Dupon tablets, a common headache remedy that could be bought over the counter at any chemist. He groaned. The only explanation he could think of was that Manu had deliberately substituted Dupon for the prescription drugs.

He was quite unable to eat the supper his wife had prepared for him, but to her consternation consumed glass after glass of raki.

'What's wrong, Elias? You don't usually drink so much and you've hardly touched your meal.'

'I have to go out,' mumbled Elias. 'I'll eat when I return.'

'Going out? Where? You don't usually go out in the evening.'

'Mind your own business.' Elias raised his hand to slap her and she moved adroitly out of reach. 'I have to meet with someone and it is none of your business where I go.'

Elias left his shop at ten minutes to eight, heeding Antonius's warning not to be late. The establishments in Bar Street were not open yet and the area was deserted. He walked to the end of the road where the bar called "Pandora" was situated and stood in the doorway.

Elias looked at the immaculately dressed man who suddenly appeared before him.

'I understand from my friend Antonius that there has been a misunderstanding.'

'Who are you?' asked Elias.

'I am Lucas. Antonius said I would meet you here. Do you have an explanation for me? Why did you substitute Dupon tablets for the drugs I requested?'

'I didn't substitute them; I swear I didn't.'

'So who did?'

'I think it may have been my son.'

Lucas nodded speculatively. 'So why would he do so?'

'I think he wanted some extra money. He was going away for a few days.'

'And he thought the easiest way to get it was to pilfer from you and sell them to one of the dealers?'

'I imagine so. I honestly didn't know they had been substituted.'

'And where is your son now? Maybe I could have a few words with him and hear his explanation.'

'He's not here. He's in Crete.'

Lucas raised his eyebrows. 'What is he doing over there?'

Elias shrugged. 'I understand he's in custody. He threatened someone with a knife.'

'That's not a very sensible thing to do.'

'He's somewhat impulsive. I'm sure he didn't mean any harm.'

Lucas sighed. 'That is what everyone says.' He pressed a bell on the door and it opened immediately. 'We'll go inside and discuss this problem further. I'm sure we can come to a solution.'

Elias was waved to a chair and two large men stood behind him.

'I think a little drink is called for,' smiled Lucas.

Elias was relieved. Lucas obviously believed that the substitution of the tablets was not his doing. His relief was short lived and turned to fear as the two men immediately seized his arms and held his head back whilst Lucas poured a quantity of whisky down his throat. Elias gagged and some of the liquid spilled down his shirt. He tried to struggle free, but the men were holding him far too tightly. Lucas removed the bottle and Elias gasped for breath.

'Please, I didn't substitute –'. Before he could finish his sentence his head as pulled back and more whisky was poured down his throat. His head hurt, he was choking, and he was also very frightened.

With a smile on his face Lucas continued to pour more whisky down Elias's throat until the bottle was empty and Elias was virtually unconscious.

'Dispose of the rubbish on your way out,' called Lucas as he walked out of the door and rapidly away from the premises.

Stenos saw Monika and Litsa safely through into the departure lounge. He was sure they would catch their flight as agreed, but he was conscientious in his duties. He had asked to be their escort for the day as he knew Monika slightly and had a good deal of sympathy for her. She was a decent young woman who had made an unfortunate mistake when she married Manu.

He waved as he saw them go up the steps and board the plane. He rather wished they had been staying longer and he could have got to know them both better. It would be interesting to know what plans for the future the street girls and Litsa had been making. With a shrug of his shoulders he returned to where he had parked his car. He would call in at headquarters and report that all was well and he had returned the keys to Litsa Kokanides. It had almost been like having a day off.

As Stenos entered the New Town two police cars and an ambulance, their lights flashing and sirens blaring, were making their way along the Mandraki Harbour road. It had to have been an important incident for them to be travelling at such speed. It was nothing to do with him; he was officially off duty an hour ago.

Litsa chatted gaily during their flight home, saying how pleased she was that Natasha was expected to make a full recovery in time and how clean and tidy the shop was; the only defect being the mouldy fruit and vegetables and some sour milk.

'I wish the girls had helped themselves to those. I wouldn't have minded and I would have preferred to know they were being used rather than thrown away.'

'So what else did you talk about to the girls?' asked Monika. 'You said they had been making plans for the future and you would tell me on the way home. I imagine you didn't want Stenos to know what they were going to be up to.'

'No, I just didn't want you to make a scene in front of them.'

'Me? Make a scene? Why should I do that?'

'When Natasha first comes out of hospital she'll need someone to look after her and the girls can't be expected to spend their days with her. I'm coming back to Rhodes.'

'Mamma!' gasped Monika. 'But where will you live?'

'At the shop, of course. I can have a bed in the little back room where I used to sleep and open up the shop each day. It will only be until Natasha is well enough to take over properly. I should have thought about it before we came over today. I could have brought some clothes with me and stayed tonight.'

'What about the work you've agreed to do in Elounda?'

'It's not exactly important work. I'll speak to the taverna owner and tell him I'm not going to be able to iron his tablecloths any longer. I'm sure he'll soon find someone else and I wasn't enjoying spending a morning ironing when it was hot. The couple whose child I meet from school must have other friends or relations who could help out until they find someone else permanently. The thing I shall miss most is doing the church flowers with Brenda. I have really enjoyed her company.'

Monika shook her head in disbelief. She was used to having her mother with her in Crete but she also knew that if her mother had made up her mind and promised her help to Natasha and the girls she would not go back on her word.

'I'm going to miss you, Mamma.'

'It won't be for long. Six months at the most. You could always come over during the winter when your shop is closed and stay for a while.'

'I suppose so,' answered Monika doubtfully. She was not sure she wanted to return to Rhodes for any length of time. Her work and her friends were on Crete now.

If you have enjoyed reading Emmanuel, you will be pleased to know that the next book is planned for publication in June 2018.

Read on for a 'taster' of what is to come......

August 2014

Stenos telephoned Poppi to say he was on his way home although a little later than he had anticipated. When he finally opened the door of their apartment Poppi gave a relieved smile. 'I was beginning to think you had been called back in to work.'

'I was held up coming through the town. There has been an incident somewhere and the traffic was being diverted from the harbour road. I was pleased I was already off duty or I may have been sent out, then I really would have been late home.'

Poppi placed his supper before him. She should be used to her husband's irregular hours by now, but it did not stop her from worrying about him when he was late. On those occasions she was always waiting for a telephone call from the hospital to say he had been attacked by some drunken youths and was unconscious or worse.

'Did you go anywhere interesting with those people?'

'Not really,' smiled Stenos as he helped himself to a slice of bread. 'I had to go to the hospital for them to visit a friend, then one of them needed to go to her shop and I was able to leave her there whilst I escorted the other one to the library.'

'And that took all day?'

Stenos shrugged. 'They seemed to have a good deal to talk about.' He did not mention his visit to the girls in the street. They were part of an ongoing investigation into the assault on Natasha.

'You know what it's like when women get together.'

Poppi nodded; she knew she would not get any more details from her husband. He did not believe in bringing his work home and confiding in her.

'How was your day?'

Poppi pulled a wry face. 'Much as usual. Builders coming in to place orders and complaining that we didn't have exactly what they wanted in stock. I did have an English woman come in who wanted handles to take back to England with her.'

'How do you know she planned to take them back to England?'

'I said if they didn't fit or she wasn't happy with them she could return them. She laughed and said the cost of returning them from England would be more than she had paid for them. She said she couldn't find any handles she liked in England for her bathroom, but she thought the ones we had would be perfect.'

'Handles are handles,' remarked Stenos.

'I called in on my parents on my way home and Mamma asked me to take her prescription in and collect her medicine. When I arrived at the chemist he was closed. He's usually open until quite late each evening.'

'Probably going out somewhere to meet up with friends and decided to close early. Is the prescription urgent? I could take it to the late night chemist if so.'

Poppi shook her head. 'No, I can take it in tomorrow.'

Stenos nodded, pleased he did not have to go out again. 'Well, as I've had an easy day what do you say to having an early night?' He raised his eyebrows at Poppi.

'I ought to wash up first.'

'Leave it until tomorrow. It won't go away.'

'That's what I'm worried about,' but Poppi argued no further and followed her husband into their bedroom.

Stenos entered the police headquarters with a smile on his face. He felt quite energised after spending the previous day with Monika and her mother, despite having had to wait at the airport until the couple he had escorted all day were safely boarded and the flight taken off. It had been a pleasure to have an early night and they might even have been successful this time in conceiving the child they both longed for.

'Anything I should know about?' asked Stenos.

The sergeant handed him a type written list and Stenos scanned it quickly. Three youths arrested in separate incidents for causing an affray, one drunk who was sleeping off the effect of the alcohol in a cell, four shop lifters had been apprehended, and a body pulled from the harbour.

'Who was the floater?' asked Stenos. 'Any idea?'

'You'll have to ask Tomas, he attended. All I know is that it was a man. Tomas will be able to tell you more if you're interested. He'll be in shortly.'

Stenos grinned. 'Curious more than interested. It will be his case, not mine.'

Stenos pulled the topmost file onto his desk and opened it. Four shop lifters, all foreigners. He looked at the passports that had been removed from their possession; they had all entered the country on the same day from Spain. He had a feeling they had been working together and would all claim to be ignorant of the language and it was a misunderstanding that had caused their arrest. Having retrieved the goods they had stolen it was unlikely the shops would want to prosecute and the girls would have their passports returned and be free to move on elsewhere. It was just a question of waiting for a Spanish speaker to arrive

The next file was no more interesting. The three young men who had been arrested for causing trouble were also visitors to Rhodes. Stenos smiled to himself; no doubt in each case there was a local youth involved, but there was no mention of his arrest. Having spent a night in the cells the men would be told to go on their way and not cause any more problems.

The intoxicated man was a regular and once he had sobered

up he would be apologetic, promise it would not happen again, and shamble away to the nearest bar. He was just a nuisance who had to be arrested for his own safety.

Tomas entered, a cup of coffee in his hand. He yawned widely. 'Just my luck. I was off duty in ten more minutes and then a call came in to say there was a body in the harbour.'

'I heard,' said Stenos. 'I imagine that was the incident that caused the closure of the coast road as I was going home from the airport.'

'Lucky you going home. I didn't leave the site until almost two.'

'Any idea who he was?'

Tomas shook his head. 'Autopsy this morning so we should find out a bit more then. Probably one of those idiots who have too much to drink and think a swim will sober them up.'

'May have been thrown in by his friends as a joke.'

'In that case they'll have a murder charge to answer. If he was thrown in they probably panicked when they saw he was in difficulties and ran.'

'Who called it in?'

'Couple out walking their dog. I spoke to them and they are coming in this morning to make a formal statement. They say they saw no sign of anyone and it was the dog who alerted them. He went down to the water and started barking.'

'Any identification on him? Anyone reported missing?'

Tomas shook his head. 'Not yet. I thought at first it could be our usual drunk, but he was already locked up for the night.'